Dark Forge

Masters & Mages
Book Two

MILES CAMERON

GOLLANCZ
LONDON

First published in Great Britain in 2019 by Gollancz
an imprint of the Orion Publishing Group Ltd
Carmelite House, 50 Victoria Embankment
London EC4Y ODZ

An Hachette UK Company

1 3 5 7 9 10 8 6 4 2

Copyright © Miles Cameron, 2019
Maps copyright © Steven Sandford, 2019

A CIP catalogue record for this book is
available from the British Library.

ISBN (Hardback) 978 1 4072 5140 0
ISBN (Trade paperback) 978 1 473 21771 3
ISBN (eBook) 978 1 473 21773 7

Typeset at The Spartan Press Ltd,
Lymington, Hants

Printed and bound by CPI Group (UK) Ltd,
Croydon, CR0 4YY

www.traitorsson.com
www.gollancz.co.uk

Dark Forge

Also by Miles Cameron from Gollancz:

The Traitor Son Cycle
The Red Knight
The Fell Sword
The Dread Wyrm
A Plague of Swords
Fall of Dragons

Masters & Mages
Cold Iron
Dark Forge

Writing as Christian Cameron from Orion:

The Chivalry Series
The Ill-Made Knight
The Long Sword

The Tyrant Series
Tyrant
Tyrant: Storm of Arrows
Tyrant: Funeral Games
Tyrant: King of the Bosporus
Tyrant: Destroyer of Cities
Tyrant: Force of Kings

The Long War Series
Killer of Men
Marathon
Poseidon's Spear
The Great King
Salamis
Rage of Ares

Tom Swan and the Head of St George Parts One—Six
Tom Swan and the Siege of Belgrade Parts One—Seven
Tom Swan and the Last Spartans Parts One—Five

Other Novels
Washington and Caesar
Alexander: God of War

*Just as the forge's anvil is not shaken by the storm or the darkness,
even so the wise are not affected by praise or blame*

Tirase, *Questions on Metaphysiks*

THE GREAT CITY OF
MEGARA

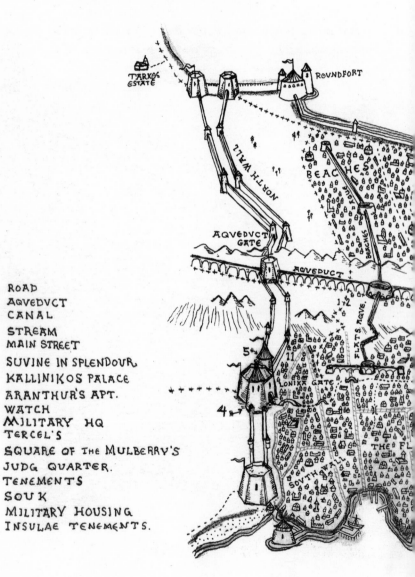

┼ ┼ ┼ ┼	ROAD
∿∿∿	AQVEDVCT
▨▨▨	CANAL
≈≈≈	STREAM
------	MAIN STREET
1.	SUVINE IN SPLENDOVR
2.	KALLINIKOS PALACE
3.	ARANTHUR'S APT.
4.	WATCH
5.	MILITARY HQ
6.	TERCEL'S
7.	SQUARE OF THE MULBERRY'S
8.	JUDG QUARTER.
9.	TENEMENTS
10.	SOUK
11.	MILITARY HOUSING
12.	INSULAE TENEMENTS.

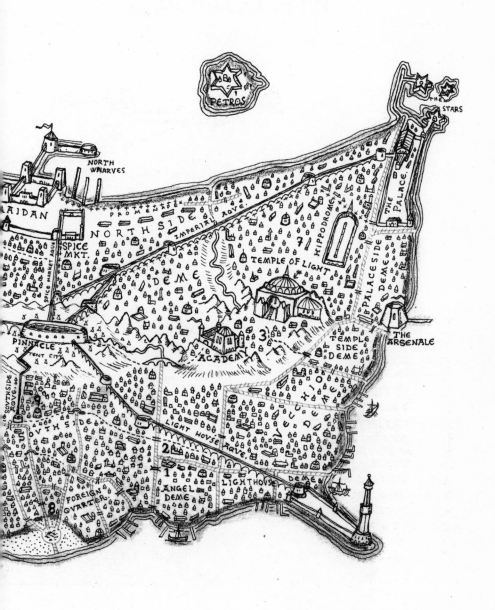

Prologue

As is usual in the life of a soldier, almost nothing was as Val al-Dun had been promised.

He might have wished to spit in disgust, but the desert wind and the grit in his mouth made it unwise. Instead, he stood in his stirrups and looked back up his column.

'Why have we stopped?' one of the *Agha* asked.

The *Agha* were the Disciple's inner circle: the *Exalted Ones*.

The *Agha* were strange figures who never seemed to look with their eyes and always knew... things. Most, but not all of them, wore robes of scarlet. This one, masked in white, had robes so red that in the brilliant sun it appeared to have a life of their own, billowing and turning around the *Agha* like a living embodiment of light.

In his head, Val al-Dun called them 'they' because... they never seemed like single people, single souls. Even their voices betrayed some sort of alliance, fragile at best.

They were terrifying in their harmony.

Val al-Dun had learnt not to roll his eyes or give any appearance of insolence. Four days before, the Disciple had stopped in the middle of a salt flat and had not moved for hours; no explanation had been offered.

The Disciple and its *Agha* never explained anything. The road from Stephion had cost the column three consecutive commanders who had failed to understand the Disciple's needs.

Val al-Dun hadn't even been an officer when the Master summoned the militia, but half a dozen of his seniors stared without blinking into the void now, their heads removed for various failures. The road behind them was thick with corpses of the *sowars* who had disobeyed orders or simply failed to keep up. It had become worse since they reached the cursed Kuh Desert. Val al-Dun was a survivor; he'd watched the errors made by his predecessors and tried to learn; he was determined to survive this debacle if he could.

'Exalted One,' he said carefully, 'the Masran guides we were promised have not been provided. The horses and camels need water, Exalted One. I have my best people looking for water.'

All around them, the Safian Tufenchis were sitting in the small shade of their saddle blankets, with their camels or horses crouched in the sun. The better troopers had put sunshades over their animals' heads, but there was always some lazy bastard...

Hussan, his *havildar*, approached.

'People need a rest,' he said, very quietly.

Val al-Dun never took his eyes off the *Agha* in front of him.

'If it serves your will, Exalted One, we will have a two hour rest.'

Hussan blanched under his heavy beard. Val al-Dun had a moment to reflect that the execution of six senior officers had its merits; discipline was improving. The Tufenchis were regular troops of the now-fallen Safian Empire, but they were really just expert militia; six hundred mile forays on camelback were not their usual fare.

And Val al-Dun had to protect them. They were his neighbours and his kin – some his friends, some not, but very few of them were what the Pure called 'True Believers' – and Val al-Dun was aware of just how expendable they were held to be. His *Ghole* had been chosen because they were *not* trusted. He understood that. The Master and his Disciples were not so very different from the run of other rulers: demanding, capricious, and probably fallible.

'We do not have time to look for water,' the *Agha* said in its odd, high-pitched, flat voice.

'Exalted One, if we do not find water, my people will die. Today; perhaps tomorrow morning.'

Val al-Dun waited for the sword. The *Agha* were inhuman – so fast that they could not be faced in combat. He had seen his former chief, Nafir Khan, killed. It had been so fast that he hadn't even seen the sword drawn.

I probably won't even know, Val al-Dun thought. *I wonder if I'll be able to see when my head hits the sand.*

And Nafir Khan had been a veteran bandit chief, *Beglerbeg* of five hundred sabres; a deadly man. He'd told the *Agha* what he thought...

The *Agha* didn't move.

'We must be at the Black Pyramid,' it said. 'Tonight.'

Val al-Dun looked at the stones and gravel at his feet, so different from the high, arid desert of his home. This was a disgusting desert, all dirty stone and grit. Not clean.

It is difficult to debate with a being that does not look at you and has no facial expression.

'Exalted One, I beg of you one hour in which to find water.'

'No,' the *Agha* said. 'We march.'

It inclined its head slightly, to indicate that the interview was at an end. The *Agha* turned fluidly, red robes swirling, and walked back to the covered palanquin carried by four camels.

'Hussan!' Val al-Dun called.

Hussan was helping one of the youngest and most inexperienced of their Tufenchis to arrange her sun-screen. The *havildar* shrugged and came back, his riding boots raising small puffs of the deadly grit.

'Great Khan?' he asked with mock reverence.

'We ride. It is an order.'

'Blessings be on the Exalted One,' Hussan took a very small sip of water and held it in his mouth, then swallowed. Then he roared, 'On your feet! Ready to ride in two minutes! Listen for the drum!'

Mikal, the kettle drummer, was an old man – a true veteran, with the scars of a life of violence on his face, his arms, and his soul. He stripped his sunshade, stowed it expertly, and had his camel on its feet in three motions. He was already mounted, his sticks in his hand. Mikal had a foreign barbarian's face and a badly set nose that seemed to go diagonally across his scarred face. His blue eyes were like a burning reprimand for the incompetence of others.

Kati, the youngest, was serving in place of an older brother who was necessary to push a plough. She was too small to mount a camel easily, she didn't know how to live off the land, and every time she stopped, she scattered her kit over the entire desert. She looked ridiculous with a *jezzail* that seemed twice as tall as she. On the other hand, she was Hussan's third cousin, and everyone liked her. She was a cheerful mite, and smart, and Hussan said she had training in the *Ruhani*, the world beyond. *Ferenhu* training in foreign magik.

They had lost one hundred and twenty-six men and women crossing the lower Stai, the gritty desert that divided Safi from Masr. Val al-Dun had been a bandit most of his life, and he wondered to himself why he had decided to try and keep the rest alive. Something had changed in him.

He shrugged.

'March,' he said to Mikal, and the old man slammed his sticks into the huge drums on either side of the camel: *bam-bam. Bam-bam.*

The people might have cursed, if their mouths hadn't been so dry. They moved off.

'We don't know where we're going,' Hussan said quietly.

'That's right,' Val al-Dun said.

He stayed at the head of the column, setting the slow pace he thought would keep everyone, people and animals, alive. They crossed a sparkling gravel flat full of some sort of jewel-like stone, and his troopers were too tired to behave like children and investigate. Then they came to dunes – the first decent, clean desert they'd seen in days – and Val al-Dun, whose scouts were all *somewhere*, had to ride ahead himself. He found them a track along the back of two great dunes and then cut back, the whole column, six hundred animals, following like a great snake.

His mare was flagging. Thera was the best horse in the column, and when she was failing, that meant other horses were near death.

He was running out of choices, and the line of dunes was going to cut them off from his scouts. He was too tired to waste time on curses, although it did occur to him to speak his mind to the *Agha* and die with a clear conscience.

'Fuck it,' he said to Hussan. 'Keep going.'

He turned his horse's head and put her at the back of the dune.

Thera was brave, and she wove her way up the back to the great dune, her hooves almost silent, quick and sure. When she crested the top he reined her in and she stood, trembling slightly but apparently unmoved by her exertion, and he loved her.

Below him, the long snake of the column turned again, almost backtracking to pass along the back of yet another great dune.

But he had chosen well, and from the top of his dune he could see a line of hills, perhaps a parasang to the south and west. And he could see that the line of dunes was not so wide; indeed, they'd chosen a reasonable place to cross the dune belt. He nodded, and took a sip from his canteen.

'Come, best beloved, and let us see if we can live to the ending of this day,' he said to his mare.

He dismounted, and together they slid down the front face of the dune. They were cautious, and still they spilled a dozen sand-slides as they went. Val al-Dun stood in a pool of hot sand at the base of the dune, with more tumbling down. He had to mount ignominiously and Thera had to leap clear to save them.

Before they rejoined the column, he gave her the rest of his canteen.

Then he led his people off to the left.

Hussan raised an eyebrow.

'I know what I'm doing,' Val al-Dun said.

'I've heard that before,' Hussan said.

Late afternoon. The heat was dissipating quickly, and the range of low hills was fully visible as they moved across a parasang-wide salt flat. The salt was thickly crusted and made for easy travelling, but it got into everything – eyes and mouths parched from six days without water.

Val al-Dun became a brutal bully. He didn't bother to cajole – he struck, he cursed, and he pushed. Now he rode at the rear of his column while Hussan led them to a gap in the distant hills. The salt flat was like a frying pan; the sun beat down and reflected back up.

Kati's camel had stopped moving. Val al-Dun turned Thera under him and his *katir* sank two inches into the haunch of the stricken camel. The beast leapt forward with an indignant roar.

'Keep moving, little witch,' he spat.

Kati hunched, miserable and very small, but her beast continued to move across the salt.

Less than an hour later, two of his best men, old criminals like himself, cantered back to the column. They had big sacks of water on their horses and they shared them.

Draivash looked his part; a greasy velvet khaftan and a pair of silver puffers couldn't hide his small stature and fox-like face.

5

'Water,' he said. 'Maybe an hour. Good water. Best thing in this fucking wasteland.'

'But our Masran guides?' Val al-Dun asked.

Draivash shook his head. 'Bethuin tracks at the well. Days old.'

Bethuin were the old nomad tribes of the south. They had no particular allegiances and it was unwise to provoke them. There were Bethuin throughout Safi, but they spoke another language and they tended to stay in the remotest wilderness. 'As secret as a Bethuin' was a Safian saying.

Val al-Dun shrugged. 'Fuck,' seemed an appropriate reply.

He gave his mare two cups of water and then left her to take a breath or two while he walked back to the palanquin. Four white camels carried a litter as big as a small castle.

All four of the *Agha* were there, as usual. Val al-Dun had never seen who – or what – was in the litter.

'Exalted One,' Val al-Dun called out.

The scarlet-clad inhuman stalked across the sand towards him. The same one? A different one?

'Speak,' it said.

'Exalted One, our scouts have found water. However, we have no contact with anyone from Masr.'

Again, Val al-Dun waited for the sword.

The *Agha* was, as usual, completely unmoving, shaven, beardless head bare in the late-afternoon sun.

'We must be at the Black Pyramid tonight,' the *Agha* said. Again.

'Exalted One, I need more information. What time tonight? Can *you* guide us?'

Val al-Dun almost cringed. He'd never asked one of them a direct question.

A few heartbeats passed.

'Do you not feel the Black Pyramid, Val al-Dun?' it asked.

It knew his name.

'No,' he said. It was the simple truth.

A few heartbeats, and then a few more. A breeze touched them; some grit flew like a small banner of smoke.

'Ahh,' it said. A simple nod. 'Go to your water, and we will guide you to the Pyramid.'

Val al-Dun walked up his column, trying not to think.

Midnight, or close enough. A full moon hung out over the desert, but the column was cresting the line of barren hills. They'd had an hour's rest and their fill of water.

The full moon lit the valley at their feet.

A long, sparkling, spilt-ink ribbon of river ran from far in the east towards the west. They rode through blasted stone hills, as if fire and lightning had formed them, but at their feet were green fields and pastures of late-summer grass. Trees lined the distant riverbank; the black water was wider than any river that Val al-Dun had ever seen. The Azurnil. The Great River – the Mother of Rivers.

On their side, the north bank, stood a city. Even at midnight, it was well enough lit to seem to glow along the river, and brilliant boats and illuminated barges cruised on the inky waters of the river. Val al-Dun assumed it was Al-Khaire, the great city of Masr. Its vastness made the size of his raiding force a joke. The city seemed to fill the plain at their feet; he could smell the smoke from a parasang away.

A single bridge crossed the river, a needle of stone across the black ink ribbon.

And there, on the other side, placed like a jewel of jet in the moonlit darkness, was the Black Pyramid. It rested in a setting of four pale pyramids around it, and beyond them, on the south side of the river, the fertile plain was covered in pyramids – perhaps twenty of them, or more, their shapes lost in the darkness. The four guardians of the Black Pyramid were ancient; so ancient that three of them had lost most of their brilliant marble cladding, and they appeared as pale blobs in the moonlight. The fourth was like a beacon, and Val al-Dun looked away and back, twice, to see if it was lit from within, and still he could not decide.

The Black Pyramid itself appeared like a primal form; the outline, in as much as it could be seen in moonlight, appeared perfect and smooth, and reflected no light.

Then the column passed over the crest, and low, scrubby trees began to obscure the magnificent view. The scarlet *Agha* led them down the steep, rocky slope. It seemed unconcerned by mortal concerns like tracks or trails. The whole column passed down a slope of broken shale, losing two horses and a middle-aged woman in the process. Val al-Dun bit his lip until it bled, but then they were through the shale and moving on a track that turned into a road.

Somewhere off to the left, a fire was lit, and a high-pitched gong began to sound.

'Exalted One, that is an alarm,' Val al-Dun said.

It said nothing, but continued to stride into the darkness, red robes flowing like moving blood.

'We will have to fight,' Val al-Dun said.

'Yes,' it said.

And later, he asked, with the boldness of desperation, 'How will we cross the river?'

'The Disciple will provide,' the *Agha* said.

'Exalted One, we lack the numbers to seize the bridge.'

Even if we could break in one of the gates.

'You are wise in your many fears. Nonetheless, all will be accomplished.'

Fuck, Val al-Dun thought.

Two hours later, the column had halted at the riverside. They had brushed aside a patrol – local militia, or suchlike. Hussan had dealt with them, and a dozen ravens were gorging on the result.

Val al-Dun dismounted, and took the time to empty the sand and grit out of his riding boots. He used river water to rinse his spare turban-cloth, to wash his face and hands.

Then he felt something change. It was not something he saw, or heard, exactly, but he became aware of the presence, the change. He turned, dropping his towel, to see Kati prostrate on her face, and all the rest of his troopers dropping, and he threw himself on the ground.

The light from the open door of the palanquin was blinding. He'd felt the light as well as seen it. He lay on the packed mud of the riverbank and covered his eyes.

The light grew.

He tried to pray to the Lady. He'd always liked the Lady, and the Thunderer, although he wasn't sure what he believed.

The light emanating from the Disciple was so bright that it penetrated his eyelids, like a bright dawn fills the room of a man with a hangover. He forced himself to remain perfectly still. At a remove, he heard the mortal sound of shoes or sandals slapping on the packed mud.

He tried to pray.

Ah, my child, said the Voice. *You have done well, and you have nothing to fear. You have brought us to the banks of the Black River. Be calm, my child.*

The feet clapped on the ground, and stopped.

There was a *pulse,* as if all the world flashed into the void for one brief instant and then reasserted itself.

Hurry, mortals. This will not last for eternity. The voice in his head was not his own.

The light was gone. In its place was a flat, featureless bridge. It was not apparent what material formed the bridge; the surface was matt, and in the dark appeared to be the same colour as the surrounding mud banks. The bridge had no visible supports and was not arched.

Val al-Dun sprang to his feet.

'On your feet!' he called. His first attempt came out as a hiss; his throat was tight with fear. 'On your feet!' he roared.

Hussan had his horse by the bridle, and he had a hand on Kati's elbow, and behind them, Mikal had his camel moving. Men and women were dusting the dirt from their garments and groaning as they flung themselves into their saddles.

Hussan approached him. 'Are you all right?' he asked. 'It ... talked to you.'

Val al-Dun blinked. 'Still hungry, thirsty, tired, and frustrated,' he muttered. 'So I reckon I'm fine.'

'There's soldiers behind us. Draivash says there're sixty, maybe eighty of them.'

As if to punctuate Hussan's statement, there was a scattering of shots off to the north.

'Take all of Draivash's kin and all your own,' Val al-Dun said. 'Keep them off the bridge until we're well out, and then come yourselves. Don't die here. No one is going to accomplish much chasing us over this bridge.'

He walked over to the palanquin, which was now dark and silent.

'Exalted One,' he called out.

Three of the scarlet people stood silently. The fourth whirled.

'Speak, Khan,' it said.

Val al-Dun had never been addressed as 'Khan' and he was taken aback. Nevertheless, he bowed his head.

'Will we return from the far bank by this wonderful bridge?' he asked. 'Should I hold the bridgehead?'

He stood, head bowed, for so long that he began to wonder if he'd been heard.

'We will not return,' it said.

Perfect, Val al-Dun thought. *We are dog meat. One-way trip. I knew it.*

The palanquin began to move, and the four *Agha* went with it. The bridge that the Disciple had made was just wide enough for the four camels, and yet the *Agha* walked swiftly, as if unaware that their feet were as close to the edge as the width of a boy's belt.

The rest of the Tufenchis were arrayed, and they crossed in order: Val al-Dun's kin, the Safians, in the lead. They were hard-pressed to keep up with the palanquin, which moved so quickly that the column began to spread out, and Val al-Dun cursed. He had enough water in his mouth to curse, now.

The crossing was as strange as every other part of the journey. The river was flat and the surface moved swiftly in the moonlight, and the low bridge passed a mere handspan above the surface of the water, so that looking at the water could be disorienting. The bridge itself did not vibrate or make noise, or sway.

A third of the way across, Val al-Dun heard a burst of firing behind him. He halted and listened, and then watched. He could see figures on horseback hurrying towards him. He waited.

Then a scream, and another. And then the sound of hooves pounding.

Suddenly the air itself seemed to pulse with *Ruhani*. The flickers of light were like pulses of summer lightning, and the whole structure on which they stood seemed to vibrate like the skin of a drumhead struck by one of Mikal's sticks.

Val al-Dun turned his horse and began to organise a rearguard out of a handful of Zand tribesmen he had. But the precaution was unnecessary; Hussan was with him before he'd ordered the Zand to dismount.

Hussan was all but whimpering with pain, and he was a tough man. Val al-Dun got his spare turban from his saddlebag and tied Hussan's right arm, shattered by a musket ball, tightly against his chest after examining it.

'More than a hundred,' Hussan said.

Draivash shook his head. 'Some kind of *maguv*. We lost people when they ...' The bandit lacked words. 'They used sorcery against us!'

'They broke off a piece of this bridge,' Hussan muttered.

'Sweet Lady,' Val al-Dun muttered.

'They'll kill you for that,' Hussan said.

'Boss, we need to get our arses back to robbing caravans,' Draivash spat.

Even as he spoke, Draivash was loading the long *jezzail* slung across his back.

'Keep moving,' Val al-Dun said.

'I can drop a few,' Draivash said.

Val al-Dun shook his head. 'All we have is speed. See to your cousin.'

He pushed forward along the column, avoiding falling into the water or pushing others, moving carefully, obscurely happy to see the small form of Kati still alive. Now he was a different kind of leader; he slapped backs and teased, prodded, mocked, joked. Among the Safians, he was with family – distant cousins and his brother's strait-laced sons. It was impossible to be the 'father of fear' to his own; they needed to be cajoled and flattered.

He went to the small woman, Kati.

'Your cousins say you can work the foreign sorcery,' he said.

She shrugged, her eyes bright under her veils. 'It is forbidden.'

'Nonetheless,' he said.

I need some help here, girl.

She made a motion with her head, mostly lost in the darkness and the veils, but he took it to mean that she was aware.

'If my poor skills can help family, I will do what can be done,' she said cautiously.

Val al-Dun nodded. 'Good,' he snapped.

He left her and went to the front, kept them moving, trying not to look out at the inky water that flowed so unnaturally under the unnatural bridge. He tried not to wonder what would happen if a floating tree struck the construction, and he tried not to imagine what some Masran Magos had done to the whole construct.

And then the whole bridge *moved* again – this time a sudden shock. Twenty Tufenchis fell in and drowned. His brother's second son fell so close that he leant from his horse, but the man was gone in a gulp and a swirl. Choked screams told of other drownings. One young man was saved when his brother grabbed his hair and held him until other arms dragged him back onto the bridge.

'Hang on!' Val al-Dun roared.

He dismounted and received a painful kick from Thera, who was terrified, her ears laid back like a cat's.

'What in all the hells?' asked Namud, his sister's eldest. Many Safians worshipped the old stone gods, and their endless hells. Not openly. Never openly.

'Lie down,' Val al-Dun called. 'Get your animals *down!*'

He could feel the bridge move. Back behind them, there was a ripple of white fire and a pulse of *power*. Even he felt it, and he was renowned among his acquaintances for his lack of attunement to the immaterial.

The bridge tilted, and then righted itself. More screams.

Val al-Dun gritted his teeth. He was on his knees, his arms around the neck of his mare.

He made himself raise his head.

The bridge was moving fast. He could only gauge by the lamplights of the distant city and the passing of the moon across the sky, but the whole bridge appeared to be moving across the surface of the river, as if it was held at one end and the current was . . .

Like a real bridge, he thought.

He'd once seen the pontoon bridge across the summertime Effrathes give way at one end, with catastrophic results.

'We're going to hit hard!' he yelled. 'Hold on to your mount!'

Again, your fears make you wise. Again, the voice in his head was not his own.

They struck. The non-material surface was neither slick nor rough, and the shock of the strike knocked people and animals flat. Men and women went into the water, but this was shallow, muddy water, and fewer were lost, although once the first horses went in, the *kuramax* struck, their pointed, reptilian heads and savage rows of teeth gleaming in the light of two moons.

The first one hit like an explosion of flesh, and it was so fast that a small horse and its rider vanished in the froth of mud and blood in the moonlight.

There was more than one *kuramax*.

The horror of it hit his tired Tufenchis and they panicked. Riders went off the wrong side of the bridge; a few leapt their weary mounts onto the slippery mud of the far bank. Further up the remnant of the bridge, most of the Zand and the Tarkars and the Ugrs made it onto a stone breakwater. But at the end where the Safians were, there were reptilian monsters in the mud and the actual bank was ten long paces away.

Val al-Dun kept his wits together. He pushed men and women off to the left, where the magikal bridge rested on stone. He screamed, and used the flat of his sword.

So he had his sword in his hand when the *kuramax* came for him. He saw the snout a moment before it opened, and the eyes. His cut severed the last five fingers of its reaching mouth, taking away the cruel incisors and leaving it gushing blood. The great jaws snapped shut on empty air, and Thera pounded a panicked hind-hoof into the thing as it darted away.

Even in moonlight, it left a slick of its oily, alien blood on the surface as it dived away. The water around them was churning. Men and animals were dying. The smell of the rotten river mud churned up by the ambush was like the vomit of a god of death.

Val al-Dun looked to his right and saw the palanquin, still facing the mudflats.

He ran to the nearest white camel. There stood the inscrutable figure of an *Agha*, its usually pristine robes spattered with mud.

'This way!' he screamed at it.

Yes. Go with him.

'Why don't you help us?' he screamed.

He could no longer control himself. The darkness was full of monsters now; there was fighting on the bank above them.

We must save ourselves for the contest.

And yet . . .

Suddenly one of the *Agha* detached itself from the palanquin. From its robes it produced two swords of white fire, and it leapt into the water.

The palanquin turned and made its way towards the stone embankment, a hundred paces distant.

Light now illuminated the carnage under the water – the light of the *Agha*'s two swords. Where it was, colour was: brown like river mud and sudden starts of scarlet, robes and blood flowing freely in the dark water.

It was so fast that Val al-Dun had trouble following the action. But he pushed his kin up onto the stone, still warm from a day in the sun, and glanced back to see the *Agha* climbing out of the water, the scarlet robes of billowing silk now stretched across it like wet kelp. It had taken wounds. It moved, not with unnatural grace, but like an old, old person forced to climb steps.

That was all in one glance. Because at the top of the stone embankment, Hussan was dead, and chaos reigned.

The night was lit by a volley – a single pulse of fire – and another half a dozen of his Tufenchis were corpses. Val al-Dun couldn't even see the Masran enemy; but he was out of options. There was only one possible answer.

'Brothers and sisters!' he called. 'On me! At them!'

He looked for Mikal, and the old man was there – mounted, alive, sticks poised.

'*Charge!*' Val al-Dun barked, putting all his fear and anger into that one word.

Bam-bam. Bam-bam. Bam-bam. Bam-bam.

The noise was like thunder.

Perhaps forty of his people were mounted and ready. Dozens more had lost their mounts, and when they charged, they were an undisciplined, desperate mob.

The invisible Masrans greeted them with a disciplined volley. The crash of fire betrayed them, close, under some sort of *baraka* cloak that hid them.

Women fell. Men screamed. Horses thrashed, but the one explosion of musketry was not enough to stop their desperation. They crashed into the Masrans, and it was hand to hand with mere men – shaven-headed men in black kilts who stood in four neat ranks and fought silently and with great determination.

Val al-Dun found himself deep in the Masran ranks, facing a rank of men with long spears all reaching for Thera. He leant so far back in his saddle that his back touched her rump. His *katir* flicked up to twitch one spear aside and he was under them. He took a blow to the head from a shaft, and another to his right arm, and his sword was gone in the darkness. Thera was his weapon, and she turned, her jaws and hooves savage, and the men of Masr – soldier-priests, as he later learnt – stood and died.

A pulse of red fire lit the night. It fell on a shield of white, and on some of the Tufenchis, who burned like screaming torches. The shield rose from the palanquin on the dark stone behind them, and the surviving Safians learned to stay within its white net. And the palanquin unloosed its own storm of white fire on the soldier-priests. Finally another *Agha* came forward into the chaos of fire and shadow and produced two swords of fire.

It threw itself into the fight.

The soldier-priests did not break and run, and neither did the Tufenchis, but the *katir* and buckler were better weapons in the darkness than the matchlock butt and the spear, and the men of Masr died.

They died hard, and they focused their attacks on the *Agha*, who, covered in mud and gore, waded into their ranks. In the end, the soldier-priests died, but they took the *Agha* with them. It lay still, sightless eyes open as in life, limbless in the moonlight.

Val al-Dun was covered in small wounds, but when he dismounted, Thera was untouched. He kissed her, and closed his eyes.

We must keep moving. Dawn is close.

He was close to refusal. But after all, why had he come at all?

Because I was never offered a choice. Serve or die, he thought.

He gathered his survivors. There were a hundred of his own dead mixed in with the Masran soldiers, their combined fluids making the gravel both slick and sticky, and another forty dead in muddy water. Two *Aghas* were dead, if dead was the correct word. The one that had attacked the monsters in the water was floating in the reeds at the very edge of the moving water, scarlet robes now black. The limbless one lay where it had been hacked to pieces by the Masrans.

We must go now, my Khan. Dawn is close.

Val al-Dun looked at the corpses of his friends and family, and he couldn't allow himself to think that this was for nothing. He couldn't let that thought go deep. Instead he found the Magos, or maybe he was the chief priest. His skin was mostly burnt off, and his charred skull seemed to wear an evil smile, as if mocking his endeavours, but what had attracted Val al-Dun was the ring with four big keys on the man's belt. They were still warm, but they weren't melted. He took them, and the black obsidian dagger the man wore.

15

'On me!' he called, his voice rough.

They followed him, even Kati, without complaint. Or comment. They had reached the point where there was nothing but the shared sense of fatigue and despair.

After less than half a parasang, the river path became a stone walkway above an embankment down to the river. On the landward side, a stone wall towered above them, perhaps as high as two tall men. At the corner was a tower, perhaps three storeys high. Beyond the tower, the stone walkway continued along the riverside to a vanishing point.

Someone in the tower had a *carabin*. He fired at long range, and hit a horse.

Something was swelling in Val al-Dun. Perhaps it was the thought that Thera might die here. Somehow, that was worse than his own death. She was a servant, a loyal servant, and deserved better than this.

He touched his heels to the horse and leant forward, and she responded with all her usual heart. She burst forward, before the sniper could shoot again.

Behind him, half a dozen of his people dismounted. They took their long *jezzails* and began pelting the tower.

He stayed low and let Thera work her muscular magik. They flew along the smooth stone of the riverside road until her iron-shod hooves struck sparks that showed in the darkness.

Thera passed the tower and her hooves clacked away along the stone road. The stone was a dark basalt, veined in white – featureless, well jointed, without any apparent mortar.

Val al-Dun was no longer in the saddle. It was a bandit trick; he'd never done a running dismount in the dark, onto stone. Both of his booted feet hurt, but he was there, in the shadow of the tower's doorway. His horse clattered away into the night, and he wished her well.

The sniper fired again. And then again. So there were at least two – maybe four.

The tower door was locked. But the second key, the browned iron one, fitted it well enough.

The keys made noise, and night is silent. Far out in the desert, he heard a hyaena, and then another.

He waited.

The *carabin* fired again.

He turned the key. It grated, and squealed, and he burst into the tower with a puffer in one hand and his *katir* drawn, to find the ground floor empty, a single room with a set of steps leading *up*.

He ran for the steps.

A black-kilted Masran shot at him from the head of the stairs, and missed, the smoke from his discharge hanging in the thick warm air.

The steps seemed to go on forever. But Val al-Dun had stormed a building before, and he knew he needed his puffer for the second man.

The musketeer swung his heavy weapon at Val al-Dun and he covered the blow, his sabre braced by the pistol in his left hand. The blade flexed under the heavy musket butt, but the sword didn't break. Then Val al-Dun was in close, the curved blade flaying the half-naked man until the point found his adversary's throat.

Even as the man fell off his sword, Val al-Dun shot the second sniper with the puffer. It was a hasty shot, under the dying man's outstretched arms. The wounded man's return shot with the *carabin* only finished Val al-Dun's work, striking the musketeer in the middle of the back. The Safian dragged himself past his victim, pushing the dying man to the floor with his puffer, and already trying to engage the third man.

There were too many of them.

Their swords were short, and broad, and the hand guards on their short stabbing swords were not sufficient to protect their hands from his expert cuts, and they weren't very well trained. That, and the brilliant *sihr* light that illuminated the second storey, was all that kept him alive. He cut and cut and covered and cut, and it was ugly, but he put both men down, hacking their hands until their fingers failed and then cutting... wrestling...

He stood and bled, and panted.

One of the men he'd killed was a mere boy.

He spat.

Outside, there was a dramatic change in the light. Val al-Dun moved to one of the riverside firing slits, carefully avoiding the ones that faced his own friends. He could hear that they were still shooting at the well-lit embrasures. He thought that it would be stupid to get hit with one of Draivash's rifle balls.

He looked out.

Al-Khaire, the great city of Masr, was on fire.

He almost choked. There were sheets of flame. He'd never seen anything like the fire, as if it was a live thing, feeding off the darkness.

Tongues and banners of flame leapt hundreds of feet into the air, as if fire elementals were dancing on the wreckage of the works of man.

The flames lit the waterfront below him, and he could see loyal Thera standing patiently, a little further along the stone road. Then, out of the back loopholes, he could see the mighty pyramids. The black one thrust up like a mountain, its front side firelit and still utterly black, so that the ground around it and the sides of the four guardian pyramids reflected the death of Al-Khaire, but the great pyramid was... black.

He went slowly past his corpses, and down the steep steps to the lower floor, and then out into the firelit darkness. He noted another door in the back of the tower, and he opened it.

In a night full of astonishing sights, he saw another. A flat plain ran from the door to the base of the Black Pyramid, but it was dotted irregularly with stelae of stone, some black, some white, some veined or marble or even iron. One was bronze. They were different heights and sizes and they were unevenly placed, but the ground between the stelae was gravelled in white marble, and as flat as the *maidan* where he played polo at home.

But almost every stele was surrounded by a nimbus of light – red or blue or green, sometimes pure gold. Some of the magelights were very bright; a few were very dim. It was all *eversher*, deep magik, to him. He made the sign of the Lady, and backed into the tower and then went to the door.

Draivash almost killed him. The scarred bandit with the crooked nose was just slipping in, dagger high.

The two men faced each other for one heartbeat. Val al-Dun hoped his comrade never noticed that his finger had pulled the trigger of his empty puffer.

'You live! You were born to be hanged, you bastard,' Draivash said, and embraced him.

'More lives than the Peacock of Shahinshah,' muttered Mikal, who, despite his age, was the second man in the storming party.

'Where are the *Agha*?' Val al-Dun asked.

His men, and some of the tribal levy, were already climbing the stairs.

'Gold!' shouted Draivash.

Nothing could stop the frenzy of looting, nor did Val al-Dun have any interest in trying. He slipped out into the orange night and found the palanquin at the very foot of the stone road, the great white camels standing silently, their strange eyes glowing with the reflection of the holocaust across the river.

Two of the *Agha* stood, scarlet robes whispering in the wind. The city was burning so fiercely that a cross-river wind had come up, feeding the rising column of fire and smoke.

'Exalted Ones, I have found a door into—'

Yes. You have done very well. Hide your eyes. Turn and go, and we will follow you.

'Exalted One, there is . . . magik.' He shrugged.

Fear no baraka. *I am here.*

A great blast of heat reached them across the river, and the sound of screams – thousands, or perhaps tens of thousands of screams.

Only minutes remain. Go!

He had no choice now, but to go. He managed to find the sense to order Kati and a dozen other of the smallest and youngest of his troopers to hold the horses. He went back through the tower, and then, without much conscious thought, he went through the back door and into the gardens of stone and metal. Tens of thousands of grave markers, rolling away in perfect disharmony to the south and to the west.

Every one of them guarded by a spell.

There were perhaps sixty of his people still following. He was pleased that he was leaving most of his own band of robbers in the tower, looting, and all his kin. Draivash might survive to work his evil on the world – a safe, petty evil that harmed only a few people at a time.

Unlike the blaze of living light behind him, now illuminating the fields of stone. Because in the death of Al-Khaire across the river, Val al-Dun read the future, and the intention of his lords and masters.

With the courage of absolute despair, he walked across the gravel, and through the spheres of coloured light that marked the charms and cantrips and watchful curses of a thousand generations. He had very little contact with the hermetical world, but the power of these old spells touched his mind like the brush of skeletal fingers on a living man's skin.

Dyar, one of the *jezzailis*, turned and began to scream, his high-pitched screams short and terrible. He tottered a few steps and fell, his mouth, ears, nose vomiting maggots. Then his screams became choked sobs, and then he was gone, and there was only a heaving, man-shaped mass of larvae writhing...

Another man, one of the Zand, paused, puzzled. Then he seemed to bend down, and in one horrible moment realisation dawned that his bones were melting. He collapsed like a deflated water bag, unable to draw breath or scream. His last sounds were liquid, and lacked even the resonance of human despair.

Val al-Dun forced his eyes to look to the front. He found a door along a wall to his right, and he made for it. It was the only entrance he could see. The Black Pyramid, half a thousand paces away, gave his eyes nothing – no door, no recess, no shadow or reflection.

He found himself running. He was detached by terror and by despair – and above both, a sort of anger that his people were dying, and his masters were so remote, so alien, that he couldn't understand their goals. But the flames of the city across the water told him something that he, a hardened killer, had not wanted to know. A prince's greed was different from a bandit's in order of magnitude, but the Disciple and his *Agha* were...

His mind closed around the word. *Evil.* A word bandits generally shunned.

He shook his head as if to clear it.

The gate was of old wood, black with age. A low altar stood to one side: white marble, deeply stained an old brown on top.

The golden key fitted in the keyhole, and he turned it. He was not acting on his own volition – he was the tool of another consciousness – and that relieved him of anxiety and yet filled him with violation, dread, and bitter rage.

His hands were swift and sure.

The gates opened.

A long corridor stretched to his right and left, running north back towards the river, as could be seen by the light of burning Al-Khaire in the distance, and to his left, magelight and running figures. The magelight was too bright and too white and it seemed harsh.

Forward.

He turned to the left and began to walk forward like an old farmer walking into a storm. His people came with him, weapons in hand.

The corridor was huge – wide enough for ten abreast, with a stone roof of the same veined dark basalt from which the tower and waterfront had been built, but inside the corridor, everything was carved in fine bas-relief. Some of it was painted or gilded; red, ivory, black and gold were the only colours, lit with the harsh white of the distant magelights. The carvings were very strange: eagles and daemons and ravens and bulls seemed to make war with armies of men without heads.

He felt the moment when the Disciple followed into the magnificent corridor. The supernatural white light of the Disciple's presence warred with the brilliant white of the magelight. Where the two whites met and fought, stone cracked and paint boiled, and more of his people died, their skin flayed away or desiccated or burst asunder from inside.

He stopped moving forward. The grip on his mind was gone.

He looked up.

Ahead of him, perhaps fifty paces away, were men and women – perhaps twenty of them, or even fewer. He knew that they were Souliotes because he had seen Souliote caravan guards.

'Stop!' commanded a bearded *badmash* with two gold earrings and a long rifle like a Safian *jezzail*.

Val al-Dun stopped. But one of the *Agha* brushed by him, flowing down the overlit corridor with the grace of a *nautch* dancer.

The *Agha* stopped and raised its arms.

'Run,' it said, its voice sibilant. 'We are here to save the world, and you are in our way. Stay, and you will all die.'

'Fire!' roared the *badmash*, and his band of Souliote mercenaries vanished in a cloud of powder smoke.

Val al-Dun watched, unbelieving, as the *Agha* was ripped to shreds by thirty muskets. It fell, and thrashed. And stopped moving.

The Souliotes had vanished behind a veil of golden light.

Val al-Dun had not known, until that moment, that the *Agha* could be killed so easily.

No! *I am too close to fail*!

The unbearable light passed him. He fell on his face, at least in part because he expected another lethal volley of musketry. But the Disciple went forward, and stood like a pillar of perfected light.

The golden veil pulsed through a series of colours.

And went black.

And fell.

The man revealed by the collapse of his shields turned to ash before

Val al-Dun could fully recognise what he was looking at. But the Souliote and his companions were gone.

The Disciple went on down the corridor.

Val al-Dun lay on his arms for a while longer, until the spots in front of his eyes died away and he could see in the now-darkened corridor.

He looked back, and saw his people, watching him.

'I . . .' he began, and his will was taken. Again.

I need you it said. The voice was no longer inside his head. Now it was his voice. It had seized his being.

He fought this time, for a while, but it dragged him through the litter of charred and broken corpses and up a long set of steps – wide, magnificent black steps, under a great golden roof with images of eagles and ravens worked in repoussé, over and over, the ravens enamelled in black glass. He had lots of time to look at them, and at the glyphs of spells set into the gold, because he paid no other attention to his mortal frame. It was a puppet, and he was like a passenger in a chariot, carried by runaway horses.

He climbed. At the top of the steps, set between two pillars of jet-black marble as big around as two men are tall. Towering above him into the darkness was a great gate – the entrance of the Black Pyramid.

He might have paused, but he was not controlling the horse, his body, and he went forward.

To his right and left came his surviving troopers. And he couldn't open his lips to tell them to go back.

He took a candle-flicker's worth of comfort that he had left his best friends looting the tower.

And then he began to climb the winding stair.

He went up.

Up.

Up.

It was a nightmare – black stone, the very heart of darkness, the very absence of light – and he was not able to control anything. He watched, and there was nothing to see. He listened, and the only sounds were his own footsteps, his laboured breathing, and his people on the steps behind him, and he had not one iota of control over any of it.

His sweat rolled down his chest, down his face; he climbed and climbed, his feet sure in a stygian black.

At his back, Fama, one of the veteran women of the Tufenchis, spoke to him, long and low, and again. He couldn't understand her words; perhaps he was losing control even of hearing. Or he was fading in and out, as the WILL driving him rode over his own . . .

'Are you insane?' she screamed. Her voice rang and echoed in the winding stair.

He turned, and in perfect darkness, he felt his sword cut her neck. Fama fell away with a gurgle and he was climbing again, climbing forever into the dark.

Yes. Come.

Now there was a faint light ahead. Gradually, as the stair wound, it went from a glimmer to a palpable light, and eventually resolved into the brightness of his lord, standing in a pillar of white fire.

He couldn't even turn his eyes away.

They were in the very top of the pyramid, in a room that dwarfed them, the walls joining into the ceiling above them.

The Disciple stood by a plinth of black rock. The rock was covered in deep cut runes and glyphs, and the whole of the inward sloping walls, and all of it was lit, if black can be a colour of light. It was not a scene that Val al-Dun could ever remember accurately.

And the Disciple seemed to speak from within him, even though it was no longer in him.

Where is it? screamed the Disciple.

Its anger was palpable; heat flowed off it, and Val al-Dun threw himself to the floor, his tie to the Disciple's will broken by the instant requirements of self-preservation.

Val al-Dun peered from under his crossed arms, through the veil of his turban, and saw another Masran priest, his feather-cloak charred, standing revealed, unbowed. He was tall and very thin, with skin the colour of old wood. He wore a black linen kilt criss-crossed with esoteric patterns, and was muscled like an Ellene statue despite his age.

'It is not here, blasphemer. It is gone.' The priest spoke flawless Safiri.

YOU LIE! roared the Disciple, and his rage exploded.

Light, fire, ice and earth passed through the air; waves of heat and cold reached Val al-Dun.

Stand aside. You have failed.

'I will never surrender my charge,' the priest said. 'If you continue on this path, you will destroy the world.'

I will save the world.

'Any fool can say as much,' the priest said.

His staff whirled through the air so fast that it seemed to make a perfect wheel, and the Disciple's torrent of sorcery fell into that wheel and vanished.

If you continue to resist, I will release all of them. You hear me? All of them!

The priest was silent.

You know I am right.

'I know that you have destroyed my city and everyone I love,' the priest said. 'And I know what you came for. It is gone.'

The whirling staff stopped. A great pulse of blue, like a gout of ball lightning, formed at the tip and then rolled down the room with the slow inevitability of the rising moon.

The column of white was outlined in blue fire.

And then the priest and his blue fire were *gone*.

NOW. WE WILL HAVE IT NOW.

An arm of white fire came from the Disciple. It took Yeshua, a Zand Tufenchis, and put him across the plinth, and smashed in his skull.

There was a scream, as if a human child had seen her mother murdered. A tender, despairing scream from the stone itself.

Where is it? Where is it?

The black plinth shattered. Shards and flakes of stone blew throughout the chamber, flaying flesh and wrecking the chests and boxes of scrolls and treasures.

Too late, the Disciple whispered in his head. It had gone from anger to fear.

A breeze began to blow from above. When Val al-Dun looked up, he realised that the top of the pyramid was gone, and that he was in full control of his body.

Unearthly laughter rang in his ears, and a voice speaking in Masri. And another voice, deep and malevolent, and wicked in its amusement.

The Disciple lashed the room with *power*.

What have you done? Where is it? Give it to me!

Val al-Dun's left side was lacerated by the plinth's detonation, and his ears rang. The moment he understood that he was again the captain of his own ship, he rolled for the head of the stairs, stumbling to his feet when he'd put one of the huge altars between his frail body and the white light of the Disciple.

He looked back. A dozen of his people were with him. The rest seemed frozen, and the white arm of fire had taken another, dragging the unresponsive victim towards yet another black plinth.

Take this.

The rage of the Disciple was so vast that it drowned his own. And as he started down the steps, he saw the arm of white fire seize the last of the *Agha*, where it stood, two white-fire swords in its two hands.

No!

Yes.

OH YES said the amused, horrible voice.

Val al-Dun didn't care. He ran down into the darkness. He went down and down. Perhaps there were gods, and a Lady, because he didn't fall; he didn't trip on the corpse of Fama; he didn't roll to his death on the thousand steps. He stayed on the outside, broader treads, and he thought as little as he could. Then, his knees like water, he was under the golden roof of the portico, passing under the black archway, and it was as if a mighty curse had been lifted from his soul.

The breeze had become a wind, and it raced through the corridors and the tunnel. And despite his failing strength and his empty lungs, he sprinted down the corridor, leaping the charred corpse and running for the gate.

It was still open. A Zand lay on the threshold, one of his Tufenchis, and the doors could not close on his corpse.

Val al-Dun passed through into the clean air of the desert night, and found himself in the garden of magiks – the long lines of grave stelae lit orange and yellow in the death throes of the city burning across the river. To his right, the Black Pyramid towered...

And yet...

And yet, from the very apex a white fire seemed to sear the heavens. The world seemed to blink. Existence itself seemed...

He was aware that he was floating in burning metal, in hell. Daemons were pulling him in two, while some sort of monster rubbed him with bone chips, grating away his flesh and muscle. He screamed...

'Got him,' Draivash said.

He lay on a smooth stone floor. It took him time to recognise that he was lying in the black tower that he had stormed, what seemed like a lifetime ago. There was blood still dripping between the upper storey floorboards and falling in wet pops close to his head.

I am alive, he thought.

'Khan?' a voice asked, close to him. 'Does he live?'

'I do,' Val al-Dun answered.

'Now blessed be the Lady and the Eagle and any other god or friend of man who can hear me,' Mikal said. 'We need you. The world is ending.'

Outside, on the stone road, the youths still had the horses.

He tried to herd his thoughts into any semblance of a plan. The bridge would be gone, and home was on the other side of the river. He stumbled to his feet, his side a battlefield of lacerated flesh, his head pounding, and got a hand on the door frame.

Kati had Thera by her reins, and her feed bag was over her head.

He looked around. There were, all told, fewer than ten hands of them left, and only two hands had been in the pyramid. They were easily identifiable, as they were all burnt and abraded by flying stone.

'We will ride west,' he managed. 'We can steal boats in the Delta.'

'Oh, gods,' said one of the Safians outside, and he fell on his knees.

Even as he spoke, the air seemed to fill with energy. Hair stood on end. The horses snapped their heads up. Every loaded musket fired, as the energy built and burst into light and static charge.

The sun was rising from the rim of the world, a ball of red fire in the east, and when the first tongue of the red light touched the Black Pyramid...

The charge blew out of the air; a fine black powder seemed to precipitate. For a moment, everything hung in the balance...

And then they heard the crack. The sound, like a lightning strike, seemed too close, and then they saw it.

The Black Pyramid began to split. The split was difficult to follow at first. It raced from a barely visible flaw in the perfect darkness at the very apex to an ever widening chasm. A third of the apparently solid stone suddenly subsided into the earth, as if a great chasm had opened. The dark life seemed to pass out of the thing, so that it was *merely* black, instead of the living, breathing heart of *black*.

Val al-Dun thought he heard the Disciple scream in terror.

Book One
Second Intention

When a combatant performs an action that is not intended to strike home in the first *tempo*, but to draw a predicted response from the adversary, against which the true assault is made, this is spoken of as an attack in the second intention.

Maestro Sparthos,
unpublished notes to the book *Opera Nuova*

1

The Imperial Army of Expedition, Eastern Armea

Five days earlier...

A ranthur's eyes opened in darkness. He was, for a moment, completely disoriented, and then he knew; he was in a very small tent, and his hip was pressed against that of Prince Ansu, who was in the process of putting on breeches. His wriggling...

'I'm sorry,' Ansu said. 'I can't sleep.'

Aranthur rolled over, and clutched his borrowed wool blanket closer.

After a long moment in which he almost passed into sleep, he heard the faint but unmistakable sound of Dahlia...

Making love.

He sat up.

'Exactly,' Ansu said.

Aranthur failed to restrain a string of Darkness imagery.

'Black darkness; fucking thousand hells...'

'Let's go for a walk,' Ansu said, equitably.

Hence you were putting on clothes, Aranthur thought.

It was odd to see Prince Ansu in Byzas clothes – almost a military uniform. He had leather breeches, an elaborate blue doublet and a small round hat with a turned-up brim.

'You'll find that it's almost dawn,' Ansu said. 'Don't imagine we'll get back to sleep.'

Indeed, when Aranthur's head poked out of the white wedge tent, he understood why it had been so easy to find his kit. Although true dawn was half an hour away, the sky had the iron grey cast of what the Nomadi troopers called 'The Wolf's Tail'.

The campfires at the end of the tent rows were crowded with Nomadi. Many were sharpening blades or clicking puffers. A few were eating. Some stared into fires.

Dekark Lemnas raised a steaming cup.

'So nice of you *gentlemen* to join us,' she called out.

The nomads laughed. But it was good-natured, and Ansu bowed elaborately. One Steppe veteran slapped his thigh.

'I thought I'd be the first one up,' Aranthur admitted.

Lemnas shook her head. 'Day of battle,' she said. 'Ever seen a battle?'

'Day before yesterday,' he said.

She barked a laugh. 'That wasn't even a skirmish, *boso*. Bah, perhaps a skirmish. Today, we will all get our feet wet.'

One of the regiment's handful of Kipkak tribesmen spat.

'Battle is for fools.' Then he grinned. 'I'm a fool.'

Their laughter had an edge to it.

'Good luck today, Syr Timos. I won't pretend we wouldn't all like to have your *aspides*, and Myr Tarkas too, with us. But I've heard—'

'I didn't wake him.' Ansu turned. 'We're riding as couriers for the General.'

Aranthur nodded. 'Well, I volunteered, way back in Megara.'

He began sorting his kit. He noted that old troopers like Vilna, the Kipkak, had everything laid out in one neat pile atop his saddle blanket: saddle; riding boots; sabre; two puffers; *fusil*; breastplate; saddle and headstall and coiled, polished leather tack.

Aranthur spent a nearly desperate half-hour finding all of his, spread over two tents and the horse lines. By the time he had Ariadne tacked up, he could hear Dahlia demanding *quaveh* and Sasan asking for some oil.

Vilna came by, his short-legged rolling gait announcing him even in the murk.

'Sword sharp?' he asked.

Aranthur bowed and handed over the old, heavy sword.

'Hmm,' Vilna grunted. 'Huh.' He ran a thumb over the edge and raised an eyebrow. 'Good sword. Old is good. Sharp like fuck.' He bowed, as if Aranthur was a little more of a human being than he'd expected. 'Bridle but no saddle, eh? Saddle here. Long day. Life is horse. Keep horse fresh. Best, have six horse.'

'Thanks,' Aranthur managed.

He was fine, mostly, but every few minutes a new set of fears rose to choke him. His body would flood with a sense of danger; his hands would tremble.

It was exactly like his first duel. He had no idea what to expect, and that was the thing that made him afraid.

When Ansu was feeding his mount, Aranthur asked, 'Have you seen a battle?'

Ansu laughed. 'Syr Timos, I come from civilisation. We have law, and just rule, and hundreds of drakes to tell us when we err. We haven't had a battle in two hundred years.'

Aranthur bridled at his friend's smug superiority.

'But you fight duels,' he snapped.

Ansu shrugged. 'Not as . . . frequently . . . as you Byzas.'

'I'm not Byzas,' Aranthur said.

'I misspoke. I will apologise—'

'Nah. I'm cursed snappish.'

Afraid, Aranthur almost said. Instead, he turned and embraced the Easterner, and felt the prince's somewhat diffident return clasp.

'Hah, this is a good custom, and one hug is worth a great many words,' Ansu said. 'My hands are shaking.'

'Mine too.' Aranthur admitted.

'Listen.'

Far off, in the direction of the enemy, there was a long roll, like the rise of summer thunder in the hills above Soulis.

It reached a crescendo and stopped.

And started again.

'By the Lady, what is that?' Aranthur asked.

Ansu made a face. 'Our foes two days back had drums.'

Sasan came up with two feed bags.

'Morning, friends.'

Aranthur found it impossible to hate the Safian man, even when he had just been making love to Dahlia.

'Morning, Sasan. Are those drums?'

'Oh yes,' Sasan said, a trace of bitterness evident in his speech. 'Every *Beglerbeg* has at least a pair of big drums, for signalling and for status.

31

They'll form in front of his tent every morning. The more powerful officers will have six or even ten drummers – big men, mounted on camels with a pair of big drums.'

A new drum storm began.

Sasan's eyebrows went up.

'That's a great many drums,' he admitted.

All along the cook lines, men and women were peering out east, where the sun was just cresting the rim of the world. The drums had a supernatural quality, and they rolled again, long and deep.

Aranthur shrugged to his friends.

'I'm ready,' he said. 'I'm going to the General.'

Sasan was just tacking up two mounts and Ansu was still drinking *chai*.

'Go with the gods,' Ansu said. 'I'm not in a hurry to do work, and that's all she does.'

Aranthur nodded, and walked off across the camp, leading his horse. He walked to the head of his squadron street. He was not actually a member of the Imperial Nomadi, but his own militia regiment – the Second City Regiment, often called 'The *Tekne*' – was in a different camp, and his officer was also a Nomadi officer . . .

The army was like a large, sprawling, complicated family.

'His' squadron was a street of fifty tents, twenty-five on either side, each holding two troopers and all their tack. At the head of his street was his centark's pavilion, a fine silk tent with heraldic bearings.

Centark Equus stood in front of his tent, fully armed, with his light armour on. He smiled, Aranthur threw a barely competent salute, and Equus bowed with some irony.

'Good morning, Syr Timos,' he said.

'Good morning, syr,' Aranthur said, formally.

'Try not to put your head in the way of a cannonball, there's a good chap.'

'I'm going to find the General.'

'Off you go, then.'

Equus went back to drinking his *quaveh*, his eyes on the eastern horizon.

Aranthur walked across the dry grass, trying to imagine that the cheerful Equus might be afraid. He saw no sign of it.

The General's pavilion was in the exact centre of the Imperial camp.

Her personal standard fluttered from the central pole, and her pavilion had three peaks and seemed as large as a palace. There were four sentries, all very alert, and behind her tent, an entire squadron of City Militia cavalry stood by their horses, armed and armoured, booted and spurred.

Even as Aranthur walked his horse across and through the camp, everything changed. The rumble of the enemy drums was drowned out by the sound of wheels and heavy horse tack, and a dozen great *gonnes* – more – rumbled past. Each great *gonne* had a bronze barrel twice the length of a man, or longer, the muzzles cast like fantastical monsters. Each *gonne* had a pair of lifting handles, made to look like leaping, swimming dolphins, cast so well that they almost seemed alive in the red light of morning. Each *gonne* had the touch mark of the casting master, and the coat of arms of the donor, the noble or merchant who had gifted the Imperial Arsenal with the cost of a great *gonne*. Their carriages were like heavy farm wagons, with wheels as tall as Aranthur's head, bound in iron. All the carriages were painted sky-blue, and some had iconography painted on the *gonne* chest between the trails. Dragons and drakes predominated, but one heavy piece had the Lady rising from the waves, and another had Coryn the Thunderer pointing his war hammer.

Each *gonne* had an attendant ammunition wagon, and the *gonne* and wagon each had six horses in draught and forty men and women to serve the bronze monsters. The train rolled past Aranthur on the dry grass, raising dust even so early in the day. He had to slip between one team and another, taking his life in his hands before battle was even joined, because the drivers were not going to stop their charges for a mere man.

Behind the line of *gonnes*, companies and banners of infantry were forming on the grass strip that ran down the centre of the camp. It looked as if the whole population of Megara had been transported to Armea. There were thousands of men and women in each stand of pikes and arquebuses. The line seemed to extend into the dust at the edge of the world.

He saw people he knew – a wheelwright, an apprentice leather-worker, a tall, foppish man with whom he'd fenced. And then he saw Srinan, at the head of a troop of jingling City cavalry. The nobleman saluted with his sword.

'Morning, Timos,' he called.

Aranthur took his helmet off and bowed.

Apparently, on the day of a battle, everyone was friendly. Even Srinan, who was no friend of his.

He walked his horse to the picket in front of the General's tent. There were a dozen chargers already there. Ariadne was the smallest horse, but, for Aranthur's money, the handsomest. He gave her a pat and a carefully hoarded turnip and then went to the door of the tent.

One of the guards, an Imperial Axe, nodded.

'She's with General Roaris,' he said. 'I'd wait. If'n I was you.'

The man paused. His fellow Imperial Axe, on the other side of the door, spoke without visibly moving any muscle in his body.

'Which you ain't,' he said.

'Ain't?' the first Axe asked.

'You ain't him.'

'Sod off, Narsar.'

'Bollocks to you, Gart.'

The two blond giants stood as solid as statues of iron.

Aranthur walked back to his horse, fiddled in his saddlebag and found a pipe and some stock. He filled and tamped his pipe, but he didn't light it. Instead he put it back, carefully; pipeclay broke too easily for rough handling. Instead he took out his *kuria* crystal, ran a thumb over it, felt its *power*.

He put the chain over his head, and tucked the crystal into his shirt under his doublet. He took a deep breath, and then another, and used just a touch of the crystal to drop into a light meditation state, from whence he began to review the *workings* he could effect.

The Secret Walk. The first *working* he'd ever managed, it could hide him, but not unless certain preconditions were met – darkness, or shadows, or a preoccupied adversary. It was a simple, weak *working*, and not for battlefields.

The Purifier. A very simple *volteia* that made water safe to drink. Almost every person in the Empire could cast it.

A complex *occulta* called the *Eye of the Gods*. It was actually a cantrip of light with a vast array of modifications that adjusted the very air into a pair of lenses. It was a required element of first-year casting, and people failed out of the Academy because working it was so hard. It was not his best *occulta*.

The Red Shield, or *aspis* as the Magi called all the protective *occultae*.

34

He was merely adequate at casting it, as his brushes with combat had shown. But it cast quickly, and he was learning to trust it. It *could* be a very powerful protection, but he needed practice...

Leon's Pieasi, or compulsion. Leon was a long dead Byzas Magos, and his compulsion was both powerful and simple. A first year *working*. Aranthur had only ever used it on a friendly dog, in class.

The Safian Enhancement. Despite being a much more complex *working* than any of the others, he was confident that he could cast it in any condition or situation. The experience of writing his will on that particular *working* while near to death had forever imprinted it on him. It was *his* in a way that no other spell except the casual spark of fire was his.

A variety of cantrips or *volteie* that adjusted or made light.

A simple visual enhancement that allowed any caster to 'see' *sihr* and *saar*, the powers that fuelled *occultae*. Or rather, the powers that fuelled most of the Academy's *occultae*. The Safian spells were all powered by the caster's own will, a surprisingly different process.

Lately he was working on a *Safian Transference*. He could cast it, but without sufficient result to justify the expenditure. What ought to be like a puffer shot at close range was more like a breath of foul air. He took it out and played with it in what he imagined as a child's sandbox, an internal meditational demi-reality that he'd learnt in the first weeks of first year, as if a piece of the *Aulos* could be sealed off for his own research, which, just possibly, was exactly true. The Master of Arts had told him, repeatedly, that his sandbox would be essential to him later. Only now, on the edge of a battle, did he realise what a useful tool it was.

He held the *Safian Transference* in his head and rotated it to look at the *working*. He couldn't see his flaw. He needed to go back to the grimoire, or perhaps he had the starting conditions in a flawed way...

'Timos,' said a deep voice.

He released the trance.

The *Jhugj*, Drek Coryn Ringkoat, stood at a safe distance.

Aranthur bowed. 'Syr Ringkoat.'

'Syr Timos,' the *Jhugj* said. 'General Jackass has taken his orders and left us. It's safe to come in. She's in a mood, but then, so am I. You playing with fire there, Timos?'

Indeed, the grass under his left foot was smouldering.

Aranthur stepped away, and considered. The smoking grass had a pungent, piney smell, not unpleasant. The sole of his left foot was hot.

Something in his transference was draining *saar*. Into the ground. Interesting. Distracting.

'Come back to us, little sorcerer.' Ringkoat grinned.

Aranthur shook his head. 'I'm with you.'

He followed Ringkoat into the great pavilion. A dozen of the General's Black Lobsters were in the outer room, most of them fully armoured.

'Syr Timos, ma'am,' the *Jhugj* called out.

'Timos? Message,' the General snapped.

She was also fully dressed, in a long velvet coat with an incredibly embroidered buff coat over it, lined and slashed in silk, the hide brushed like tan velvet itself and so thick it would turn almost any sword cut. She had a fitted breastplate over the coat and Myr Jeninas, the Buccaleria Primas of the Black Lobsters, was holding her helmet.

'For the Capitan Pasha,' she said. 'Go. Compliments. Praise. Do the civil.'

That was all. Aranthur took the scroll tube and mounted as the General's black unicorn was brought from the horse lines. The animal was so big that it dwarfed the big cavalry horses, and its golden eyes seemed to glow. Aranthur could feel the thing's occult power.

He edged around it and let Ariadne have her head. In three strides he was galloping up, over the ridge, and down into the chaos and jumble of the Attian camp. Here, too, tens of thousands of men and women were forming – a veritable tide of horseflesh off to the left, and in the centre, six great blocks of the famous Yaniceri. They had standards with black horsetails, and drums of their own, and four sweating slaves carrying bronze cauldrons at the centre of every regiment. Aranthur looked at them with fascination, as they were the traditional enemies of his folk, at least in tales. Up close, they were heavily bearded, and his father or his uncle could have dropped into any of their regiments and vanished; the same height, the same noses, the same look.

He raised a hand in salute, and a Yaniceri officer raised a mace.

He galloped by. There was no need to ask directions; the Capitan Pasha's pavilion was the largest. It was also bright red, and set in the centre of the apparent chaos of the Attian camp.

Aranthur slowed to a canter, and then reined in, and the Sipahis, the Attian knights, parted for him. The Capitan Pasha wore armour of blued steel and gold over the finest maille Aranthur had ever seen, and under it, a deep, rich purple khaftan of silk that shone through the maille in the rising sun.

'Now let all the gods and goddesses rejoice, and be praised,' the Capitan Pasha said. 'A messenger from our dear Myr Tribane.'

He held out a strong white hand on which the fine red hairs stood out.

Aranthur handed him the tube.

The Capitan Pasha cracked the wax and took out a scroll. Inside the scroll were six silver sticks.

'Ah! Wonderful.'

The pasha was speaking in Armean. The Attian court spoke mostly Armean; Attian was for peasants, or so Aranthur had been told at the Academy.

'Any message?'

'No, my lord,' Aranthur said. 'Except Myr Tribane's compliments. She wishes your highness a glorious morning and the day of a hero, with a sunset of felicity.'

'See now! Here is the tongue of a poet in a barbarian!'

The Capitan Pasha slapped his back. The Attian commander was a large man, almost a giant. Up close, he smelled of spikenard and lemon.

Aranthur backed Ariadne a few steps. He was conscious that twenty fine horsemen were watching him.

The pasha shook his head. 'Eloquence and diligence deserve a reward.' He reached up, to the saddle of his warhorse, which waited behind him, and took from the saddle a long, gold-mounted puffer. 'Here. Kill our enemies with something beautiful.'

Aranthur leant out and took the puffer. Despite its length, it was fine and well-balanced. The butt was shaped like an eagle's talon holding a ball, which proved to be a detailed globe of the world.

'Highness, I am unworthy,' Aranthur said in his middling Armean. He waited, expecting an answer.

The pasha was reading the scroll. A hand twitched.

'You may retire,' a younger officer said. He said it with a smile. 'It's a battlefield, not a court. And your compliment was well-turned, syr. I am Ulgat Kartal.'

'Aranthur Timos,' he responded. 'Arnaut.'

'Hah!' Kartal said. 'My hereditary enemy! Many times, we raid your cattle.' He offered his hand.

Aranthur shrugged. 'I'm sure we've come for yours as well.'

He dropped the magnificent puffer into his empty saddle holster. City militia were expected to provide their own puffers. He'd acquired one in a fight in the City; now he had a second, although it was a hand's breadth longer and the eagle-claw butt stuck up out of the holster. The rain cover would not go over it.

A problem for another day, Aranthur thought, looking at the brilliant sunrise.

'Of course! Well, today, we are friends. Fight well!'

'And you!' Aranthur paused. 'What if he has an answer?'

Kartal waved with the same negligence that Tiy Drako might have. 'The pasha is a great lord, and has his own messengers.'

Aranthur understood. He saluted, and he turned Ariadne and was away. He gave her the signal to gallop, and let her go – a little showy, but there was something about the Attian camp that made him feel that he was on stage.

He reined in at the General's tent. The sun was fully up; most of the regiments were formed. Across the parade, one of their two regular infantry regiments was filing off from the centre.

Off to the east, the drums rolled, long and low.

'Timos?' the General called. She was standing by her monstrous mount. 'Message. Anything from the pasha?'

'No, ma'am,' he said.

'Hmm. Get a fresh horse. Roaris. Fast as you can.'

A liveried Imperial servant gave him a saddled horse and took Ariadne. He sprang into the saddle and took the tube as he passed, flashed a salute and was away, off to the west, where he knew Roaris to be.

He found the Imperial general fifteen minutes later, sitting on his chestnut warhorse at the top of a long hill behind the end of the ridge that held the camp, watching the opposing ridge. He was surrounded by his staff, which was much larger than General Tribane's.

'Messenger,' someone called.

Aranthur rode up to the general, whom he'd seen twice but to whom he'd never been introduced.

Vanax the Prince Verit Roaris was a very handsome man: almost

38

exactly the same height as Aranthur, strong jawed, with a short beard, a magnificent moustache, and the long nose, brown skin and green eyes of the oldest Byzas families. He rode a fine charger with an elaborate red and gold saddle cloth, and he wore the black and gold colours of his own ancient house, and of the Lions, the party of which he was the acknowledged head, instead of an Imperial uniform. By him was his standard, a golden rose embroidered on a black field, the exact reverse of Tribane's device.

Prince Verit was pointing at the ridge opposite, speaking to a long-nosed Byzas youth in a magnificent fur-trimmed doublet.

'War is a science, my boy, not some sort of slapdash tomfoolery,' Verit Roaris said. 'The slattern has no idea of how war functions, or what it's all for. I'll let her wallow in error a little, and then maybe I'll rescue her from her childish decisions. Or not.'

'But, my lord, we could lose the first line,' the young man insisted.

Aranthur felt he might have seen the young man at Mikal Kallinikos' home, or perhaps at a fencing *salle*.

'Shopkeepers and grocers? Always more where they came from, Syr Kanaris,' Roaris said. 'Best to thin the herd from time to time, anyway.'

Aranthur cleared his throat.

The aristocrat started, surprised by Aranthur's quiet approach.

'Who in a thousand iron hells are you, syr?' Roaris spat.

'Timos, syr.'

'One of Tribane's bed-warmers, eh?'

The general took the scroll tube and opened it. He flicked the scroll open. It too held several silver sticks. He took them and dropped them into a pocket in his buff coat. He smiled slightly, as if he had a private joke, and then nodded.

'Tell her that I understand. She already *deigned* to inform me of her *plans*. We are the third line. When the effeminate Attians melt away like butter, we're to come and save Myr Tribane from her foolishness and her trust of foreigners and her plan to run the world with shopkeepers. Carry on.'

'An Arnaut as a messenger?' laughed one of the staff. 'At least you know they can't read over your shoulder!' he jested.

It was Djinar. Aranthur's stomach muscles tensed and his horse fidgeted.

Djinar smiled. 'Toady. Informer. Liar, cheat,' he said.

Aranthur bowed.

'Aranthur Timos, at your service.'

He smiled easily as he said it, despite his inner turmoil, and he was pleased to see an instant flush of anger on the other man's face.

Aranthur backed his horse, and Djinar turned away ostentatiously, as if he was beneath the man's contempt, but Aranthur was trying to imagine...

It was just ten days since he'd seen Djinar on the steps on Rachman's jewellery shop. With Iralia by his side, and Ansu, they'd faced down the Servant, and captured the poisoned *kuria* crystals.

He was almost sure that the masked man he'd faced in the shattered doorway of the jeweller's was Djinar.

And now *Djinar* was on Roaris' staff.

Aranthur dashed back to the General's tent, a distance of almost a mile, trying to imagine how to express his fears. Trying to imagine for himself what it was he feared.

By the time he reined in, most of the infantry was off the parade ground by the officers' lines. The last of the militia regiments were filing off down the long streets of tents towards the enemy.

The General was gone, as was her bodyguard and her banner. And his precious Ariadne.

Aranthur trotted along the ridge until he could see clearly down into the plain. The black unicorn was easy to spot, and he turned his borrowed mount and galloped down the ridge. On his way down he passed a long line of Attian *gonnes*, drawn for the most part by bullocks, but just as big and just as magnificent as the Imperial *gonnes*.

He cantered up, his horse slowing without direction from him. He dismounted by the General. The borrowed horse fidgeted as his weight changed. It flinched away from the General's unicorn, almost spilling Aranthur in the dust, but he made a dancer's recovery.

Two grooms took the horse's bit and pulled it away.

'Timos,' the General said.

Prince Ansu was standing close to her, his reins over his arm. Dahlia was just behind him.

'Ma'am, Vanax Roaris understands he is the third line.' Aranthur couldn't stop himself from raising an eyebrow to indicate what he thought of General Roaris. 'Ma'am, I wish to say—'

'He had better understand,' she said acerbically. 'Message. Ansu.'

Prince Ansu stepped forward.

'Vanax Silva,' the General said. 'She's somewhere near the banner of the First in the front line. Ansu, try to find out which of the Attian officers is taking command of their front line.'

'Front line?' Aranthur asked Dahlia.

'We're fighting in three lines. Big lines.'

'Message. Tarkas. Vanax Kunyard. This message. And then find Centark Equus and tell him to get his arse up here.' The General shrugged. 'We don't have enough cavalry to let some wait around combing their hair.'

She waved Dahlia away and pointed at the next messenger.

'Sasan. Message. Capitan Pasha.'

The Safian stood out in his fine maille and tall helmet. He waved at Aranthur and cantered away.

The line of messengers shuffled forward. Aranthur was now half a dozen from the front: three women and a man he didn't know, and a man he'd fenced with, who gave him a casual wave. He didn't have the General's attention, and as strongly as he desired to share his sudden suspicions, the middle of a battle did not seem the time.

'You knew Kallinikos,' the man said.

'I liked him a great deal,' Aranthur said.

'As did I. I'm Strongarm.'

It was a Northern name – maybe even a Western Isles name – although the man looked perfectly normal, in a dark blue coat with an elaborate black and gold breastplate.

The women and the other man in the messenger queue introduced themselves. The man, as tall as Strongarm, leant forward, as if studying Aranthur carefully.

'By the Lady,' he said. 'You're the lad who saved my bacon in the street, the night of the riot.' He extended a gloved hand, and then stripped the glove with his teeth. 'Marcos Klinos, House Klinos. Imperial War Staff.'

Aranthur grinned. They had fought back to back, for no better reason than that they were attacked.

'Syr. I am Aranthur Timos. Pardon my laugh – everyone I've ever met seems to be here.'

The man grinned. 'At the least, I owe you a cup of wine,' he said, and then his name was called and he rode off.

In front of them, the Yaniceri regiments marched into the front line and deployed. The Attian infantry had the right half of the front line. The two Imperial regular regiments were alternating with the most reliable Imperial militia in the centre. The rest was filled in with squares of City Militia, their pike heads glittering in the strong sunlight. Aranthur had seen at least one regiment of Arnauts, too.

'There we are, then,' Myr Tribane said with satisfaction. 'Jennie, we've got the front line formed. Go back and tell me how the third line is doing.'

Her *Primas* saluted and rode away.

The General turned to Aranthur.

'Don't worry. Your turn is coming. You have a question?'

'Ma'am, when does the battle start?'

'When does any story begin? It started when we decided on this gambit, a year and more ago.' She smiled.

Up close, Aranthur found that her hands were shaking very slightly.

'But today began before dawn, when two thousand Attian irregular cavalry struck their horse lines.' She shrugged. 'They weren't brilliant, but they screwed my opponent's plans for a rapid approach march, and bought us the time to deploy. Once we're deployed . . .'

The drums rolled from the opposing ridge, loud and long. The sound was like the approach of a storm, or the sign of an impending doom.

'Message, Timos,' the General said. 'Oral only. Go to the First, and tell the bandmaster, with my compliments, that he may play. We have music, too.'

Aranthur didn't know whether he should be offended at such an inconsequential errand, but he bowed, and took yet another borrowed horse, and galloped down the ridge. The second line, where the General was standing on a low dimple of a hillock in the centre of the ridge, was almost five hundred paces behind the first line. The first line was a mile and a half wide, and Aranthur's rapid calculation suggested there were fifteen thousand soldiers in the first line alone.

He knew the flag of the First from drills in the City. He rode up, and saluted the senior centark.

'From the General, for the bandmaster,' he said.

'Be my guest, syr.' The commander was *not* a nobleman; in fact, from his accent, he was an Arnaut. He pointed to a tall man in an elaborately plumed helmet. 'Carry on, brother. You are an Arnaut?'

'Yes, syr.'

The centark smiled. 'Go pass your message, lad.'

The officer looked magnificent in a velvet fustanella with a breast-plate, and an aquamarine silk turban.

Aranthur saluted, and then trotted to where the bandmaster stood. Another rumble of drums from over the next ridge.

He saluted the gaudy bandmaster.

'General Tribane says you may play.'

The man grinned. 'All my life I've waited for this!'

He turned, and behind him, forty bandsmen took up their instruments – mostly long fifes and heavy, cylindrical drums. Then he took from a pouch at his belt a short, green stick. He broke it. Aranthur had seen message sticks before; a whole section of the Arsenal was dedicated to their manufacture, and senior students at the *Studion* often participated. But the military had their own, with special protections.

'Imperial March, on my command,' he said into the stick.

Aranthur looked at the ranks of pikes. The First Regiment, the oldest in the Empire, were all professional soldiers, men and women who spent most of their time building roads and policing villages. But they had excellent armour and their tight lines and obvious discipline contrasted with the next regiment, a City Militia regiment, where bellowing dekarks were still trying to get the most difficult people into their ranks.

In front of the regiment, its two companies of musketeers waited patiently in lines. From a distance, they looked like the sleeves on a person's doublet, with the pikes as the body of the doublet.

Aranthur took one more look and remounted.

'Ready!' the bandmaster said, and raised his mace.

Even in the militia regiment on the left, Aranthur saw the band-master's mace go up.

A single note sounded over the battlefield, high, wild, and shrill. And a single drum beat three times. One.

Two.

Three.

The sound swelled. Suddenly there were four hundred drums and four hundred fifes.

A crash of trumpets.

Aranthur felt as if his blood was on fire.

He rode up the ridge to the sound of the Imperial March rolling like disciplined fire from the front line. By the time he dismounted, most of the other messengers had already returned, and he handed in his mount and rejoined the queue. The General waved at him, as if acknowledging the sound. It was slightly attenuated by distance in the second line, but still loud and clear.

'Well,' said his one-time fighting companion, Klinos, 'we've won the music contest.'

All of the messengers laughed.

From their position, it was easy enough to see the whole formation. The first line was almost entirely infantry – ten formations, all with gaps between them. The Yaniceri had slaves digging ditches in front of them. The Imperial troops stood easily under their pikes.

In the second line, cavalry, mostly Attian, alternated with infantry, mostly militia from both Atti and the Empire. In the very centre, though, stood the General, and with her was a company of Imperial Axes, as well as her own Black Lobsters and the whole of the Imperial Nomadi. Just to her right stood the Capitan Pasha, with two large squadrons of magnificent Sipahis. In front of them was a large block of blue-coated men with big helmets and huge pole axes.

Just behind the second line, Attian slaves and Imperial engineers were digging like ants. Aranthur watched a dozen grooms move the messengers' horses as an engineer ran a rope line right through the former picket line. Even as the grooms hurried to move the horses, a wagon began dropping pre-woven gabions like empty baskets at intervals.

'Lady, give me two more hours,' the General said. 'Right then. Everyone mount. On me, now.'

The General suited her action to her words, and vaulted onto the back of her monster. It gave one curvet and settled, and she trotted to the left, down off the little hillock and onto the slope of the ridge.

Instantly a pair of engineers, stripped to their shirts, began to drive stakes into the ground. Artillerists appeared with picks and spades.

'Doesn't she have messages for us?' Aranthur asked.

Klinos shrugged. 'I've never seen a battle like this. But usually after the message sticks are handed out and opened, we sit and get lectures on warfare.'

'But there's nothing to do!'

'Be lucky she doesn't make us dig,' Ringkoat said. 'She has, afore this.'

'She's won many battles?' Aranthur asked.

Ringkoat croaked a laugh. 'You know what Roaris calls her, eh? The General who never won a battle.' He shrugged, his massive muscles raising the armoured shoulders a handspan. 'She's never fought a real battle. But she's studied them all her life.' He looked out over the plain. 'Truth is, no one in the Empire has done this – on this scale – in five generations.'

'That's . . .' Aranthur couldn't think of a useful thing to say.

'Exactly. Look. Here they come.'

Over the far ridge came a rustle and a glitter, and even a mile away, the ground seemed to rustle.

'That's a lot of people,' Ringkoat said after a few minutes had passed.

'Quite enough of everything to give us a warm day's work,' the General said. 'Well, there's one question answered,' she went on.

'What's that?' Ringkoat asked.

The General nodded. 'They're going to fight. By now they must know that Atti isn't in a state of civil war, about to collapse. But hells, maybe they believe their own propaganda. We all usually do.'

'Maybe they just think they can win a straight up fight,' Ringkoat said.

'That's my hope, Coryn.' The General watched the movement of her enemy, and then shook her head. 'They're not waiting. Where are my *gonnes*?'

No one spoke.

'Timos. Master Gonner. Time until she can open fire.'

Aranthur got a foot into the stirrup. Ringkoat all but threw him over the saddle.

'Top of the little hill we just left. Red velvet coat, stupid looking wig,' the *Jhugj* said.

Aranthur rode off. It was a short canter. The woman in question was obvious: thin as a rail, her red velvet coat filthy, her wig like a stage witch's hair.

'General Tribane wants to know how long until you can open fire?' he asked.

'Tell Myr Tribane that if she'd have allowed me to dig in last night, we'd have had rounds in the tubes ten minutes ago!' the woman shouted.

A heavy *gonne* was rolling forward into a shallow pit at the brow of the round hillock. Three *gonnes* were already in place, with fascines that were being filled even as the *gonnes* were traversed.

A very young woman sprinted forward, the weight of a heavy cannonball apparently nothing to her. A big man took the ball. Behind him, two others opened a parchment cartridge and pushed the contents down the wide mouth of the bronze drake.

A clod of turf followed the powder, and then the ball.

'Ready number four,' called a Byzas voice.

'Tell her nibs I'll be firing in . . .' The woman glanced at a *kuria*-powered device. 'Two minutes.'

'Thanks. Two minutes,' Aranthur said, and he was going back down to where the General waited.

A servant took his horse; he sketched a bow.

'One minute from now,' he said.

She was watching the plain.

A whole line of shambling infantry were coming down the opposite ridge. They were still half a mile away, and they were slow.

'Magi,' the General said.

A short, portly older man stood up.

'Give me a close look at that infantry line,' she said.

The Magos spread his hands and cast. Aranthur felt the *saar* going into the winds of chaos and being written on reality; he almost understood it. He knew the *working*, admired the ease with which the man cast the *Eye of the Gods*.

A wedge of air in front of the General changed shape, oscillating.

'Sweet Light and bitter Darkness,' the General cursed.

Aranthur was close enough behind her to see what she saw. A line of women and children.

'Lady,' he swore.

'Finer resolution,' the General said. 'Track left. Now right. Eagle almighty. *Subjugated?*'

'Working,' said the Magos.

Aranthur noted that there were six men and women seated on camp stools. He didn't know any of them. He assumed they were the Empire's much vaunted *Polemagi*. The Battle Magi.

'Dorotea!' the General snapped.

'This,' said the portly man. He didn't appear to do anything.

A short woman stood up. She tossed a *working* with a rapid fluidity that Aranthur could only admire again. It was a heavy, complex *working*, but it went like a whip.

Just to the left of the enemy centre, the long, thick line of stumbling women and children came unravelled.

'I took out their *subjugation*,' the short woman said.

'What the hell is that?' another of the Magi asked.

As a few hundred of the rail-thin women ran, they revealed a tall figure swathed in scarlet. Before anyone could comment, though, a barrage of red balefire fell into the shields and burned through them in two places. The portly man fell, gasping. Before he was all the way to the ground, there was a soft, sloppy *pop*. The rush of air, the heat, and the smell of burnt soap told of a massive release of sorcery, and the *sihr* rolled away, black as death.

Aranthur's face was suddenly warm and wet. He wiped blood off his face. The portly man was dead, his head exploded from some terrible *puissance* that Aranthur hadn't even felt.

Above him and to the right, the first *gonne* fired.

The distance viewing spell was gone, dead with its caster.

Another line appeared behind the first, this one not shambling.

'I need a view,' the General spat. 'That's cavalry. The infantry isn't a serious attack – it's slaves being driven forward to demoralise us. Timos! Tell the Master Gonner to concentrate on the cavalry.'

A third caster left his camp chair.

'Someone shield us. Lady, you lot have practised all this, have you not?'

'Agathur . . . was our best . . .' the third caster muttered.

Still, even as Aranthur put his foot into his stirrup – his own beloved Ariadne, he noticed – he saw the new man raise a viewing lens as a fourth caster evinced a pale, glowing *aspis* over the whole command position.

Aranthur rode out from under it. He cantered up the hill again to the Master Gonner.

All the *gonnes* were silent.

'The General says to fire on the cavalry, not the infantry screen,' Aranthur said.

'She needs to make up her mind. She just told me to cease fire.' She waved a broken message stick.

Below them, just two hundred paces away, a series of lights and explosions played across the pale golden *aspis*.

Aranthur was confused, and he didn't like the play of *sihr*, the more violent magikal power, on the shield. His confusion passed through his hips to Ariadne, who began to fret.

'I'll ride back and confirm the order,' he said.

The Master Gonner spoke into her stick. Aranthur heard the sharp tone of the General in her reply.

'She says cease fire,' the woman said. 'All in a rush to get my *gonnes* up, and then tells me to sit silent.'

Aranthur saluted and rode down the hill. The flow of *sihr* was less; he timed two attacks and rode through the shield in the next interval.

Another of the Magi was down, burned black.

'Well?' the General snapped. 'Timos? Why are our *gonnes* silent?'

Aranthur was dismounting; a groom whisked Ariadne away and out of the golden *aspis*.

All the Magi were on their feet. Aranthur could feel the incoming attack. He felt how the enemy caster had built a rhythm, a *tempo*, like a swordsman setting up a deception, and now . . .

All that in far less than a heartbeat. Aranthur reached out, put a hand on one of the Magi, and passed a steady pulse of *power* through him into the shield. He knew a lot more about channelling than he had known when he let Iralia pull *power* from him until he was *saar*-sick. He pushed the *power*; it flowed, all in the *tempo* of the attack.

The *aspis* went black, and then, slowly, recovered to pale gold.

'Dahlia!' he called.

'On it.' She stepped in among the Magi. So did Prince Ansu.

'Sophia, wise and true,' whispered the Magas. 'Thanks, youngsters.'

The General was looking through the viewer.

'Timos, why have my *gonnes* stopped firing?' she repeated.

She seemed not to know that they'd just *barely* survived a massive magikal assault.

'Ma'am, you ordered the Master Gonner to cease fire.'

Her head snapped around. 'I what?'

'You ordered the . . .'

Timos was more anxious about the General's palpable anger than about the *tempo* of magikal attacks.

'I told you to order her to put fire on the cavalry,' the General spat.

'I told her that, ma'am. But she spoke through her message stick and . . .'

The General whirled. 'Fuck.' She raised a gold message stick. 'Vanax Kunyard.'

There was a crackle and an indistinct sound.

'Kunyard, report.'

More indistinct crackle.

'Timos, on me.' She turned to her groom. 'Horse.'

In moments the two of them were mounted. Aranthur followed the General, on one of her own messenger horses, as they rode further to the left, along the second line.

Vanax Kunyard's command group had two layers of shields over it. Aranthur's instant summary was that Kunyard had a better battle magik staff than the General, for whatever reason.

Kunyard was a big man; he was on horseback, and he saluted with a baton. By his side was the Pennon Malconti, in full armour. Malconti raised an eyebrow at Aranthur.

'Vanax. Message me.'

Kunyard shrugged and raised a silver stick. He spoke into it.

Nothing emerged from the General's gold stick.

'Destroy it. The enemy have our codes.'

The General's voice had developed a pinched sound, as if she was angry at the whole world.

Kunyard cursed, and broke the stick in his hand in a dozen pieces.

'Messenger only, then,' he said. 'That'll be slow and clumsy.'

'Least of our problems,' the General said. 'Their *Ars Magika* is better than ours. How the fuck can that be?' She shook her helmeted head. 'Never mind that. I need you to outflank those flanking columns—'

'I wasn't born yesterday, Alis.'

The two smiled at each other like old friends, or sparring partners.

Below them on the long slope, the first line was waiting. The enemy line of infantry, whether slaves or not, was plodding down their own hill. They would have to cross a very small stream, mostly just damp ground.

'Timos, on me.'

Together they swept along the second line, informing each commander that the coded message system was compromised.

'Go to the pasha,' she ordered. 'Tell my *gonnes* to start firing!' she yelled as he rode away.

Aranthur rode across the back of the second line. He delivered the message to the Master Gonner. She tossed her message sticks on the ground in disgust and started yelling orders. Aranthur was already gone, angling up the ridge to where he could see the pasha and his magnificent Sipahis.

Behind him, the *gonnes* began with a crashing salvo. Twenty big *gonnes* were incredibly loud, firing in a rolling volley; smoke billowed out over the ridge. Aranthur tried to watch the fall of the shot, and could not, but he saw the long, thick line of enemy cavalry ripple.

A pulse of red fire flashed out of the centre of the enemy ridge and fell on the *gonnes*. There was a flash, and the *gonnes* began to fire again. Someone had defeated the enemy spell – Aranthur had no idea who.

He tore his eyes away from the battle and rode up the ridge to the pasha. The pasha dropped his message sticks into the dust with a look of disgust and spoke in rapid, musical Armean to one of his own long-robed Magi.

'Tell the General I will have my own *barakas* attack the enemies,' he said. 'We can't just wait for them to cut us apart.'

Aranthur heard the Magos say, in Armean, 'He is very strong, *Effendi.*'

'Hit him, *Hakim.*'

Aranthur wondered, given that he was only a third-year Academy student, why all the army's Magi were not in a single choir, for maximum effect. But his thoughts were swept away by the sheer spectacle of the battle that lay before him, as his position on the ridge gave him the full panorama.

To the left and right, heavy columns of enemy cavalry, shining horses and glittering steel, swept to envelop his army. In the centre, the long, slow advance of the thick ribbon of enemy infantry was backed by six big blocks of cavalry.

From near the very top of the opposing ridge, light sparkled. And death fell on the first line – thin, distant screams, and flashes of light where local casters and amulets countered some of the effectiveness of the adversary.

Aranthur thought of fighting against the Servant in the Square of the Mulberry Trees – of the success of his thrown sword in a fight otherwise entirely conducted in the *Aulos*. He leant forward, and urged his messenger horse to a gallop. One more time he raced up the hill that dominated the artillery position.

'You again?' the Master Gonner asked.

'Ma'am. You see that sparkle?'

Aranthur pointed, and the Master Gonner called for a viewer and looked.

In the magikal viewer, the area looked as if it was bathed in a thick ivory light. Nothing distinct could be seen.

'That's the focal point of their *buvu* attacks,' Aranthur said, using all his languages, trying to get his point across. 'The *zori* magik. The *sihr*.'

'The General wants me to switch fire?' the Master Gonner asked.

Aranthur shook his head. 'No, ma'am. It is my own observation.'

Another line of red fire fell on the first line. And the enemy infantry line was crossing the bottom of the valley.

But the Master Gonner was nodding.

'I'm willing to give it a try. Betha! Look lively. Ranging shot—'

'If you try the range, he'll get his shields up,' Aranthur said. 'I'm a Magos – I am not making this up.'

A green and gold casting from behind them – the pasha's choir. It passed like a beam of sunlight on a cloudy day.

The response was immediate: an explosion of ruby light, and a single white beam.

'Got it,' said one of the gonners.

Two men were moving the trail of one of the bronze monsters while Betha tracked her target by eye.

'There--dyce. Ready, *gonne* three.'

'Ready one!'

'Ready seven!'

'Ready four!'

'All together!' the Master Gonner roared. 'And—!'

Linstocks went up all over the position.

'Fire!'

All the linstocks went down. Most of the *gonnes* had quill primers in their vents, and they all went off together. A few, more old-fashioned gonners set fire directly to the excess powder atop the touch hole. Two brand new Imperial *gonnes* had flintlocks that fired immediately, faster than the linstock-lit *gonnes*. The whole salvo took about four beats of Aranthur's heart to fire.

Aranthur watched the far-off point on the enemy ridge, but there was no apparent effect. The Master Gonner ordered a second salvo while Aranthur remounted and rode down to where the General had mounted her unicorn at the head of the Black Lobsters. Dahlia and Ansu were maintaining shields with the short Magas and her single remaining partner, a nondescript man in the brown robe of a priest of Aploun. There were a number of corpses in the command position. Two of the messengers were down, and four Magi, and one of the grooms.

Another messenger galloped in behind Aranthur.

'Timos?' the General asked.

'Pasha says his Magi will target the enemy magisters,' he said. 'He destroyed his message sticks. The Master Gonner is trying the enemy magisters too.'

'Best news I've heard all morning,' the General said. 'Jennie?' she called.

Primas Jeninas was sliding off her mount.

'Ma'am, he's fucking *withdrawing*.'

'What?' General Tribane, who had kept a fairly mild demeanour up to now, snapped. She flushed red. 'What in ten thousand iron hells?'

'Vanax Roaris says he is withdrawing the third line, and recommends that you extricate yourself. From what he calls "Tribane's disaster".' Jeninas was red with anger. 'I spoke my mind, ma'am. He told me to fuck off, in just so many words. Ma'am, he says he is not now, nor has ever been, your subordinate, and he's exercising his independent command.'

General Tribane stood in silence for as long as it might take a child to count to three. Above them, the *gonnes* fired another salvo. No red fire had fallen on the front line; Aranthur had a feeling, a hunch, that the pasha's Magos, or perhaps the *gonnes*, had won them a respite.

'Well,' Tribane said.

Aranthur had seen his father do the same: shrug off bad news and go on with the work. It was a very special type of courage. She glanced around, winced at the flickering shields above her, and pointed.

'The Second line must advance,' the General said forcefully. 'If we retire, we lose a generation of our citizens.' She pointed at the militia infantry in the front. 'Kunyard better know what he's doing out on the left. Now I have nothing to send him.

'Klinos! Go to Vanax Kunyard. Tell him to go for the cavalry column to his left front. If he can spare Malconti, send the Pennon to support the left of the . . . The Second Dacan and Fourth Arnaut and the Twenty-third City. Understand?'

'Yes, ma'am.'

The nobleman mounted a horse and he was away, his mount's hooves raising dust.

'Tarkas – no, I need you here. Timos. Back to the pasha. Tell him we're moving to support our infantry line and he might want to do the same. Make it sound nice, but it's an order.'

'Yes, ma'am.'

'Sasan, Master Gonner and then down to Vanax Silva. Tell her to withdraw one hundred paces.'

Ringkoat shook his head. 'Ma'am, the Yaniceri have dug in. They can't withdraw.'

'Fuck,' the General said.

That was the last that Aranthur heard. He was already mounted. His legs were tired, his hips stiff, and it was not yet breakfast time in Megara. If he was home, he might just be purchasing *quaveh* for the Master of Arts.

The Pasha had moved two hundred paces to the right. Aranthur rode past a row of dead Sipahis and at least one of the pasha's staff, horribly burned. One man's *katir* was bent like a melting candle in the skeletal claw of his desiccated hand.

Aranthur's eyes passed over the horror and he reined in amid the pasha's staff.

'Lord of Glory.'

He saluted the pasha. He hoped he remembered the phrase correctly from a poem.

The pasha smiled. 'You are a charming barbarian.'

'Myr Tribane is throwing our cavalry at the left-hand horn of their attack.'

'And she hopes I'll do the same? I concur.' The pasha nodded.

'We are moving up to support our first line.'

The pasha shrugged. 'My Yaniceri need no support. Not against that rabble.' He leant forward. 'One of my grooms says that your Vanax Roaris is... hmmm. Farther away? Than he was before. Leaving my Prince Atbey sitting with my reserve Ghulami and no friends, eh? Do I need to know something, young knight?'

Aranthur had no idea what the proper response was.

'I... have no orders on this matter.'

'Eh. Well, I would like a report. Tell the General, if Roaris is withdrawing, we are in deep trouble, and allies talk about these things.' The pasha's eyes were hard. 'I have just lost a good friend. Tell the General that we should meet. In fifteen minutes, I think. As soon as I have seen the cavalry fight begin.'

He turned and began to rattle orders, and his own messengers began to ride away to his right flank cavalry.

Aranthur assumed that he was dismissed, and rode for the centre. His horse was fresh; the long string of messenger remounts made sense. He galloped across the back of the second line. Now there were stray bolts of *power* striking around the second line. A line of red passed over him before he could raise an *aspis* and moved on, burning a black line into the sandy soil and the summer grass.

The first line was about to engage.

Aranthur rode up. The General had also moved. She'd gone down the ridge three hundred paces, and most of the cavalry to her left was gone.

Half a mile off to the left, there was a rising column of golden yellow dust.

The *gonnes* fired.

Aranthur slid from his mount; a groom took the gelding, and Aranthur bowed. He repeated the pasha's message while the thickset Magas adjusted the General's expanded magikal view of the first line.

The view passed across the Third City Regiment.

The two sleeves of musketeers stood ready in front of the block of pikes. Just beyond them, several hundred thin, hungry looking women and children shuffled to a stop perhaps forty paces from the levelled muskets. The view was so clear that Aranthur could see the minute snakes of smoke rising from the burning matchcords of the musketeers.

'Fire,' whispered the General.

But the Third held its fire as the women and children shuffled slowly forward, despairing eyes down.

'*Fire* for the love of the Lady,' the General said.

But the militia shuffled, and looked at each other. An officer went out from the musketeers, hands extended. They couldn't hear what he had to say, but his open arms spoke for him.

Aranthur felt the casting. So did Ansu, whose head snapped around. So did Dahlia, massaging her golden *aspis*.

In the viewer, the thin figures transformed from victims to predators. And they dashed forward like hungry wolves on a weakened prey.

They were only twenty paces from the musketeers.

'Lady, no,' the General said.

Some of the musketeers fired, silent blooms of smoke from their muskets showing that their resolve had cracked. Others held their fire – altruism, or shock, or horror. A few of the scarecrow wolves fell, but not enough.

The musketeers broke. Many were too slow, and they died in a red haze of dust and blood, the blows of their suddenly galvanised foes too rapid to follow. But more did as they had been taught, and ran for the cover of their pikes, a few paces behind, rolling in under the protection of the long shafts.

The pikes were as surprised as the musketeers had been. In several places, panicked musketeers burst straight into the formation, forcing their comrades to raise the lethal pike heads so as not to impale a friend, a son, a sister.

The human wolves were only a pace or two behind, running their prey. They flowed into the cracks and crevices in the pike block, and the whole block began to shred, the formation collapsing back.

Down the ridge, at the point from which the women and children had started their assault, there stood a single, scarlet-clad wraith. The *Exalted* waited with patience, arms crossed. Aranthur watched the red figure, even as the pikes fell back.

Then the red robes whirled, and the still figure became a streak, almost impossible to follow. It accelerated through the surviving fringe of musketeers – two knots of men and women fighting desperately and hopelessly – and left a mist of blood in its wake. In each hand, the figure had a sword of white light. When the scarlet streak went into the pike block down an alley created by the feral children...

The Third City died. Fifteen hundred prosperous, well-trained, well-equipped grocers and leather-workers and cutlers and paper makers; apprentices and journeywomen and masters; nobles and commons.

As the General watched, unable to tear her eyes away, they died.

2

Eastern Armea

As Aranthur watched in horror, the Third City died.

The line of women and children struck the whole front line. The Third was not the only regiment overcome, unable to respond. The General put a hand to her mouth as the magikal viewer swept along the front line.

'Lady,' she breathed.

But the disaster was not mirrored everywhere. Almost at their feet, the First Regiment, the road surveyors and engineers of the regular army, fired a crashing volley at point-blank range into the oncoming line of apparent captives. They had a fraction of time to appreciate what had happened to their left, to the Third City. An officer ordered the volley, and the regular soldiers obeyed. The volley smashed the women. The survivors went forward and were met by the second volley from the rear two ranks, firing like a clockwork automaton. The whole sleeve withdrew into the forest of pikes as if they were on parade. No scarlet streak eventuated; perhaps a *gonne*, or a dozen musket balls, had ended it.

To the right, a Yaniceri regiment failed to break the charge. They fought for their lives at the edge of their trench, hand to hand with a rabble of *enhanced* peasants and not one but two of the red horrors. To their right, another Yaniceri regiment stood their ground, shot down their opponents and then charged, clearing their front, ruthlessly butchering the survivors. On the far right, repeated magikal attacks had already decimated an elite Yaniceri regiment, and it was broken. Worse, in their flight, they panicked the Ulaman militia above them on the ridge, and they ran without firing a shot. On the far left, too, several Imperial regiments shared the fate of the Third: farmers from Bagas died in a scarlet mist. A regiment of artists and fishmongers, weakened by an hour's pounding from the enemy sorcerers, broke when it was charged, was run down and massacred.

The General watched. Beyond the enemy 'infantry' were big squadrons of cavalry – well armoured, on fine horses. They were manoeuvring, preparing to exploit the portions of the first line that had collapsed.

'I was wrong,' the General said. 'The infantry was the real attack. It's all fucking real, and they have our communications and they have superior magikal support.'

'Their magik hasn't launched a tangible attack in the real for some time,' Dahlia said.

The General shook her head.

'I hear you, Myr Tarkas, but I think we're in a different phase. Our enemy has a playbook. We're fighting a doctrine.'

The *gonnes* fired, a timed ripple. All twenty *gonnes* fired at the mass of enemy cavalry in front of them. The results were spectacular, and Aranthur could see, even five hundred paces away, the chaos in the enemy ranks.

'I need time. Time that can only be bought by heroism. Timos – first line. Find Vanax Silva. Prepare for cavalry. Tell her I'm coming. Tell her to *hold*.'

'Yes, ma'am.'

Aranthur tried not to think that Sasan had not returned from his earlier mission.

He mounted yet another horse, and leant forward. The First had its musketeers back out. They fired a volley into the gruesome horde that appeared to be feeding on the dead of the Third City. A knot of the enemy broke away from the last stand around the Third colours and began to lope towards the First.

Aranthur slipped off to the right, towards the melee where the Yaniceri were still struggling to clear their ranks of their adversaries. Half a company of the First's musketeers stood, muskets primed, in an agony of indecision.

Aranthur galloped in behind them. He found Vanax Silva on horseback under the First's great blue and silver standard – a flag so old that some people worshipped it and the gilded eagle at the top of the staff. Aranthur automatically made the Eagle sign.

'Myr Tribane says, prepare for cavalry, and, she *is* coming,' he panted.

He pointed into the dust. Down here, nothing much could be seen more than fifty paces away.

Silva shook her head.

'If the Attians go down, I'm fucked anyway. Screw the cavalry – that's a problem for later.' She turned to the Arnaut centark. 'Iskander! Take the . . . musketeers. Help the Attians.'

The Arnaut officer drew a magnificent blue and gold *kilij*. He trotted his horse to the waiting body of musketeers.

'Draw your swords!' he roared.

The regulars had swords, and bucklers too. They dropped their heavy matchlocks and pressed together.

'Coming, brother?' the officer asked in Souliote.

Aranthur drew his long sword. It warmed in his hand. As it had been the morning of his first duel, he found himself curiously eager, carried away on a tide of his own excitement.

Ahead of them was the flank of the dying Yaniceri regiment. There were two obvious eddies in the fighting, and in the middle of both, through the dust, Aranthur could see scarlet.

The other Arnaut grinned.

'That's the spirit, brother,' he said. 'Let's go!'

The clump of musketeers jogged forward. It wasn't a charge, because they were entering a confused fight, but as soon as they made contact they changed the engagement. Tired Yaniceri gained heart.

Until they reached the first scarlet vortex. Aranthur was among the first. He cut at a woman who was swinging a *tulwar* with both hands, and behind her was the *Exalted*. He'd seen one in the skirmish, two days before, and he thought he had an answer.

But he miscalculated, and then he was on his back, on the ground, and his horse was dead, its two front legs cut clean off by a white scythe of *power*. Aranthur's leg was pinned under his fallen mount's weight, and he felt as if his left hip was smashed. The glowing red thing looked at him and moved on. Almost too fast to see, it turned and killed the Arnaut officer and two veteran Imperial musketeers. Its blinding white weapons cut through bucklers and armour, swords and limbs, so that it never had to stop moving.

Aranthur reached inside, found the fire, and wrote on reality.

Enhancement flowed through him. He wrenched his leg from under his dead mount in a faster *tempo* and the battle around him seemed to slow to crawl. A Yaniceri took his death blow in agonising hesitation, his last exhalation prolonged like the climax of an aria. One of the regular musketeers managed to stay alive against the tide of women slashing at him. Their slashes were in Aranthur's time, now, while the musketeer's parry seemed sluggish. He flowed to his feet, accelerating into a higher phase. He was, indeed, with the gods. He found his sword and picked it up in the same *tempo* as the *Exalted* gutted another musketeer with a rising sweep of its left sword of light.

Aranthur went at the scarlet killer.

It turned.

Operating in the same *tempo* as the red storm gave Aranthur the chance to really see it. It was tall – taller than a man – and androgynous, with pale skin spattered in blood, white hair tied in a tight queue, now soaked in gore, and a white mask, and elaborate lines of tattoos like jewellery on wrists and neck.

Aranthur put his sword behind him, in a deceptive guard his master favoured against an unknown opponent. He had never faced anything quite so completely 'unknown'.

The blood-soaked assassin turned and faced him.

It was obviously surprised. In the moment of its hesitation, Aranthur closed the measure, lifting his foot to avoid the entrails of a dying Yaniceri. The thing tracked him, as if time had stopped.

But it hadn't. One of the musketeers shot it. She was only three paces away. Her weapon seemed to come up with glacial slowness, but the *Exalted's* entire attention was fixated on Aranthur.

The musket ball tore away its jaw.

Aranthur struck. He was perfectly aware that his sword wouldn't parry one of the bars of white fire, but he was who he was, and he was at his measure with a sword in his hand and the power of surprise. His point came up from behind his right side, edge first.

Yes said a woman's voice in his head.

And then, as if in joy, '*Now we are revealed.*'

The *Exalted* stumbled, and got its right arm up, cutting straight at Aranthur's head.

His sword crossed the bar of light...

60

And held it.

His sword burned a brilliant blue. He was blinded, stunned, but not as stunned as his adversary, who fell back a step.

Aranthur's body acted without him, his wrist turning, his deceptive cut rolling off the heavy cross. It was not a matter of thought. He never thought it.

The *Exalted*'s right hand fell to the ground, cleanly severed.

A mortally wounded Yaniceri cut its hamstrings from behind with a hooked knife.

Even with two death wounds, the *Exalted* whirled. Falling, it beheaded the Yaniceri left-handed. It tried to reach Aranthur but it was down, its left leg unable to support it.

Aranthur cut off the left arm with a simple cut, and the white swords went out.

Even in his massively enhanced time, Aranthur saw the focus on the face of the musketeer who had shot the thing, and he turned.

The second *Exalted*.

It came for him. As if called. Summoned.

Aranthur felt the *kuria* crystal on his chest grow warm, as if he had cast *saar*.

This time, there was no pause in the *tempo*. Both swords reached for him.

He covered. Again, his old, heavy sword burned like a brilliant blue-white diamond lit by a volcano. *He made both parries.*

While they crossed, someone shot them with a puffer. The ball passed through Aranthur's coat, although he didn't know it until later, and struck the *Exalted*.

It attacked again.

It only seemed to know how to attack.

Aranthur was trying to process everything, from his own fear to the sheer lethality of the white swords and his own, which seemed to have no remedy except themselves; nothing seemed to tangle or stop them. A missed parry was death. Even his own sword looked as if it would kill him if it touched him, and none of that was conscious thought.

Aranthur rotated the thing, backed to avoid the second blade, and struck into its attack, because it moved in a false *tempo*, leading with a step like a novice swordsman. His back-cut left it without hands, and its fantastical speed could not save it from a wave of enraged musketeers and Yaniceri, who tore it down like hyaenas on a kill.

Aranthur had time to realise that he couldn't really communicate with them. He was too far *enhanced*.

He ran to the front of the melee, but with the *Exalted* down, the Yaniceri were mastering their position.

He looked up at the enemy ridge, and saw the enemy cavalry through the dust. They were closer.

It was very difficult to read them. His own *tempo* was so much faster than the mortal *tempo* that he couldn't immediately decide if they were standing still or coming forward.

Aranthur turned, and passed his now ordinary sword through a very young boy with a spear. And then, with gritted teeth, he hamstrung a woman facing a Yaniceri with nothing but a stick. The Attian killed her.

Aranthur's *tempo* made every one of these actions murder, not combat. The Safian women and children were not nearly as *enhanced* as he was himself, as if their numbers attenuated even the Enemy's spell effect, and he could kill them so easily . . .

So easily . . .

He killed a dozen before he couldn't make himself kill another.

He stood, in the middle of a desperate fight, unable and unwilling to simply murder women and children who were probably both *Subjugated* and *Enhanced*.

Nor was he willing to watch the Yaniceri and the musketeers die. He trapped some weapons from behind. Then he had to watch as his allies slowly butchered his helpless victims.

He wanted to retch.

Instead, he turned and ran at the enemy cavalry, who were preparing to charge. They were close – perhaps waiting for an order, perhaps hesitating at the trench.

He burst into their midst out of the haze of dust, and he was the nightmare. He released all his anger and his disgust at murdering children and women on them, but it was still murder. He flowed through them, and they died. He could kill a man and then kill the man behind him before the first victim's severed head struck the ground.

The horses, wiser than their masters, panicked. Three hundred veteran cavalry fled, leaving a dozen of their brothers in the dust. He stood alone, and the sword burned like blue-white fire in his hand.

He released his will on the *enhancement* and he almost fell. His legs felt as if he'd run a dozen parasangs and his shoulders ached.

But the Yaniceri had cleared their trench and were meticulously killing the wounded. The surviving musketeers were huddled by the body of their centark.

He began to walk back towards his own side. It wasn't very far, but it seemed to take him forever, and he felt as if he was walking in glue.

'How'd you do that, syr?' asked one of the regulars.

Aranthur stood, breathing so hard he thought his ribs might crack. The next thing he knew, he was walking again, one hand across the shoulders of a regular dekark, stumbling across the upcast of the Attian trench and then, all but sobbing with fatigue, being carried into the solid square of the First's pikes.

An Imoter leant over him and he was lying on the ground. Nothing made sense – he couldn't seem to put events into a sequence...

'I'm not hurt...' he muttered.

'That's an interesting *theory*,' the Imoter said.

He ran his hands over Aranthur's left arm, and Aranthur felt the man's *saar*.

His entire left sleeve was sodden in blood. He saw that he was cut so deeply that something pale glistened at the bottom of the cut as the Imoter held it open. The pain was...

Aranthur came back to the surface of reality with no idea of how much time had passed. He sat up, and realised that he was lying on the grass, and there were ants, and in front of him a line of pikemen.

His left arm was heavily bandaged. He felt as if he'd been clubbed, or as if he was wrapped in wet cloth; everything seemed sluggish, even sound.

With real difficulty, he clambered to his feet. He had to concentrate, and he failed on his first attempt. In the end, he had to put one hand out, roll on his side, and get his right knee under him, like a drunk rising in some reeking alley. He was so hungry he couldn't really focus on anything else.

There were twenty or thirty other bodies lying on the dry grass. Everything smelt of sulphur and the acrid tang of *saar*, and the burnt-soap smell of *sihr*, as his mother had once said.

The light itself seemed grey.

Dust rolled over him, coming from in front. The sound of the forge of war – close, personal war – beat into his ears like the sound of a blacksmith's hammer shoeing a horse, multiplied a thousand times.

All around him, the pikes of the First regiment, locked in a tight square, faced a cloud of racing horsemen – dark-clad Pindaris, light horse with no particular allegiance but to loot. They circled just beyond the points of the pikes, throwing javelins and occasionally trying to close. The clouds of dust they raised from the hard-packed soil were obscuring the sun.

The First had lost most of its musketeers saving the Yaniceri. It could only endure, although a handful of survivors loaded and fired as quickly as their weapons allowed.

All this, Aranthur took in with a glance. Even in his current state, he understood the deadlock.

Vanax Silva glanced down at him from her warhorse.

'Glad to see you back with us, dekark.'

She was watching the Pindari horse; her glance conveyed interest, but not much concern.

'I wonder if I should return to the General,' Aranthur asked.

The Vanax smiled. 'I don't think you'd make it very far, just now. In a few moments, I expect these thieves to be gone.'

To their left, a party of armoured cavalry tried to break into the square – not Pindaris but better armed men, in full maille. But the pikemen baffled them, and their horses wouldn't close. When one brave man pressed into the pikes, a dekark killed him with a spear. Aranthur drew his sword, ready to sell his life dearly, but the pikemen around him looked more bored than grim. Aranthur noted that his sword had returned to being perfectly normal. Old, heavy, and sharp.

'Be easy, syr,' one muttered. 'Unless they bring up big *gonnes* or a Magos, they can't touch the likes o' we.'

Aranthur realised with a sense of unreality that it was the dekark from the road surveying party, who clearly did not recognise him.

Out in the dust, there was a mighty rumble. The earth, already vibrating from the hooves of a thousand Pindari ponies, suddenly shook as if the mountains were moving.

The Pindari cavalry vanished like mist on a sunny morning. Suddenly Aranthur could see plumed horsemen everywhere, on both sides of the pikes: magnificent Attian Sipahis on big horses, with plumes on their helmets and horses' heads – scarlet and orange, blue and green and lavender. They thundered by and left silence in their wake, and more dust.

The front ranks of pikes, who'd held their weapons horizontal for far too long, allowed their pike heads to slump to the ground. Kneeling men and women rose with groans.

The dekarks ordered the pikes erect when it was clear that the threat was gone.

The First's lines were still crisp, and through the dust, the Yaniceri were still lining the edge of their trench. They gave a cheer.

The First answered the cheer.

'Dekark?' asked the vanax. 'The General's right over there. I haven't got a horse to give you, but you might catch her.' The commander reached down and handed him a small flask. 'Drink this. It'll put hair on your chest.' She laughed.

Aranthur took a swig, and felt immediately refreshed.

The vanax smiled. 'Not too much, mind. But I hear you put down one of those fucking witch things. A Scarlet – the boys and girls would do anything for you, just now. No, she's right there.'

The vanax pointed through the dust, and Aranthur could see the General, mounted on her black beast. She had a baton in her hand and was pointing up the ridge.

Aranthur pushed through the pikes and shambled across the open ground. There were a surprising number of dead and wounded Pindaris on the ground, and he was sickened at their youth. Most of them were beardless boys, fifteen years old or even less. Here and there lay an older man with a henna-dyed beard. All of them had lines of black tattoos.

The General was dictating orders to Syr Klinos, who had an arm in a sling and blood on his face. Before Aranthur could stumble up, the man saluted and rode away. He was replaced by Sasan, still straight as an arrow, the horsetail plume on his helmet twitching in the fitful breeze.

Dahlia was managing the shields; Aranthur could feel her *saar* before he saw her. Beyond her, Prince Ansu sat on horseback, eyes closed, deep in concentration. Ringkoat had the General's personal standard. Just beyond him was a familiar face, dark as good leather. The man smiled at Aranthur and put a hand on his shoulder.

'You look . . .'

It was the Masran Magos that Aranthur had met as 'Harlequin'.

Today he wore a long khaftan of figured blue velvet, covered in dust, and high boots. At his touch, Aranthur revived a little, and he thought that perhaps the Magos had channelled *saar* straight into him.

'You faced their *Exalted*,' Harlequin said.

Aranthur grinned, despite his fatigue.

'Two,' he said.

A groom brought him a horse. Best of all, the groom brought him Ariadne, and he mounted carefully. The young man offered him a leg up, and he took it gratefully.

The dust was everywhere, and the only way Aranthur could see anything was to get a glimpse into the viewing image cast by Prince Ansu. But even after several minutes of looking, he couldn't piece together the images he saw with the terrain. He saw a cavalry battle, and a confused running fight, but he had no reference to their locations.

'Harlequin', the Masr magos whose real name, according to Dahlia, was Qna Liras, pressed him for details of his encounter with the adversaries he called '*Exalted*'.

Aranthur shook his head.

'They are *enhanced*,' he said. 'In fact, the *enhancement* seems to be a standard of the enemy. The slaves they used against our infantry were also *enhanced*.'

Qna Liras nodded. 'That accords with what we think we know.'

'Who is "we"?' Aranthur asked.

The dust was settling. The sun was still shining, and the long, grassy ridge down which the enemy cavalry had come now appeared empty.

A flash of black and red.

Dahlia held it.

'Timos!' called the General.

Aranthur bowed to Qna Liras and turned his little mare.

'Yes, ma'am.'

'Find Centark Fird, Twenty-third City. Probably the leftmost in the line, if they held. Tell him that we will begin a general advance when he sees a flash of blue light from the centre. Then off to the left and find Kunyard. I need a report. As soon as you can.'

'Yes, ma'am. General advance, blue light, Vanax Kunyard, report.'

'Go!' Tribane shouted, and he was cantering away, his legs curiously slow to find the rhythm of his horse's movement. Everything hurt; he felt as if he'd been dragged over stones.

The Twenty-third City stood third to the left of the front line; their senior centark was on foot. They were one of the best City regiments, in scarlet vests and short fur hats, and their lines looked untouched. In front of them, the enemy dead lay like flotsam left by a tide that was now receding.

Aranthur saluted and delivered his orders.

'About fucking time,' Fird snapped. Then he smiled. 'Don't tell her I said that.'

Aranthur saluted and rode away. Ariadne was much fresher than he. Her explosion into a gallop almost unseated him, and he had to lean forward to stay mounted.

But as soon as he cleared the regular Second regiment, in their small red turbans and buff coats, he could see the cavalry battle. As far as his eye could see, men and women and horses were intermixed – thousands, and even tens of thousands. They milled just beyond the flank of the first line. Aranthur glanced back to find that there was no longer any second line; the General had committed her reserves. At the top of the ridge, the Capitan Pasha's third line was advancing to take the ground that the Sipahis had just left.

Aranthur let Ariadne carry him up the ridge, skirting the edge of the cavalry fight on the left. Even from higher ground he couldn't pick out Vanax Kunyard or his staff. He couldn't even find the red-gold shimmer of their *saar* shield.

Ariadne raced up. Aranthur passed what had been the position of the second line, now occupied only by the great *gonnes* of both armies and an impromptu field hospital guarded by the Imperial Axes who usually attended the General.

He could now see the Nomadi reforming. They were rallying on their horsetail standards, and he could see Centark Equus, perhaps two hundred paces away.

Aranthur put his head down, pointed Ariadne across the ridge at the red-khaftaned cavalrymen, and let her flow into a gallop. He came up as the ranks had settled. The whole regiment might have been on parade.

'Dekark Timos, as I live and breathe,' Equus said. 'Good to see you, old boy. Forgot to duck, what?' he asked, pointing at Aranthur's left arm.

'Something like that. General Tribane sent me to find Vanax Kunyard.'

'I see them, Tsari!' Equus roared to some unseen officer. Then he turned back to Aranthur. 'See the Whitecoats? See the City Cavalry?'

Aranthur did see them.

'He's somewhere there.'

Equus waved with his horsetail riding whip by way of a salute, and turned away.

'Squadron will advance,' he said to his trumpeter.

Aranthur trotted along the back of the regiment he'd spent a week with. Fifty saddles were empty; he didn't see Dekark Lemnas of the carabiniers anywhere.

He passed the left end of the Nomadi and passed across open ground. A little clump of enemy horse watched him, and one man rode at him. Ariadne easily outdistanced the man, who dropped back like a lion balked of an antelope, slowing as soon as he knew his horse to be inferior.

Aranthur pulled up among the dusty white coats of one of the City Cavalry regiments. The Nomadi had charged, and the whole mass of enemy horse had flinched away, unable to match their close order.

'I'm looking for Vanax Kunyard,' he asked the city troopers – men and women just like him, part-time soldiers.

They looked exhausted, their horses done in, but they were formed in ranks. Most of them were drinking from canteens and trying to get their horses to take a mouthful of water.

'There's his adjutant, Uschar,' one of the troopers said. 'Bright blue coat.'

'I have her,' Aranthur said, and he was off again.

'What in ten hells is going on?' shouted a militia dekark behind him, but Aranthur needed to catch the blue-coated officer before she rode off. She was bare-headed, her bright blonde hair like a brass helmet. She was shouting orders to another detachment of City Cavalry, urging them to get water into their horses.

'Damn it! I need you one more time!' she called.

Aranthur rode up from behind. She shot him a look, one hand on her pistol holster, and then turned her horse.

'You are?'

'Timos, General Tribane's messenger. The General requests a report on—'

'This mess?' she snapped. 'We haven't lost yet. No idea why. They

68

have ten to one in numbers but they keep backing off.' She turned back to the city troopers. 'Are you ready?'

Someone had the energy to shout 'no' and half a dozen weary troopers laughed.

Uschar allowed a very slight smile to flit across her face. Then she spoke to Aranthur.

'Sorry I can't be more help, but the Nomadi have just opened a hole in our line and someone needs to patch it.' She waved a puffer at Aranthur and trotted off. 'Follow me, Fifth City!'

With a clatter of hooves on stony ground, the militia cavalry trotted off, forming in close order as they moved forward into the gap created by the charge of the Nomadi.

Aranthur watched them gather speed. Their horses were so tired that they barely passed a heavy trot, but the enemy cavalry dispersed in front of them, the whole cloud of them racing away into their own cloud of dust.

Kunyard was nowhere to be seen. The cavalry melee went on, off to the left, as far as Aranthur could see through the dust, which rose to the heavens like an offering to the God of War. He sat on Ariadne, nearly choked with dust, in an agony of indecision, until Uschar's ponderous charge came to a halt, far off down the plain.

He knew very little about war. But it seemed to him that the cavalry had at least cleared the flank of the first line. Kunyard and his staff were nowhere to be seen.

He pointed Ariadne's head back down the ridge, at the just-visible standards of the Second Regiment, and let her run. She was tiring now, and he was not much better. He took a moment to gather a little *saar* from his crystal, and it refreshed him so much that he drew more.

He passed behind the Second and then behind the Twenty-third City, waving as he passed. Then the Second Bagas and Ninth City and the Fourth Arnaut and the First South Getas. Then the wreck of the Third City, a hundred survivors still huddled around their standard, and then he was with the General.

'Well?' she asked.

Behind her, the Black Lobsters stood like statues.

'Ma'am, I couldn't find Vanax Kunyard. I found Myr Uschar – she believed that the cavalry fight is a draw. Ma'am, she said she's outnumbered ten to one, but that the enemy don't press.'

'Hmm,' the General said. 'How helpful. Well, syr? What do you think?'

'Ma'am, I've never been in a battle.'

'Syr, none of us has. Not like this.'

'Well, then, for my money, the Nomadi just cleared the flank of the first line and there's cavalry supporting them. That's what I saw.'

Aranthur shrugged, as if to disclaim responsibility for his own report.

Tribane looked left, as if the dust might part for her. He saw her face set, saw the moment of decision.

'Jennie? Ready with the blue light?'

Ringkoat smiled. 'We're attacking?'

Tribane shrugged. 'When in doubt, attack.'

She pointed at Jeninas, who, kneeling a few paces from her horse, lit the fuse on what looked like a child's rocket. The General smiled at Aranthur.

'Not magikal, so it can't be tampered with.'

The fuse hit the powder and the black tube spat fire. In one breath, it climbed away through the dust. Suddenly it was engorged in blue flame, rushing into the heavens. It only lasted for a count of three – then it burst in a rain of blue stars.

To their right, the First's drums began to beat. Beyond them, the Yaniceri crossed their trench, and then, like a tired wrestler, the whole of the Allied army stumbled forward. Almost immediately, they came to the low ground between the two ridges, and the marshy stream there, and they slowed again.

Aranthur waited for some response from the distant enemy. It was all very slow. Tribane cursed and cursed again, and he was kept busy warding a sudden swarm of flies off Ariadne, as if the little muddy stream was full of insects. Off to the left, the survivors of the Third City came forward – a thin line of survivors unwilling to await the conclusion of the day. Beyond them the banners of three more regiments could be seen. A second line regiment, the Seventh Souliote, came from the second line and filled the gap where the Third City had been. The survivors vanished into the fresh regiment's ranks.

With Ansu and Dahlia he helped repel a veritable barrage of *workings*. He stopped counting after the sixth attack, and he spent all the *saar* he'd borrowed from his crystal and more besides. Dahlia appeared to be grey, her hair limp, her face lined; he had a glimpse of the hard-faced older woman she might be. Ansu channelled to her, too inexperienced in shielding to cast himself. Harlequin worked brilliant spot defences, tiny *aspides* that functioned only exactly where they were needed, a technique that Aranthur had never seen before.

And then the whole line was across the wet ground and still unopposed, and the moment of danger was done. They were moving – moving at a brisk, swinging pace, as if the men and women of the Attian infantry, the Byzas and the Arnauts were gaining energy and spirit from every step forward.

The Yaniceri began to sing, their band playing a magnificent march – cymbals and drums and shrieking fifes – and the line surged forward towards the crest.

A paroxysm of supernatural rage lashed the Allied line. Five hundred soldiers died – immolated, crushed, desiccated, blood-boiled or bone-jellied – as the front line's *saar* shields failed, as individual *aspides* and amulets failed. The whole horizon seemed to be aflame with the enemy *workings*.

The Attian music never faltered. The drums beat on, and the Yaniceri's singing was picked up by the Arnauts on the left of the Imperial line. Women stepped over the ruined corpses of their friends; men slogged forward, slipping on the intestines of their comrades.

As the front line went forward, it closed to the centre without an order, so that pikes began to compact to the centre, where the enemy sorcerers were. And behind them, all the Attian *gonnes* and all their own fired constantly, pounding the enemy Magi. The enemy magikers, in their turn, cast heavy charcoal-coloured shields to resist the cannon, but the shields themselves gave the *gonners* a better target. Every enemy Magos casting shields was one fewer to be throwing fire at the Allied line.

Aranthur found himself riding between Prince Ansu and General Tribane, with his red *aspis* cast and hanging in the air in front of them, spread as widely as he could cast it.

The next onslaught of *sihr* struck them. This time, the carnage was only half that of the first great strike, and the front line began to cheer. On the left, the Attian third line units, the reserve, began to sweep forward. The Capitan Pasha could be seen leading his Household Sipahis off to the right, a wall of Attian chivalry crushing the lighter enemy horse and breaking the enemy left.

'Well?' Tribane asked fate, and her enemy. 'Do you have a reserve?'

The enemy sorcerers broke. A hundred paces away, they were mounting horses and camels and running. A dozen stood their ground, casting as fast as they could, the air full of their fire.

A pillar of light exploded among them, tongues of lightning lashing out.

'It's killing its own people for running,' the General said with satisfaction. 'And it doesn't have a reserve.'

She turned to Qna Liras Harlequin.

'This is your show, ain't it?'

Qna Liras shrugged.

'I have no idea if I can take it. I'd like some help,' he said agreeably, as if he was moving furniture.

The pillar of light began to retreat.

'That is a Disciple,' Qna Liras said. 'A real one. The first we've ever seen alive.'

'Not the first I've seen,' muttered Sasan.

In front of them, just to the left, a body of enemy cavalry were forming as a rearguard – perhaps two thousand armoured men.

Tribane turned to the Black Lobsters at her back.

'Companions!' she roared. 'There is our foe! Defeat the men, and leave the pillar of light to our Magi. Ready!'

There was a growl, and the pillar of light was getting farther away. Some of the infantry regiments were slowing. There was nothing to fight, and beyond the crest of the ridge could be seen the enemy camp.

'Klinos! Tell the Capitan Pasha to keep the heat on and not to stop to pillage the camp and I'll see to a fair distribution of the loot. Beg him!'

Klinos saluted and rode off.

'Here we go, Companions!' the General called in her high, clear voice.

The Black Lobsters began to trot.

Their heavy black horses made the earth shake.

The enemy cavalry that was supposed to protect the enemy's sorcerers broke and began to flee in all directions. Off to the right, the remnants of the Pindari cavalry turned and fled, and the whole enemy right began to give way.

And in the very centre, the Magos in the blue velvet khaftan rode up the last of the ridge, alone against the pillar of light.

Aranthur turned to Sasan and Ansu.

'I'm going to try to help,' he said.

Dahlia laughed. 'Of course you are.'

Sasan grinned. It was an ugly grin. 'I would give my life to strike at that thing.'

Dahlia cast a layered shield over the four of them, a swirling mist-shield, another *proaspismos* technique that Aranthur had never seen. He, for his part, drew deeply on his crystal. He took more *power* from the *kuria* than he'd ever taken.

He glanced at Sasan.

The Safian met his eye as if reading his mind.

'Absolutely,' he spat. 'This thing has killed my land and enslaved my people. Let's do it.'

Aranthur turned to Ansu, who was checking the prime on his puffer.

'Wouldn't miss it for the world,' he smiled.

The four of them rode up the hill behind Qna Liras.

Qna Liras reached the crest of the great ridge and raised his arms.

The pillar of white fire seemed to hesitate, and then it swelled, its light bright like the sun, unbearable; a hemisphere of brilliance. Around the Masran light bringer grew a rainbow of light-effect, becoming a hemisphere of glittering, opalescent *Aulos*, as if an oily perfume had been poured into an eggshell and then coated in gold powder. Where the two effects met, there was a cataclysm of sound and colour and texture, as if rival realities contended for possession of the space and the means to fill it; in the contended zone where the two shields crossed, colour, light, and sound were a vivid but irrational display; moments of intense blackness shot through with alien stars; images of carrion birds, all coming and going faster than thought.

What impressed Aranthur most was that he could detect no particular *working*. It was as if Qna Liras and his adversary contended with their very beings – as if their *workings* flowed from them without beginning or end. Next to the flow of the Masran Magos, Aranthur's casting was as pedestrian as a man slowly ploughing behind an ox is to a racehorse galloping free without a rider.

'Holy shit,' Dahlia said.

Aranthur kept riding. He rode well out from the pillar, but he crossed the ridge, and Sasan stayed with him.

'Stop!' Dahlia said. 'We can't change this!'

Aranthur thought she was wrong.

'Sasan!' she called. 'Don't die for nothing!'

'Somewhere in the centre of the pillar of fire is a man,' Aranthur said. 'We can get to him, and at the very least, we'll interrupt his casting.'

'You think that you can just ride through that curtain of white fire?' she asked.

'Yes.'

Aranthur was heavy with the fatigue of battle and the added burn of the *enhancement* he'd used earlier, but he was certain, nonetheless.

Ansu's thin face wore a set smile. He checked the priming in his magnificent matchlock, the lacquered stock catching the sun.

'You are all three fools,' Dahlia said, shaking her head. 'I don't want to watch you die, so I might as well come along.'

Ansu looked at Aranthur.

'So your plan is . . . ?'

'Distract it,' he said. 'There's a man in the midst of all that white fire. I'll wager my life on it.'

'You are wagering your life,' Sasan said. 'And ours.' He nodded. 'But I, too, believe there is a man – or a woman – in that fire.'

'So?' Dahlia asked.

'We ride up behind it, shoot with our puffers and cut our way in,' Aranthur said.

'That's your plan?' Ansu asked.

'Do you have a better?'

Prince Ansu shrugged. 'No. But I expected . . . Never mind. Of course – let us do this desperate, stupid thing.'

'Puffers?' Dahlia asked.

Aranthur shrugged. 'Muskets worked on the *Exalted*. I have a theory . . .'

'Oh,' she said, her tone heavy with sarcasm, 'that's all fine then. You have a theory.'

Nonetheless, she took her puffers from their holsters, and checked their priming.

They were well past the pillar of white fire. It was still drifting backwards, even as it contended with Harlequin's. Where the two of them passed the ground was often scorched down to rock; indeed, rocks in their wake glowed a dull red. Aranthur could feel the heat. It was a little like watching theatre or the opera in Megara. Unbelievable.

74

'You can't be serious,' Dahlia said.

Sasan leant over and kissed her.

'I think you should stay here and live.' He raised an eyebrow at Aranthur. 'Couldn't you magik me again? Or a horse?'

'He's too spent already,' Dahlia snapped. 'Just look at him. He can barely speak. This is *crazy*.'

Aranthur shrugged.

'Look at them,' he said, pointing at the surreal combat. 'We can do this. We're—'

'Perhaps this is not for Dahlia,' Sasan said. 'We—'

'Keep your male bullshit for another occasion,' she snapped. 'You are not leaving me out of this just because I'm wise enough to know we're doomed.'

She drew a puffer and checked the priming.

They all did.

'Ready?' Aranthur asked.

The four of them turned their horses, and charged.

The ground was smooth, the grass tramped flat, and their horses, tired though they were, managed a hand-gallop.

About forty paces out, the white pillar spat a tendril of fire. It engulfed Dahlia's shield of mist, contending with it.

A second bolt struck Aranthur's red shield, which burned black and collapsed.

A third, in almost the same *tempo*, struck Dahlia's creation from another angle, and it blackened.

Twenty paces out, they were naked.

Aranthur, slightly in front because of Ariadne's speed, cast his red shield again. He had it ready in his mind, and he flowed into it, raising it as soon as he was conscious of the other falling. In the same *tempo*, the white fire struck, and struck again. He had an odd moment of realisation, in the midst of battle, that his ability to recast was almost infinite . . .

Something enveloped the white pillar in its moment of distraction. It had no more *sihr* to spare for the four riders. Indeed, the pillar seemed to shrink, and become smooth. It lashed back, flailing a whip of embodied thought at Qna Liras, whose hemisphere also sank in around him.

Aranthur, ten paces from the smooth white fire of the Disciple, put the barrel of his puffer at the very centre and fired.

The fire rippled, and Sasan fired both of his puffers, turned slightly in his saddle like a trick rider. Ansu shot as he turned to the right, over his bridle arm.

As far as Aranthur could see, the Disciple's shields shed all the bullets.

Dahlia turned to the left to have a clear shot.

Aranthur and Ariadne went forward into the fire. He had the Capitan Pasha's puffer in his left hand, and his sword in his right. His mind screamed as they passed through the edge of the Disciple's white fire. The barrel of the weapon tracked the shape of the *man* at the centre of the white pillar, fear and elation cancelling the pain of his wound and the totality of his fatigue. The weapon seemed to fire of its own accord and he was through the other side, turning Ariadne, who was panicked by the fire and yet had proved true to her salt, overcoming her fears.

Aranthur had to turn in a wide circle, and he missed fifty heartbeats of combat, struggling with Ariadne's fears. When he looked back, the white pillar was gone. Harlequin stood with his staff pinning a writhing, wounded creature to the earth.

Aranthur touched spurs to Ariadne, and she responded, angry at the spurs but still willing. He reined in just in time to see the thing under Harlequin's staff begin to char, as if burning from inside. He had a single distinct image that haunted his nights, of a child's face set in a look of hate.

And then it was gone, burned to ash.

Aranthur dismounted, and walked up. Sasan was close, his sword in his hand. Dahlia was just beyond him, her shields up and steady. Prince Ansu was loading his puffers.

Qna Liras smiled at Aranthur.

'That was very timely,' he said, as if they were at a party and Aranthur had fetched him a glass of wine.

Then Harlequin went down on one knee, faced the sun, and began to pray.

3

Eastern Armea

It was a victory, but the cost was hellish. Aranthur – despite near *saar* exhaustion, despite already feeling the effects of having used the Safian *enhancement*, despite a suppurating wound from his left elbow to his wrist – helped Sasan and hundreds of other men and women to collect the survivors from the front line regiments that had collapsed in the face of the *Exalted*. There were enough survivors to make the search worthwhile. As the light faded, and the hyaenas and vultures and ravens arrived in vast numbers to make speed the more essential, he found himself clearing the very ground on which he'd fought the *Exalted*. He carried a Safian woman up the ridge to the Imoters, her severed hand and broken arm hastily bound. He went back and helped a regular musketeer carry a big Attian Yaniceri. He went back a third time and stabilised the blood flow from a drummer girl discovered in the litter of corpses from the destruction of the Third. He carried her up to the hill and went back again into the darkening valley, his clothes sodden with blood and ordure.

It was on the fourth trip into the valley of death that Aranthur found himself standing over the corpse of one of the *Exalted*, and he flinched. It was as if he expected the thing to spring back into new life. He had never seen anything so terrifying, so beautiful and lethal, in his life. Now the corpse was like an alabaster statue, except for the tattooed lines around the wrist and throat.

Aranthur knelt by the corpse, and touched it. And then he grew less hesitant, although the skin was *wrong*.

It was all wrong. The skin was more like vellum or parchment than like a corpse's skin.

Feeling like a ghoul, he took his razor-sharp eating knife off the scabbard of his dagger and, after a long moment of fear, cut the skin above the wrist. The skin was tough, like vellum.

The bone flashed silver, like metal.

Aranthur recoiled. He flinched, but curiosity drove him back to the corpse.

The skin was already brittle. The stench was incredible; even in the moments he'd been kneeling there, the skin had passed from milk-white to a sort of ivory-tan. The blued-steel eyes, open in death, were rotting.

He turned the wrist. From his belt purse he took his student's book, a book he'd bound himself in happier days, and the lead pencil bound in brass that he used when he had a good thought about an *occulta*. He thumbed to a blank page, past a sketch of Dahlia lying on his bed, and another of the Master of Arts' hand on a grimoire, and a formula for gunpowder, and a recipe for lavender soap.

He knew the characters on the wrist. They were in the Safiri script. They ran in a perfect circle, like the worm Ouroboros, eating its own tail – the beginning of the invocation was the last character of the end as well.

Binding.

The same invocation and characters on the neck.

He shook his head to clear it, and rose from his knees. Darkness was falling, and full exhaustion was hitting him, and the deep depression of fatigue and violence.

The ravens came suddenly and in vast numbers – thousands of the big birds, summoned from the wooded slopes of the Alti by the smell of a battlefield. The hyaenas came in packs, their blood-matted muzzles and carnal stink an embodiment of the reign of death on the night-time battlefield. Twice, Aranthur used his sword to force one of them off a pile of dead and wounded. The guardians of the underworld would stand a few feet away, bloody teeth bared, daring him to relinquish their prey. Aranthur was trying to find the other *Exalted*, but darkness was coming too fast. The Wild had come for its share of flesh, and he could not keep it at bay. He stumbled back, and back again, and found himself straddling a boy of perhaps twelve, clutching his gut, which proved to have a deep stab wound.

78

'Water,' the child begged, in Safiri.

Aranthur raised his shields to keep the hyaenas at bay and lifted the boy, who gave a weak scream. He struggled, but Aranthur carried him. Everything felt as if it was made of lead, but he was determined to save this one child. It became his light, his beacon, and he trudged heavily up the ridge towards the Imoters. The climb, which Ariadne had managed in heartbeats, appeared eternal. He went up, up, one foot in front of another, a different kind of combat.

And then other hands took his burden, and he fell forward into a haze of light, or it seemed that way. There were hundreds of them on the ground. The rows of wounded stretched off to the edges of the darkness, and the magelight was pitiless in showing their wounds. There weren't enough Imoters – a dozen of them struggled to keep death away – and Aranthur thought of the hyaenas. His gorge rose.

'Aranthur?' Ansu said.

Aranthur could only collapse outside his tent, mind empty of anything but a creeping feeling of despair and the pain in his arm. Ansu sat by him, silent. His knees were drawn up to his chest, and he rocked back and forth slightly, like a child in great sorrow. Dahlia came, and sat, and Sasan, who seemed better off than the other three. There were campfires; the smell of a rich fish stew penetrated Aranthur's head.

He made himself rise.

'I need food,' he managed. 'We need food, and water,' he croaked, when Ansu didn't respond.

Dahlia struggled to get to her feet. Aranthur could see that she was utterly spent; the dark circles under her eyes made her look as if she'd been beaten.

Sasan pushed her down.

'I'll get things,' he said kindly. 'You stay here.'

The two of them went to the Nomadi fires and literally begged bowls and food. There was Dekark Lemnas, alive; she found them bowls.

'Staff whallahs,' she said with a smile. 'Nay, brother, I know you had a hard day. I can see it in your face.'

As soon as the food hit his mouth, he needed more; it was as if his body wouldn't allow him any other action but eating.

'I saw your charge,' Aranthur said, between his first and second bowl of stew. 'I didn't see you and I feared...'

She shrugged, as if death was something one couldn't be worried about.

'Which time? We charged six times. I lost two horses.' She shrugged again. 'And six friends.'

'You saved us,' a voice said.

The General materialised out of the darkness, with Centark Equus and the Masran Magos, Qna Liras.

'Everyone saved us, really,' she said agreeably.

Aranthur thought that Myr Tribane was perhaps a little drunk.

The Dekark smiled. 'Nomadi! General Tribane is at your fire.'

Men and women stood up, wherever they were. They rattled their spoons on their bowls.

Sasan took the bowl out of Aranthur's hands.

'I'm going to feed Dahlia,' he said gruffly.

Aranthur turned to go with his friend, but the General took his arm.

'Stay a little. I know what you did,' she added, almost as an accusation. 'You fought the *Exalted*, and you put a pistol ball in the Disciple.'

Aranthur shrugged. 'Maybe.'

The General swayed.

'Know what you did,' she said agreeably. 'Eh, Nomadi? This boy went sword to sword with one of the Scarlets.'

Lemnas smiled. A few of the Nomadi rattled their spoons on bowls.

'Always knew you was a *bahadur*,' Centark Equus said.

'But my question,' said the General, 'is how your sword survived.'

Not so drunk.

'My question, actually,' said the man Aranthur knew as Harlequin. 'May I see your sword, young hero?'

Aranthur turned to get it. It was wrapped in his sword-belt, on his sleeping pallet.

'Never mind,' the General said. 'Time for that tomorrow. Have some wine.'

She poured an abundance into the silver cup in her hand and gave it to him. Equus was handing a full flagon to Lemnas, and she was sharing it out.

Aranthur drank his off without a qualm.

'More?' the General said.

She made a circuit of the Nomadi, talking to them, listening. After a few minutes she turned to Aranthur.

'Take me to your friends.'

Aranthur led her through the tangle of tents and tent pegs to where his friends were eating fish stew.

Sasan had saved him a bowl. He devoured his third while the General – with her own hands – poured a cup of wine for them and shared it around.

'What happened?' Dahlia asked. 'By the Lady, Alis! Why did we have such poor magikal support? Where is Roaris?'

A servant opened a camp stool and Tribane all but fell into it. The servant produced a second bottle of wine.

'I have no fucking idea what happened,' Tribane said wearily. 'In early spring, when we decided to support Masr by attacking Antioke, I think we sent too many of our Magi and Imoters that way. We had no idea back then what we were up against.' She blinked. 'But today... I had tactical and strategic surprise, I had a better army, far better infantry, and the numbers were equal, and ten thousand hells, I almost fucked it away.' She had poured a cup of wine for Dahlia, but without thinking she knocked it back herself. 'Thanks,' she said to Dahlia, giving her the empty cup. 'I am perfectly aware that without you and the prince, I'd have been burned to a crisp ten times.'

Sasan took the bottle and poured the cup full. He took a long pull at the wine.

'Milady, you are a fine Magas yourself...'

Aranthur knew the answer to that one.

'It's a matter of concentration.'

Tribane shrugged.

'I have some *saar*,' she agreed. 'But I've never trained enough and I lose concentration too easily – especially when everyone is looking at me...' She shook her head. 'Fuck,' she muttered.

Ansu raised his head. 'At your service, ma'am.' He smiled a certain way.

The General laughed.

The two of them crossed eyes; Aranthur knew they had been lovers. It occurred to him, then, that this was how life was – a tangle. He imagined being in an army studded with his loves, and how that might be.

'Now what?' Dahlia asked. 'If a mere volunteer can ask the *Pru Vanaxa?*'

The General sighed.

'The pasha mounted something of a pursuit, but all those Pindaris escaped, and I fear that they will explode out into Armea and even Atti, burning, raping, looting. It's what they do. They come in brotherhoods, like societies of assassins – they rank themselves by their atrocities.' She shook her head. 'I shouldn't be telling you any of this, but I want to advance into Safi, if only to let the survivors of the Pure know that they can be beaten. But I cannot let the Attian heartland be plundered.'

She drank more.

'You know,' she said, as if they were talking about love poetry, 'I have spent my entire life studying war.'

They all drank.

Out in the valley, hyaenas fed noisily, and the raucous sounds of carrion birds filled the night with horror.

'There was a general – a Qin general. Qin was the empire before Zhou... yes? I digress. I cannot remember his name.' She shrugged. 'I'm drunk. But he said the only thing worse than winning a great battle was losing it.' She stood, unsteadily. 'I worry that I know nothing, and that our adversary is as pleased by today's outcome as by any alternative in which we're all dead and the Disciple is drinking the wine. I have no idea what drives a mind that enslaves starving peasants and uses them as a shield. This... *thing*... didn't need to fight. It should have slipped away.'

She turned to Aranthur.

'Walk me to my tent. Goodnight, good people. I will see all of you are rewarded. I will find Roaris and kill him with my bare hands. I promise it on the corpses of every dead man and woman in the valley.'

'Some of the reserve came forward without orders,' Qna Liras said.

'Yes,' the General said. 'Yes, most of the reserve cavalry came back.' She shook her head. And then caught Aranthur's eye and smiled.

Prince Ansu put a hand on Aranthur's arm.

'She is looking for a lover. Is that what you want? It's what she does when she is nervous, or upset.'

Aranthur thought of Lecne and the General, and then of his own relationships.

'That I... understand,' he said.

But he took the General's arm and walked off into the darkness.

She was in no particular hurry to reach her pavilion. In fact, a train of servants waited in the darkness with a stool, more wine, more cups. And they went from fire to fire, along the lines. Aranthur watched her sit at a fire with the silent survivors of the Third City, and saw her laugh with the Attian Sipahis, who were dancing, their gold-laced yellow boots slapping the hard ground in time to a drum and a tamboura.

Aranthur stood by while she and the Capitan Pasha embraced.

Ulgat Kartal emerged from the firelight and threw his arms around Aranthur.

'Now we are battle-brothers,' he said.

The embrace felt good.

Aranthur introduced his Attian friend to the Masran Magos.

He bowed. 'I'm afraid that I only know you as Harlequin,' he said. 'I have heard that you have a name...'

The Masran Magos smiled.

'I am Harlequin, in your tongue. In my tongue, I am called Qna Liras.' He bowed. 'I confess that is only a use name. But I am a priest of the Secret Fire – I do not have a name, as you know names. Indeed, that is all that kept me alive today.'

Ulgat looked at the tall black Lightbringer.

'You fought?' he asked.

It was difficult to believe, as the man was immaculately clad in unrumpled silk.

'He defeated the Disciple,' Aranthur said.

'Now, by the Twelve, by Coryn's beard and the seven sacred swords!' Ulgat bowed deeply.

'It is possible that it was *you* who defeated the Disciple,' Qna Liras said. 'He had a pistol ball in his back when I reached him.'

'Hah, I share my fire with a Lightbringer!' Ulgat shouted.

Almost instantly they were surrounded by Sipahis. Even the Capitan Pasha strode over, scattering lesser men, to embrace 'Harlequin'.

'I think you may be the first Lightbringer I have ever touched.'

The pasha's henna-dyed beard was red as blood in the firelight. His silk khaftan deceived the eye; his gold lace glittered like stars.

Qna Liras received the praise with unbreakable humility, bowing, and refusing to accept that he was the hero of the hour.

'I have never been in this position,' Qna Liras admitted in an aside to Aranthur. 'We do not work like this, on battlefields. We work in secret.' He shook his head. 'Kurvenos said that we must...' He glanced at Aranthur. 'He said you desired to be a Lightbringer. Or that you spoke of it.'

Aranthur was wishing that someone would pour some *arak* for him. The tamboura player was as good as Tiy Drako.

'I did,' he admitted. 'I admire . . . you – all of you.'

'You kill very easily,' Qna Liras said. 'But I feel your *power*. You have the . . . *baraka*.'

'How does a person become a Lightbringer?' Aranthur asked.

'By making choices,' Qna Liras said, enigmatically.

Aranthur wondered if he was being mocked.

'Oh, really?'

Qna Liras handed him a flask.

'Here, drink with me. Listen, you make me feel so young I don't know how to talk to you. Have you ever . . . reached a point . . . where you knew that you could *not* do something? That to do that thing would change you?'

'Many times.'

Aranthur was thinking of the duel in the courtyard, and then of the frenzied, *enhanced* women he hadn't been willing to kill while he was himself *enhanced*.

He had no idea how much time passed, but the Magos passed his hand over Aranthur's eyes.

'Tell me,' he ordered. But it was not a *compulsion*.

Aranthur drank some of the liquid in the flask. It was marvellous, light and sweet and very alcoholic. He drank more.

'I have an *enhancement*. It is Safian in origin . . .' he began.

'I know,' said the Masran.

'I used it in the battle – when the first line was . . . falling.'

Aranthur was suddenly there, lying on his back in the sand.

He spoke for a little, describing. And then he came to the women.

'I couldn't kill them any more. I . . . can't explain. They had no chance. It was not war. It was merely murder.'

There was a silence, punctuated by the wild notes of the tamboura and the pounding feet of the dance.

'Mayhap it is all murder,' Qna Liras said. 'Mayhap you perceive some difference between killing in a contest and killing in cold blood, but you must admit that both are killing.'

Aranthur shook his head. 'I admit it, but . . .'

Qna Liras smiled. 'I killed today. I have killed before. Perhaps I will again.' He shook his head. 'I prefer it to be the very last choice, the final resort. Listen. As you grow, you will make choices. No one makes you a Lightbringer. There is no school, no training camp. One day, you find yourself on the edge of a precipice.'

'And if you don't jump, you are a Lightbringer?'

Aranthur was almost unbelieving that he was having this conversation, and he drank more of the wonderful cordial.

'Must you drink all my wine?' the Masran said with a smile, taking the flask. He looked at Aranthur, his face almost as close as a lover's. 'No, my young friend. If you elect to spend the rest of your life teetering on the edge of the abyss, then you are a Lightbringer. Some jump. Some retreat. Only a few stay.' He drank deeply. 'Few stay long...'

'I don't understand.'

Qna Liras shrugged. 'Who am I to teach you? But listen. When you are ready to make choices, when you learn that there is never a simple answer, when you know no nation or race or clan is *better*... When you see so clearly that the despair can choke you, and yet you choose to act for the best in a dirty grey world, then you are a Lightbringer. But the other side of the cliff beckons – if you ever think you truly *know better*, you instantly become the enemy.'

'I don't understand,' Aranthur said again.

'Bah, neither do I.'

Aranthur had a thousand questions, but then the General came and dragged him to where the Sipahis and a dozen Imperial soldiers were dancing. There were more tambouras and some drums and an oud. The oud player was Sasan, and he lay with his back against a saddle and Dahlia's head on his shoulder. There were also hundreds of soldiers dancing, both Imperial and Attian. The music almost drowned out the sounds of the battlefield, the thin cries and the hyaenas' madness.

Aranthur ate again, a full meal at an Attian campfire – a rich lamb stew with raisins and saffron – and then he allowed himself to be pulled into the dance. He was drunk enough to move easily, and not yet ready to fall over, although his hips and knees protested at the additional effort after a day of near exhaustion.

He followed the General.

The dances were not any more elaborate than village dances in Soulis; indeed, many of them were identical, or close enough. He whirled through an all-male dance well enough, and then found himself part-nered with a musketeer from the regulars with no memory of asking her to dance. They managed well enough, and he caught her leap and turned her sufficiently well as to get a smile from her and a burst of applause from the drunken onlookers.

Now there was a line of fires, all along the slope, and the dance wound between them. Fifty musicians were playing a raucous sound with no clear leader, but with a driving beat provided by a bass drummer from one of the infantry regiments and echoed by a pair of Yaniceri.

Prince Ansu whirled by with the General, doing some Zhouian dance of labyrinthine complexity. Aranthur went back to his musketeer, only to find that she was now dancing with Syr Klinos, who bowed to him but whirled off with his friend.

Ulgat Kartal stumbled up.

'Didn't you say you wanted *arak*?' he asked. 'I got you some, but then I drank it, and then I got you more . . .'

Aranthur took the cup. He drank deep, and the stuff burned like fire. 'Ahh,' he said.

He asked Ulgat what dance they were doing.

'It is a Steppe dance, and I'm not sober enough,' Ulgat confessed, but then he began to dance, the cup in his hand.

Aranthur followed his movements, and Vilna and Lemnas material-ised out of the darkness and took charge, teaching them the move-ments. Sasan came to their group and brought a drummer. Gradually the nomad music began to fill the air, and the intricate beat began to filter through the fumes of wine and make sense to Aranthur, and he danced, leapt, and danced again. It was an ungendered dance, and he went around the circle once with Ulgat, who was delighted to have recaptured something of his own youth, and then with Lemnas.

He landed with her by Sasan, who grinned.

He bowed, like a Byzas noble, to kiss the Nomadi officer's hand. In the firelight, he could see that she had blood under her nails, and her right cuff was soaked in it.

As was his own.

His gorge rose. But he kissed her hand and stumbled away, suddenly drunk despite his success at the dance, or because of it.

He wandered away from the fires and pissed into the darkness, but away from the dancing, he could hear the horror of the battlefield down in the valley. He paused, and prayed for the first time in a long time, although he couldn't have said whether he prayed to the Eagle or to the Lady.

Let them all be dead and at peace.

Because being left on a battlefield and eaten alive had become his new nightmare. He thought of all the enslaved women and children used as fodder. His gorge rose again.

And he vomited.

Empty, he felt better, and when he went back to the fires he found water, clean drinking water, and swallowed a pint or two. He felt much better, and he found a handful of troopers at the Nomadi fires. A Steppe woman offered him more fish stew and he ate again.

'There you are,' the General said.

'Yes, ma'am,' he said.

'Call me Alis.' Her voice was very slightly slurred. 'I thought you'd gone off and left me. I don't *order* people into my bed. Although I suppose in the end I will.' She shrugged elaborately. 'What's a girl to do?'

She handed him a cup which was, as it transpired, full of mead.

He drank some, looking at her over the top of the cup. She made no effort to be beautiful: she dressed in military clothes and never wore make-up; her hair was always tied back in a queue so severe that it stretched her skin; she wore a high white stock that hid her neck. He had no idea how old she might be; people said she was well past forty.

For some reason he thought of Alfia Topaza. It was a strange juxtaposition, but there it was – Alfia did have something of the General's absolute self-assurance. And Dahlia did too, for that matter.

'Syr Timos, do you like what you see?' she asked.

'Even without the perfume,' he said.

She laughed. It wasn't a giggle, but a whole laugh, and she almost doubled up, and then, rather suddenly, she sat down.

'Horse sweat. Erotic as all the hells. Oops! Drunker than I thought.' She smiled at him. 'That was funny, and I need some funny.'

He reached out a hand and pulled her up, and she, with a grace that belied long practice, put her lips on his and kissed him. There was nothing tentative about it. It was more than a little like an erotic cavalry charge, and Aranthur's whole body responded.

As did hers. Hands wandered, and time passed . . .

'I don't think that my reputation would bear making love in the grass in public,' Alis Tribane murmured. 'Come.'

Her hand was iron hard, with ridges of callus that spoke of reins and sword hilts. She dragged him along, and he laughed at her urgency, and then he could see her red pavilion, lit from within by a lantern.

Standing in the door was Coryn Ringkoat. He smiled at Aranthur.

'Are ye sober, General?' Ringkoat asked.

'Not even a little,' she said. 'And horny as hell, so—'

'Too bad. General Roaris is here.'

'Fuckwit.' The General spoke loudly.

'Absolutely, but he's sitting in your tent.' Ringkoat raised an eyebrow to Aranthur. 'Another time, perhaps.'

Aranthur smiled. 'I understand.'

'Fuck,' muttered the General.

She took Aranthur's hand and very softly bit it.

Aranthur laughed and walked off into the darkness. Behind him, he heard her voice raised in anger, and then he heard Roaris spouting insults.

Lemnas, of the Nomadi, handed him some *arak*.

'From Atti,' she said and hiccuped, which was very funny.

He sat with her, and with Vilna, on a saddle blanket, and watched the stars.

'Tomorrow we *pursue*.' Vilna sounded perfectly sober. Aranthur wasn't sure he'd ever heard a word imbued with so much meaning. 'Let's go to bed.'

Lemnas laughed. '*Subjhar*, I almost died today. I may just choose to stay up all night.'

Vilna got to his feet.

'Perhaps. But the horses will require work at dawn – the tack will still have to be oiled and cleaned, and then—'

Lemnas threw a cup at him. But ten minutes later, Aranthur was alone. He collapsed on his blankets and slept.

Morning came far too early, and Aranthur's hangover was a nasty wraith sitting in his head and driving silver spikes into his skull from inside. But someone was pulling insistently on his foot. He kicked, failed to make contact, and eventually found himself looking at the severe face of Vilna.

'Drink this and don't spit,' Vilna said.

Aranthur drank. It was foul, but he'd had other such concoctions, usually amid pranks at the Academy. He drank it off and sat up.

'Oh, Lady,' he moaned.

Vilna laughed.

'Horses don't feed themselves,' he said. 'Come. You were one of the most sober.'

Aranthur was very tempted to tell the Nomadi veteran that he wasn't actually on the strength and couldn't be made to do shit duty like currying horses the day after a battle, but there was something about the wiry little man that made it impossible to sputter such stuff.

He flung off his blankets. He was still fully dressed in his battlefield clothes, liberally doused with blood and other fluids and now stinking like rotten meat.

He pushed through his tent flap and vomited for the second time in ten hours.

'All better? Curry horses,' Vilna spat. 'Next time, spew outside of tent lines or pay fine.'

He laughed, slapped his thigh, and went off down the tent row.

Sasan and Dahlia's tent was empty, and there was no sign of Prince Ansu.

Aranthur spent an hour working his way down the picket line. He started with Ariadne, who gave him a look meant to indicate her feelings about her condition. Then he did the other horses: Dahlia's and Sasan's, and then Ansu's gelding, and on down the long line.

Vilna came, checked some hooves and a coat, and handed him a big bowl of honeyed gruel and yoghurt.

He slurped it down before considering whether he was still too hung over to eat. Vilna produced a cup of steaming *quaveh*.

'Bless you, Vilna,' he said.

The sun was rising in the east. The valley was still full of ravens and hyaenas.

'We will move today,' Vilna said.

'Lady!' Aranthur spat.

Vilna shrugged. 'No point to win fucking battle. Unless pursue, ride, kill.' He shrugged again. 'Don't stop. This is victory. Win battle – worth my shit. Pursue – destroy. Then victory.'

Aranthur didn't understand. He was filthy, and his head hurt, and

89

the sun was blazing, and it was all he could do to continue working. He went down the second picket line, and was well into the third when a trooper he didn't know appeared with a bronze canteen of water, another cup of *quaveh*, and another bowl of meal.

Aranthur ate and drank while the new trooper curried. The new man didn't speak Byzas; they had a halting conversation in Attian, which neither of them knew well enough, and then exchanged smiles and went to work. With a second pair of hands, the horses went better, but it was mid-morning before they had a dozen more pairs of hands at work, and the horses gleamed.

Centark Equus appeared and tacked up his own charger. He clucked a few times over his horse's condition, saw Aranthur, and smiled.

'The man of the hour, what?' he said. 'Enjoy being a lowly groom, young Timos. I hear you are to be promoted.'

Aranthur smiled. But he kept the brush going in circles.

'He's not going to want to do much today,' Equus said, referring to his mount, a big Nemean stallion. 'We're moving in an hour. You're with us.'

'Am I?' Aranthur asked. 'I think I'm on staff...'

Equus smiled. 'Trust me, young Timos. I have your best interests at heart. I'm taking the light horse out now. You ride with me.'

Aranthur went back to Ariadne, who was, all things considered, in fine shape; after all, he'd had remounts all the day before. He put her bridle on, saddled her, and stole her a double handful of oats from the General's manger.

'I packed your kit,' Prince Ansu said.

He looked as if he'd been beaten, with deeply hollowed eyes and lines by his mouth.

'Are you all right?' Aranthur asked.

Ansu laughed. 'No, I was in a terrible battle and then a party nearly as perilous. By the hundred and forty-four.'

'I curried your gelding.'

'I knew you had heroic qualities,' the Zhouian said. 'I'll try not to humiliate myself.'

'I've thrown up twice. It helps.'

'*Child, dost thou think I knoweth this not?*' Ansu asked in passable Armean. He managed a smile.

Less than an hour later, silent and mostly surly, they were moving. Aranthur and Ansu rode with the centark.

'From this morning, I am, at least temporarily, a Vanax,' Equus said.

'Congratulations,' Aranthur said.

They were just cresting the ridge, so that the remains of the enemy camp, which both armies had looted enthusiastically, lay at their feet.

'I am commanding the pursuit, at least on this axis,' Equus said.

'How long will the pursuit go on?' Aranthur asked.

Equus looked back at them, his face unreadable.

'A pursuit goes on until the victors are too tired to continue or the losers are destroyed. I rather think it'll be the latter, don't you?'

'Destroyed?' Dahlia asked.

Equus turned his horse. 'Dahlia—'

'You mean, until we kill *even more* of them?'

Equus shrugged. 'Just so. All of them, if we can manage it. The whole point of winning a hard-fought action like yesterday's is that afterwards, the defeated usually disintegrate. They can't manage an organised resistance unless they have a rearguard. We'll see what this lot can manage.'

'And then we kill them,' Dahlia said.

'Precisely.' Equus' voice was gentle. 'It's war. General Tribane has ordered it.'

'Lady!' Dahlia turned her horse aside and looked down at the plundered camp. Armeans were still stripping the tents. 'Did *you* get anything good?'

Aranthur shrugged.

'You didn't go into their camp?' she asked.

Sasan shrugged.

'He was helping the wounded,' the Safian man said.

'As were you,' Dahlia said. 'I see. You two are working on sainthood, perhaps?'

Aranthur smiled at Sasan.

'Luckily,' Lemnas said, 'the General guaranteed an equal division of spoils to all.'

Dahlia flushed.

Equus nodded. 'Myr Tarkas, I know you are not under military discipline, but anything you ... found ... must be handed in to be shared.'

Dahlia sighed. 'I thought I'd averted poverty for a year or two.'

Equus was standing in his stirrups, looking at the ground behind the enemy camp.

'Maybe you have. There was quite a bit of gold in that camp. I say, Timos, have a gallop along to the Second City Cavalry and tell them to shake out into a skirmish line after we pass the camp.'

As Aranthur turned his horse, he heard Dahlia spit, 'We're going to massacre people, but we have rules about dividing the spoils?'

'Precisely,' Equus said.

Aranthur rode along to the regiment that was, by rights, his own. He saluted the centark commanding and passed the message.

The centark raised an eyebrow.

'You're this famous Timos?' she asked.

'Yes, ma'am.'

She laughed. 'Well, I've never met you, but apparently you brought honour to the regiment yesterday.' She reached out and shook his hand. 'You know you're to be promoted?'

'I heard it mentioned, ma'am.'

She smiled. 'Well, wear it well. I could use another centark. We lost half our officers yesterday.'

'I really know nothing—' he began.

She cut him off with a wave.

'I'm a mercer, Syr Timos. What do I know of cavalry skirmishes? But here we all are.'

He saluted and trotted back up the column to the Nomadi, who were already forming line. He fell in behind Equus.

'What are we doing, syr?' he asked.

Equus stood in his stirrups again.

'Can you cast that far-seeing *occulta*?' he asked.

Aranthur nodded.

'I'm a little beaten up by yesterday,' he admitted. 'I'm not exactly full of *zori*.'

'*Zori*?' Clearly the Ellene word puzzled him.

'*Saar. Power.*'

Aranthur cleared his mind. His horse immediately sensed his relaxation and began to crop grass.

Aranthur found the *volteia* and summoned his *saar*. He took his time, and built the whole construct in his sandbox, and then nudged it into the *Aulos* and the viewer burst into reality, fully formed. It floated in front of Equus.

It seemed very difficult to find the *power*. There was dark *sihr* in the ground, and in the air – the Aulian equivalent of death. But the *saar* was thin and difficult to manipulate.

It occurred to Aranthur that with his *transference occulta*, he might be able to link the viewer to the user so that it would stay in one place relative to the user. But he lacked the talent to do it. Theoretically he could add all sorts of things to an *occulta*; at a practical level, they simply became too complex at a point – uncastable.

Equus looked out across the plain. In the distance there was a river; in the viewer, it sparkled, and there was a bridge and a dome. He tracked to the right and left, but the bridge was the only significant feature. There were several patches of woods, one large, and in the left centre of the plain, a domed hill, as if someone had upended a bowl there.

The line started forward. Aranthur carried messages, as did his friends. As the line of light cavalry moved across the plain to the river, it thoroughly explored the woods and a detachment seized the top of the bowl-shaped hill. The line began to gather prisoners – wounded men abandoned the day before, or men who'd lost their mounts, or who were dazed, or who simply wanted to be done.

Sasan made it his business to collect the prisoners. Aranthur came across him several times, as the prisoners were gathered in the shade of a grove at the base of the hill.

No one offered any fight, and the line continued forward, cautiously examining every building, every projecting stone, every stand of trees or patch of rough ground. By mid-afternoon they'd come miles. The hill was a dim hump behind them, and the horses could smell the water of the river. It was difficult to hold them, and many of the militia cavalry were already having trouble with their mounts, too tired to go on.

Equus sighed.

'I want to see that bridge,' he said. 'Let's finish what we started.'

He rode along the line, reassuring his officers in person, and then the line went forward to the sound of a trumpet. Many horses walked, heads down, tails like wilted flowers. Their riders were not in much better shape, but the line made it to the water, and veteran file leaders made sure that the watering of the horses was orderly.

The bridge had been broken by *sihr*. The edges of the magnificent stone structure were burned black, and there was a hole in the centre; an entire span was missing. In the water below were dozens of corpses, some burnt, some merely drowned.

'You can't hold a bridge from one end,' Equus said. 'Lemnas? Find me a good ford.'

'Wait, syr,' Aranthur said, just as Ansu raised his hand imperiously. Both men rode forward.

'Dahlia?' Aranthur called, and she rode carefully down the bank to the water's edge.

'Lady,' she muttered. 'That's a *stigal.*'

Aranthur could see the thing, which appeared to be black. It was hanging from the broken beam of the middle span of the bridge.

Aranthur leant forward, and a wave of *wrong* passed over his face like a foul smell.

Someone *moaned.*

Dahlia's head snapped back to him.

'What was that?' she asked.

Aranthur's sword hilt was warm to the touch.

Ansu turned his horse. 'It's a very powerful curse, anchored to that artifact suspended from the beam.'

'But what made the noise?' Dahlia asked.

Up above them, on the bridge's apron, Dekark Lemnas put her *carabin* to her shoulder. There was a flat *crack* and the artifact spun off into the water with a splash. Immediately the sense of *wrong* passed away. Aranthur could actually *feel* the curse being moved downstream. It was also sinking; the curse was struggling with the water.

He ignored the noise and the warmth of his sword hilt, which had felt as if it was vibrating. He put his horse's head at the top of the apron and Ariadne sprang up the bank.

'Centark, the enemy have left . . .' He shook his head. 'Sorcerous traps. Only the Twelve know how many, or where.'

'Barbarous,' Equus said with a shiver. Then he straightened. 'It is my duty to find their rearguard if I can. Dekark Lemnas, find me a ford, but do *not* cross.'

'Yes, syr.'

Lemnas carefully completed the loading of her short, rifled weapon and then gathered a handful of her troopers. Aranthur noted that they

94

had the best horses. The old Steppe nomad, Vilna, took two men and a woman and went the other way.

'Kunyard is off to the north somewhere. Attians to the south of us. We should be seeing their dust.' Equus took a deep breath. 'It's big out here. A thousand cavalry can just vanish in the haze.' He paused. 'I don't like these sorcerous traps.' He was looking at the bloated corpses in the water. 'Terrible way to die.'

'A sword in the gut is better?' Dahlia asked.

Equus shrugged. 'A sword in the gut is a risk that I understand. It's an odd thing – the nomads hate magik, mostly. But they like you lot.'

'Steppe people have their own ways into the place you call *Aulos*,' Ansu said. 'They distrust your way much as you distrust sorcery.'

'Well said, Highness.' Equus was watching the dust to the north, where Lemnas was cantering along the riverbank. 'But General Tribane is worried, and if she is worried, I am worried.'

'The General is worried?' Aranthur asked.

'The General is paid to worry all the time,' Equus said. 'Give me that viewer thingy again.'

Aranthur cast. It was much easier the second time. And the *saar* seemed more plentiful.

'And there she is – Lemnas has a ford.' Equus looked all along the eastern horizon. 'Now, does our beaten enemy have a rearguard, or not?' He glanced at Aranthur. 'You are allowed to comment.'

'I don't know anything, syr.' He looked at Prince Ansu.

Ansu leant forward.

'I think our adversary is happier trusting his *sihr* than mere people.' The Zhouian looked rueful. 'Also, I observe that we left his corps of Magi largely intact, but his soldiers were badly beaten.'

'Fair enough,' the centark said. 'So you mean that instead of a rearguard, we have these traps.'

Aranthur nodded with Ansu.

Equus' pleasant round face took a sterner look.

'Right, then,' he said. 'Follow me.'

Aranthur cancelled his viewer with a faint *pop* as the shaped lenses collapsed.

He followed Equus to the ford.

'Do you have a *proaspismos* ready to hand?' Ansu asked Dahlia.

'I do. I don't like it.' She turned to Aranthur. 'You know that every time you access the *Aulos*, Magi can find you?'

Aranthur nodded.

'I'm sure I knew that, some time,' he said ruefully. 'I've never actually had the *polemageia* class.'

'I've had it in second year. That was enough to teach me how different battle magik is. I know that the *Polemagi*, the Battle Magi, are trained to cloak their castings as they perform them. I watched them yesterday. That was their failing – they were better at cloaking than at casting.'

'But out on this plain, anyone can see everything we do,' Ansu said. 'What we need is a drake. A drake could see anyone use any kind of *power* – could track a mouse.'

'Do you take drakes to war?' Aranthur asked.

'There is a great statue in our old palace of a drake in armour. So it may have happened.'

'A drake would indeed be handy just now,' Equus said. 'Aranthur, with me. Myr Tarkas, if you'd be so kind, get the Second City Cavalry and ask Centark Domina to cross after the Nomadi. The other regiments are to stand down and make open camps. To be alert for bodies. Myr Tarkas, you are to provide . . . hmm . . . *magikal* support to Centark Domina if she needs it.'

'Yes, syr.'

She didn't quite salute, but her wave was not casual.

They rode up to the ford, where Dekark Lemnas waited on the beach. She was wounded.

'Corpses on the far bank,' she reported. 'Some bastard with a *jezzail* killed Manax and winged me, syr.'

The ford was hidden by a low bluff, and on the far side, there was a sandy beach. A low, muddy spot beyond that rose to a small farm, with a mud-brick house. There were lumps on the sand, like piles of rags.

'I don't like the look of that,' Equus snapped. 'Get Dekark Lemnas to an Imoter, please. Timos, viewer, please.'

Aranthur managed it, but his limited supply of *saar* was stretched. He kept enough to shield himself . . .

Equus looked through the viewer. The little beach was littered with corpses, and there were more of them on the other side.

'There's one here, too,' Aranthur said immediately. 'Another *stigal*.'

Lemnas cleared her throat. 'I can't see it this time.'

Equus cursed. 'Blood and Darkness. Fucking cowards.'

'Will a *proaspismos* stop a *stigal*?' Aranthur asked Prince Ansu.

The Zhouian was casting, singing softly in his own tongue. A nimbus of light gathered around his left hand, and then around his horse's muzzle.

Aranthur prepared his *aspis* but left it uncast. He accessed the jewel on his chest for *saar*.

'I need this ford,' Equus said.

'I'll do what I can,' Aranthur said.

Ansu smiled. 'I'm game if you are.' He smiled again – a companionable challenge.

Aranthur laughed. 'Let's do it!' he shouted.

He leapt his horse down the bank and splashed across the river, the first man to cross. His chest tightened and he watched the overgrowth at the water's edge, expecting a sudden fusillade or a shower of arrows, or even the crack of sorcery, most of all the sudden stink of *wrongness* from the *stigal*, but Ariadne scrambled for purchase on the gravel shoal and then they were up the bank. There were dead men in the reeds, and corpses on the flat, marshy ground beyond, as if fifty men and women had simply decided not to live any more, and fallen to the ground. Aranthur dismounted, and flipped a corpse; as he'd expected, it had no wound. He'd now seen enough dead people to know – no pool of blood, no stain, and surprisingly few flies.

'I think this was *sihr*,' he said. 'But I cannot feel the *stigal*.'

He looked at Ansu, who came up the bank and circled his gelding around the corpses. Ansu reined in, throwing one leg over his horse's head in a showy dismount. He walked among the corpses, looked at two, and then made a noise.

'Let me do it,' he said to Aranthur.

If he cast at all, Aranthur couldn't see him do it. Instead, he sang a little, and shook his head.

'Is that the Zhouian way of magik?' Equus asked Aranthur.

The Nomadi were forming a column on the other side of the ford. Aranthur could just see Dahlia leading the Second City Cavalry beyond the bluff.

'These were all killed by sorcery this morning,' Ansu said. 'After the sun rose.' He pointed inland. 'There will be more over there, and over there.'

Aranthur spat. 'Were they deserting?' he asked.

Ansu shrugged. 'How would I know?'

Aranthur rode down to the water's edge and shouted, 'Don't go anywhere yet! Please, halt your people, centark!'

He turned back to where Prince Ansu was singing softly through his nose.

'Ansu, could the . . . curse . . . still be functioning? Did someone cast a magikal protection on the ford, or the east bank?'

Ansu paled, and he sang again, raising his hands so that a tablet of light appeared between them.

'Ten thousand devils!' he said. 'It's in the house. It is a curse – we're already infected.'

'Back!' Aranthur shouted to Equus.

The Nomadi crowded back from the water, those at the back wheeling their horses. For long moments the column was in chaos.

Ansu was working; he'd abandoned concealment. Aranthur *altered* himself to be able to see *sihr* and *saar*. The black stuff seemed to pool around the corpses, but he could see lines of emergence from the distant house.

'How badly off are we, old chap?' Equus shouted to Ansu.

The prince shook his head. To Aranthur he said, 'We're only alive because these poor bastards died. They took a lot of the sting out of the curse.' He paused. 'But I can feel it going after my heart – can't you?'

Aranthur shook his head. 'No.'

He could, in fact, see a faint dark line like a spiderweb connecting the house and Ansu. But there was no such line to him.

'How's the curse fashioned?' he asked. 'I can see that it's in the house, but not what it is.'

'Beyond me.'

Ansu sat suddenly, as if his hamstrings had been cut. His face grew pale.

Aranthur looked at him, made his decision, and moved. He went for the house, watching it in the *Aulos*, his long sword tapping the ground behind him as he ran. And as soon as he passed the bodies, a faint line, a silken thread of darkness, reached out, brushed at his *aura* . . .

And fell away.

Aranthur went forward.

Another thread reached for him. He sensed, rather than saw, that he was exerting a field, like an *aspis* of *saar*.

He had no idea why. Or rather, he had an idea, and it was irrational.

He was close to the mud-brick house's only door, and he drew his sword.

Almost instantly, a pulse of light flashed through the *Aulos* and a dozen reaching threads shrivelled away, burned like silk thread touched with fire.

Aranthur was stunned. The sword ...

There was no time. He burst through the door, which hung drunkenly on rusted hinges, and ...

There ...

Was ...

The ...

Focus.

The child had been tortured before he was killed. Aranthur had a moment to remember the taste of all that pain – the pain that Syr Xenias di Brusias had suffered at the hands of his captors, before he died. He'd tasted it back at the Inn of Fosse, and he'd asked if there were Darkbringers.

And now, in a farmhouse in Armea, he saw what a Darkbringer might do. It was terrible. The worst of it was that the child's face reflected the despair, the horror, the humiliation, the sheer awful unfairness of his death. And the body had been painted black, and was mutilated to look as if it had wings.

Aranthur didn't hesitate. He slammed the sword into the focus of the curse, the mutilated child's corpse.

There was a sound in the mortal world, a *pop* of displaced air. And to Aranthur's *enhanced* vision, there was a sudden hole in the mortal reality around him. It didn't last long, but for a few beats of his heart, there was a jagged gash in his perception of the world and the *Aulos*. He saw ... something else, something other – raw, ugly, unformed.

It was ...

More than his mind could fathom. He stood for some time, until Ansu's hand was on his shoulder.

'Ten thousand frozen star-hells,' Ansu said. 'Oh, gods. The poor thing. Who the *fuck* does this?'

Aranthur blinked. The gash in *everything* was gone, and he doubted it had ever been. The sword in his hand was almost hot, but it was just an old sword, a First Empire long sword with a complicated hilt.

The dead boy was just a dead boy. Mutilated, terrible, but dead.

Ansu gave him an odd look.

'You did this?' he asked. 'The *stigal*? You ... cancelled it?'

Aranthur nodded. 'I ... think ... so.'

'Go and get your centark,' Ansu said.

'You can work the *Aulos*!' Aranthur said.

'Of course I can. I wanted to learn *your* way.' He stood over the thing that had once been a human boy. 'Go and get the cavalry. I'll do my best to dispose of this poor victim.'

Aranthur was deeply shaken. He made his way back to the riverbank, caught Ariadne where she was munching grass, and called for Equus, all in a black tunnel of his thoughts – all while trying to make time pass with simple functionality.

He splashed across immediately, followed by Dahlia with her mist-shield over both of them.

'Aranthur, what just happened?' she asked.

He shook his head. He was still seeing the boy. And the void, or the chaos, or whatever he had glimpsed. The unformed ...

'What did you do? Where's Ansu?'

Aranthur shook his head to clear it.

'Syr, the *stigal* is destroyed and the way is clear. Prince Ansu is using his own powers to dispose of ...' He blinked. 'The victim.'

'Gods,' Equus said. 'Right then.'

He whistled, and a young woman with a long trumpet tore across the stream.

Equus made a hand motion, the trumpeter blew an order, and the Nomadi began to cross. Again.

Two hours later, the Nomadi and the Second were encamped, with an *abatis* of felled trees around the camp as a quick defence and a corral for their horses, which were on picket lines. A full quarter of each regiment were on duty. Just as darkness fell, four wagons arrived from the rear with an escort, bringing up food, oats for the horses, and orders, as well as Sasan.

The Safian had wine. Aranthur was sitting by the fire, staring at it.

Dahlia hugged Sasan and shared out a half-bottle of red wine, and Aranthur drank his share without looking up.

Dahlia turned back to Aranthur.

'Tell us again. Your *sword* defeated the *stigal*.'

Aranthur nodded. 'Yes.'

Ansu drank off his wine.

'You may say I am as crazy as our friend, but I thought it was his sword that made the moaning noise, back at the broken bridge.'

'It talked to me, in the battle,' Aranthur said.

'What?' Dahlia asked.

'It said something about being revealed.'

Aranthur shrugged. He was feeling better; time, and food, and wine, had restored his balance a little. So he smiled at Dahlia.

'I was a little busy at the time.'

'May I see your sword, please?' she said.

Aranthur felt a faint hesitation in handing her over.

Her?

He handed the sword to Dahlia, who drew it.

Her.

It was an old broad sword, on a long sword blade. It was too heavy for Dahlia, but she hefted it, made a mock cut, ran a thumb down the blade.

'It seems to be a perfectly ordinary sword, to me,' she said.

Ansu nodded. 'That *stigal* was ... very powerful. It resisted my best effort to unmake it, at a range of perhaps fifty paces.' He scratched under his chin. 'I'm not a particularly powerful Magos, but in Zhou we say that unmaking a static *occulta* is merely a problem of leverage, yet I could not gain a purchase on this one.'

Dahlia handed the old sword back to Aranthur.

'How long have you had this old sword?' she asked.

Aranthur shrugged. 'I bought it at a street fair ... before last Darknight. Before I walked home.'

Dahlia nodded. 'Interesting.'

The subject changed, and Sasan spoke at length about the Safian prisoners.

'They are tools, mere cannon fodder,' he said bitterly. 'Bah, they are no different from the Shah's armies – they do as they are told, for money and loot. However despicable, they are merely men.'

'And women,' said Dahlia.

Sasan shook his head. 'A few, but not as many as I would have expected from the Steppes and the northern clans. The Pure do not trust women,' he added. 'That was obvious when they started coming at us five years ago.' He looked at Aranthur. 'Your Myr Tribane has offered to let me recruit from among the prisoners.'

Dahlia sat up. 'That's insane,' she said.

'Is it?' Sasan asked. 'I will not sit on my hands. If the gods stand with me, I will not go and hide in *thuryx* again. I will take the fight to the Pure.'

'You?' Dahlia asked.

Aranthur winced at her tone.

'I was once a warrior,' Sasan said. 'Perhaps I will earn the right to call myself such again.'

Dahlia bit her lip.

Ansu nodded.

'It seems fitting, to me,' he said.

'Me, too,' Sasan said. 'What could be more fitting than a horde of murderous turncoats led by a *thuryx* addict?'

'Sasan!' Dahlia said.

Sasan shrugged. 'That's what you were saying, were you not? From the immense height of your superiority?'

'Sasan!' she spat.

Aranthur couldn't prevent the slight smile that crossed his face. He knew her tone.

'Syr Timos,' called a voice.

Aranthur sat up; it was the young woman who served as Equus' trumpeter.

'Here,' he called.

She bowed.

'The Vanax is asking for you at your earliest convenience,' she said formally.

'Which means, right now,' Aranthur groaned.

Dahlia ignored him, eyes locked with Sasan.

Ansu rose with him.

'I think he wants to see me, as well,' he said sweetly.

'Oh, no . . .' the young woman began, but Ansu stepped past her smoothly.

'Trumpeter, I know Centark Equus fairly well. Besides, I have something to tell him.'

'And you want clear of that camp fire,' Aranthur said with an uneasy smile as they walked away.

'Exactly,' Ansu whispered.

Equus was lying on his blankets, with his head pillowed on a saddle, looking up at the stars.

'Timos.' He rose to his feet as if it pained him, and perhaps it did. 'The convoy brought us orders. You are promoted, as of today, to centark.'

Aranthur, despite his fatigue and the feeling of doom that had clung to him since he looked at the gash in reality his sword had made, managed a genuine smile.

'Centark?' he asked.

'Yes. In the Nomadi. And Centark Domina has also asked for you – the Second lost most of their officers in the battle.' Equus nodded. 'I've asked for you, too.'

'I know nothing of the duties of a dekark, much less a real officer,' Aranthur said.

'That is why I am sending Dekark Lemnas, who is long overdue for promotion, to the Second to act as a squadron commander. She took a wound today. You can take her place leading the *carabins* for a few days with Vilna as your dekark. I feel that the scouts might need your *polemageia* for the next few days, and you'll learn the basics of leading a troop of cavalry.'

Aranthur bowed. 'Perhaps Syr Vilna can teach me.'

Equus nodded. 'I see us in a long war,' he said. 'Training and experience will be everything.'

'I . . . have other duties . . .'

Aranthur didn't know what to say about the Safiri grimoire, or the whole world of Cold Iron, which seemed so far away.

Equus shrugged. 'Well, to me, you are promising, even if you are one of Drako's effete gang of thieves and cut-throats.'

Equus' trumpeter poured him wine and he handed Aranthur a cup.

'And any way you cut the loaf, you belong to me for a few days. I want to make better time tomorrow. I propose to send you and your Academy friends out with my scouts to try and locate and eliminate any more of these traps. Can you handle it?'

Aranthur looked at Prince Ansu. Ansu shrugged.

'I confess that this is probably not what my father thought I was coming here to do.' He spread his hands. 'Despite which, I accept.'

Aranthur nodded. 'I think we can do it.'

'At speed?' Equus asked. 'I'm sorry, Timos, but none of us have ever done anything like this. I don't know *how* to look for your sorcery while riding across country. But Tribane is marching at dawn – she'll pass through this position tomorrow. We're going into Safi. I will not tell you more, in case you are captured.'

A feeling of horror passed through Aranthur's shoulders and down his back.

Captured.

He thought of the child, tortured to death merely to power an occult artifact.

4

Safian Borderlands

The next morning, after a briefing in late night moonlight, Aranthur 'led' his first cavalry patrol forward into the darkness beyond the line of pickets. He'd already learnt so much he couldn't really take it all in. He saw that the Nomadi had sent out a patrol before his, to make sure that there was no ambush waiting just beyond the picket lines – a strong patrol that had gone all the way around the camp. He watched Vilna examine 'his' troopers, demanding that one young woman fill her canteen, mocking another man for having too little food.

And then they were away. Aranthur rode in the middle of the column, with Sasan and Dahlia and Prince Ansu. They had six troopers well out ahead. Another six trailed them by several hundred paces. All told they had only twenty-four Nomadi.

The first hour was the worst, as they felt their way forward in near total darkness. Every tree branch was an enemy. Every horse whicker presaged an ambush. Every broken branch suggested the crack of a weapon or the casting of a spell.

They passed a lonely crossroads, and halted. The sun rose in their faces and bathed the world in blood. Far out across the plain, something caught the light brilliantly, and shone like a beacon for a few minutes. A little later, a line of white teeth appeared far off at the very edge of vision, but they, too, vanished as the sun climbed. Aranthur rode around the crossroads, but there was nothing to see except that hundreds of men and horses had recently passed.

'Leave six at crossroad,' Vilna told him.

Aranthur nodded. 'Very well.' He was watching Vilna command 'his' detachment. He smiled. 'Whatever you say.'

Vilna laughed. 'You not so stupid.'

He barked orders in his own sing-song Steppe tongue, and six riders fell out. Aranthur had time to think that only a day before, Vilna had ordered him to curry horses, and now he was an officer. He smiled to himself. He didn't feel that he was in command at all. He had more the feeling of riding a runaway horse.

They moved east, into the rising sun.

By noon, they'd come so far that they were close to the building whose tower had flashed in the sun.

Aranthur had watched it grow from a spike on the horizon to a palace out of a tale. It was red-brown, with hundreds of windows and a huge copper dome that rose like an eastern helmet to a spike. The spike was covered in gold and rose into the heavens. The temple, if such it was, was surrounded by a high wall, and there were signs of a village or substantial town outside the walls.

Aranthur looked to Vilna, but the old nomad pursed his lips and shrugged.

Aranthur trotted his horse to the head of his little column.

'Halt?' Vilna asked.

Aranthur looked at the town, and what appeared to be a river and a bridge.

'We're still in Armea?' he asked Sasan.

'This is Elmit. Still eight stages to Safi. That is the monastery of Helre, who is your Aploun. See the line of hills on the horizon? They are at the edge of Safi.' Sasan pointed south, towards another line of hills. 'Masr. Eventually.'

Aranthur rose in his stirrups, mostly because that's what Equus did when he couldn't decide what to do. He looked at the bridge.

The town offered him no answers. Distant dogs barked.

Vilna was waiting for *him* to decide.

Fine.

'Forward,' he said.

Vilna nodded sharply.

The column moved forward at a trot. A few hundred paces from the arched bridge, Aranthur saw horsemen, and behind them, men working on the bridge.

He knew in an instant that they were not *working on the bridge*. He guessed that they were sorcerers, putting down a victim. A *stigal*. A curse. And he could feel it. He snapped his *volteia* for seeing *sihr* into reality and there it was: a complex *working*, black as pitch, but unfinished.

'I want to charge them,' he said to Vilna.

Vilna smiled grimly. 'Good.'

Aranthur drew his sword and all the troopers around him did the same.

He looked back, caught Dahlia's eye.

'Get the Magi!' he shouted.

Sasan had a puffer in his hand. Ansu flicked him something like a salute, and they were off, racing along the road.

A hundred paces out, Dahlia did *something*. Aranthur missed her cast, but her *occulta* skipped the fringe of Pindari cavalry and struck among the men on the bridge, scattering them. Their arcane shields came up too late for at least two, who fell screaming, clutching their guts.

Then Aranthur was sword to sword with the Pindaris. They were surprised, despite everything, but the man who stayed to swagger swords with Aranthur was big, wore a red felt cap over his helmet, and knew his business. He cut so hard that Aranthur lost his sword at the cross and took a blow. He never felt it, and he got an arm around the man's neck and both of them fell from their horses. Aranthur's troopers swept by, and Aranthur rolled atop his opponent. He felt rather than saw the man go for a knife, and he stopped it with his left hand.

His right hand pinned the man's other blow, and they struggled, but Aranthur was stronger. He slammed a fist into the man's head, but the Pindari chief threw him off, and Aranthur rolled and rose to his feet.

The Pindari turned to face him, and drew a knife. It was long and gleamed in the midday sun, and then suddenly the man exhaled blood.

Sasan waved a smoking puffer at him and rode on. The Pindari fell forward, shot through the back. He twitched once and lay still.

Ariadne was three steps away. Aranthur caught her reins and then retrieved his sword, which lay in the dust. His right hand still felt numb, and it was only when he looked down at his numb hand that he saw the blood on the skirt of his once-white fustanella.

He stopped the bleeding himself, and stood by his horse, breathing and trying not to pass out, while his little troop of cavalry cleared the bridge. Finally Aranthur felt the wound in the top of his thigh was stable enough, after he poured *saar* into it. He mounted carefully from a low wall and rode forward. The cut to his wrist was bad.

There were half a dozen corpses on the bridge, and two more on the far side. Three of them carried staves and wore bright gold talismans – a perfect circle, like a wheel.

Past the bridge was an open market, abandoned, the stall roofs flapping in the wind. Dogs barked and howled, and the wind caught up dust devils and whipped them through the air.

Aranthur heard a scatter of shots to the east, and he pressed Ariadne forward. He found Sasan with a pair of wounded Pindaris.

'You wounded?' Sasan called out.

'Better now,' Aranthur said. 'What happened?'

Sasan shrugged. 'Dahlia went through their Magi like a wet knife cuts cheese. And when they turned their backs, our nomads butchered them. They don't like sorcery, your lads.' He smiled grimly. 'I'm taking prisoners,' he added.

'I'm glad someone is.' Aranthur was very tired of killing. 'Are you recruiting?'

'Tattooed Pindaris? I doubt it. Once they're marked, they're ... scum. They kill for pleasure. Rape, rob, kill.'

'Tattoos?' Aranthur asked.

Sasan pulled one man's khaftan back to reveal a series of hash marks and whorls in black ink on the man's pale skin.

'They take children from the parents they kill, and make them into Pindaris. Once they're marked, they're killers.'

The man whose khaftan he'd pulled up just smiled, as if he wanted to be friends.

'What do you plan to do with them?' Aranthur asked.

Sasan shrugged. 'No idea. I just can't stomach killing everyone I disagree with. Even this lot.'

Aranthur shared his feeling, and the fight with the Pindari chief had scared him. Unlike a dozen other fights, the man had almost had him at the first blow.

I was beginning to imagine I was a good blade, he thought. He looked at the cut to his forearm. *I was almost dead.*

He rode forward past Sasan, his hands shaking. Ariadne was troubled by her rider's inattention and shied at some bodies, and Aranthur was almost thrown.

Closer up, he could see that the dome of the magnificent temple was cracked, and there were scorch marks. As he picked his way through the town and passed around it, he found that the dome, perfect when viewed from the west, had partially collapsed. The town was full of rubble, and stank. There were bodies in every building, and he began to avert his eyes rather than see them, bloated and in many cases stripped naked by looters.

He pressed his heels to Ariadne's sides and she leapt forward, jumping over a fallen basalt pillar with a flowing stride that belied her fatigue. He raced down the empty main street and along the base of the precinct wall, which on the north side had been breached in two places. The corpses in the breaches were mere skeletons, picked clean of flesh – an old horror story.

He heard a horn, and then another, and then he saw Vilna blowing on a large cow horn at the eastern end of the town.

'Sorry I'm late,' he said as he rode up, and Vilna smiled.

'Bleeding,' he said, and pointed at Aranthur's right arm.

Aranthur was bleeding fairly freely, because apparently his *occultae* had failed and he hadn't even noticed. And he was low on everything.

One of his troopers gave him a length of linen – some dead man's turban. Aranthur cut a piece out and wrapped his hand and used a little stored *saar* from his *kuria* to reinforce the effect of a tight bandage.

'I think we got them all,' Dahlia said. 'This one is alive.'

She pointed to another one of the staff-bearers, who lay on the ground, his circular amulet glinting in the strong sun. There was blood flowing from a gash on his head, but he was breathing.

'All right,' Aranthur said.

He felt bad: tired, stupid with blood loss. But Vilna was looking at him, and so were the rest of his troopers.

'How many did we lose?' he asked.

Vilna smiled his grim smile.

'None. Almost lost you.'

Aranthur looked at Vilna.

'Dahlia, how about you and Sasan take the prisoners back to Equus and report? We'll leave two troopers here and press forward.'

He was looking under his hand at the blank expanse of open ground stretching to the distant line of hills: irrigated plains, criss-crossed with irrigation ditches and streams. Terrible cavalry country.

Vilna's face was expressionless.

'Your command,' he said.

Does that mean it's a bad idea? Aranthur wondered. He looked at Dahlia. She nodded.

'I have juice left. I can get this *badmash* back to Equus.'

'Sasan is back along the road.' Aranthur turned back to Vilna. 'My feeling is that we should stay on them.'

Vilna nodded. 'We should have remounts. But yes. Lost no people. Now they fear us. Forward. We will kill them, every one.'

Aranthur winced.

Two hours later, even Ariadne was showing her fatigue. They stopped to water horses at a cool stream that ran clear over stone. Aranthur purified water for the patrol, and the Nomadi thanked him in three languages. Ansu and Vilna watched the eastern horizon.

When the horses were watered, Aranthur looked at Vilna.

'Well?' he asked.

Vilna was looking east.

'If I had another horse.' He shrugged eloquently.

Aranthur nodded. 'We should go back to the temple.'

'Ayee,' Vilna said. 'Bad place, but yes.'

'Bad?'

'Haunted,' the old nomad said.

An hour later, as the shadows began to lengthen, Vilna ordered all the nomads to dismount and walk, to save their horses, and Aranthur joined them. It was the edge of darkness when they came to the cavalry sentries along the eastern edge of the temple town – men and women of his own Second Cavalry.

He met Dahlia with a bowl of fish stew in her hand.

'You need to see the temple,' she said. 'Better yet, don't.'

'What?' he asked.

'Desecration. Horrible. All the altars – every god. Broken and . . . polluted.'

Aranthur winced.

'Human sacrifice?' he asked.

'All the trimmings,' Dahlia said bitterly. 'Fucking murdered children. I'll never go to sleep again.'

But before the stars were out, Dahlia was asleep next to Sasan, and Aranthur was curled against her. The dead child, painted black... The most horrible thing was that it made no sense.

It made no sense.

It was as if the Pure committed atrocities for some sort of grotesque joy. And yet, when captured, they seemed to be men – ordinary men.

He lay awake for a long time.

In the morning, he was awakened by the trumpeter again, and he followed her to a circle of officers around a campfire. Despite the heat of the days, it was chilly.

'Can you take the forward patrol again, Syr Timos?' Equus asked. 'And thanks for joining us. Officers' call is every morning, not just feast days.'

The other officers laughed.

'Syr, I can, but I doubt my horse can do it,' he said.

'We brought up all the spares in the night,' Anda Qan, the squadron *primos*, handed him a cup of hot *quaveh*. 'I know you have a spare,' he added, a glint in his eye.

Aranthur's wounds were stiff, and Vilna ordered a trooper to tack Rasce while he sat on the ground and an Imoter worked the cut to his wrist and the wound in his leg.

'That wrist cut...' the woman said. 'Syr, you almost lost that hand.'

Aranthur shivered. But when the woman was finished, she nodded.

'Maybe not good as new, but solid enough. Who did the blood *occulta*?'

'I did,' he said.

She smiled, her teeth very white against her dark skin.

'Well done. Not many soldiers who can work *saar* like that.'

'You need a servant,' Vilna said.

Aranthur laughed. 'Vilna, in real life, I'm more likely to *be* someone's servant.'

'Real life?'

'Back in the City.'

Vilna smiled his straight-lipped smile. 'Syr, *this* is your "real life".'

Aranthur looked up at the stars.

'You might have a point. Ansu? You coming?'

Ansu was fully armed. He swung onto a borrowed horse, and they trotted to the head of the patrol, where Dahlia and Sasan were waiting. Sasan had six men with him. They had sabres but no other weapons.

'My army,' Sasan said.

The Nomadi eyed the Safian men with obvious distrust.

'Equus said we could use them as guides,' he said. 'These are the ones I trust most. Two of them are from near my home.'

Vilna spat.

Aranthur nodded.

'Please have them ride at the front of the main column. Dekark? Same as yesterday – two riders well out, then four more. Then the column – Sasan's guides, then our party, and then six troopers at the back, well back.'

Vilna nodded sharply.

The patrol set out with twenty-four Nomadi troopers, six Safian 'guides' and the four friends.

But even as they marched, the whole of the Second Cavalry was forming on the flat ground on the east side of the ruined town. Aranthur rode to the imperious figure of Centark Domina and saluted.

'Syr Timos, as I live and breathe. I hear great things about you, although I plan to keep Lemnas for ever. I'll buy her a business in the City if I have to, just to keep her in the Militia.' Myr Domina smiled.

'You mean to keep her in the City Cavalry?' Aranthur asked.

'They don't call us the "Artists and Artisans" for nothing,' Domina said. 'I'll make her a *Tekne* yet.'

'I'm taking out the advance guard,' he said.

'I know!' she said with a smile for his enthusiasm. 'I'll be about a mile behind you.'

That seemed much better than the day before, but Aranthur was aware that under his own ignorance, they were all learning. No Imperial army, much less a vast force with allies, had done any of this in hundreds of years.

The advance guard went forward at a trot to gain some ground. Aranthur passed the morning patrol with a wave. This morning, he knew the officer commanding and snapped a salute. Then they were crossing streams and irrigation ditches on the little arched bridges they had seen the afternoon before.

They were still less than a mile from the temple-town when a flash of red light alerted them. The four men on advanced picket came galloping back.

The scouts were both dead, as were their horses. The bodies were shrivelled and black, scorched beyond recognition, features burnt away, leaving skulls and teeth protruding in dull whiteness from the black ruins of flesh and clothing.

Dahlia located the focus, the *stigal*, and destroyed it.

The Nomadi stood by their horses on the road, and their faces reflected shock and dull rage in the first light of the sun.

Vilna shook his head. 'Fuckers came back in the dark. Cowards. *Gignards.* Sorcerers.'

The other Nomadi looked at Dahlia, and then at Aranthur.

Aranthur nodded. 'Vilna, tell the patrol that we will fight fire with fire – that no more people will be lost, they have my word. I'll take point myself.'

'We could just halt and demand actual Magi to support us,' Dahlia said. 'Do you think the three of us are really battle Magi?'

Aranthur glanced at her and then at Prince Ansu.

'Honestly? Yes. I think we're what Equus has.'

'General Tribane must have better,' Dahlia said. But she sounded doubtful.

'We saw them lose the magikal duel with the enemy,' Aranthur said.

'Some of them. But every brigade . . .' She shrugged. 'It seems stupid, to me. Three students against the best the Pure have to offer.' She shrugged again and spoke very quietly. 'The enemy has a clear superiority in *power*.'

Ansu was looking at the horizon.

'We felled the Disciple,' he said. 'We're still here.'

'With Qna Liras,' Aranthur said. 'I don't think General Tribane will risk her one Lightbringer clearing traps. We, on the other hand, are expendable. I cannot and will not order you. I will go, however.'

Ansu shrugged. 'I'm coming. I'm better armed today.'

Dahlia rolled her eyes. 'I thought I was cocky. Fine.' She smiled grimly. 'Do you know how to *guise*?'

Aranthur shrugged because he still hated telling Dahlia all the things he didn't know how to do. Especially in front of Vilna and the others. But honesty pushed him.

'No,' he admitted.

She drank some water.

'You were good at *subjugation*, though. I remember – you got a first. Listen, *Guise* is just a minor *subjugation* with a side of illusion. You look like someone else. It's better if backed by some acting and a good costume. Even better if you had study time. Your friend the Emperor's mistress is unbelievably proficient at *guise*.'

Aranthur winced.

'Iralia,' he said.

'Exactly. The tart.' Dahlia wiped sweat from her eyes. 'Here, I'll show you. Just like a *subjugation*, it helps if you play on your audience's belief. Hard to be a giant lizard. Not so hard to be a Pindari scout.'

Vilna made a sign and backed his horse out of the little circle. Chimeg, one of the Pastun from the Steppes, muttered '*Baqsa*' and said a charm.

Dahlia ran Aranthur through the *occulta* twice. Aranthur learnt it easily; it really was just a form of a *working* he already knew.

'Better if we could get some Pindari clothes,' she said.

'Yuck,' Ansu said. 'There are limits on my willingness to "play soldier".'

'We'll do whatever it takes,' Aranthur said. 'Right. We're on point. Let's ride.'

Dahlia smiled. Softly, she said, 'One day at this and you sound like an officer.'

Sasan laughed. 'Good luck, friends! I'll just stay back here with my cut-throats.'

The three of them rode forward and took the point. Vilna appointed four new troopers for the support to the point, and they were off.

They rode perhaps four hundred paces to the next arch. Aranthur raised his magesight, and the span appeared clear, but his heart raced as they passed over it.

'I'm awake now,' Ansu said.

'I think this is the stupidest thing I've ever done,' Dahlia added.

'I'm assuming – hoping – that I will see the *stigal* in the *Aulos*.' Aranthur winced at his own lack of assurance.

'A real *polemagos* can hide his casting in plain sight.' Dahlia shrugged. 'I have my sight up, too. And some other things.'

They rode forward. Two terrifying bridges later, they all stopped to drink water.

'I'm not sure I can do this all day,' Ansu allowed.

Aranthur nodded. He breathed deeply and tried to calm his nerves. A mere sword fight seemed like a possible relief.

As they approached the next bridge, Rasce shied, and Aranthur reined in, just as his sword moaned.

'Stop,' he said. But he was too late.

The red flash was so intense that Aranthur was blind for seconds. Ansu fell from his horse.

The horses panicked, and Ansu was kicked.

Aranthur managed to control Rasce and all he could see was spots. 'What happened?' he called. 'What the hells?'

'Oh, Lady,' Dahlia said.

Aranthur's vision began to clear.

Dahlia was sitting on the road, and Ansu lay on his back, holding his ribs. The bridge was destroyed, and the dark water rolled just beneath Rasce's front feet.

'My shields caught it,' Dahlia said. 'Holy Lady Fuck.'

She turned and spat blood.

Aranthur dismounted and walked down to the edge of the stream. It was the clear stream they'd watered at the day before. He could see the focus, and nothing showed in the *Aulos* in his magesight.

He shook his head. But then he started testing what he saw – looking for traces. He found *sihr* on the ruined bridge and on the ground.

'Dahlia, can we refine magesight?' he asked.

She looked at him.

'If we confined the sight only to *sihr*,' he said, 'could we achieve a finer resolution?'

She got to her feet and drank from her canteen, spat, and drank again. But when he showed her the focus, she nodded. She cast her seeing *volteia* three times. The third time she smiled.

'Jackpot. Not just *sihr* but their "style" of *sihr*.'

'Style?' he asked.

'Another time.'

She taught him, quickly and efficiently, how to alter his school-learned *volteia*.

She managed a smile.

'In *Ars Magika*, they taught us that a *volteia* is too simple to be altered,' she said. 'Almost like a *glyph*. But my sister taught me how to open them up. They're not all solid the way you think.'

Aranthur felt as if a whole new world of self-designed *volteie* opened before him. A way to avoid over-complex casting.

He could see again, and when he used his *kuria* to power his new cantrip, he could see the focus quite clearly.

'Don't destroy it yet,' he said. 'I want to see what my range is.'

She nodded, and then the four support troopers galloped up, having already reported. Aranthur was touched by how happy they were to find him alive.

He rode back and forth until the whole column caught up. He ordered Prince Ansu escorted to the rear; his broken ribs made breathing difficult.

By the time all that had been organised, he had a better idea of what to look for. Less than a mile later, he and Dahlia caught a *stigal*.

This one was different, however.

Aranthur was just aiming his *carabin* at the focus, which looked to him to be a shrivelled human heart, when he heard the crack of a *fusil*.

Dahlia yelled.

Aranthur saw movement, turned, and pulled the trigger. The Pindari was aiming a *fusil* and he went down.

Behind him, a dozen enemy cavalrymen reined in. They were waiting . . .

Aranthur began to reload. He was about forty paces from the focus, and he had its range defined to the width of a woman's finger. He knew Dahlia was somewhere behind him.

She was hit. He could hear her moaning.

He backed away, calling to Rasce, who ignored him.

Two of the Pindaris had *fusils* and both were aimed at him. Suddenly the combat was very personal. He could feel the barrels tracking him. Both weapons fired together, and one ball went through the skirts of his fustanella. The other hit his military turban and tore it from his head.

But they didn't dare come forward, because they feared the *stigal*. They'd triggered the ambush too early.

He found Dahlia's horse. It was lying down, dead, a musket ball in its head. Dahlia was pinned beneath, her leg badly broken.

He heard hoof beats; his own cavalry. He lay down by Dahlia, laid the barrel of the *carabin* on the horse's rump, aimed, and fired.

Missed.

Reloaded.

The Pindaris shuffled around on the road. Two of them shot at him. One ball thudded into the carcass of Dahlia's dead mount.

Aranthur got another bullet down the barrel. He thought of casting his *enhancement* but his level of fatigue was so high that he wasn't sure he could get it off. Besides, he was learning to load quite quickly – and to do so without much thought, like a sword form he'd practised so often he could let his thoughts run free while he practised.

He took more careful aim. The range was over a hundred paces; the short, rifled barrel was not ideal . . .

Crack.

One of the bandits went down.

The others waved weapons.

'We'll be fine,' Aranthur said.

'You have the oddest definition of fine, Aranthur Timos,' Dahlia said. 'Oh, Lady. I've worked on the pain, but I can't touch the break until this beast is off me.'

The Pindaris fired again, and he heard a horse cry, and knew they had hit Rasce. The big horse hadn't followed him back to Dahlia. He felt terrible and stupid for leaving the gelding, and he prayed . . .

Aranthur was reloading when the rest of the patrol came up. At a crisp order, the whole patrol dismounted. Horse handlers took the horses and a dozen shots rang out.

The Pindaris retreated up the road.

Sasan got his 'cut-throats' to lift the horse off Dahlia and she fainted.

Then Aranthur led his people forward.

Aranthur found that the Pindaris had shot Rasce. The horse was lying at the edge of the stream, still kicking. Aranthur had to work very carefully to the point where he could see the focus. He made himself ignore the suffering of his horse – a companion who had taken him across the Soulis mountains and had ploughed fields for his father.

He aimed very carefully, but it took him three shots to destroy the focus, and by then he was crying. He ran forward, heedless of the fire of the Pindaris. Vilna led the troopers forward, and they passed him, leaping the stream.

He knelt by his horse, but the big brute was already dead.

Chimeg, one of his female Pastun troopers, brought him a Pindari pony.

'Good horse?' she asked.

He nodded. He was crying, as he had not cried for any of the dead or wounded after the battle.

'Yes,' he managed.

He was sobbing, and felt foolish and guilty, all together.

The woman took some leaves of stock from a pouch at her waist and threw them over the horse. She said something Aranthur could not understand.

'Come, syr,' she said.

She scrambled back up the bank and gave him the reins of the Pindari pony. Then, as if he was a child, she patted his hand, went back, and got his saddle and puffers from Rasce.

'Thanks, Chimeg,' he said.

With her help, he tacked up the Pindari pony, who was small, but appeared very tough.

Sasan's little troop of Safians passed over the bridge.

Vilna came up and saluted.

'Chimeg and Omga take point,' he said. 'No lose officer.'

Aranthur thought of the good woman who'd just thrown stock on the carcass of his horse.

'No, I'm in front. Everyone else one hundred paces back, in case I screw up. We're going to catch these bastards.'

His fatigue – his increasing depression at the endless stress – was replaced by a burning desire to kill the Pindaris and their sorcerous allies. Aranthur understood that, under his rage and fatigue, he wasn't thinking well, but he pushed forward.

Vilna saluted. It was the first time he'd saluted Aranthur, as he had cause to remember as he rode down the empty road, alone. His new mount had a temper and bad manners and a mouth that was used to a spiked bit. Aranthur had to concentrate hard to stay in the saddle and also maintain his refined magesight, but he was wary, and he expected another attack.

He picked up the *stigal* – not at a bridge, but on the open road, in a culvert where a farmer had placed terracotta tile to drain his field. Aranthur couldn't get at the focus, so he rode back to Vilna and led his patrol north, over the open fields.

'How do you feel about taking a risk?' he said.

Sasan gave him a thumbs up. Vilna raised an eyebrow.

'They are on the road,' Aranthur said. 'Vilna takes half and goes south two hundred paces. I take Sasan and the rest and go north. We ride like hell.' He made a fist as he indicated closing on the rearguard that he was sure they were pursuing. 'Leave ... Chimeg here to tell Centark Domina what we're about and what to avoid.'

Sasan nodded.

Vilna's eyes narrowed.

'If works, fine. Otherwise, stupid as fuck,' he said. 'What of black sorcery in fields? In ditch? Buried in dirt?'

Aranthur had only been a patroller for a day, but he felt that he understood his enemy.

'They can't be that good. We beat them like a drum, Vilna. They're *running*.'

Vilna shrugged. 'You centark.'

His disapproval was obvious.

Sasan nodded. 'I say, do it. Or turn around and go back. I've made a little war, Aranthur. The whole trick for these bastards is to break contact after every fight and give themselves time for the next trap, the next ambush, so all we do is walk into their shit. I've *been* them.' He shrugged.

Aranthur turned to Vilna.

'You know that I am a ... A *baqsa*,' he said.

Vilna made a sign of aversion, a pair of horns with his fingers.

'Never, *Bahadur*. You are Magos, not *baqsa*.'

'Wrong word,' Aranthur muttered. 'Listen, though. I understand these bastards. They only have so much *power* in a day, and casting takes time.'

Time we're wasting in an argument.

Can I really go against what this veteran wants?

Vilna frowned.

'You centark,' he said again.

'Then let's go,' Aranthur said.

He wasn't actually happy to leave the road, and the next field had been left ploughed, with deep furrows, and the horses struggled to cross it. The long, low hedgerow at the eastern end looked like the perfect cover for an ambush . . .

But they passed it, and then they had to cross a deep ditch, and the whole idea seemed absurd, but minutes later they were on hard gravel, moving briskly. Aranthur could see the dust of Vilna's wing, and they went forward, due east. The next time they came to a ditch they all jumped it and swept on, moving faster than they had all day.

As the sun peaked above them, frying every man and every horse, Aranthur saw the twinkle of sun-dazzle on metal. Immediately he turned further north, passed a fringe of date palms, and led his half-troop along the far bank of a shallow, dry ditch.

'Ready now,' he said.

Sasan turned to his six.

'Now I see whether you are true men,' he said in Safiri.

Each man put his right hand to his face.

Aranthur checked his girth and the priming on his pistols.

'I can't shield us like Dahlia,' he said to Sasan.

Sasan shrugged. 'Why don't we pass them? Then come back on them like a fish-hook?'

'Brilliant,' Aranthur said.

'See, I've actually done this before.'

Sasan rattled something in Safiri to his six, and they laughed.

Aranthur waved a casual salute and they all mounted. They rode quickly down the long line of date palms until Aranthur, his heart in his throat, hoped they were well past the twinkle of metal. Then they followed a line of very dusty vegetation, mostly thorny scrub, back towards the road.

'We've come too far.' Sasan shrugged. 'Better than not far enough.'

He smiled, like a man truly enjoying himself.

Aranthur waited for the surge of confidence that usually came before combat, but nothing came, and he got them to the road, afraid of . . .

Everything: ambush, combat, magik, traps . . .

They were moving fast. There was almost no cover, and nothing but speed, and Aranthur's pony broke into a gallop, and the Nomadi and Sasan's 'guides' followed him.

There were men ahead, and horses. A scatter of shots, a hasty *occulta* turned on his *aspis*, and they were in among the Pindari horse, scattering them. Most never stood; they rode off, south, abandoning two circle wearers. Aranthur rode one down, turned his pony, and cut down as the sorcerer raised his staff.

The sword went through the staff as if it was not there. Aranthur's sword went a hand's breadth into the man's skull. He fell, screaming incoherently, and the sword burned him with blue-white fire.

Aranthur turned his pony, pulling viciously at the reins, but the other sorcerer was riding away, galloping south.

He made it to the next irrigation ditch, and then there was a volley, and all the Pindaris dropped. Vilna waved.

Aranthur had a moment of solid satisfaction.

Omga brought him a better horse, but Aranthur had begun to respect the pony, who, despite an ugly head and a temper like a drunk, tended to do more than Aranthur expected. They watered the horses, and he went through the dead sorcerer's effects. He had three human hearts; Aranthur looked at them and shivered.

Sasan was still mounted. His six had bloody sabres and looked as if they had fought.

'Let me go east,' he said. 'Those were cut out of victims not two hours ago.'

One of the Safians, until then silent, leant forward on his mount.

'There is a post,' he said. 'Not far. Maybe a parasang.'

Vilna shook his head. 'No. My pardon, syr. But no. After the shots? And these men of yours.' He shook his head again. 'No. But all of us.'

'Preserve the hearts,' Aranthur ordered. 'Leave six people here – the rest of us will drive on.'

Vilna nodded. 'Not much further, *Bahadur*. Horses are almost done.'

'One parasang,' Aranthur said, indicating the Safian guide. 'But not on the road.'

Three miles later, they found the post. There were four corpses on the road, and signs of a hasty abandonment. They saw dust in the distance, and Aranthur reined in.

'Vilna, will you pursue?' he asked.

'And you, Centark?'

Aranthur pointed back down the road.

'Four bodies. So one heart is in a sorcerous trap.' He pointed behind them. 'On the road. Leave me Omga.'

Vilna watched the distant dust.

'Ayee!' he cried, and thundered off.

Aranthur felt very alone, even with Omga. He felt even more alone fifteen minutes later, when he detected the *stigal*. But Domina's cavalry would be coming, and he made himself go forward. His hands shook, and he took two shots to hit the focus, and even then the spell was not broken. He had to hit it again, and by then he had only three round balls left in his pouch. Then they made their way forward until they reached the *stigal* under the road. Aranthur walked wide of it, out into the fields, looking for an angle, but Omga was more direct. He made a grenado out of his spare cartridges, and threw it into the culvert on a javelin, with an expert flip that belied years of practice.

The explosion was small, but it wrecked the curse, and sickly black-yellow smoke rose over the road.

He ordered Omga to ride down the road to the column. As soon as he sent the man away, he began to worry about everything again: whether he'd just sent a trusting young nomad to his death.

But he turned and followed Vilna.

He didn't have to go far. Vilna came trotting towards him, raising dust; he still had fourteen troopers.

'We found them,' he said. 'They are right there – perhaps ten hundreds of paces along road.' He grinned.

Aranthur waved behind him.

'I sent Omga to fetch the *Tekne*.'

And to his immense relief, before the sun sank another finger's width, the vanguard of the Second Cavalry, the *Tekne*, appeared with Omga riding proudly by the Centark. They were trotting.

'We caught their rearguard,' Aranthur said. 'Or rather, Vilna says it's more of a panicked mob and some wagons.'

Domina smiled the thin smile of a feral cat.

'How splendid,' she said.

He played no role in what followed – it was not a fight but a massacre. The city cavalry were more cautious than the regulars might have been, but they nonetheless captured a thousand horses and drove the enemy farther along the road, and Domina sent her reserve squadron in further pursuit. They were as ruthless as only tired, angry men and women can be, cutting their way through the enemy's hasty camp. It was brutal, grim, and utterly one-sided.

'Don't fight the rest.' the centark ordered. 'Just herd them along so we know where they are.'

The enemy army – what was left of it – was breaking up in all directions. It seemed incredible; the Second City Cavalry were terribly outnumbered, but the 'enemy' were now just desperate men trying to ride foundering horses away into the dusk. There wasn't even a show of force from the enemy Magi. Four more were captured.

Centark Domina turned to Aranthur. She smiled grimly.

'If they stay in contact, you won't have to do this again tomorrow. By Coryn, young man – you and your friends are like *Drabants*.'

The *Drabants* were the band of heroes who had been the bodyguard of Rolan in the War of Wrath.

Aranthur was too tired to enjoy the praise. He was too tired to drink wine. He found an Imoter and visited Ansu, who was almost recovered, and Dahlia, who was in worse shape. By the time that darkness fell, he'd explained the day to Equus and he was asleep. But his dreams were dark, mostly of watching despairing men hacked down by Imperial cavalry.

The trumpeter woke him, and Omga had all his gear laid out, and a little hot water for a hasty sponge-bath. He was presentable when he dragged himself to the morning officers' call.

'So pleased that you could join us,' Equus said.

Vilna put a cup of *quaveh* into his hand.

Anda Qan was dictating morning orders to a scribe. Centark Domina was describing the kind of business she would buy Dekark Lemnas, to general merriment. Aranthur shared half his cup of hot *quaveh* with Sasan, who drank it off and handed him a roll filled with almond paste, which Aranthur thought might be the most delicious thing he'd ever eaten.

'Good morning, companions,' Equus said. 'Last night, as you know, our forward elements caught the enemy and the "Artists and Artisans" did yeoman work carving up their baggage. We kept in contact all night, at least with what remains of their forces in front of us, and this morning, General Tribane will join us to storm what passes for their camp.' He shrugged. 'Seriously? We could storm their camp now. The Pindaris are cutting their losses and running. The baggage is mostly abandoned, and all their *gonnes* are right across the river.'

'So why are we waiting for the General?' a *Tekne* officer asked.

'We're out of Magi,' Equus said. 'And that's the one thing our opponents seem to have in plenty. Timos, are you up for another day of patrolling?'

Aranthur managed a smile. 'I'm new to the army. Am I allowed to say no?'

Everyone laughed.

'Not really,' Equus said.

'Well, then, I can hardly wait,' Aranthur said.

But his humour was forced. The whole thing sickened him.

Equus seldom let his mask slip. But he read Aranthur, put a hand on his elbow, and took him aside.

'Maybe two more days,' he said. 'It is necessary. It must be done.'

Aranthur nodded. But when he rode away, he wasn't convinced. And for the first hour of the day, the ground was virtually carpeted with dead Armeans and Safians.

Pursuit.

Now he knew why the Nomadi said it the way they did.

His orders were clear, and much less dangerous than the orders of the last two days: he was to prowl south and east, looking for the outriders of the Attian army. He and Vilna and Sasan and their troopers moved quickly across an empty landscape of abandoned farms and broken irrigation ditches.

Just before midday, with sentries out in all directions, they took a break and watered their horses at a fish pond watered by a stream from the mountains that were no longer distant. Sasan kicked at the collapsed bank where an irrigation ditch should have received water from a broken dam.

'No one has farmed here for a year,' he said. 'Maybe two.'

'When did you leave Safi?' Aranthur asked.

'Two years ago. Maybe more. There was a fair amount of *thuryx*, brother. It makes time flow like molten metal.' Sasan shrugged, looking at the mountains. 'There is my country, right there. Do you think the Pure are beaten?'

Aranthur shrugged. 'Ask Myr Tribane.'

'But you don't think so.'

'How is Dahlia?' Aranthur asked, changing the subject.

'She's not a good patient. She was taken back west last night. Ansu, too. Ansu is really too important to be serving as a cavalry scout, much less as an hermetical point man.'

Aranthur shrugged again. Fatigue was settling on him like a blanket. He sat on the earthen bank.

'How long ago do you think the Pure hit this area?' he asked.

Sasan shook his head. 'This kind of intensive agriculture needs a stable labour force. A lot of peasants. And regular upkeep. And infrastructure.' He watched the fish. 'If the Pure started raiding here when we were collapsing – that's three years back. That would explain the cut dams. We've crossed a dozen of them, all deliberately wrecked.'

'And not repaired. The peasants flee, the irrigation fails, the crops aren't planted—'

'And people starve. In big numbers – these plains are the breadbasket of Armea.' Sasan stood up. 'Or used to be. By the Thunderer... My band of brigands is looking restless.'

'Can you trust them?'

'Not at all. It's like dealing with a band of *thuryx* addicts. I can't believe a word they say, but by the gods, if I am patient, I may just habituate them to me. I picked up a few more yesterday night – wounded Safians left in the camps.'

'You aren't afraid... they'll just kill you and run off?'

Sasan shrugged. 'If they do, that is the will of the gods. I am trying to repair... something. It starts here.'

He extended a hand to Aranthur and dragged him to his feet.

They rode south, hugging a big, dry irrigation ditch for almost a parasang. A large town with a pair of tall minarets was visible to the south and east.

In early afternoon, they saw horsemen to the south. Vilna led them cautiously along a fringe of big date palms, and then across a patch of thorny scrub and sandy rock that looked more like open desert than tilled land.

The horsemen to the south sounded a trumpet, and began to coalesce like a school of fish attacked by tuna on the great ocean.

'Attians,' Vilna said. 'Good horses. Too good to be Pindaris.'

Aranthur touched Ariadne with his spurs and he and Vilna rode forward, their red coats plain to see. A bey rode out from the mass of riders, followed by a woman with a horsetail standard and a man with an arrow on a viciously curved bow.

'Now Sophia be praised,' the Attian officer said. He gave a perfunctory salute with his sabre and sheathed it. 'Byzas?'

Aranthur, even in the depths of fatigue, found it funny that an Attian nobleman thought that he, an Arnaut, and Vilna, a Pastun nomad, were Byzas. But he returned the salute.

'We are from the advance guard of General Tribane's army,' he explained.

There followed a deeply confusing hour, wherein Sasan, two of his men, a dozen Attians and Aranthur all tried to explain to one another where – exactly – they were, where the Capitan Pasha was, and where the remnants of the enemy might be.

Aranthur tried to draw a rough map, but neither the Attian bey nor Sasan accepted his picture as accurate. The best that they could do was to establish that the name of the town to the south was 'Al-Bayab' and that the pasha's advance guard was there.

'We have flown like arrows from a bow,' Vilna said. 'And each of us has flown in a different direction. The Capitan Pasha is far, far more south than anyone thinks.' He shrugged. 'If Vanax Kunyard is as far north as Pasha is south . . .' He looked east.

He returned to find the General's scarlet pavilion set up in the midst of what had been the enemy camp, and four of the Imperial regiments camped around her. Despite his fatigue, he had to report to Equus, and then, when he had reported, Equus dragged him to see the General.

She was sitting at a table, writing. Prince Ansu, arm in a sling, sat in another chair. He leapt up and kissed Aranthur on both cheeks.

The General kept writing. She glanced up, nodded, and went back to her work. Vlair Timash, her military secretary, hovered nearby.

'Two copies of this – different couriers. Direct to the Emperor's hands.' She read over what she'd written. 'Copy my orders out for me to review.'

She handed the pages to Timash, who bowed.

'Equus? And Syr Timos. To what do I owe this pleasure?'

She sounded as tired as Aranthur felt.

'Centark Timos made contact with the fringe of the Capitan Pasha's advance guard at Al-Bayab. I brought him in case you wanted to question him.'

'Parsha, have you had this poor young man out on patrol for four straight days?' she asked.

Equus smiled and twirled his moustache.

'He's shaping into an officer. That's why you sent him to me, ain't it?'

Tribane sat back. 'Show me on the map,' she said. 'Al-Bayab. By Rolan's sword, that's *five parasangs* further south.'

She had an actual map on a second table. Aranthur found it fascinating; he stood over it, trying to make the web of irrigation ditches and little bridges and roads match the lines on the creamy new paper. The current location was marked with a pin and a red and black flag. He was able to follow the line of the pursuit, and then...

'Which town is Al-Bayab?' Tribane asked. 'Show me, Aranthur.'

Aranthur ran a finger south and east, trying to estimate the distance to the mountains, which were marked with ^^^ marks and whose shape was only roughly sketched in. But the big irrigation ditch was correctly marked, and it ran almost due south for almost six miles. Aranthur even found the fish pond where they'd watered the horses.

'Here,' he said, pointing at a town. 'It has two minarets and a temple – I assume it's a temple to Sophia.'

Tribane flashed him a thin-lipped smile.

'You've heard about the desecration at the monastery of Helre? At Elmit?'

'Yes,' Aranthur said.

The General was looking at the map.

'We're spread over a twenty mile front.' She looked at the map. 'You know what the prisoners say? This was just a thrust – an interruption, like a stop-thrust. They were to beat us and then turn south into Masr. We even captured their water-train – twelve hundred camels.' She shrugged. 'So far, the captured Magi won't talk. One suicided, one killed two guards and was in turn killed.' She shrugged. 'They behave like feral animals.'

'Masr?' Equus asked. 'They were to turn south to Masr?'

Tribane smiled. 'For once, thanks to Drako, we're ahead. We attacked them at Antioke in the spring, mostly to support Masr.' She shrugged. 'That was a secret. Too many of our best troops and best Magi, too. Well, and it was *our* feint. Or stop-thrust.' She shook her head. 'Why Masr, though?'

She looked up and her eyes met Aranthur's.

127

'Am I allowed to know where Roaris is, ma'am?' Equus asked.

'On a ship home, I hope.'

'He'll make trouble at home.'

'I'm fully aware of that, Vanax.' Tribane sounded pettish, and tired. 'In my considered opinion, he was making more trouble here.' She stood back from the map table. 'Right. We stay at it. I want all those sorcerers. They can't be far. I don't really need to know why they planned an elaborate feint before invading Masr. I can just kill their sorcerers.'

'I'm almost out of fodder, and there's nothing to forage here,' Equus said. 'I noted that in my evening report.'

'So noted.'

'Ma'am...'

Tribane turned. Her profile against the candles on her writing table was like an old first Empire statue: the nose sharply defined, the lips chiselled.

'Parsha Equus, please shut up, there's a good fellow. We will pursue as far as we possibly can, and then a little farther. I assume that any reasonable sentient is tired of killing the defenceless, but we'll keep at it another day and then we'll have their fucking sorcerers. To the best of my knowledge, no one has handed the Master a defeat in the field before. We have to make it count. The territory we're standing on is worthless. We're not liberating anything, and we sure as the ten thousand hells are ice cold can't hold the ground. I have all his *gonnes*. I have his baggage. Now I want his little coven of sorcerers who take human hearts out of fucking refugees to make roadside curses. I want them all. Then I will declare victory and march home to deal with fucking Roaris and his craven arse.' She took a breath. 'Or maybe to Antioke. I'm worried by the silence from there – we should have taken it in a matter of weeks. Now...'

Equus saluted. 'Yes, ma'am.'

They walked out of the pavilion, which glowed red behind them.

'I love her, and she's the best general the Empire has produced in three hundred years, but...'

Equus was walking across the trampled grass in the dark, and Aranthur didn't know if he was meant to hear all this.

'But?' he asked.

'But if we run out of food and fodder, we could lose this army as fast as a defeat in battle. In a battle, you lose maybe ten or twenty per cent of your people. If you run out of food . . .' Equus spat. 'Go and get some sleep. You've earned it.'

Aranthur didn't even remember lying down.

But he awoke, suddenly, from a terrible dream. It was dark; the inside of his little tent was almost pitch-black.

Something was wrong.

Very wrong.

He stumbled out of the tent, buckling on his sword, and bumped into Dahlia.

'What the hells?' she asked.

'Something . . .'

'I feel it too,' she said. 'Potnia's fecund pussy, Aranthur. What time is it?'

'Almost dawn.'

'Darkest before the dawn.'

'What the fuck?' Sasan asked. He wriggled out of the tent he shared with Dahlia.

'You feel it too?' she asked.

Aranthur's feeling of unease only increased, and the absence of alarms somehow made the apprehension worse. He found Ariadne, slipped her picket and mounted bareback.

He trotted her along the bank of an irrigation ditch, and then slipped down a line of trees, silent and dark against the stars, but the sentry was right where she was supposed to be. She challenged alertly. Aranthur gave the reply and rode further south into the light of the new moon, was challenged again, and cantered back to the edge of camp, where he found Sasan tacking up his horse with Centark Equus.

'Anything?' Equus asked.

'Everyone's alert,' Aranthur said.

'All the Steppe people are awake. Most of 'em are praying,' Equus said. 'Something is very wrong out there.'

Aranthur raised his magesight, and it flared, shining like a beacon, until he controlled it.

'Sorry,' he muttered.

He felt like a first year student, losing control of a light spell.

But there was nothing untoward to be seen: a smear of black *sihr* where people had died in the storming of the camp; another, deeper ink blot of *sihr* where the enemy Magi had butchered people to make the foci for the *stigali*. Several spots of *saar* where, for example, the General had a magelight burning.

'I'll look at the northern sentries,' Aranthur volunteered.

'Please,' Equus said. 'I'm turning out the quarter guard. Vilna!'

The quarter guard was literally the guard of a quarter of the camp. Usually, it was a reserve on duty, ready to deal with a surprise. In slack units, it was a pile of men sitting sleepily together.

In the Nomadi, it was a full troop, all mounted and with weapons loaded.

Aranthur trotted north with Dahlia and Sasan. He moved along the semicircle of Nomadi pickets, but they were all alert. When he passed on to the pickets of the Second City Cavalry, the *Tekne*, he was pleased to see that they were just as alert. Two pickets along the line, he met Lemnas, coming the other way.

'You feel it too?' she asked.

Aranthur nodded and pointed back.

'The whole picket line is intact and awake,' he said.

'Good. We won't all be murdered in our beds.' She laughed, but the sound was hollow and lost in the darkness. 'It's cold.'

'It is damned cold,' Dahlia said. 'Something is happening. I can feel it. It's in the *Aulos*.'

Aranthur rode back along the picket line, but he stopped as the first rays of the sun began to lift over the eastern mountains. The feeling of unease spiked, and for a moment, he felt as if he could hear a man screaming.

Ariadne laid her ears back.

'What the fuck?' spat Dahlia. 'It's as if the world is ending.'

There was an almost imperceptible rumble, like the tremor of a distant earthquake.

Sasan looked back and forth between the two Magi.

'What is it?' he said. 'All I feel is that I've lost an hour's sleep.'

'Do you hear the scream?' Aranthur asked.

Dahlia's face was white as parchment in the ruddy light.

'I do,' she said, her voice tinged with horror.

Suddenly she raised her shields. The last five days had strengthened her, despite her wounds. Her shields rolled out like the rapid flowering of a garden of golden roses, the petals blossoming at the speed of thought until the three of them were covered. And in the same instant, Aranthur engaged his own shields. While they lacked the elaborate layers of Dahlia's, his too had evolved in constant combat. They rose like a snowstorm of red-gold flakes and his flashing red *aspis* was like the morning sun, deep and intense.

Dahlia slipped off her horse. Sasan's mount began to plunge, and she grabbed his bridle. He dismounted, put a corner of his cloak over his horse's head and waited.

Behind them, the Nomadi made a sound like a low scream, the sound of Steppe men and women who had lost someone they loved. Their keening was eerie; the sound rose over the terrible red light.

Aranthur turned and looked south. The feeling now had a direction – not east, towards the enemy, but south, towards Masr.

There was a sound like the crack of a mighty thunderbolt, and Ariadne reared.

A mighty wind rose in the south and began to blow sand at them, and Aranthur murmured to Ariadne.

The feeling was like a pressure in Aranthur's head, and the pressure grew and grew, almost exactly like the headache of having overspent on *saar*.

'Lady, it *is* the fucking end of the world,' Dahlia said. 'What in all the hells is going on?'

Off to the south, something...

Blinked.

There was another crash. This time, it was as if every *gonne* in the Imperium had fired together – a short, incredibly loud pulse of sound.

The spike of pain in Aranthur's head seemed to penetrate to his heart.

And then, in the blink of an eye, the sky changed.

A crack appeared in the dawn, out over the south. Where the sky had been a salmon pink, brighter towards the distant eastern mountains, paler and greyer in the south, suddenly a ragged rent appeared, like a crack in the sky, shaped like an anvil. Even as Aranthur, clutching his temples in agony, watched the crack, it formed, widened, and opened.

Men and women in the camp were screaming.

The wind was like a storm. It had picked up sand, leaves, debris of war and peace, and the wind lashed them. Aranthur pulled the scarf of his turban over his face and tried to keep Ariadne calm.

His sword was making the moaning noise.

And a voice, a woman's voice, said: '*No. No, you fools!*'

With a flare of darkness, the anvil in the sky widened until it appeared to be the width of a child's finger.

The wind howled against their shields.

'Ware,' Aranthur said, just before the wind of *sihr* and *saar* struck them.

It came, not from the *Aulos*, but from the south. Aranthur felt as if he was enduring the primal wind of chaos. It swept his shields away, like paper in a deluge of water. Dahlia's shields didn't last more than a heartbeat longer. They were naked to the storm of magik.

Aranthur stood alone on the vast empty plain of the *Aulos*. And then he was not alone.

Nenia turned to him. Her dark eyes looked into his.

'Do you speak this language?' she asked.

Alfia took his hand.

'How foolish are you?' she asked.

Iralia's hair burned with a net of white fire.

'Stand with me,' she said.

She extended her hand. Somehow she was more real than Alfia.

There was *power* everywhere – more *saar* than he had ever experienced, so that he might have powered every *occulta* he knew at the same moment.

And then Dahlia was beside him.

'Do I fight it or accept it?' she asked.

Qna Liras reached out and took Iralia's hand.

'Accept it.'

And a woman's voice said, 'And thus are two thousand years of victories wasted in an instant.'

Aranthur guessed that there was no fighting the mad rush of *power*. Instead, he opened to it. It was like attempting to swim in the floodgates of a dam, and he was swept away on a rising tide of light and dark.

He had Iralia's free hand in his. And she held him in a grip of adamant.

His heart beat like a dancer's drum, so fast that he couldn't count the beats; terror was the horse he rode. It seemed to him that the foundations of the world were broken like the dams of the irrigation ponds, and he was being carried outside the world – or perhaps the world itself was dying in the torrent of magik.

'Take my hand,' said the woman's voice.

Aranthur put his free hand in the woman's hand. She wore armour, and stood like a pillar of light, buffeted but unbowed.

He never saw her face – it was turned away, facing the east.

'Save Dahlia,' he said.

'I have,' she said.

She sounded as if she was crying.

'The Emperor!' cried Iralia.

'I'm doing what I can,' the armoured woman said.

A pulse... a blink. *As if for a moment, there was* nothing.

'And now it is all to do again,' she said. 'Why are we such fools?'

Book Two
The Universal Parry

The universal parry is such that, if executed correctly, the student will cover all lines and cross any blade in a single action, preserving his life at the cost of initiative and *tempo*. Only to be deployed when truly desperate.

Maestro Sparthos,
unpublished notes to the book *Opera Nuova*

1

Eastern Armea

The cataclysm killed both men and women, horses and cattle. Almost a tenth of the Army of the Empire died outright, or never recovered. More than twice that number refused to look at the sky, or shuddered uncontrollably every time sunlight or the rising moon showed the gaping rent in the eastern sky.

Ariadne threw Aranthur at the height of the tumult, but then remained true to her salt and stood by him. He rose, his hip bruised, but his mind intact, to find that Dahlia and Sasan had both survived the assault on their minds and their perception of reality.

Sasan even managed the ghost of a smile.

'For the first time,' he said, 'my life as a *thuryx* addict has prepared me for something.'

Dahlia lay on her back with her eyes open to the sky for a long time. Then she sat up.

'Aranthur,' she said softly. 'Who was the woman in armour?'

'You saw her too?' Aranthur asked.

'She took our hands,' she said. 'Was that the Lady?'

Sasan looked at her. 'What?'

'I think I just met . . . God,' she said. 'God.'

Aranthur shook his head, but only to clear it. He had a different notion, but the sound of screams and the sounds from the horse lines drove every thought from his head.

The stampede of the army's herds was unstoppable. The best that the survivors of the storm of magik could do was to follow on the handful of mounts who remained. Then begin the painful task of collecting the horses, the draught bullocks and camels of the train, and the cattle they drove for meat.

Aranthur had difficulty recalling that day. He rode and rode, because Ariadne was one of the few horses that stood her ground. He gathered riding horses and brought them back to mount more people, who rode out to gather more mounts...

Aranthur covered seventy miles or more, that day and the next, when General Tribane sent him south to make contact with the Capitan Pasha. The army of Atti was in the same case – shattered, decimated, and in a state of anarchy, with its camp blown flat by the physical winds and an even higher casualty rate. The Capitan Pasha himself was silent, his eyes downcast, and the bey of the Sipahis seemed to be giving the orders.

'Tell your general we must retreat,' he said.

Aranthur was careful of Ariadne on the return trip, although she seemed to be made of grey iron. He walked beside her across a salt pan and up a narrow ridge of sand hills.

He was recovering rapidly – so rapidly that he used the return trip to experiment with the new world. Because, to a Magos, it was a new world: a world with a third more *saar* available at all times, and winds that boosted that amount even more, although they came and went with dramatic intensity. In one flood of *power*, he cast and cast the variants he'd imagined to his far-seeing spell, powering and dispelling his *occultae* with reckless abandon. Before the tide ebbed, he'd cast more *saar* in an hour than he would have cast in a month at the academy.

And then he was back. The General's camp had been struck, and the army was already moving north and west. General Tribane was with the rearguard: her own black-armoured cavalry, and the Imperial Nomadi, and the *Tekne*.

'The Attians are retreating,' Aranthur said after he had saluted.

He could see Ansu, his arm now free of a sling, and he smiled, despite everything. Dahlia was with Ringkoat and Jeninas. Sasan was nowhere to be seen.

Tribane looked haggard, and older than he had ever seen, but her eyes, far from avoiding the flaw in the sky, seemed drawn to it.

'Any idea what has happened?' she asked. 'In the Attian camp?'

'No, ma'am. Although they have a thousand dead.'

His mind shied away from the lines of corpses.

She nodded.

'Ma'am, where . . . Where is the Lightbringer? Qna Liras?' Aranthur asked.

'Only the gods know,' she said wearily. 'He stayed at the Temple of Helre. He . . . warned me of something dire.' She frowned. 'Syr Timos. Centark Timos. If you have any notion of what is happening, I'd be *happy* to hear it, even if it was purely speculative.'

Aranthur looked at Ansu.

The prince gave a minute shrug.

'General, something . . . was broken. Like the keystone of an arch.' Aranthur shrugged. 'You are a Magas. You must know that we are suddenly flooded with *sihr* and *saar*.'

She was looking at the hole in the sky.

'Yes.' She shook her head. 'We were so *fucking* close.'

If the retreat never quite became a rout, it was mostly because of Alis Tribane, who rode up and down the column. Whatever face she might display in her pavilion, on the march she was calm, dignified, and somehow, present everywhere. The day was hellish; the steady southern wind brought heat and sand off the desert of Masr. The soldiers trudged along, heads down, many afflicted with what everyone called *the darkness*, a heavy depression, sometimes complicated by other factors – battle fatigue, homesickness, terror.

The hot wind blew; the winds of magik blew alongside it. Men lay down and died, staggered away from the column in the grip of hallucinations, or sank to their knees from pure dehydration. A few victims of *the darkness* seemed to have physical symptoms. One woman vomited black and then died, and the rest of her regiment shied away from her corpse.

Alis Tribane was everywhere, and so was Equus, and Dahlia, and Aranthur. They cajoled and promised, ordered, healed; Sasan played music and made jokes.

The column stumbled on.

And, despite every disaster that beset them, when the army marched into Elmit a day later, there were two hundred wagons waiting with supplies. It wasn't very much; but somehow, those supplies – a night's

wine, grain for tired horses, bread and meat for every man and woman
– meant that some part of the world was still there.

They raised their tents on the same fields they'd occupied just four
days before. Aranthur, who, with Sasan, had spent the day riding to
Vanax Kunyard and back, rode in to find grain for his horse and a stew
of salt cod waiting for him, as well as orders to attend the general at
'his earliest convenience'.

Ulgat handed him a bowl of fish stew.

'Eat,' he said. 'Lady Khan can wait.'

Aranthur agreed. He inhaled a bowl of the salty stew and then
another, and he and Sasan drank two cups of wine, unwatered. Only
then did they cross the *maidan* to the red pavilion. As he entered, the
Lightbringer, Qna Liras, was standing, his hands clasped as if in prayer.

'They will not recover,' he was saying quietly. 'The ones in the hospital who do not move – their brains are burned away. The ones who
fear the sky are savable. The other ones who lie quietly will starve to
death, and there is nothing I can do to prevent it.' He looked up, and
saw Aranthur. He smiled. 'You lived.'

Aranthur was young enough that he had already begun the process
of recovery, or rather, he'd already begun to forget the trauma.

'Yes,' he said. 'I felt you, when the wave came, and the Rift appeared.'

Alis Tribane was writing. Her forehead was in her free hand, and
her eyes were haunted.

'If I had *lost* the battle I would not have lost this many,' she said.

Qna Liras shrugged. 'You would have lost this many, and then again
when the cataclysm struck.'

'Can we even resist this enemy?' she asked.

Qna Liras sighed. 'I do not know if we can,' he said. 'I only know
that we must.'

'Can you tell me what happened?'

Qna Liras scratched at his short beard. He looked as if he had not
slept in days; there was more grey in his hair than Aranthur remembered.

'Something terrible has been done,' he said. 'I guess it is in Masr.'

The silence went on too long.

'What do we do now?' Tribane asked.

Qna Liras shook his head. 'I will guess something, but I need more

140

evidence. I fear to be wrong – I fear that events are balanced on a knife edge.'

'I can release you from that fear,' Tribane said, dully. 'We are consuming the last of our supplies tonight. We will have to dash for the coast, and pray that the navy is there to save us, and not blown to kingdom come. And may all the gods save the City, and Ulama too.'

'I sent a warning,' the Masran Magos said. 'When I first felt it. The old cities have protections.'

He swayed, and Aranthur steadied him, and then fetched a folding chair and put the priest into it.

Tribane waved a hand. 'Never mind. That's for tomorrow. Tell me what happened.'

'It will change nothing,' Qna Liras said. 'And I'm probably wrong.'

'Try me,' she said.

Qna Liras pointed at the great, gold-domed monastery temple.

'The altars of this ancient place were defiled. When I saw the way in which they had been defiled, I elected to stay and investigate them.'

'I know,' Tribane said. 'You have a strong stomach.'

'These were not merely rapacious brigands,' Qna Liras said. 'These were dedicated in slighting thousands of years of worship and rendering it as if it had never been. Breaking, if you like, the temple's link to the . . . sacred.'

'The *Aulos*?' Ansu asked.

Qna Liras put his head back as if he was about to fall asleep.

'Do you believe in the gods, Highness?'

'Of course!'

'There's a traditional answer.' The Masran Magos smiled thinly. 'So you know, or at least you have heard, that there is another plane which is to the *Aulos* as the *Aulos* is to us?'

'I have heard this,' Prince Ansu said.

'I have, too,' Aranthur said.

'And then, theoreticians suggest that there is another plane, or perhaps status, above that. And perhaps another and another – perhaps an infinity of stacked levels of power and experience, each charged with the—'

'Stop!' commanded the General. 'Is this fact or mere academic meandering?'

Qna Liras spread his thin hands.

'Sometimes, academic meandering is the closest we can come to fact. Will you suppose for a moment that there is a higher plane than the *Aulos*? And that people can access it through prayer, perhaps in much the same way that we "harness" the *Aulos* through will, discipline and practice?'

Tribane shook her head. 'And these defilements are meant to break this bond...?'

'And the older these bonds are, the more powerful,' the Magos said, although he made it sound more like a question. 'So that the White and Black Pyramids in Masr would be very powerful indeed.'

'Lady,' muttered the General. 'Oh, gods. You mean, I'm trying to defeat them on the ground, and they are breaking the corners of the world so that the war will be fought with magik.'

'You have leapt ahead of me,' Qna Liras said, his voice hollow with fatigue. 'But that is where I was going. Nor do I think that they are done. They must intend to break more – to open that hole in the sky wide. So that the whole tide of chaos washes our shores, and only those who can use the magik that is offered will have any... power.' He spread his hands. 'I'm no loremaster. I have heard that the temples of Masr contain ancient things. Entities. I have heard that we have captured them... Perhaps the Great One is released, although to release any of the Old Ones sounds like madness. The ancients died to stop the Old Ones. Only the truly malign would release them.' He shrugged. 'But it is all madness.'

Tribane leant back. She motioned at Ringkoat, and he began packing a pipe.

'You think they have other... rituals? To complete?' she asked.

'I know nothing!' Qna Liras shouted. 'I'm guessing! By all the gods, woman, the world is being destroyed and I am fucking helpless!'

She took the lit pipe, drew deeply on the smoke, and leant back.

'Well, I like a fight. Let's imagine that the Master plans to knock the foundations off the world. Where are they?'

'Necropolis in Safi,' Sasan said. 'They took it two years ago.'

'Lost to us now,' the General said.

'Haghia Sophia,' Aranthur said. 'In Megara.'

'The Sufiat Dome in Ulama,' Tribane nodded.

'The Muyyayit Temple of Light in Antioke,' Qna Liras said. 'They've had it for six months.'

'Maybe we took it back,' the General said. 'We acted in secret, but we sent some of our best.'

'There are a dozen temples of impeccable age in Zhou,' Ansu said. 'If this Master wishes to break the foundations of the world, he will have to take Zhou.'

The General breathed smoke out of her nose and put the pipe down on her writing desk.

'Exactly,' she said. 'It is ever the way of men to break things they don't understand, but equally, it is also the way of men to overreach. There is a hole in the sky, but by all the gods, friends, if we were beaten, it would already be evident.'

'A thousand dead, an army defeated, and a hole in reality...' Qna Liras said.

The General sneered. 'Bah. What can be broken can be repaired.'

Aranthur thought of the woman's voice: *'And now it is all to do again.'*

'I can send birds to Ulama and to Megara. Today, this very hour. And Antioke... may once again be in our hands.'

Qna Liras looked up. 'How?'

'Another expedition. Originally a feint, but the Pure didn't respond, so the feint became a siege.' She steepled her hands. 'I think you should go to Antioke, Lightbringer. With my dispatches and some orders.'

'I am more interested in going to Masr,' the Lightbringer said.

Tribane raised an eyebrow. 'To the scene of the crime, so to speak?'

'Yes. I can get your messages to Antioke by way of Masr. In ten days. Fewer, with luck.'

Tribane looked at him with obvious unbelief.

'How?' she asked.

He scratched the base of his chin and pointed at the map.

'We're deep in Armea. We cannot cross the Kuh here – the mountains are like a wall. So to reach Antioke, we would have to go all the way to the coast, and then down the coast almost to Masr. Yes? So look, my dear General. Instead, we cross the mountains right here, on the old smugglers' pass, and cut the corner of Safi...'

'You'll just ride into the lion's den,' she said.

'Yes. We cut the corner of the Safian Plains, and cross the Kuh at its narrowest. We come out opposite Al-Khaire and I'll put your message on a boat. It races downriver and out through the northern Delta – your messenger will be on the dock at Antioke a day later.'

'If you aren't all killed, or better yet, captured by the Pure,' the General said. 'But that is very fast, I agree.' She leant over. 'I'm worried for Atti and for Masr, too. I'll wager you a golden crown against a dirty glove that this "Master" only intended the army we defeated to make trouble – a giant raid, if you like.'

'Why?' Qna Liras asked.

'A hunch, no more. But look at the composition – all those Pindaris, all the Safian cavalry, and yet very little disciplined infantry and almost no artillery.' She shook her head. 'He plays a deep game, this "Master". He doesn't expect every army to win. He has another army, or two, with all the better troops.' She looked up at Qna Liras.

The Magos nodded. 'The amount of *sihr* that their casters exerted controlling and *enhancing* the mob of refugees and captives they used as shock troops,' he said, waving one hand. 'They were effective, and they shocked our militia. But it was incredibly wasteful of *power*.'

'And yet they virtually destroyed my magikal staff,' the General said. 'I can't face a major action again until I have replaced all my casters.'

Tribane glanced at Aranthur.

'You'll need a escort,' she said.

They rose before the sun. Aranthur was moved to find that Equus got up to see them off; the Nomadi officer embraced him.

'You're taking my best man,' he said with an easy smile. 'See that you bring Vilna back.'

Aranthur smiled. 'He's more likely to bring me home.'

Vilna said nothing. This morning, he and six of his troopers were dressed in Steppe clothes with no vestige of uniform: caribou-hide khaftans carefully painted with intricate designs, cotton trousers and short, soft boots. Most of them wore fur hats of various degrees of shapelessness.

All seven of them were armed to the teeth, with multiple puffers, lances, swords, bows; Vilna himself had a small axe and his saddlebow, and Chimeg had a lasso of woven horsehair. Aranthur himself had given up his sweat-stained fustanella and his red military turban for a silk khaftan borrowed from Equus and a black lambskin *kulah*. Sasan's ruffians wore the usual selection of outlandish Pindari dress. Dahlia had joined them; she was tall enough to vanish among them, and she was a fine rider. Prince Ansu, on the other hand, had chosen to consult Vilna. He appeared as an Eastern Steppe nomad, except for the long and outlandishly curved sword he wore at his belt.

Only Qna Liras was unchanged. He wore a Byzas velvet coat, and his own long hair in a thousand braids tumbling down his back. But he had a robe – an enormous Bethuin robe – that he promised to put on if circumstances arose.

'I have other ways of avoiding conflict,' he said.

All of them had multiple horses. Four days of victorious pursuit had filled the army's picket lines with spare horses, and every person had two remounts, carefully chosen.

At the last moment, General Tribane appeared. She was plainly dressed, already booted and spurred.

'Listen, Aranthur,' she said. 'You need to get my dispatches into Antioke at the earliest moment. But there's more to this little jaunt. Sasan says you will have to cross the Farach Plain to reach Masr – Qna Liras agrees. I need to know...' She looked around. 'I need to know everything. Literally, everything. You will be the first *exploratores* into Safi for...' She shrugged. 'Many years. I leave it to you – both as an officer and as a sword of Cold Iron. Go to Safi, on to Masr, report back to me. Take my messages into Antioke and return – any of those, or all of them. You will have to make many decisions. I need to make decisions too – whether to stay in the field or keep retreating, for example.'

'How would I find you?' Aranthur asked quietly.

'Qna Liras has ways to communicate with me. But here is a pair of our communications sticks. You understand – the enemy seems to be able to manipulate them. I assume they're still good for one message. I may be wrong.'

Aranthur took them. They were bright gold, and he slipped them into the lining of his hat.

She smiled at him. 'I wish I was going with you. A simple, terrifying scout, instead of an endless profusion of choices. I'm not sure that I love command.'

'You won a great battle.'

She smiled, but the smile never reached her eyes.

'Praise me when we are home. I am afraid of everything now.' She was looking at the anvil-shaped patch of starless darkness now visible with the first flush of dawn. 'Get you gone. Before I desert my army and go with you.' She held out her hand. 'Tell Vicar Dukaz at Antioke that I will come, if I can. Tell him that. It may matter.'

She squeezed his hand, and suddenly Aranthur wondered what it was she *wasn't* telling him.

He mounted Ariadne, saluted the General and Equus, and then they rode away, east, into the hazy dawn, pink as hope, with the black scar of the rift marring it.

Aranthur had been over the ground twice, and he led them for most of the first day: south, along the ridges to the former Attian camp, and then another day due east again to Al-Bayab. The Attian army had decamped, but there were still patrols of their light cavalry, and at Al-Bayab, one of their beys remained encamped. Aranthur's little troop was well fed on stolen mutton and regaled with ghost stories at a roaring campfire.

'There are no people!' one woman said in broken Armean. 'The bastards slaughtered the whole population.'

'Bullshit,' said an older Attian. 'They all live in my street now, in Ulama.'

The Attians laughed, but Aranthur sensed that the empty country oppressed them.

The next day they rode away south before the anvil could be seen in the sky. When they passed the *vedettes* of the Attian *Delhis* they were beyond the very farthest reach of the allies, riding into a land that was at best hostile.

At first the countryside *was* utterly deserted. Vilna had riders out at the edge of their sight all the time, and he rotated them often. Aranthur rode with the leaders on the road, with Dahlia, looking for signs of *sihr*. The rest of the little column followed them, and Qna Liras brought up the rear, apparently lost in thought.

They rode a day, and then another, and the mountains didn't seem to grow any closer.

But on the third day out of Al-Bayab, when the sun was high in the sky, they began to climb.

Sasan waved. 'This is the Low Pass. We call it *Devea-Boyoun*, the Neck of the Camel.'

Aranthur would have sworn his friend sat straighter.

'Aya!' shouted one of Sasan's brigands. 'So we will live to see home again! I never thought it.'

The former Pindaris and the Safian outriders were beginning to achieve acceptance from the Nomadi; they felt it, and spoke up more. Some of them began to be individuals, to Aranthur. Haran was big, bold, outspoken, a little too clever. 'Asid was silent and haunted, his long nose and heavily scarred face more full of sorrow than Aranthur would have expected in a bravo. Kalij and Hissin were hard men who spoke only to curse, and yet could make men smile. But despite Vilna's constant warnings, Aranthur thought that they were loyal to Sasan.

The dusty plain gave way to hills. Among the hills was more and more water, and then the hills themselves were steeper and grass covered. There were still no people – just cairns of stone – but as they climbed, there were signs of life: a pair of sheep on a hillside; a big buck sprinting across open ground at the edge of some woods.

Vilna took the buck as a good sign. Indeed, all the Nomadi made a sign over their hearts with a closed hand. At Vilna's order, they dismounted and gathered birch bark and firewood and loaded the spare horses.

After the high woods, the road had become a track, but the ground was easy on a horse's hooves, and they made good time. Ahead, the grassy hills suddenly became a wall of stone.

'This used to be a smugglers' route,' Sasan said. 'Too steep for wagons.'

'You said this was the low pass . . .' Aranthur said. The weight of command was heavier than armour.

'There is a high pass, off to the north another sixty parasangs.' Sasan smiled, pointing at the wall of stone. 'And then the Great Gates, even farther north, at the edge of the Altai.

They climbed. Horses tired and they all changed, and climbed, over grass-covered slopes and then between two spectacular cliffs, each surmounted by rows of statues so high above them that Aranthur could not make out what they were.

'This is the low pass?' he asked again.

He couldn't see the top, or a break in the massive cliffs that towered ahead. It looked as if their little valley was a dead end.

Sasan shrugged. 'The pass turns at Ilija. You cannot see the top yet, but it's not bad. I'm more concerned that the old fortress is manned, or that there will be patrols. I rather hoped we'd find some tribal people. This area should be full of sheep, and nomads driving them. They know ways around the fortress. Bethuin, for example.'

They rode on, into the afternoon. The air grew cooler. The last trees fell away behind, and when Aranthur looked back he could see the carpet of Armea spread behind him, gold and brown and green all the way to the river halfway across the plain. Due south, the walls of the Zagan Mountains rose like a monster's teeth, barring the road to Masr.

At mid-evening, the scouts returned. After a hasty consultation, Aranthur agreed to Vilna's plan that they camp in a shallow depression above the road. The dimple commanded a long view up the pass, but might conceal a small fire.

Aranthur had the uncomfortable experience of having Sasan and Dahlia and Vilna all look at him, waiting for him to make a decision that each of them might have been better suited to make. Dahlia was a Byzas aristocrat and a natural leader. Sasan knew the terrain best of any of them. Vilna had led a thousand patrols.

Why am I in command? he asked himself, but the answer was obvious.

Because the General told them I was in command.

He acceded to Vilna's plan gravely, trying not to laugh at himself, and they rode into the little dell. Immediately, the Nomadi troopers dismounted. The horses were picketed, and Omga began to curry them all while Chimeg and two other troopers took cooking gear off a packhorse.

'We'll need food in two days.' Vilna took a filthy clay pipe from his khaftan and began to fill it with stock.

'If we sent a pair of riders out now . . .' Aranthur began.

Vilna actually smiled, the corners of his mouth rising to interrupt the thousand ridges of his wrinkled face.

'Very good,' he said.

'I'll go,' Aranthur said.

Vilna frowned. 'No. Never.'

He turned and spoke a dozen syllables in one of the Steppe dialects, and two of the Nomadi troopers, without so much as a shrug, grabbed ponies and rode out, headed up the pass.

Sasan watched them go.

'Even my people fear them,' he said. 'How did your emperor ever acquire their loyalty?'

'History, habit, and rich rewards,' Aranthur said. 'I did a little Steppe history at school. I wish I spoke even a little of their language.'

Chimeg was gutting a rabbit that had miraculously appeared.

'I'll teach you,' she said. 'This is *typpan*'.

She pointed at the rabbit. Then she began pointing at various objects and naming them.

Qna Liras sat on his saddle, looking back into the vast bowl of the Armean plain. He, too, had an old clay pipe, and he was filling it.

'They have a dozen languages.' He pushed the stock into the bowl of his pipe and lit it with a coal, like any other person, instead of with *power*.

Aranthur watched him inhale the smoke.

'I take it we should not be casting,' he said.

Vilna paused, his own pipe unlit.

Qna Liras shrugged. 'Probably safe enough here. But why take a risk? The more empty these lands are, the more likely we are to be seen when we play with forces.'

Aranthur was fascinated. It was like having one of his professors all to himself.

'Is magik easier to hide in a crowd?'

Qna Liras shrugged again, and lay back on the pile of cut turf blocks that Sasan's men had generated when they dug the fire pit.

'When we manipulate *saar*, we toy with life forces. When we are surrounded by life, it's easier to mask.'

Aranthur, who was growing accustomed to keeping his magesight engaged almost all day, had already arrived at a similar notion. When he looked for *sihr*, for example, it showed up as bright splotches of purple-brown on a monochromatic world. The *sihr* itself could 'light' surfaces around it; a cursed artifact, like the traps that had been laid for them, could radiate a sort of 'unlight' that he could 'see', although the whole concept was allegorical.

Dahlia had a skin of wine and she poured some for each of them and then sat gracefully, like a Safian, her legs crossed.

'So, are the Pure clearing the lands around them to more easily detect intruders?' she asked.

Qna Liras narrowed his eyes. 'That is a very disturbing thought. But I suspect it is more of a by-product than an intent. The chaos at the wavefronts of their assaults empties whole regions. People cannot live in the midst of a war. The Pure have been quite efficient at driving a wave of people before them.' He sat back and smoked. 'It is much easier to conquer an empty land. Perhaps to put a more trustworthy population into it.' He nodded. 'I will consider this.'

'How can we know so little?' she asked.

'They strike very quickly, with a maximum of shock and horror. They drive off the population, who carry with them a message of defeat and confusion.' Qna Liras shook his head. 'We only noticed them two years ago. And I confess that I still don't understand where they came from.'

Sasan looked away. 'Two years ago.'

Vilna reached in and took a twig and lit his pipe.

'Where did these Pure come from?' he asked. 'Not the Steppe, I promise you.'

The sun was setting, and Qna Liras' black eyes seemed to glitter with reflected light.

'Another excellent question,' he said. 'I'll give you another. Who is the Master? I'd wager he's one of us.'

'Us?' Dahlia asked.

'I'm wondering who you imagine "us" to be,' Ansu mocked. 'An Arnaut student, a Zhouian royal, a Safian poet, a Masran priest, and a Byzas aristo...'

Even Dahlia laughed. And the Lightbringer joined them.

'And yet, we all get along well enough, do we not? Because we share the teachings of Tirase. We share the generations of work done by our scholars, whether in Zhou or in Safi – the grimoires and the logic exercises. Look at a hundred Magi, and you will see that they have more in common with each other than with their supposed cultures.'

Ansu made a face. 'Perhaps. But what does this tell us?'

'That the Master knows us well. He knows our societies and their many flaws. He is not an alien entity attacking from outside. He's a worm eating from the inside. He has looked us over like a man buying a horse, and he is attacking at the weakest points.' He smoked, and looked at them over his pipe. 'Let me ask another question. What are these *Exalted* and Disciples? Are they truly some sort of alien?'

'Assuming that we reject that they are actually disciples from a higher being...' Aranthur said.

'Assuming that,' Qna Liras said.

*

The next morning, a pair of riders went out at first light, and then another pair, riding close around the camp. Half an hour later, they were all mounted, moving along the track towards the top of the pass.

After an hour's ride, they came to a small town: a dozen roofless stone houses, as many burned shells of wooden houses, and the soot-blackened remnant of what had once been a fine blue temple shaped like an onion's top.

'Yezziri,' Sasan said, and one of his men made a sign, like a new moon, with his fingers.

'Yezziri?' Aranthur asked.

'Worshippers of the Sacred Fire. An old religion – older than the Lady or even the Twelve. They live in the mountains. I have been to their festivals, in happier days. They put the statues on the hillsides, and they carved the great runes you'll see at the height of the pass.'

'No bodies,' Chimeg reported. 'No *corpses*.'

And they rode on.

Just before noon, they descended a steep and rocky ridge into a high valley, and crossed a river that, even at the height of summer, ran swiftly over gravel and round stones. The arched stone bridge of three spans was broken and blackened with eldritch fire that had burned away a portion of the stone. Qna Liras spent several minutes running his hands over the stone as he sang a song.

It took them an hour to cross – the horses feared the water, and the Nomadi muttered.

'*Malas*,' Chimeg spat. She pointed her riding whip at the fire-burned stone.

Vilna spoke sharply to her, and then turned to Aranthur.

'They say the water is cursed.'

Aranthur rode in close, and looked into the water. So did Dahlia. He cast; Vilna flinched.

Dahlia shook her head. 'Tell them that it is very, very difficult to maintain any kind of *occulta* in running water.' To Aranthur, very quietly, she said, 'I thought we weren't casting?'

'I have to keep up my *sight*.' He shrugged.

Dahlia crossed her hands on the cantle of her saddle and leant forward.

'True enough.' She glanced at him. 'Do you know what you're doing?'

Aranthur looked around at the massive cliff ahead, the mountains, the sheer grandeur of the scenery, and the thirty men and all their horses.

'No,' he said.

He twitched his reins, and Ariadne went forward into the water, which was icy cold, and they crossed. Twice she slipped on the round stones, but then they were up the sandy bank, warm in the bright sun.

Aranthur found that he was looking at the hole in the sky.

Chimeg, the next across, nodded and pointed at it.

'It looks like an anvil,' Aranthur said.

Chimeg nodded. 'We have named it *Karkar Byn Boprok*.'

Aranthur watched Omga leading a line of packhorses, loaded with fodder and firewood, across the treacherous ford.

'What does that mean?' he asked.

'The Dark Forge, or the Black Anvil,' Chimeg said. 'Our *Baqsa* says there is a prophecy.'

'*Baqsa?*' Aranthur asked.

'Spirit tamer. Witch. You Byzas have so many names for the . . . *malas*.' She shook her head.

'Am I a *baqsa?*' He meant it to be funny.

She frowned. 'Hope not. They have their balls cut off.'

'What's the prophecy?' he asked, wriggling in his saddle.

Chimeg shook her head and curled her lip. 'Best not to ask.'

Once they were across the river, there was a good road, neat cobbles laid in sand and gravel. They followed it up and up, over two unbroken bridges, until they reached the top of the ridge and the road turned. There, a few stades away, was the village of Ilija.

There were no people, no livestock, not even a chicken or a cat.

Aranthur listened to the scouts, glanced at Vilna, and motioned towards the top of the pass.

'Let's move on.'

Vilna nodded, but his face betrayed hesitancy.

'Too fucking empty,' he said.

Aranthur didn't like that Vilna was shaken. But he pretended to be unfazed; he imagined that he was Equus, and he met the news with a bland smile.

'Ah, well,' he said. 'At least we'll see our foes coming.'

He almost added 'old chap', he was so attuned to Equus in that moment.

The track came to the foot of the incredible cliffs, and turned sharply to the right – the south. The track ran along the base of the cliffs, through a rubble field of fallen rock: boulders as big as temples, some half buried in the gravel, some standing proud like sculptures. And above them on the cliffs, an incredible line of old Safiri runes. Aranthur rode out into the field beyond the fallen rock to look at the runes.

'Varestan?' Aranthur asked Sasan.

The Safian nodded. 'You are a good scholar, my friend. Better than me. Do you know what it says?'

'I only know the rune for "King", which I see two times. Maybe a third. There's been a rock fall.'

Sasan nodded. 'King of Kings, ruling over kings. It is the most famous inscription in Varestan that is left to us.' He glanced at Aranthur. 'They ruled the world, my people. And now . . .'

Aranthur frowned. 'I thought Varestan was a Dhadhian language.'

Sasan shrugged. 'My people are part Dhadhian. Or so the legends say.'

By mid-afternoon, Omga had come back with two of Sasan's riders to say that the old border fortress sat with its gate wide open and the barracks inside thoroughly looted. An hour later they rode past it, and they started down the long trail into Safi. Sasan's people all gave a long war cry that echoed down the valleys.

Vilna changed the outriders. He trotted over to Aranthur, who was dismounted, resting his pony.

'Listen, *Bahadur.* I am worried.' He glanced at Sasan. 'I do not want to send this riff-raff out in their own homeland. They will never come back.'

Aranthur thought a moment, and then walked over to Sasan. There was rain in the air, and the Safian was fishing in his saddlebags for gloves.

'Can I trust two of your people to go out as scouts?' he asked bluntly.

Sasan thought for a moment.

'Haran,' he said. 'And 'Asid.'

Aranthur nodded.

'Haran and 'Asid,' he said to Vilna.

'If they betray us, I . . .' He narrowed his eyes. 'I know this Sasan is your friend.'

'Haran and 'Asid.'

Aranthur got a foot in the pony's stirrup and mounted.

'Ayi, *Bahadur.*'

Late afternoon: heavy, wet fog and light rain. Aranthur was already aware that their outriders had vanished, even before Vilna reported.

'I'll find them,' Sasan snapped.

He put spurs to his horse and was gone into the mountain mist that swirled around them.

'They are gone,' Vilna said darkly, but he was quickly proven wrong. The three riders came back up the trail, and Sasan reported.

'Haran here wants us to go across the next stream and bear away a little to the north.' He raised his hand. 'Only for tonight. I went and looked. He's right – a good campsite and easy to secure. We're high up – it will be cold. We want a fire.'

'We need food,' Vilna said. 'And I worry.' But he smiled at Haran. 'This was well done.'

'The mist ends just ahead, and then you can see forever.'

Haran was smiling, all his teeth showing. Aranthur thought that he knew exactly what Vilna thought, and was testing them, or playing some game.

'I worry too,' Aranthur said. 'I worry about everything. Right now I'm worrying that there is *no* story to explain who we are. There's no traffic here – no wagon ruts, no hoof marks, no nomads.'

Vilna nodded.

Qna Liras shook his head.

But as they rode, they passed through the edge of the mist, and suddenly they were in a sunny day, and the whole of Safi seemed laid out at their feet.

The Masran reined in and pointed off over the rolling hills of Western Safi, towards the distant ridge that they all knew marked the edge of the Kuh.

'Two days at this speed,' he said, 'and we're in the desert.'

Vilna nodded, but later, when rations had been cooked over a tiny fire, carefully set under a magnificent birch tree, hundred of years old, to spread the smoke, he sat down with Aranthur.

'Safi bad,' he said. 'Desert very bad.'

'I know,' Aranthur said.

Vilna shook his head. 'We need food,' he said again.

Aranthur nodded. 'So much to worry about.'

In the morning they rode down the pass, but not by the main track. Instead, following Haran, they went a little farther north before going east. They toiled up a thickly wooded ridge and came out on a grassy slope that seemed to continue into a grey and rainy infinity.

'I like rain,' Chimeg said. 'We can't see the fucking *Karkar Byn Boprok*.'

It was true, and Aranthur felt it too. He also felt it in a lessening of the winds of *power*.

They smelt the woodsmoke before they saw the village at midday. Then the heavy rain hit them, and they were in the squalid village before the scouts could warn them. A handful of terrified Yezziri cowered in the tiny village square. They were so poor that the men wore only simple tunics, their legs were bare, and the women were wrapped in old scarves and heavy wool coats.

Sasan rode forward and spoke, the rain rolling off his turban and down his back.

Aranthur understood everything Sasan said, but not much of what the villagers said.

'This is what we used to call a "two chicken" town,' Sasan said bitterly. 'It's been taxed to the point where most people just move away.'

'Two chickens?' Ansu asked.

'In the whole town, there might be two chickens,' Sasan said.

Ansu smiled without mirth. 'That's . . . terrible.'

'They think we're Pindaris, and I'm letting them think that. The head woman is afraid we're collecting taxes.' Sasan grimaced. 'I'm afraid I let her believe that, too. No one will comment on rapacious Pindari tax collectors.'

They gathered a day's worth of grain from the hollow-eyed villagers. Aranthur felt shame at oppressing such poor people.

Vilna was disgusted. 'Dirt men,' he said. 'They should fight.'

Aranthur shook his head. 'Not that easy. They don't know how to fight.'

Vilna made a sign. 'Everyone knows how to fight.'

155

They rode on. In late afternoon they came to another village, this one destroyed. There were perhaps a dozen residents living in the ruins. They looked too feral to be fully human, and they vanished like wraiths when the scouts rode into the town. But to the south and east of the town they found a farmstead – probably some nobleman's country house. There were bodies in the courtyard, or rather, skeletons, a few with bits of hair still on the skulls. Animals had not been kind.

In the outbuildings, Sasan's men found grain: a huge store held in grain jars set in the floor, big *pithoi* large enough to hide a man. They refilled all their stores and added sacks of oats and wheat. After carefully combing the house, Aranthur agreed that they could use it. Despite Vilna's entreaties, he kept the evening patrol for his own command. He went almost a parasang south and east before turning for home, riding a long circle around the manor house before checking his night pickets.

Dahlia declared the beds unfit for people, so they all laid out horse blankets on the boards of the manor house hall, and slept around the hearth.

Aranthur was awakened by the sound of horses, and he was out of his blankets, the sword in his hand, before he heard familiar voices. Sasan went to the door, a long-barrelled puffer visible in his right hand. The Safian looked back as Aranthur lit a candle.

'Haran,' he said.

The Safian brigands had been trusted with some watches, usually with a pair of Nomadi to supervise them.

Haran came in, followed by a stranger.

'A traveller, or so he says,' Haran commented. 'I think he is a holy man. One of ours.'

A lean man in a magnificent green silk turban bowed deeply. The rest of him was as scruffy as a beggar, but he had across his shoulder an ornate axe inlaid in silver and gold.

'Now, all the gods be with you, masters,' he said. 'Surely you have made of this ruin a *Daru's-safd*, the very abode of delight.'

Sasan stepped forward and took the man's hand.

'I am Sasan Khuy. You are a Seeker of the Gods?'

'I am Mir Jalu'd,' the green turban said. 'And I do indeed seek, although for the moment, I would be delighted to accept some of that

156

soup, and perhaps a little stock that I smell in the air, and then we can all get to know one another better.' He smiled around.

Vilna had a puffer aimed at his head. Dahlia was holding a spell, the pale blue lines of *power* leaking from her hand like talons of beauty. Qna Liras... was not there.

'A witch!' Jalu'd said. 'By the gods!'

He went to her, and raised his hand in greeting, and Dahlia stepped back.

'Another move and I blow a hole in your head,' Vilna said.

Jalu'd looked around, and then very carefully put his great axe on the floor.

'I am a poor seeker for wisdom, sworn to poverty,' he said. 'I am no threat to anyone.'

Aranthur glanced at Haran. 'Couldn't you have just sent him on his way?'

Haran looked down, obviously embarrassed.

'He took me by surprise, Lord, and he is very... persuasive.'

Sasan handed the man a bowl of soup from the pot on the hearth. Jalu'd sat down, bowed three times to north, south, and east, and ate the bowl with noisy appreciation.

'I've known a dog with better manners,' Dahlia said in Byzas.

'Do you keep your dogs two weeks without food, Lady?' Jalu'd held out the bowl, and crossed his hands on his forehead. 'More, please, for the love of the gods. Witch lady, I will be your slave. Just seeing you with the Secret Fire on your fingers makes me feel that there is yet hope in this fallen world.'

Sasan took the bowl and filled it. Vilna kept his puffer aimed at the man below the folds of the huge turban.

'Are you not an *Eversham*, yourself, brother?' Sasan asked.

Jalu'd looked around, his mouth already busy with the second bowl of soup. Ansu handed Jalu'd an oatcake; Aranthur had attempted to make his mother's oatcakes, with modest success.

Jalu'd devoured it, though it was mostly burnt. Aranthur gave him the remnants that the others had spurned. Then he went back to the soup.

Dahlia folded her *working* away into the *Aulos*.

'They'll be here in about six hours,' Jalu'd said.

'Who will?' Aranthur asked.

'The Pure. Perhaps a Servant, perhaps an *Exalted*,' he said, in sing-song Byzas. 'Any spark of *power* and they come. I'll guess they saw you yesterday. I know I did.'

'How do you know that?' Dahlia asked.

'I am alive, where most of my order are dead. Once I would have told you that I was above the petty struggles of men – that I sought only the truth of the gods. But three years under the Pure and I know a new truth. There are times when the search must be put aside until the Evil Ones are defeated.' He sat back and unleashed a long belch. 'Delicious. I would accept a cup of wine.'

'Wouldn't we all,' agreed Aranthur.

Jalu'd shrugged. 'It seems a poor return on your provision of a meal for my poor starving self, but perhaps we should move on.'

'How did you find us?' Sasan asked.

Jalu'd smiled. 'I was wandering, as I do. I heard a bird in the air say that the Pure had been defeated on the plains of Armea, and I thought, perhaps it is time to wander that way. And then I met a fox who said he had dined on cooked bones from men with many horses, and I knew you must be outriders of some foreign army. And then I meet villagers who say that Pindaris came to their town, but took only grain, killed no one, burnt nothing. And I think these are no Pindaris I've ever heard of.' He shrugged, still sitting, Vilna's puffer still pointed at the nape of his neck. 'And yesterday, I felt *baraka* in the *Eversher*, and not the dark stuff the Pure spew. So I listened with my heart.

'And I think many things. But mostly I think, these people, if they are foreign, they will camp somewhere. Why not Kirman's fine house, where you and I both know there is grain under the barn floors?' He sat back and crossed his hands on his naked belly, which, despite his posture and his heavy meal, showed heavy muscle. 'Nomad, if you will kill me, let me only say that it is kind of you to wait until my belly is full, for the first time in two years.'

Vilna looked at Aranthur. Aranthur looked around for Qna Liras, but his eye caught Sasan's.

'He is a Seeker,' Sasan said. 'I have met dozens of them.'

'He could still be a spy of the enemy,' Vilna said.

Sasan shrugged. 'I cannot imagine a Seeker doing such a thing. They do exactly as they please, and if they are killed, they say, "So be it!".'

Dahlia laughed. 'I like the sound of that. Perhaps I should be a Seeker.'

'I would be happy to have you as a disciple,' Mir Jalu'd chuckled. He made a lewd face. 'Or as a lover, if you like.'

Dahlia frowned. 'I'm not available.'

Jalu'd nodded. 'I am, though. Almost always. Especially lately.' He looked around. 'Shall we go?'

'We cannot go anywhere without Syr Qna Liras,' Aranthur said.

Qna Liras stepped out of the deep shadows on the other side of the hearth.

'I'm right here,' he said.

Jalu'd stood, and faced the Masran Magos. Then he bowed at the waist, as supple as a dancer. The Masran repeated the gesture, and each man extended his hand, and they brushed the knuckles of their hands.

'Now let all the gods be praised, each by name.' Jalu'd began to sing a hymn in Safiri.

'He is as he calls himself,' the Lightbringer said. 'We should heed him, and flee. Dahlia, you cannot summon *power* here.'

Dahlia flushed, as she had not a moment before.

'Yes, Harlequin,' she said.

They rode south into the darkness, and eventually the sunrise in the east lit their path. Riding in the dark had its dangers, and one of Sasan's men, the dour Kalij, fell into a gully and broke his hip. The whole column had to halt; the man could not ride, and had to be put in a litter between two horses.

He seemed very surprised that he wasn't left to die.

They moved on, and the light grew.

The high birches and the broad, weed-choked fields were giving way to drier ground with fewer watercourses. The rain had stopped, and they rode into an increasingly hot day.

Omga came galloping back, reporting that there was a band of mounted men across the next valley.

'I wasn't seen,' he said with Steppe smugness.

'East and east,' Vilna said.

They left the road at a stream bed chosen by Sasan, and they rode up the stony stream bed for perhaps five stades. Then they went over a sandy ridge. Beyond it, to the south, was a broad plain and a distant river. In the south, the line of jagged mountains had become a mere smudge of hills.

Sasan sat on the ridge, looking east like a man in a dream.

'Shabriz, and Farfaz across the river,' he said. 'Half of Safian poetry is about these places. Oh, gods, I have missed home. Smell the cypress? The jasmine?'

Ansu pointed. 'Civilisation.' He was looking into the middle distance. 'Look,' he said. 'Smoke. Charcoal burners, I believe.'

Aranthur looked, and then looked away, and looked back.

'I'm not sure. I swear I can see an army camp. Look at the layout.'

Vilna nodded. 'Too far.'

'Do not cast,' Qna Liras said. 'I can feel the enemy. Down there somewhere.'

Aranthur stood in his stirrups.

'I will ride down the ridge and look . . .'

Vilna waited until he had his seat.

'A word with you, syr?'

Vilna's Byzas was not always the best, but this one phrase he had with aristocratic fluency, leading Aranthur to smile slightly at how often the Steppe officer must have said it to young Byzas officers. He dismounted and walked his horse back over the ridge, to a small stand of trees.

'Vilna—'

'Syr – no. You will not scout down the ridge. Please. It is the wrong thing to do.'

Aranthur was frustrated.

'You do not think I can do it?'

Vilna shrugged. 'I do not think it is your duty. Your duty is here. I cannot command these people. You can. You are not a scout, not a lone hero. You are *our* centark.'

'They would take orders from you.'

'Not the Safian gentleman. Not Myr Tarkas. Not the Zhouian.' The Steppe man shrugged. 'I know what I'm saying. Please believe me. We are deep in a hostile land, syr. We do not need to "muck about".'

Aranthur grunted. But he remounted, and rode back to the others. Jalu'd nodded at him, almost as if he'd heard every word.

'Tonight I will show you something. But now, we need to stay on this path.'

'What path?' Aranthur asked.

'The one at our feet. Look, it runs along this ridge, so that we cannot be seen from the east, and we can see anyone coming from the west. Follow me.'

Aranthur suddenly realised with a shock that Jalu'd was mounted on Ariadne, and his cheeks flushed.

'That's my horse!' he spat.

Jalu'd smiled. 'Ah. A fine animal. The best.' He shrugged expansively. 'Your people said to take whichever horse I liked. I like this one.' His smile broadened into a clown's grin. 'Besides, you cannot own a horse. They have their own likes and dislikes, like people. She says—'

He gave a start and suddenly slid off the saddle.

'She says she belongs to you,' he said, all contrition.

Aranthur rolled his eyes. 'We should follow this mountebank?' he asked Qna Liras.

Qna Liras looked tired. But he managed half a smile.

'Yes. There are many forms of power.'

Aranthur frowned, while Jalu'd grinned.

'Very well. And you may ride Ariadne – if she will have you.'

'You are the very soul of kindness, and your wisdom flows from your mouth like the rivers of Shariz,' Jalu'd said.

Sasan barked a laugh.

The column turned and started south along the ridge, and Sasan rose in his stirrups and trotted to Aranthur's side.

'Shariz is at the edge of a desert,' he said.

Aranthur laughed. 'Well, he's got me pegged. That's exactly how wise I feel.'

But Vilna merely nodded.

2

Southern Safi

The ridge grew higher, and still the ground below them was green. A hundred fields of barley and rye stretched out along a watercourse that was too straight to have been made by nature. But the ridge was arid, a taste of what awaited them.

'Asid reported that there were horsemen to the west.

Jalu'd knew where to find a trail, and where to find water. He led them south, over two deep gullies, and then down a third to a huge pool of clean water flowing over gravel. The walls of the gorge were white marble, and entirely carved in runes.

Sasan paused to run his fingers over the runes in wonder. Interspersed with the runes were glyphs – pictures and symbols. Aranthur saw them with something like awe.

'Old Varestan,' he said. He looked at Jalu'd.

Jalu'd nodded. 'One of their outdoor temples. Or perhaps just a public bath.'

'What does it say?' Dahlia pushed her horse forward.

'No idea,' Sasan said. 'They say our language comes from Varestan, but I can't make it out, and the glyphs...

Mir Jalu'd shook his head. 'It is a good place, full of peace. But I cannot read this either. A little of the Varestan, but none of the glyphs.' He made a motion. 'I could entertain you with some intelligent lies, if you like.'

Dahlia grinned. 'I'll bet you could at that. I know one of those glyphs. It's *water*! I have it in my grimoire.'

Aranthur glanced at Dahlia.

'We had that in Sigils.' He looked closely at the glyph. 'It is a *working*. The whole thing. It's incredibly complex.'

Qna Liras pushed forward. 'By Aploun!'

He fell to his knees, but it was not to worship. He was kneeling on the fine white sand, reading the lower glyphs. He ran a hand over them, and it was as if the letters and glyphs filled with ink. Suddenly they were perfectly visible.

The ink glittered and became gold.

Jalu'd stood with his arms crossed, unperturbed, but the Nomadi and the Safians flinched, and backed their horses.

'Amazing,' Qna Liras said. 'I don't even know what it is. But it works. It is keeping the water clean, and it is...' He shook his head in awe. 'It is very old.'

The golden letters and symbols subsided, and once again it was carved stone. But now Aranthur noted the clever design. The inscription was carved directly into the natural rock face that leant out, so that the inscription was well hidden, and formed a sort of cave, so that the weather could not get at it.

'How old?' Ansu asked.

Qna Liras looked at Jalu'd.

Jalu'd shrugged. 'Now I teeter on the razor edge between an intelligent lie and an educated guess. I am eager to impress the clever beauty, but I do not feel that this is a good time for a falsehood, however inspired.'

Aranthur smiled at Sasan. 'He's growing on me.'

'They say whatever comes into their heads,' Sasan muttered. 'It's not always good.'

Qna Liras stood up and made a sign, very like the eagle. Aranthur made the sign of the eagle as well, from habit.

'Varestan was the language of this land two thousand years before Tirase spoke at Megara,' Qna Liras said.

Dahlia was concentrating on one glyph.

'I will trace this while you water my horse,' she said to Sasan. 'I would wager that this... was that old when Varestan was the language of the land.'

'Six thousand years old?' Aranthur asked.

'Impossible,' Sasan said.

Jalu'd chuckled. '*Hich kas' ukda'i as kar-I-jihan baz na kard, Har ki amad girihi chand barin tar fuzud.*' He glanced at Aranthur. 'Does thy scholarship include this?'

Aranthur shook his head. 'No.'

It was very old Safiri, and too complicated. *A knot? A tangle?*

Sasan sighed. 'I'll try,' he said.

> '*No one yet hath unravelled a knot,*
> *from the skein of the universe,*
> and each one came,
> *and essayed the same,*
> *but made the tangle worse.*'

Aranthur smiled as he puzzled through the words.

'Beautiful.'

Qna Liras smiled back. 'Too true. Regardless, we can water the horses, drink it, even bathe. It's safe.'

The dark-skinned Magos leant over, cupped a handful of sparkling water and drank it.

He was silent for a moment. Then he smiled.

'Delicious.'

'I have drunk it many times,' Jalu'd said, as if they were all fools.

With exaggerated care, the Nomadi brought horses to drink.

'This is a *malas* place,' Chimeg said.

'Tell me a word for "blessed",' Aranthur said.

' "Blessed"?' Chimeg asked. 'What is this?'

'When the gods make something to help you, to make life better?'

Chimeg was holding her canteen in her hand, as if weighing her options.

'We worship different gods. On the Steppe, there is no "blessed". Only *malas*.' She looked around the echoing chamber of the pool. 'It is beautiful, but so are many deadly things.'

They laid Kilij down at the edge of the pool so that the two horses bearing him could have a rest. The Nomadi were still very careful of the water; the Safians less so.

'We need to move,' Aranthur said to Vilna.

Jalu'd nodded. 'But you go to the desert, yes? And I have something to show you, *Bahadur*.' He used the title 'hero' in a way that left some doubt as to his sincerity. 'In the desert there is no water. You should fill every container here – this is the best water. And we should travel at night.'

Vilna nodded. 'It's true. How far to the Kuh?'

Jalu'd raised an eyebrow. 'One might say we were already in the outstretched fingers of the Kuh. The valleys are still Safi. The ridges are already Kuh. Here we have shade and cover. No one can see us from outside.'

Aranthur scratched his chin. He felt dirty; days of riding, and never changing his clothes or shaving, made him feel more tired than he really was.

Vilna nodded, a very small nod of agreement.

Dahlia smiled. 'I'm for it. I'll get the whole inscription, and a bath.'

Aranthur got slowly to his feet.

'Dahlia, will you . . . ? I want that inscription – it could really cast . . . meaning . . . on part of my school project.' He felt the flush spread on his cheeks and he smiled. 'School. Can you imagine?'

Dahlia laughed. 'It seems incredibly far away.' She put a hand on his – a friendly, reassuring gesture, and the first time she'd touched him for a while. 'Don't worry. I'll get it.'

'Good. I have to continue pretending I'm the officer.'

'You are a pretty good officer.'

Aranthur stepped away, unable to hide his grin of pleasure.

'Chimeg,' he called. 'Are you up for a scout? So these folks can bathe in peace?'

She shrugged. 'Let's scout.'

The two of them climbed back out of the cleft and they lay on the sun-drenched rocks until their eyes adjusted. 'Asid was on watch.

'There was dust,' he said. 'Way off there.'

He pointed west, to the foothills of the mountains, but it was no longer possible to trace clear lines; the hills seemed to tumble together.

'Easy place to get lost,' the scarred man said.

Aranthur nodded. 'I'll go across the valley and up that peak. Chimeg, have a look east.'

She nodded, and led her horse down the ridge, headed east towards the deep desert.

He went west, down the steep hillside into the valley below. It had once been fertile. There were old irrigation ditches, and weed-choked fields that should still have been rich. A pair of lonely mud-brick houses sat by a pond, its dam broken.

He passed the houses and the garbage of a dozen ruined lives: a doll; a pair of votive idols to Potnia; a scrap of garish cotton faded...

He flinched when he saw what the cotton was stuck to, and his pony spooked.

And then up the far ridge. He dismounted, tied his pony to an old stone wall and crawled carefully to the crest, which was farther than he'd expected. He looked back and saw 'Asid wave, smaller than an ant, a mere flash of movement.

Finally, after a long climb that filled his boots with gravel, he got to the top. On the other side, he could see for parasangs – well to the west, there was a column of dust. Below him, and to the right, an eagle circled.

He watched the dust for half an hour. From time to time he rolled on his back and watched Chimeg scouring the valley below them, and then the ridge off to the south. He was thinking about the *Ars Magika* – about glyphs and sigils, and the bewildering number of them used at the pool below him. He lay there, pondering what it meant to be able to write changes in the code of nature directly on reality, without the intervening failures of human thought – what that implied about speed and exactness.

A single glyph for a complex action, instead of a long sentence.

His *Ulmaghest* had long lists of glyphs at the 'back'. And the complex manipulation he called the *Safian Enhancement* was very close to the 'front'. He thought about it all, and then he thought about Dahlia. And the Academy, and Nenia and Alfia and Lecne, and his parents, and his sister, and home.

Nenia would enjoy working through Varestan, he thought. And a wave of homesickness struck him like a physical thing. His eyes filled with tears, and he lay on his stomach, as stricken as if he'd taken a punch.

Eventually, he recovered. He writhed a little in the dust, and looked again at the hills below him.

The dust that might or might not mark his enemies moved steadily south, towards the desert. If they were following him, they were in the wrong valley system and several hours away.

He got to his feet, dusted himself off, and slid down the scree to the gully he'd climbed. Then he made his way down to Ariadne as the sun was setting in the west.

Back at the marble cleft, the rocks above the pool were festooned with an entire company's laundry, shining in the last of the sun. The rocks and the dry air were baking the clothes dry with the speed of an oven. Chimeg was already in the water with fifteen other bathers, and Aranthur stripped and jumped in. The water was incredibly cold, and he had a headache immediately, but he put his head under anyway, whooped, and made himself clean. Then, as Sasan cooked salt fish from their rations, Aranthur shaved and changed his shirt.

He felt like a new man. At first, that seemed natural, but after fifteen minutes he realised the wound that he'd taken to his wrist wasn't stiff. He was so used to the pain and ache there that its absence was obvious.

'Now I show you something, *Bahadur.*'

Jalu'd took him by the hand, and he followed, collecting his khaftan and his trousers from the rock.

Aranthur waved at Vilna, who was up in the 'coopla' watching the valleys.

'I'm going for a walk,' he said.

'A ride,' Jalu'd said. 'We will be an hour.'

Vilna nodded. 'Not too far,' he cautioned.

Aranthur took Ariadne and Jalu'd had to content himself with a Pindari mare, a pretty horse that probably had some Nissean. They rode up the ridge, back to the west in silence, the only sound the horses' hooves on the loose rock and sand. Jalu'd left the track and went almost due east, up the ridge that had covered them all day. They climbed for long enough that the first stars came out, and then the darkness fell rapidly. Off to the west, Aranthur could see a pair of campfires burning. If that was a force looking for his column, they were not afraid to show a fire.

Aranthur was still looking west when they came to the crest of the great ridge. Earlier in the day it had been high enough. Now it was as if they'd climbed to the top of the world, and they were high enough that far off to the west, the edge of the sky was still light.

To the north was the vastness of the plains of Safi, all the way to the Effrathes River. The richest part of Safi stretched away east; to the west, the rolling hills they'd crossed rose and became mountains.

Aranthur couldn't see the mountains, but he could see the woods and foothills and stands of tall trees in the clear air and the last light of the sun, and a long line of dust moving west.

Jalu'd sat on his horse, murmuring to her in a series of chants, humming and tapping a rhythm on her neck with the flat of his hand.

'Safi,' Aranthur said, mostly to say something.

He looked east, and then back west. The dust worried him.

'Wait,' Jalu'd said. 'Contemplate on a Being greater than thee.'

Aranthur was not sure, as was usual with Jalu'd, whether he was being mocked.

Suddenly a tiny tongue of flame licked out in the Safian darkness, and then another. Before he could fully draw breath, there were hundreds of points of light down along the great river. Hundreds, and then more hundreds.

'An army,' Jalu'd said. 'An army of Darkness, yet we can see them by the lights they shine into the natural dark.'

Aranthur couldn't count the lights, but he knew what they were – the campfires of an army. An army that covered half of the foothills of Safi, marching west.

He whistled. 'Fifty thousand?' He was awestruck. 'How did we pass through them?'

Jalu'd shrugged. 'This is what I wanted to show you,' he said agreeably.

'But how?'

Jalu'd smiled. 'They march west. You go south. With a good guide, you passed behind them.' He sounded smug.

Aranthur was still looking at the field of fires, which seemed to mirror the stars above. He imagined General Tribane's map; they moved due west from his present position.

'They're going to Antioke,' he said. 'Or following the General, but she's three days gone already – they'll never catch her.'

Jalu'd nodded. 'What will be, will be.'

Aranthur spat. 'Easy to say. What does it mean?'

Jalu'd smiled and turned his horse and rode down the ridge, moving faster than Aranthur would have thought possible. Aranthur picked his way more carefully, even on Ariadne, and when he made it back to the track, the sky was dark. The moons were not yet up, and the starlight seemed very bright at the edge of the desert, yet not enough to keep him from rolling to his death if Ariadne misstepped.

And in the middle of the sky, the Dark Forge was like a black mouth, a hole in the field of stars.

Vilna had the column ready when Aranthur rode up, and he saluted stiffly. The horses looked good; most of the people were smiling.

'A good place,' Chimeg admitted. She handed him a bowl of fish stew. 'Horses like it.'

This seemed to represent her highest level of compliment.

He dismounted, the stew bowl in his hand, and went down into the ancient pool. When he was there, he withdrew the golden wand that the General had given him. He looked at it for a long heartbeat, and then he broke it.

'General!' he said.

There was no response.

'The Safian reserve army that you predicted is marching west to Antioke, or perhaps to the Armean plain,' he said. 'More than ten thousand warriors. I could only see campfires.'

The sticks emitted a buzzing, and then one grew hot. Aranthur dropped them into the pool, and they vanished.

He drank a little of the water, and then he climbed back out and found the column.

'What was that about?' Vilna demanded.

Aranthur smiled, but ignored the man.

'You lead,' he said to Chimeg.

She nodded, and turned her mount.

They rode south. For two hours, as the moon rose, they were still on the ridge, which now ran down gradually to the desert below them. And they rode the rocky outcroppings all the way to their very end, where five tall pillars of granite rose out of the sand and cast long black shadows in the moonlight.

'Tonight the Great Moon, which we call the Hippo, will cross the Dark Forge,' Qna Liras said. 'At least, I pray the Hippo will survive the crossing.'

'Eagle!' Aranthur swore, and made the sign with his hands. 'What do you mean?'

'I watch the heavens,' the Masran Magos said. 'I know the tracks that the stars and planets must follow. Tonight, the Hippo must cross the abyss of the rift.'

Aranthur had never given it a moment's thought, and he shuddered.

The smaller moon was red-brown like old blood, and it crossed the sky rapidly, low on the horizon. The larger moon, which Easterners called the Hippo, and which the Byzas sometimes called 'the Lady' and sometimes 'the Huntress', moved with deliberation.

After midnight, it became obvious that the Huntress would either enter or cross the abyss. The Nomadi, especially, became very quiet.

They were on the sands of the desert by then. It was cold, and a bitter wind blew from the north, picking up sand.

The Nomadi began to ride with their heads down, and Jalu'd rode in among them.

'Brothers and sisters!' he said. 'What is written is written! And what the hand of man has marred, the hand of man can remake.'

'This is not a matter for people, but gods,' Omga growled.

'There is no difference between people and gods,' Jalu'd said.

Qna Liras looked up at the stars.

'A very strange doctrine, brother.'

Jalu'd's teeth flashed in the starlight. He rode up and down the column, and suddenly he was the clown, making Chimeg laugh, making Haran hold his stomach.

Aranthur was on the same mission – trying not to watch the track of the great moon, trying not to let his mind go.

'Change the outriders,' he said to Vilna, who was staring at the moon.

'I am sorry, *Bahadur*,' he said. 'I am trying to hold her in my mind, in case she dies, so that I will not forget her.'

Aranthur looked back along the column, and then glanced up at the heavens.

'I do not think she will be disturbed in her track, Vilna. And I am still worried about the ones hunting *us*.'

The man nodded. 'I will change the outriders,' he said, and cantered off across the sand and gravel.

Aranthur wasn't sure he believed what he'd just said, but he knew that it was his role to be confident, and he played it. He rode along, reminded Chimeg to take a mouthful of water, mocked Jalu'd to Sasan, mimed his own inept salutes to the rearguard, and exchanged a wary smile with Dahlia. She was at the very back of the column with Ansu, who was asleep in his saddle. Aranthur envied him.

He turned Ariadne and cantered all the way to the front of the column. As he reached Vilna, he saw the man's hand shoot up into the air, heard the cries from all the Nomadi, and then the shouts.

High above them in the cold night air, the Huntress entered the black maw of the Dark Forge. Her light dimmed . . .

And dimmed . . .

Aranthur winced.

Behind him, Qna Liras raised his hands.

'Pray!' he called.

He began a hymn – a hymn that any worshipper of the Twelve would know, to the beauty of the silver moon. Jalu'd joined him with a clear, beautiful voice, and Aranthur sang too.

The Safians were off their horses, raising their hands in prayer, and then the Nomadi.

The Huntress grew so pale that she appeared to be made of translucent marble, but she continued across the rift. Her light withered but did not go out.

Aranthur thought of his Natural Philosophy Master, who had insisted that all gods were human fabrications and the planets were all natural phenomena.

I wonder what he would think now, he wondered.

He was kneeling in the cold sand; he had no memory of dismounting.

The Great Moon reached the middle of the dark rift.

Its light was very pale, like that of a new moon on snow, and then it seemed to stop in the sky.

The hymn rose from them. Aranthur tried to imagine in his prayer that he sang with tens of thousands of other believers – with every free man and woman. He imagined the dance of the spheres, which his people danced at Darknight and the Eagle's Triumph.

The Huntress moved. She sailed like a queen through the rift, and as she crossed the centre and made her way to the broad end of the Dark Forge her light began to increase. The hymn faltered as the Nomadi fell on their faces in the sand and roared their approval.

And then she completed her journey across the abyss of utter darkness and her light shone, pure and white.

Aranthur got to his feet. Vilna was stuffing a talisman back inside his khaftan. 'Asid was still prostrate on the cold sand.

Aranthur drew his sword. He felt as if he was in the grip of another's

171

will – or rather, he felt as if he'd been told what to say. But he agreed. He raised the old sword, and the blade glowed blue-white against the darkness.

'The Light can cross the Darkness!' he roared. 'Darkness cannot quench the Light!'

They all turned, and then Chimeg gave a yip, and there was a scream like a battle cry from the whole company.

Then he sheathed his sword, feeling sheepish. But his people were smiling.

Later, as they rode across a plain of gravel, Jalu'd rode up beside him.

'That was a Yezziri prayer,' he said. 'And well chosen, *Bahadur.*'

And later still, as the Tail of the Wolf brushed across the eastern sky, Qna Liras joined him.

'What happened?' Aranthur asked. 'To the Huntress?'

'You think I know?' Qna Liras asked. 'Let me see your sword.'

Aranthur unsheathed it carefully and handed her over, hilt first.

The Masran Magos cradled it like a child in his arms as they rode. In the early light, it appeared black and grey, the old stains of use mottling the surface of the blade.

They rode side by side, and Aranthur felt . . . odd . . . at having the sword so far away.

'I have just learnt . . .' Qna Liras began. Then he sighed. 'I cannot believe, as a mature Magos, that I have had three things like this happen in one day. The Well. The Moon.' He looked at Aranthur. 'And your sword.'

He handed it back. 'Tell me again where you received this sword? An ancient heirloom of your house?'

'No, syr. I found it on a table of scrap and kitchen implements in the Covered Market in Megara. I paid . . .' He remembered. 'Thirty silver soldi for it. Couldn't pay my rent. Had to take in extra leather work. I almost failed *Arithmetika.*'

Qna Liras shook his head, and then he laughed, and it was a long laugh, an unexpected sound in the desert dawn. Above them, the Huntress, or the Hippo, beamed.

'Thirty silvers.' He shook his head. 'You bought your fate for thirty soldi. Perhaps my fate as well.'

Aranthur couldn't read the priest's face in the dawn.

'Now you are mocking me,' he said.

Qna Liras shook his head. 'Do you know of the Seven?'

Aranthur shook his head. And then, when Qna Liras opened his mouth, he raised a hand.

'Kurvenos mentioned them once,' he said suddenly. 'Seven swords. Artifacts—'

'Seven paladins of the First Empire. Emperor Tulwar, the second emperor, ordered them killed, and their souls condemned to ride in swords.'

Aranthur shuddered.

'Six of them . . . were very dark, and how could they not be, forged in murder and betrayal?'

Aranthur tried to imagine what it would be like to have his intellect shut up in the prison of a sword blade.

'Eagle,' he muttered.

'One of them was a woman. She . . . chose a different path.' Qna Liras said. 'Or so the myths say.'

'When was this? Two thousand years ago?'

'It is a Byzas myth and not a Masran myth. Your Byzas empires do not keep records in stone like Masr. It was sometime in the late First Empire, before the wheels fell off.' He glanced at Aranthur. 'There is a tale among the Lightbringers that she protected Tirase. The sword. She . . . rode an outlaw. He became a great general.'

'Aploun! And this is that sword?' Aranthur asked.

Yes.

Aranthur touched the warm hilt. He flinched at her word.

'Does she speak to you?' Qna Liras asked.

Aranthur glanced at Vilna. 'I need to get a camp spot and get us bedded down.'

'You said that she spoke during the battle,' Qna Liras said.

'Yes.'

Aranthur didn't really want to talk about the sword, and he waved to Vilna, who trotted over.

'We need a camp,' he said.

'If the lee of a dune can be called a camp,' Vilna said. 'Does the One Who Seeks still know the way?'

'To Masr?' the Jalu'd asked. 'Of course I know the way. And the

Sickle in the Sky is above Masr, so of course that's where the hero is going, and all the rest of us.'

Vilna tapped his mount's sides with his heels and he was racing along the track south. Except that south was now a direction almost identical to every direction; the dunes ran roughly north-east to south-west, but there were enough exceptions to make dead reckoning almost impossible.

Qna Liras raised his head.

'Someone is searching,' he said.

'And in the *Aulos*,' Dahlia said, and suddenly she put her hands to her ears.

Aranthur could feel it, but not as sound. For him, it was more like a coherent beam of colour.

'Shit,' muttered Qna Liras in Byzas.

Aranthur watched the mottled patterns move along the desert floor. They swept over the column and went past.

'Damn, damn,' Qna Liras said. 'I didn't think they could do that.' He shook his head.

'An ancient Dhadhian artifact that still works, an incredible lesson in cosmology, a magik sword.' The Magos closed his eyes. 'And now a search beam of coherent *sihr*.'

'It's coming back,' Dahlia called.

'Everyone freeze!' Ansu shouted. 'Do not move.'

He reached inside his khaftan and produced a jade perfume bottle, which he opened.

Instantly a breeze of fine scent seemed to caress them, and then to fly away. Ansu pointed west and north, and the breeze moved with a flutter of uncountable tiny iridescent wings.

The mottled colour swept past the caravan and pounced on the fluttering, but the wings seemed unaffected. They moved very fast, and the mottled colours tried to move with them and vanished.

'What was that?' Dahlia asked. 'Ansu, you are an endless surprise.'

The prince bowed in the saddle.

'I endeavour only to please you, fair lady.'

They slept, or at least rested, through the blazing heat of the day. Aranthur found it impossible to settle to sleep with the brilliant light of the day just beyond his eyelids. Every time he began to nod off, he thought of the sword which he had clutched to his side.

But when he assumed he would never sleep, he rose, drank some water, and looked at the horses, stumbled around to his three outposts and checked his guards, and then went almost instantly to sleep under an awning of his military cloak. He awoke to the smell of salt fish in water.

'Surprising news,' Qna Liras said, when he was awake and had a cup of hot *quaveh* in his hand. 'Kilij's hip and pelvis have knitted.' He rubbed his jaw. 'In one day.'

Vilna was roasting a tiny piece of meat on a skewer.

'And all the horses . . .' he said. 'The lame are healed. The old look younger.'

'The Well,' Qna Liras said.

'The other glyph I could read was *Youth*,' Dahlia said.

'Are we younger?'

Aranthur wasn't awake enough to be having this conversation. But his wrist told him that the story was a true one.

'How old does that make our guide?' Ansu glanced at Jalu'd, who was standing atop the dune, facing the setting sun. 'He said he's been drinking the water for years.'

Aranthur shook his head. 'I feel as if I'm going mad, or perhaps living in a myth brought to life, or maybe just an opera.'

Dahlia nodded. 'I knew your sword was an artifact, for what it's worth. I thought you knew it too.'

'Two thousand years old? With a woman's soul in the blade?' He shook his head again. 'But she has spoken to me.'

And then, fascinating as the sword might be, or the speculation between Ansu and Qna Liras about what the passage of the Huntress meant, he had to see to his pickets, look at the horse herd, and round up all his people.

'Rations for two more days,' Vilna reported.

'So half rations from tonight,' Aranthur said.

'At least the water's good,' the old nomad said with a quarter of a smile.

The night was uneventful. As the Red Moon rose, they entered a vast salt flat. Everyone tied scarves and turbans across their mouths, drank a mouthful of water, and settled in for a long ride. When the breeze picked salt up, it burned their eyes and nostrils, and the horses fidgeted.

Twice, Aranthur ordered the column halted so that the riders could wipe their mounts' eyes.

And again, after the Great Moon rose, it had to cross the abyss, but the column kept riding. All of them felt fear, but it was not the gripping beast of the night before, and they rode on until the Huntress burst out of the far side of the Dark Forge, and again they cheered.

Early in the new morning they climbed out of the salt flats and came to an outcropping of rock.

'The Island!' called Qna Liras. 'Jalu'd, you are the very prince of navigators.' He turned to Aranthur. 'It is the only outcropping on the whole floor of the desert – it has water . . .'

Vilna was beckoning to him. Aranthur walked over to find a desiccated corpse, headless, and the head a few paces away on the ground.

'How long ago?' he asked.

Chimeg moved one of the dead arms and then picked up the head. She shrugged.

'Hard to know. Very dry here. A week? A month?' She looked at Aranthur. 'Look at the cut.'

The neck was cleanly severed, and there was black, scorched skin at the edges of the cut.

'*Malas*,' she said.

Aranthur couldn't be sure in the moonlight, but it didn't look like magik to him.

'More like the swords of one of the *Exalted*,' he said.

They refilled their water skins, ate half a meal, and went to sleep.

And in the evening, they did it again. They rose and stretched, cooked a little food, and drank deep of the water before settling into another night of riding.

The line of hills, or mountainous dunes, was growing closer.

'How far to Masr?' Aranthur asked Jalu'd.

Jalu'd smiled. 'As far as it must be, of course.'

Aranthur smiled in amusement. 'So, how many days must it be?'

'Ah, now you want prophecy. I will prophesy, then. Two days to the area we call "The Belt". Then two days to Al-Khaire.'

'Four days?' Aranthur thought of the sand, the gravel, and the lack of fodder.

'You worry too much. We are in the hands of the gods. And you especially, *Bahadur*.' Jalu'd nodded. 'All the gods watch you.'

'And yet you say the gods are but men and women.'

'We are all kin, we and the gods. Who knows? Perhaps you will become a god, or I will, or Dahlia. In fact, I could easily worship your Dahlia. She is . . . perfect.' He laughed.

'I do not know if you are the holiest man I have met, or the greatest blasphemer,' Aranthur said.

'Good. I make you think, and that is good. And the only blasphemy is not to seek knowledge.'

Jalu'd saluted with his riding whip and rode away, his axe glinting in the moonlight.

Aranthur roved his column for a while, and eventually fetched up by the Lightbringer. He generally rode alone.

'Tell me more of being a Lightbringer,' Aranthur said.

Qna Liras glanced at him. 'I am a terrible Lightbringer.'

Aranthur smiled at the other man's humility. 'Really?'

'I have no idea. There are no meetings, or awards. I don't even know who else is a Lightbringer, except Kurvenos and a handful of other men and women.' He shrugged.

'Is it all about choices?' Aranthur asked.

Qna Liras turned and looked at him. 'Choices about power.'

Aranthur nodded. 'You kill.'

'Too often,' the Lightbringer said.

'Kurvenos does not kill.'

'He doesn't kill with a sword. But he leaves a fair number of corpses.'

Aranthur had heard the man say as much with his own lips. He rode along for a while.

'My powers are . . . greatly increased. Since the rift opened.'

'I'm not surprised,' the Magos said. 'Mine as well.'

'I have a theory about the superiority of the Pure's magik to ours. In the battle.'

He glanced at the Lightbringer, but the man was muffled against the wind and his veiled face gave nothing away. Aranthur found that he craved the man's good opinion so much that he was hesitant to voice his wild guess.

But Qna Liras turned and pulled his face veil aside.

'Tell me,' he said.

'What if the Pure have recovered the use of glyphs? A whole lexicon of sigils and glyphs. They'd cast faster, and their castings would be more certain. And more... massive. The red fire. They cast it again and again.'

Qna Liras toyed with the end of his turban.

'Ahhh,' he said. 'I believe you may be on to something. Speed, but not subtlety. The glyphs cannot be altered to circumstance, you understand. Indeed, I suspect that's why the Dhadhi stopped using them.'

Aranthur shook his head. 'I don't understand.'

Qna Liras nodded. 'Imagine water. Now, when you write the glyph for *water*, what you get is water in a single, ideal state. But what if you want muddy water? Or some other kind of water?'

Aranthur wasn't sure he understood, but he let it go.

'You get water – but faster,' he said.

'Very fast. When we faced the Disciple, he was incredibly fast, and yet not very good at dealing with rapid change.' Qna Liras nodded. 'Glyphs. Varestan glyphs. I believe you are correct.'

Aranthur thought of the *Ulmaghest* that awaited him in Megara.

'People died to bring this to us,' he remembered the Master of Arts saying.

They didn't mean the spells. They meant the glyphs.

'Still want to be a Lightbringer?' Qna Liras asked.

Aranthur smiled. 'Two things I'm not good at. Celibacy, and keeping my sword in its scabbard.'

Qna Liras laughed. 'So to speak.'

Aranthur shook his head. 'I didn't mean—'

'There really ought to be more humour in the world,' Qna Liras said. 'Listen, Aranthur. The essence of what we call a Lightbringer is a strong desire to do as little harm as possible, while willingly facing what is wrong or evil. Ill-considered actions of any kind can do harm. But we are women and men with lives and needs and desires.'

'Is killing the symptom, not the disease?' Aranthur asked.

The dark-skinned Magos smiled. 'I promise you that for the men and women you kill, it's the disease.' He took a swig from his canteen, and looked up at the Dark Forge. It was almost directly overhead, a stain on the jewelled brilliance of the heavens. 'But yes. That is an excellent way of expressing a horrible truth.'

'Killing can be a habit.'

'Indeed. A little violence can appear to solve most problems.' Qna

Liras sipped a little more water. 'The problem is, sometimes it is *the only way*. And it *does* solve some problems.'

'The Pure,' Aranthur said.

Qna Liras shook his head. 'I'm not sure. I have a theory... that the Master is one of us. One of the Magi. A man, I assume, as he certainly seems to dislike women. Could be a woman full of self-hatred, but most self-haters can't master themselves, much less control empires.'

Aranthur could not stop looking at the Dark Forge.

'But really, are we sure we can't just talk to him? I admit, I'm reasonably sure. If it is possible to know a man by his works, then the being we call "The Master" is a dark bastard indeed. And then we have to ask, would killing him actually change anything? People tend to follow leaders with whom they agree.'

Aranthur nodded. 'So the knife edge of which you spoke is about the use of power.'

'Any power,' Qna Liras agreed. 'Sex, violence, oratory, magik, birth, family, strength, weakness...' He hung his canteen from his saddle. 'I mean, it's easier to kill with magik than with family connections, but you see where I'm going.'

Aranthur nodded. 'How could we talk to the Master?'

Qna Liras looked up at the Dark Forge.

'I have no idea,' he said after a pause.

'Did the Master cause that?' Aranthur's eyes were also on the Dark Forge.

Qna Liras shook his head. 'I doubt that he meant to. Or mayhap he did. If so, he's more of a fool than I thought.'

'Can we fix it, like Jalu'd said?'

'I knew it was dangerous to start answering your questions. But I like the way you think. I don't know. I will know more when I see whether this actually happened as I fear. I would like to believe that what we can break, we can repair. I'll say one thing, one tantalising thing – the Great Moon crossed the sky *behind* the Dark Forge. You saw?'

'I did.'

'Only that means that the Forge is much smaller than I feared, and much more local. You understand?'

Aranthur nodded. 'Geometry.'

'Exactly. The most hopeful thing I've seen since the fabric was broken.'

Qna Liras looked away.

Aranthur thought of the small . . . hole . . . in reality that he had made when he destroyed one of the *stigali*.

'Would it heal itself?' he asked.

Qna Liras nodded. 'Maybe. But if the General is correct, whoever made it will seek to open it wider.'

With that cold comfort, Aranthur went back to the mundane problems of taking a column across the desert.

'Tomorrow we will have no more fodder for horses,' Vilna said.

'I know,' Aranthur commented. He was looking out across the sea of dunes in the dying light of the fourth day. 'I had not expected the Kuh to be so beautiful.'

Vilna nodded. He even smiled.

'Now, to me, this is the most foolish thought ever,' he admitted. 'What is beautiful here? I cannot feed my horse, the gravel gets into his hooves, the salt stings his eyes, and there are scorpions when I want to piss.' He shrugged. 'But I am glad that you see some beauty in it.'

Aranthur laughed. 'I think you just told me that I'm a fool.'

Vilna shrugged. 'You do well enough, *Bahadur*.'

But the fifth evening, Mir Jalu'd found them a small oasis with good grass and a few date palms and even a fig tree – a gigantic fig that looked as if it was as old as the world. The water in the well was fresh and cold.

'Someone ate all the figs and killed the people,' Omga said. He held up a scrap of turban and a broken rein with a brass disc. 'Pindaris, or maybe Safians.'

There had been six small houses of baked mud, and all of them had had their roofs caved in; their beams were burnt.

They killed a lame horse, and ate it roasted in fig leaves, to the disgust of their Safians and the delight of the Nomadi. They found enough rice under one of the houses to give everyone a handful. The rest of the mounts cropped the green grass and drank the water.

'I know the way from here,' Qna Liras said. 'I used to come here as a boy. There is a temple to the east, in the deep desert, and this is the way station.' He looked sad. 'Or it was. Even the Bethuin did not raid these people. But the Pure will kill anything.'

*

They left at nightfall, travelling south and a little west, following a track. They came rapidly to the belt of mountainous dunes – dunes so high that the riders couldn't always see the top. In the shifting valleys between the sand mountains, there was no wind, but it was cold.

Qna Liras led the way, with a pair of Nomadi. The huge dunes created a maze of valleys, and twice the entire column had to backtrack out of a dead end, or continue around a vast mound of sand to cross their own trail.

But long after midnight, at the rising of the Ruby, the small red moon, they came down a bank of soft sand, treacherous for their horses, so that they all had to dismount and their boots filled with sand. But when they shuffled clear of the soft sand, they were on a great plain in the cold moonlight of both moons. The huge dunes were left behind, and they were passing over a salt pan with patches of deep gravel.

'A warning,' Qna Liras said. 'An immense battle was fought here – men and *Jhugj* against Dhadhi. With drakes on both sides.' He shrugged. 'We have no idea why. But they killed all the life here, for a hundred parasangs. It is in our lessons.'

Aranthur shuddered.

Dahlia shook her head. 'This was done by people?' She sighed. 'Terrible.'

'Nothing more terrible than people,' the Lightbringer said. 'Except maybe the old gods.'

Aranthur walked on, looking at the ground. There were no stones larger than a pebble, as if the very rock had been splintered by the forces unleashed.

After a hundred paces or so, he saw a white stone, no larger than a fingertip, symmetrically shaped like a pointed egg, and he stooped for it. It wasn't stone.

It was lead.

He held it out to Qna Liras, who took it very carefully.

'These things are always dangerous,' the Lightbringer said. 'This is a sling stone – Dhadhian. With a glyph cast into it.'

Very carefully, he rubbed one side of the egg and revealed the glyph, marvellously detailed.

Aranthur put it in the pouch at his waist and walked on, leading Ariadne to give her a rest. He found another, and then a third, and each was different.

Towards morning, they came to the line of hills that separated the plain from the valley of the great river – the Azurnil.

'I'd like to keep going,' Qna Liras said to Aranthur.

Aranthur wondered what would happen if he disagreed. He didn't feel that he had any authority over the Lightbringer; in fact, he was supposedly escorting the Magos. But he rode to Vilna.

'The horses will make it,' the Nomadi officer said with assurance.

Aranthur nodded. He rode back to the Lightbringer.

'We'll halt in an hour, as usual, and water the horses,' he said. 'After that we can keep going, if there's fodder at the end.'

The Masran Magos shrugged. 'I cannot promise anything. I am... afraid... of what I will see when we crest this set of hills.'

He looked back down the column, where Haran and Hissin were changing horses and bickering in Safiri.

'I've become quite fond of all of you,' he said suddenly. 'I will do my best to see that no harm comes to you.'

Aranthur felt as if ice water had been poured on his head.

'What do you expect?' he asked.

'I have no idea what to expect. I fear many things. But I will be plain with you. I think that someone has cracked the wards on the Black Pyramid and released something ancient and very, very bad. I am not from the branch of our priests who study the past in detail, but there are... thousands... of beings...' He paused. 'The Black Pyramid is a prison for malign entities. We call them the *Apep-Duat*.'

'How old is the Black Pyramid?' Aranthur asked. And then, fearing to sound foolish, he added, 'I mean, I've heard of it, of course.'

'Older than humanity,' Qna Liras said. 'Older than the Dhadhi.'

'Eagle,' Aranthur said, making the sign. 'A prison?'

Qna Liras nodded. 'A metaphysikal prison. Older than human beings.'

3

Masr

The sun was rising in the east, its red light burning the Azurnil as they crossed the height of the pass. The broad valley of the Azurnil stretched endlessly before them from horizon to horizon. The river was broader than any river Aranthur had ever seen – so wide that it was more like a Souliote lake than a river.

They could smell the charcoal and the woodsmoke as soon as they crested the pass; there, off to the west, was Al-Khaire. The city itself was enormous. It seemed larger than Megara, bounded only on the side of the Azurnil and spreading out over the fertile plain and almost into the desert on its northern side. In the centre was a mighty acropolis crowned with gold-roofed temples and massive spires visible even from a parasang away. The lower slopes of the acropolis were shrouded in fog. Or smoke.

'My city is on fire,' Qna Liras said.

Aranthur could hear the fear in the Lightbringer's voice.

Across the river from the city, which was hidden in a pall of smoke, stood the pyramids. There were dozens, but five stood above the others at this distance: four white pyramids in an uneven square, and the fifth, the largest of all, its darkness lit by the rising sun.

'It is as I feared,' Qna Liras said.

His voice was dead, emotionless, and his veiled face was without the least sign of an expression.

'How can you tell?' Mir Jalu'd asked.

'The Black Pyramid neither emits nor reflects light in its proper state.

Look at the reflection of the sun... Never mind. There is no more time for talk. We must ride.'

'Change horses!' Aranthur said. 'Water up!'

The column halted, and all the people slid to the sand and began the process of getting water from canteens into horses.

Qna Liras fretted. 'Can't we...?'

Aranthur bowed. 'Syr, you clearly feel we are in danger. If the danger is mundane enough to be faced by troopers on horseback, the horses need to be as fresh and well watered as we can manage.'

Qna Liras smiled wryly.

'I will restrain my impatience,' he said. But his eyes were on Al-Khaire.

As soon as the column was ready, Vilna waved.

'Remember,' Aranthur said, 'we are a caravan from Armea, not an army.'

'None of that matters now,' Qna Liras said. 'Please, let us go.'

Aranthur looked up and down the column.

'Our Lightbringer expects danger,' he said. 'Everyone be ready – puffers primed, swords loose in your scabbards.'

The column rippled in the new sun as men and women drew their puffers. Omga took his bow from his scabbard and put three arrows in his belt. Dahlia nodded and rolled the rings on her fingers. Aranthur had come to know that this meant she was preparing her *aspis*.

Sasan rode over. 'Listen,' he said.

Aranthur was watching the valley. 'All ears.'

'My lads have proven themselves. They deserve puffers. Right now they have nothing but their swords.'

He nodded in the direction of Kalij, who was looking at his sabre.

Aranthur didn't turn his head. He was watching a plume of smoke or fog that seemed to move with a will of its own.

'Vilna!' he called.

'Blessed Twelve, can't you make a decision without asking that nomad?' Sasan snapped.

'No. Vilna, I'd like to give puffers to the Safian riders. What do you think?'

Vilna crossed his hands on his cantle and leant forward, his eyes narrowing. He was silent for a moment.

'Yes,' he said.

'Good.' Aranthur looked over the column. 'Anyone with more than two puffers, give one to a Safian.' He smiled. 'You will be repaid.'

Vilna laughed. 'Never. But it's a nice thought.'

Nonetheless, Chimeg handed Haran a silver mounted puffer with a long barrel. Omga had *five* of the weapons, and he handed over two. The Nomadi shared freely; in moments all the Safians had one, and Haran had a pair.

Despite Qna Liras' glaring, Aranthur thought that it was a moment for something to be said, or done. So he rode among the Safians and exchanged a handclasp with each man.

Haran bowed and put the back of his hand to his forehead.

'*Bahadur,*' he said, 'we will not disappoint.'

The others mumbled.

Aranthur turned his horse.

'Gods only know what we're facing. Listen for orders.'

He trotted to the head of the column.

'A handful of pistol balls will not stop an ancient evil,' Qna Liras said.

Aranthur shrugged. 'A little trust might save a lot of lives. Now we can go.'

Qna Liras said nothing. He simply touched his heels to his horse, and they started down into the valley of the Azurnil. The sun rose behind them, and the waters of the great river lost the touch of the great fire and began to reflect the blue of the heavens, as their name implied. The smell of smoke grew.

When they reached the base of the ridge, the road suddenly improved immensely. It was wide, built of neatly jointed stones, and covered in mud and gravel held by marble kerbstones.

Ansu pointed at the kerb.

'Very nice,' he said. 'Civilised, even.'

The column began to move faster. Aranthur sent out four Nomadi under Omga. They spread wide across the fields of gravel, but before the first bend in the road, the gravel had given way to cultivated fields with irrigation ditches. The road ran across the fields, through a long alley of shading date palms, and bypassed a village.

There were no people working the fields.

Aranthur couldn't find the patch of fog he'd seen from the height of the ridge. But his eyes went everywhere – up and down, over every field, every stand of trees.

Qna Liras rode ahead.

Batu, one of Omga's scouts, galloped back from the direction of the village.

'Dead mens,' he called out in Byzas. 'Ugly. Ugly.'

Aranthur followed him, with Dahlia at his heels, and he raised his magesight. But first he saluted Vilna and pointed at the Lightbringer, who was already ahead.

'Guard him. Hold him back if you must.'

'Yes, syr,' Vilna said. He obviously agreed.

The latent *sihr* was everywhere. Aranthur was confused at first, until he realised that the *power* was in the corpses, and the corpses were in every house – a hundred or more.

He reined in, and pointed to Dahlia, but she already knew.

'Potnia!' she swore. 'Is this the Pure? More of these despicable Pindaris?'

The village was surrounded by a high mud-brick wall, but the gate was open, smashed in by a force so great that it had collapsed the basalt pillars that anchored it. They lay, toppled, across low buildings they'd smashed in their fall.

The little village was like an abattoir that had been left uncleaned for a few days. Bodies lay strewn about, as if thrown by the hand of a giant. Aranthur's sight told him there were dozens more in the warren of whitewashed mud-brick buildings.

'This place could be full of traps,' he said. 'But the *sihr* tastes different from that in Armea.'

Dahlia looked at Ansu, who waved a hand, as if dismissing the protest of a friend. A single butterfly – or perhaps an emanation shaped like a butterfly – emerged from his hand. Its wings beat, and it rose in the foul air.

'I do not see a *stigal*,' Dahlia said.

'We need to keep moving,' Qna Liras said.

He rode up with Vilna at his heels. Vilna made a motion with his hand, as if to say '*nothing I could do.*'

Aranthur nodded. 'I don't like leaving this behind me.' He gestured at the corpses and the pools of malevolent sorcery.

'It's . . .' Qna Liras shrugged. 'We are very vulnerable here. At least it is daylight. Look, Aranthur. The Black Pyramid is broken. Some-thing – or some *things* – have escaped. The *Apep-Duat*. They will be . . . hungry . . . after many thousands of years . . .'

Dahlia backed her horse.

'Lovely,' she said. 'We go all the best places.' She glanced at Aranthur. 'Arry, I'm not sure we're up to facing some ancient evil with a column of cavalry.'

He nodded.

Qna Liras shook his head. 'I will try to protect you.'

Aranthur thought, briefly, that they were supposed to be going to Antioke by the most rapid route. He wondered if the Masran Magos had ever intended them to reach their destination.

He wondered if he should use his remaining message sticks, but this didn't seem the moment.

He looked at the bodies.

'Right,' he said. 'Let's keep going.'

An hour later, they were trotting along the road, which was broad enough for a column of cavalry eight men wide. They had passed two more villages, both of them empty of either living people or dead.

Al-Khaire grew before them, the magnificent domes of its citadel plain against the sky. It was clear that part of the city was afire; there was smoke rising from the lower town, nearest the river.

Aranthur began to have doubts about their entire course of action.

The immensity of the Black Pyramid was a matter for awe. On the far side of the river, a stone wall ran almost as far as the eye could see, with a walkway beneath it and stone piers at regular intervals. There were towers, low, squat, and black, and beyond, a vast paved field, and then the pyramids, each the size of a small mountain. Aranthur could not see more.

Closer in, he found traces of *sihr* on the road, but no more obvious sign.

Ahead of them, the magnificent acropolis of Al-Khaire towered in the smoky air above the devastation below it. The temples still glowed with golden light in the sun.

The road turned away from the waterside at what appeared to be a ferry dock. There were a dozen dead. Aranthur dismounted to look at them: three dead Safians, instantly identifiable by their headgear, and the rest some sort of local militia.

'Why weren't they buried?' he asked.

'We need to keep moving. I think there is an *Apep-Duat* on this side of the river, and it will stalk us.' Qna Liras' voice betrayed anxiety.

Aranthur looked at the bodies again.

Sasan, who had confirmed their origin, shook his head.

'These all died by good old-fashioned human violence. Maybe five days ago.'

'When the rift opened,' Dahlia said. 'All these could have been killed by Pindari raiders.'

Sasan pointed back behind them.

'These are not Pindaris. These are Tufenchis – like your better quality militia. Not professional warriors, not thugs.'

'We need to move,' Qna Liras said.

Aranthur nodded. 'Let's go.'

They turned north and west with the road, away from the river.

Soon after, his scouts reported movement on the road, and Aranthur closed the column.

'Please. These are likely my people,' Qna Liras said.

'Of course,' Aranthur said.

But he brought up his magesight and went forward with Dahlia and the Lightbringer, just to be sure.

What they found was a temple priest and two eights of priest-soldiers. The priest wore all black; the soldiers were mounted on camels, and wore black turbans and black robes.

Qna Liras saluted and sang something in Masri.

'Any idea what he's saying?' Aranthur asked.

'No clue,' Dahlia said.

The priest spread his arms wide, and locked the Lightbringer in an embrace.

'Well, we're friends, anyway,' Aranthur said.

'When did you become so cynical?' Dahlia asked. 'You were such a lovely innocent.'

She smiled, as if to take the sting from her words.

Aranthur shrugged, and looked back along the column.

'Move it,' he called.

*

'I was right – there are *Apep-Duat* loose on this side,' Qna Liras said. 'The Black Pyramid is broken, but all of the White Pyramids are still functioning. Nazar here believes that the *Ammit* is itself still anchored on the other side of the river, and we face only tendrils of its *power*. Or its servants.'

'That's cheering,' Ansu said.

Qna Liras looked back along the column, now augmented by the Masran priest-soldiers on their camels.

'Not really,' the Magos said. 'Nazar says it has broken the city wards of Al-Khaire and taken or killed more than a thousand people.'

Ansu grunted. 'And the killings make it more powerful?'

Qna Liras glanced at him.

'Exactly. If we allow it too many victims, it may be able to manifest. You know this sort of lore?'

Ansu smiled. 'It is not unknown in Zhou. We also have a black pyramid of sorts, although it is neither black nor a pyramid.'

'Has anyone seen it and lived?' Aranthur asked.

Qna Liras asked the Masran priest. Nazar nodded.

'He says it looks like fog,' Qna Liras said.

Aranthur nodded.

'Perfect,' muttered Dahlia.

'Where are we headed now?' Aranthur asked.

'The Mirza Gate,' Qna Liras said. 'It's strongly warded.'

Aranthur nodded. 'Keep going,' he said, and turned out of the column.

He rode back along his people, all the way back until he reached the rearguard, which was Sasan and his people.

'Fog,' he said. 'The entity, or what have you, looks like fog.'

Sasan looked back. 'How do you fight fog?'

Aranthur shook his head. 'We don't. We out-ride it.'

He went off to the north, found two outriders, and told them about the fog. He had no outriders along the river; he was ready to ride back to the column when Batu pointed.

'Fog,' he said.

And there, crouched amid the treetops of a village with a stand of date palms, was a patch of fog, or maybe damp spiderweb. It had a yellow cast in bright sunlight, like horse-piss on snow.

'Fuck,' Aranthur breathed. He *saw* it with magesight – a gaping maw of *sihr*.

'On me. Run,' he ordered.

He waved, and Batu needed no urging, and they were galloping across a rutted field full of gravel and leaping an irrigation ditch, their horses skimming the ground as if they were flying low. Aranthur looked back, but he could no longer see the village or its malevolent occupant.

They reached the road.

'Tell the others!' Aranthur shouted.

He turned south, riding hard for the rearguard.

As soon as Sasan saw him coming, he made the right guess, and the Safians started forward at a rapid pace.

Aranthur turned Ariadne. Now he could see the blob of *sihr* off to the north, flowing over the field he'd just covered.

'Come on!' he roared.

He watched it move, tried to guess its speed.

As Sasan came abreast, he pointed at the distant cloud, and brought Ariadne to a canter.

'Go!' he yelled, and then the Safians needed no more urging.

Aranthur followed them, watching the cloud, and casting occasional glances behind. There could always be two, or even three, whatever they were.

They raced along the road, the horseshoes casting sparks even in the brilliant sun. But the yellow mist was still three hundred paces away when they passed it, and ran on, and by the time they reached the column, it was well behind.

They arrived at the gate through a slum of ramshackle hovels built outside the protection of the walls with their horses blown. Aranthur was not sure he'd ever felt quite so dirty or so tired. He'd been awake for almost two days. He wasn't sure he could concentrate to cast effectively. Ariadne, the strongest horse he'd ever known, was done, almost unable to walk after the last burst. Aranthur changed to his Steppe pony to save Ariadne, and then fretted with Qna Liras under the gate.

'Men are deserting their posts. The city is in the grip of fear,' Nazar said, through Qna Liras.

And it was obvious there were no soldiers on the walls. It took long minutes to get the gate opened, and then only when the Masran priest became shrill in his denouncements. When the gate opened, the people inside only opened a small postern, and they all had to dismount and enter the city in single file. Aranthur waited with Sasan and Dahlia, and their horses were restless.

Aranthur turned and looked back over the deserted gateside slum.

'It's close,' he said.

Dahlia nodded. 'I can feel it,' she admitted.

The line of men in front of them seemed to take forever to pass the gate.

'There it is,' Aranthur said.

In magesight, the first tendrils of the *sihr* were like rotten vines creeping across the slum – long, slimy tentacles of Dark *power*.

Aranthur's pony exploded away. He spent a terrible minute fighting for control of his mount, and when he had the horse calm, he saw that Dahlia was down, and her mount had run. Sasan gave her a hand up behind him.

One of the tendrils was just a hundred paces away. It was curiously hesitant; it moved with caution, probing, probing...

Sasan got a hand on Dahlia's horse's bridle and went for the little postern gate.

'Come on!' he called.

Aranthur wished he was mounted on Ariadne. But he backed the pony towards the gate, watching the tendrils. There were two, now – like the tentacles of a kraken, often the way the enemy, the God of Darkness, was represented in Twelver art.

The pony quivered between his legs.

He cast the preparatory for his *aspis*, so that the *working* was ready in his hand, or that's the way he framed it.

Sasan was through the postern.

'Watch out, Aranthur!' called a voice.

High above him, Jalu'd leant out over the wall, and lightning flashed.

One of the tentacles of damp darkness was moving very quickly now. Jalu'd twirled, high on the wall. A bolt of jade-green lightning struck the tentacle, and it lashed furiously.

Now the other came along the ground at waist height, as fast as a swung sword.

Aranthur interposed his *aspis* with a muttered word.

He had to dismount to pass the gate – he didn't want to lose the pony. He cast a second *aspis* and used the two shields aggressively, pushing them against the immaterial form of the tentacle. It gave, but he didn't appear to be doing it any harm. On the other hand, he could push his *aspis* quite far. Now he used his will and all the new-found *power* he could access to thrust both *aspides* away. Despite exhaustion, his desire to save his horse, and his people, fired his will.

He slapped his pony on the rump and she put her head down and followed the smell of the other horses into the darkness. He turned back, and pushed the tentacle twice, once with each *aspis*. It was baffled, but the yellow fog was coming up to the wall, and it was, if anything, growing.

A beam of sea-green struck it from the wall with no apparent effect, and then another crack of Jalu'd's jade lightning.

Aranthur longed to see if the sword would do it any damage...

No! Not now. Unless there is no other choice.

He tried another gambit, casting two more *aspides* and juggling all four like a shield wall.

'You are restraining it *in the Aulos*.' Dahlia was at his shoulder. 'Very clever. Now get your arse inside so we can close the gate.'

He felt sheepish, but he stepped back, and Sasan slammed the heavy oak door closed. Immediately, lines of blue-white fire traced the outline of the door, and then the greater gate in which the door was set. They flared, and then went out.

Aranthur was left with an after-image burning on his retinas.

'Did you see that?' he asked over his shoulder.

There were upset horses milling in the near-darkness of the gate, and dozens of men and women trying to calm them.

Whooom.

The gates rattled.

'That can't be good,' Dahlia said.

'Get the horses into the city!' Vilna called.

'They won't open the inner gate!' called one of the Safian riders.

Aranthur put a hand on the gate and pulled it away as if he'd been burnt.

'Eagle. It's attacking the gate.' He looked back at Dahlia. 'You get up on the wall. You have all kinds of offensive stuff I don't have.'

Dahlia nodded, handed him her reins, and brushed under the outstretched neck of an angry mare.

Aranthur steadied himself, grabbed *saar*, and put his hand on the gate. Then he pushed *saar* very slowly into the ward he found there, ignoring the existential pain of the attacker against his own will.

The ward took the *power*. The gate flared in the real.

Whooooom.

The gates shook as if a great wind was blowing against them. The horses began to panic – ears were down, and the younger horses rolled their eyes.

Vilna had his horse lying flat on the cobbles, and he was pulling other horses down. Most of the Nomadi emulated him.

Aranthur pushed more *saar* into the gate.

He was still working when the attacker struck, and just for a moment he was confronted with . . .

Minemineminemineminemineminemineminemineminemineminemine

It was hideous, and all-encompassing – a unitary horizon of *mine*. It was like the embodiment of a will of selfishness, and it knew no other boundary but the unitary desire to possess. It was absolutely seamless and pure in its devouring desire. Its will contended for possession of the ward, the gate, and Aranthur's mind at the same time.

Then he was out, on his knees by the gate, vomiting up his empty stomach. He felt unclean – as if the slime had rubbed over his entire body and every happy memory in his mind.

He tried to stand. His mind went back.

He stumbled.

Whooooom.

The gates rattled hard, flexing against the heavy iron rod that pinned them to the road and slamming against the massive wooden bar set across them.

Aranthur raised his hand. It took an effort of will to make himself touch the gate.

He threw what *saar* he had.

Out! he ordered in the *Aulos*.

He retreated from the bond ahead of the attacker's backlash.

Behind him, one of the priests finally got the inner gates open, and the horses began to push through into the city. Aranthur glanced back, almost blinded by the sunlight, to see fire damage and a smoking ruin. Vilna ran with the horses, holding the reins of one of his own mounts.

WHOOOOOOOM

The gates slammed against their stops, and they seemed to bend.

Aranthur took one of the *kuria* crystals he'd taken so long ago in the fight in Megara. He opened it in his mind, and placed it against the gate.

There was an explosion of light, and his gauntleted left hand stung as if it had been hit with a sword. But he felt none of the filth, and the gate felt solid under his hand.

The crystal, one of the largest he'd ever seen, was *gone. Subsumed.*

Outside, a cry like that of a bereft child.

Aranthur stumbled back away from the gate. He found Ariadne, loyal to the end, standing behind him, and he put his arms around her warm, horse-smelling neck.

'Eagle,' he murmured.

She stood there, perhaps puzzled by the embrace, and perhaps happy to have a little comfort when the world was so upsetting, at least to a horse.

And to a man.

'Show me your drawings from the Well,' Aranthur said.

They were in the Temple of the Sun, in the citadel on the massive acropolis of Al-Khaire. Qna Liras had been closeted with the priests – the surviving priests – for hours. All of the Imperials had received medical attention, and food, sparingly rationed, and fresh water. Their horses had been fed.

The city was packed with desperate people, and low on food and drinking water. One whole quarter had burned, outside the new walls, down by the ancient Temple of the Kings. The people, citizens and refugees alike, were in a state very like the horses – near panic, a smouldering fear needing only a hot spark or a breeze to become an inferno. At least one and as many as ten *Apep-Duat* stalked the land outside the wards on the city. Worst of all, Qna Liras reported that the wards in the older districts had been overcome at least once, with a consequent massacre of people.

And then the Lightbringer had gone back to his interminable meeting.

Dahlia was smoking stock, passing a pipe with Sasan. But she got up and walked to her saddlebags, rooted around for a moment, and extracted a scroll tube, which she rolled out on the floor.

Aranthur crouched over it.

'I think that I saw it,' he said.

'Saw what?' she asked.

'The sigil on the gate wards. It's in this somewhere.'

Dahlia knelt next to him.

'I did see it,' she said, chagrined. 'Of course it's a Great Ward. But why it would be on the Well ...?'

Jalu'd joined them.

'The Well, as you call it, is a sacred place of *power*. Of course it would have a ward. The world is not more dangerous now than when it was young. If anything, the converse.'

The three of them went over the scroll. In the end, it was Dahlia who found it.

'Look, it's right here. The *ward* sigil is set into the *stone* sigil.'

'I didn't even know that was *stone*,' Aranthur said.

'It's not *stone*,' Dahlia said. 'It's like *stone*, though.'

Jalu'd nodded. 'It is probably a glyph made especially for *that* stone, or perhaps for any white marble. The Magos is right – glyphs lack flexibility, unless you constantly create new ones, and then no one can read them.'

'But this glyph is certainly *ward*,' Aranthur said.

Dahlia glanced at him. ' "Certainly" seems a little strong.'

'Let's go down to the gate,' Aranthur said.

It wasn't so simple. It took the five of them over an hour to find a priest with authority, to make their way to one of the gates, and to invoke the ward by opening and closing the gate.

Dahlia rubbed her eyes. 'I agree that it's probably the *ward* glyph,' she said.

Ansu was more enthusiastic.

'Now I wonder how permanent the substance holding the ward must be?' he asked.

The priest was looking at them with ill-concealed suspicion. His superiors had ordered him to support the foreigners, but he didn't have to love them.

Dahlia started the long walk back to the citadel.

'It is my sense that the more durable the physical substance is, and the better embedded the ward is in the substance, the tougher it is.'

'Like to like,' Aranthur said.

'Exactly,' Dahlia said.

Sasan shook his head. 'You two are not much fun for those of us who don't happen to cast bolts of lightning.'

Aranthur sensed a hint of jealousy, and he nodded inwardly, aware that the events of the last two weeks had forced him to work constantly with Dahlia in a way that had to feel unfair to Sasan. And equally aware that all was not well between Dahlia and Sasan. Once that might have pleased him; now it was more like a disaster.

But Jalu'd stepped in.

'On the contrary,' he said, 'both of them speak a good deal of sense.'

Ansu nodded. 'Listen, this is one of the world's major cities, yes?'

Aranthur nodded and waved at the skyline. Even fire, assault, and invasion by godlike and malevolent entities could not utterly destroy the beauty and harmony of the towers and temples, the fine high buildings, the overhanging balconies.

'They must have armourers. What if we engraved the sigil on bucklers, or shields?' Ansu asked.

'How do we power...?' Dahlia said. 'Crystal?'

Aranthur nodded. 'It must be possible, or the gate would not have eaten my crystal.'

'A whole new technology,' Dahlia said.

Aranthur scratched his unshaven chin.

'Is it really new? Aren't we just making a more durable *amulet*?'

'Someone must have done this,' Dahlia agreed, deflated. 'So some part of it must not work.'

Aranthur shrugged. 'The glyphs are mostly lost. Did you know the *ward* glyph before... today?'

Dahlia nodded. 'No. Good point.'

The priest of Masr who was escorting them had been listening intently. Now he stopped them.

'We use your sigils and glyphs,' he said proudly. 'Perhaps these are forgotten in the north, but here in the south we know them well. Our older places are full of them.'

Dahlia looked at Aranthur, a look that clearly meant 'don't say the first thing that comes into your head.'

'Can you take us to an armourer?' Aranthur asked.

The young man nodded. 'We have the best armourers in the world,' he said proudly.

'We also specialise in arrogance,' muttered Sasan.

'Shut up,' Dahlia said.

'And we know everything,' Sasan added.

'Darling...' Dahlia said.

Sasan winked at Aranthur.

They walked through noisy streets. Up by the acropolis, the streets had seemed empty. Here, in the heart of the city, the streets were so crowded that it could be difficult to walk, with rows of stalls on either hand, and the looming wonder of the Temple of One Hundred Women, with two magnificent white towers, rising to robin's egg blue domes dominating the sky over the street. High in the sky between the two towers lay the Dark Forge, a reminder that all was not actually well. But in the streets, despite malign entities and fire and sword, children played, a street singer sang of some Masran hero, an old man sold sweet tea, and a much younger man sold fresh water.

People watched them, from doorways and from stalls. Dahlia, with her uncovered gold-blonde hair, seemed to draw every stare, but Aranthur's height and broad shoulders also drew the attention of many. Some of the women made the sign of the 'horns', an invocation of the Gazelle Goddess – but then, one young woman in a veil raised her eyes to look at Aranthur and blinked both eyes.

Aranthur smiled at her, but she was gone in the crowd.

In the square before the Temple of One Hundred Women, there were hundreds of stalls. A rich family was distributing food to the poor – good food: white bread and fresh meat and fish and measures of rice.

The priest nodded, as if this was all as it should be.

'They earn much favour with the gods,' he said. 'Generosity is one of the greatest of virtues.'

Somehow he managed to imply that, as foreigners, they needed a great deal of instruction on the virtues.

There were lanes and avenues running off the square in every direction, each of them crowded with stalls and shops. The priest led them across the square. Sasan caught a very young pickpocket and released him. Ansu became entangled with three dancing women, and left the three of them laughing.

'Those women are not virtuous,' the priest said.

'Glad to hear it,' Ansu said.

The priest frowned. 'This is the street for armourers.'

The street he indicated was more of a warren. The smell of burning charcoal and coke was everywhere. The alley seemed to be populated with black-robed priest-soldiers in black turbans. Aranthur noted for the first time that the black robes were only an outer layer. Close up, the priest-soldiers wore elaborate and colourful clothes under the robes: silk trousers, velvet jackets not unlike what a Souliote or an Arnaut might wear for a festival.

Hammers rang on anvils, punctuating the air with clear notes, higher or lower as the artisans worked their pieces. The shops seemed dark from outside, sometimes lit only by the forge fire. At street level, they often had an awning of finely woven tapestry, black with shop-soot, and under the awning would be a pair of boys or girls and a carpeted table covered in wares: pairs of gauntlets in one shop, puffers in another. A third had finely ornamented helmets with lobster-tail neck protection and elaborate bars under a sun visor. Another had daggers, hilted in antler or ivory, wickedly curved and often jewelled.

'Anyone have any money?' Aranthur asked.

Ansu smiled. He no longer painted his teeth black, so his smile was very white in the gloom of the forge-street.

'I always have money.'

Dahlia shook her head. 'We can't just live off Ansu.'

'Why not?' Sasan asked. 'Ansu, does your beneficence run to some kit for my bandits?'

Ansu turned to the Masran priest and bowed.

'I will need to negotiate some bills,' he said. 'Can you ask for a money-changer to come here?'

The priest smiled slightly. 'I can take you to a money-changer. There are three on the other side of the square.'

Ansu smiled. 'I suspect they will come to me.'

He took his pen case from his belt and, using Aranthur's back, he penned a short note. He folded it, and with a single silver coin he acquired a flock of small boys.

'Listen carefully,' he said to the boy he selected. 'And this small coin will grow much larger. Go to the money-changer with the largest table. Give him this note. If he declines to follow you, go to the next. If they all decline to follow you, come back here.'

The priest was amused.

'I have never seen anyone summon a money-changer,' he said.

Ansu bowed slightly. 'I am not surprised.' He smiled, in case his words gave offence. 'Now, let us make some purchases.'

Sasan found maille, light as air, almost magikal in its tiny complexity, and helmets. Ansu found a shield maker, and after a brief discussion with the girls at the table, they were invited into the shop. Then they walked through the shop into the back, where there was a small garden and a well. The shield maker came in from another door, wiping his soot-black hands on his leather apron.

'*Effendi?*' he asked.

And in minutes, he was with them at a small table, and Dahlia had her sketches in front of him.

'Steel? I can do it,' he admitted. 'Good steel is ... difficult in this size.' He glanced around. 'How many?'

'Thirty?' Ansu asked. 'Fifty?'

The man paled. 'I will need to work with other people.'

'How soon?' Ansu asked.

'A month?'

'I need them tomorrow,' Ansu said with royal confidence.

'My lord, there is a man to see you,' said one of the young girls. 'Papa, may I let the man in? He is a *Farounzi*, a money man.'

'Let him in and bring us tea,' the artisan said.

The girl bowed, both hands on her heart, and darted away. A moment later a young man in a long black gown appeared. He was smiling.

'I had to see what this was about,' he said, pleasantly enough. His glance fixed on Ansu. 'You are from Zhou?'

'I have that honour.'

The money-changer bowed. 'I am Bardi. Lanzo di Bardi of the Megara House.' He nodded. 'You must be Prince Ansu. There cannot be two of you.'

Ansu rose and returned the Liote man's greeting and bow.

'I am he,' he agreed. 'If I write a note on my Imperial father, will you honour it?'

Bardi shrugged. 'It depends on how good my own credit is, Highness. The truth is that these people are under siege – even hard currency has lost value compared to food, and credit is not very elastic. How much do you need?'

'One thousand gold dinars. Perhaps three times that.'

To give the man his due, Bardi didn't flinch or wince. He did smile.

'That much?'

'We are endeavouring to save the city. Listen, Syr Bardi – these shields will have movable wards. With those we can clear the infested sections and then repair the great wards. The city, at least, will be safe.'

'Tomorrow?' asked the shield maker. 'That's... impossible.'

Aranthur leant in. 'Syr, if these work, they will... be quite valuable. And perhaps revolutionary.'

'If they work?' Bardi asked.

Dahlia smiled. 'I am Dahlia Tarkas.'

'Ah, Myr Tarkas. I can offer *you* perhaps fifty ducats.'

'Very kind, but I am merely saying that we have certain... interests. In Megara. I promise you his bill is good.'

'The Emperor, you mean? You mean that you are on official business?' He smiled. 'Of course, a Tarkas would not lie to a poor banker, would she?'

'Almost never,' Dahlia said.

'Make one,' Aranthur said. 'We'll test it, and we'll know. Someone has to work the crystal side. I have several crystals...'

No one else volunteered.

'That's me, then,' he said.

The craftsman quoted a price, and the banker agreed. Immediately the man went out into his shop and let forth a rolling volley of orders to the dozen young men and women, who went in what seemed to be all directions.

'I need to be here,' Aranthur said.

Dahlia shrugged. 'We have nowhere else to be.'

Ansu smiled. 'I'll just cross the square with Syr Bardi, then, and spend my father's money.' He smiled and bowed slightly.

Sasan went out to shop for his horsemen, but before he went out, he leant over Aranthur.

'Don't you think Ansu's business will involve the dancing girls?' he whispered.

'All three of them, no doubt,' Aranthur said, grinning.

'That's just selfish,' Jalu'd said. 'He'll need help. I can't abandon him.'

Over the next few hours, Aranthur and Dahlia tried not to be in the way in a very small shop, especially as the front of the shop grew gradually more cluttered with Sasan's growing pile of purchases. An engraver was sent for, and Aranthur and Dahlia drew out a glyph for him to copy. The man had more than a little latent talent. He was very cautious of the glyph, but he rendered it neatly on to a sheet of copper with his engraver, and then set about deepening the engraving lines.

He called for the smith, and the two of them had an animated conversation in Masri. By then, the priest had changed his mind about the foreigners. Something about the banker's ready attendance on Prince Ansu had convinced him that they were worthy of his time. Now he first gave his name, Haras, and then translated the exchange.

'The smith says, why do you interrupt me, I'm working, you do your work and I do mine. The engraver says, this is all *baraka* and must be done in sequence, and how will this complex *working* be powered? The smith says, Oh! Gods save my house. The engraver says, these are evil days. Then he says, let me engrave the iron, before it is hardened in the furnace. And he also says that he could do it faster, and perhaps better with wax and acid, in his own shop.'

'That's not engraving,' Aranthur said. 'That's etching. I'm not sure...'

Dahlia shook her head. 'Let it be. Anything that is faster is better.'

Aranthur pointed at the practice copper.

'When you build the shield, put this behind the steel,' he said.

The engraver smiled.

The shield maker frowned.

'Too heavy,' Haras said for him.

'Try it,' Aranthur said. 'I'm fairly strong.'

Dahlia turned to Haras.

'What do you do, when one of these things attacks inside the city?'

'We die,' Haras said. 'The only tactic so far is to set fire to a street of houses. The entities fear fire.' He winced. 'Sometimes.'

'And they are getting stronger,' the banker said. He had returned after an hour. He glanced at Dahlia. 'I have scraped together enough credit to cover your friend. It's mostly my own money, and honestly, I'd rather not die here.'

He glanced at Aranthur, who was working on a sheet of leather he'd acquired from the harness-maker a street farther north.

'What news of the General?' he asked.

Dahlia sketched the events of the last two weeks.

The banker shook his head. 'We heard here... that you lost.'

'What?' Aranthur looked up, his burnisher in his hand.

Bardi shrugged. 'That's what we heard yesterday, from Antioke.'

'No, we most definitely won,' Dahlia insisted. 'We broke their army, captured their horse herd and all their guns, and killed or captured most of their magikal talent.'

Bardi leant back. 'That's . . .' He looked first stricken, and then delighted. 'That's amazing. So the General is not dead or captured?'

'I saw the General with my own eyes, as close as we are, seven days ago,' Aranthur said.

Bardi blinked. 'Someone is misinformed. Bankers can't afford this kind of error. Thankfully, I've had nowhere to wager my money.'

Aranthur kept working. He cut out leather backing for the shield, and then worked the glyph on the rough side, facing out. Then he added some routine decoration, and made a strap. A teenage girl in an apron came and took his work, and fifteen minutes later, they had the shield about the same time that Ansu and Sasan returned.

The shield, which was really more of a buckler, had a steel outer face. It needed a great deal more polishing than it had received, but polishing hardened steel takes time. The glyph was very clear in fine engraved repoussé, and the light polishing had tended to hit the high points, so that the glyph glowed against the fire-scale and roughness of the less polished portions. The copper layer was barely visible, riveted close to the steel layer, and the leather was held by the same rivets. The strap had a nice steel buckle.

'You do good leather-work,' the smith said. 'I have three more on the way. Give me another two hours. They will be . . .' He looked at Haras.

'Etched,' Haras said. 'Not engraved.'

'How do we test it?' Sasan asked. 'Oh, fuck me, I didn't mean that.'

'We go out into the bad neighbourhoods and find ourselves an *Apep-Duat.*'

Haras flinched when Aranthur used the Masri word.

'You have no idea what you are saying,' the young priest said. 'The *Apep-Duat* are unholy. They are like gods, but . . . no one would ever seek one. They are—'

Dahlia nodded. 'And then we see what we can do to it. When we were at the gate, I took careful note of what hit hard and what didn't. Jalu'd had an emanation that I've never seen – it appeared to do damage. The Lightbringer was less effective.'

'He was too afraid. I merely danced for it – a little love can be very confusing to the wilfully evil.'

Jalu'd nodded, as if throwing love as a weapon was a commonplace.

A young man came in and said that food was to be served for all of them in 'just a little time'.

Sasan nodded. 'Good. I'd like to eat before I go wandering around looking for something I can't fight.'

'You cannot do this. You will die, and you might stir one of these horrors up and it will devour more people.' Haras was indignant.

Aranthur shook his head. 'Qna Liras makes it sound as if all casters have all these talents in common. But you and Ansu are as different from Dahlia or me as chalk from cheese.'

He was talking mostly to himself; while he spoke, he was fiddling with a small *kuria* crystal.

He handed the shield to Sasan.

'Engage the crystal,' he said.

Sasan did as he was told, and the shield glowed a cold blue.

'If it is fog,' Aranthur asked, 'can it be moved by wind?'

Dahlia tapped her long fingers on the table.

'Interesting. Have you learnt the *Safian Transference* yet?'

'I've learnt it, but I don't get the result that I was told to expect, and I don't have the grimoire here to see if I misunderstood. Somehow, my casting creates heat...'

Dahlia nodded. She turned to Haras.

'Can you ask the artisan for the use of an old clay pot or two? They will be broken. I hope.'

The young woman ran off with a bow, and returned with ceramic vases under each arm.

'Both cracked. Go ahead.' She spoke through Haras. 'She asks, do you use that sword? Are you a warrior?'

'Watch out,' Sasan said. 'Masrans are the most conservative people in the world.'

Haras shrugged. 'We have no women as soldiers, it's true. Women are too important as the makers of children to waste them on war.'

Dahlia smiled at the girl, but then looked at Haras.

'So women's ability to rear children is more important than war?'

'Of course,' the Masran priest said.

'More important than politics, would you say?'

'The very most important thing.'

Dahlia grinned. 'So naturally—' she began, and Sasan put a hand on her arm.

She looked up at him.

'Guests,' he said.

She leant back. She looked at the girl.

'Yes, I wear a sword, and use it. And I can work the *Ars Magika*, and I will eventually sit on the Council of Thirty that makes the laws of my City.'

The dark-haired young woman nodded. She glanced at Haras, shrugged, and walked over to the wall without reply.

Haras looked back and forth.

'Show me your *transference*,' Dahlia said.

Aranthur raised it, and wrote it in his mind. It was fluid, and easy, and the *power* came . . .

He leapt in the air.

'Darkness falls!' he swore.

His left boot was smouldering, and he pulled it off with a string of curses.

Jalu'd leant forward.

'I know this a different way,' he said. 'You cannot hold the summoned *saar*. It must flow through you, not pause. In your pause—'

'I don't pause!' Aranthur said.

Dahlia shrugged. 'I think he's right.'

'Damn it,' Aranthur said.

'It is only practice,' Dahlia said. 'And you need to eat more.'

Aranthur took a deep breath and then used his *kuria* meditation to steady himself and avoid anger. He knew they were right – but he now thought of himself as a skilled caster and it was embarrassing to make simple mistakes.

The second time, he wrote the *volteia* in his mind, and then let the *saar* flow into it, so that, in his imagination, the letters lit with fire from right to left in a single, not quite smooth progression, as if a scribe were writing them. All this in less time than the beat of a butterfly's wings.

His bare foot was warm, but the nearest vase exploded in fragments, and one cut Aranthur's face. The young man carrying a tray of fragrant rice flinched, and there was rice on the floor.

'Exactly!' Jalu'd said. 'Much better. It must flow, like dance. This is why I use dance as my focus, because these manipulations are all about balance and timing.'

'Perhaps you should sing your *working*.'

Dahlia was mocking him, but he saw the virtue in the notion. And in that moment, a cascade of insights took place; no time passed, and an entire universe of technique seemed to expand before him.

'Eagle,' he breathed.

He took a step back.

'Everyone stand back,' he said. 'I don't want to spoil more of our dinner.'

He whistled a tune to himself – a fairly juicy Arnaut tavern song. He imagined playing it on the *tamboura*. He fitted the *volteia* to it the way lyrics might fit a song, and he cast.

'Now I see,' he said.

'Of course you see,' Sasan said. 'You blew a hole in his wall.'

Dahlia put a hand on his shoulder.

'I was ... making a joke,' she said. 'But that worked.'

Aranthur was shaking his head. 'Oh, that's just the beginning. By Sophia. What if I fitted my *workings* to the movements of swordsmanship? Like dance, but for combat ...'

Dahlia's eyes widened. 'Damn.'

'Can we eat first?' Sasan asked.

And indeed, as the table filled with dishes – roast lamb with saffron rice and raisins, several bargains, and a marvellous vegetable soup – Ansu summoned all the workers to the courtyard.

'He ordered it,' Sasan said. 'There's not much food in the city. I swear he bought it all.'

The workers dug in, eating quickly, and Haras passed some of the discussions along.

'We'll pay them to work all night,' Ansu said.

Various voices were raised in protest. Aranthur discovered that he was ravenous, and he wolfed down the rice, and even took a piece of lamb, despite the Academy's prohibitions. Not eating meat was seemingly irrational in a world so full of violence, but he hesitated with the lamb at his lips, and then put it down, and had a fish curry instead. It was delicious, and he had a second bowl and then a third.

A boy came in; he shouted something, and suddenly everyone was on their feet.

Haras shook his head.

'There is a fog rising – a real fog, from the river,' he said. 'But the entities are moving under cover of the fog. The killing has started.'

Aranthur got to his feet. He felt the familiar urge – to go at the danger, to attack it.

'Let's go,' he said.

Sasan frowned. 'Not so fast.'

'People are dying,' Aranthur said.

'You're dying to try your toy. How are we going to fight it?'

'Wind, the shield, direct sorcerous attack.'

Ansu stroked his chin, and flicked more rice into his mouth.

'And,' he said, when he'd chewed and swallowed, 'I want to try cutting it off from its host. These things have tendrils, but they are themselves merely the reaching arms of the thing . . . that the Pure released. Do I have that correctly?'

'This is what I have been told,' said Haras.

Ansu nodded. 'Keep it in one place for a little while and perhaps I can sever it from its roots.'

Haras looked suspicious. 'Only a senior priest can attempt such a thing.'

Sasan looked around. 'But we don't *know* that we can hurt or even contain one of these things.'

Ansu smiled. 'Life is full of risk.'

Sasan looked at Dahlia. 'You're the one who—'

She smiled brilliantly. 'I'm the cautious one, you mean. But not here. People are dying.'

Sasan leant very close. 'Answer me this, then. Qna Liras is one of the toughest Lightbringers. He's one of the Masran priests, and not the greatest among them, correct? So check my logic. They can't handle these entities. Why can you?'

Aranthur met Sasan's eyes.

'I admit, it is a sobering thought.' He shrugged. 'But I think it is because they are human, and feel defeated. We . . .'

He wanted to say something noble, but nothing came to him.

'We're young and arrogant,' Ansu said. 'Let's go and die trying. Really, is life worth so many questions?'

'See, that's exactly what I'm afraid of,' Sasan admitted. 'I can't even fight back.'

'I'll protect you,' Dahlia said.

Sasan sighed. 'The things I do for love.'

His humour sounded forced, and Dahlia frowned.

Out in the dark streets of Al-Khaire, their confidence did seem arrogance, and utterly misplaced.

The fog was thick. Torches on houses and corner lanterns were mere smudges of light in the thick darkness, and their glow could be as confusing as the darkness itself.

Aranthur prepared a variety of magelights, and in the end, cast two, one on each knee. Lights low to the ground appeared to throw a better light, although the movement of his legs could make the fog seem to be alive, an illusion that didn't help them at all.

Dahlia put her own magelight at her waist.

The streets were empty, and they walked south through the warren of alleys behind the market, headed for the riverside, where the poorest neighbourhoods were, and from where they'd received rumours of attacks.

Aranthur raised his magesight.

'This way,' he said.

He was looking for *sihr*, and there was a bonfire of it burning almost due south, past the Temple of Aploun, who in Masr was known as Lyra. They entered the Square of Lyra, with more than a hundred statues of the god, some standing and some seated, all in ancient, stiff styles, the bodies curiously rendered, half-turned away.

In the fog, they were unearthly. As they moved along the square, each statue loomed up, as if summoned, and the shifting magelights brought the stone to restless life.

Far in the distance, there was screaming. It appeared to come from everywhere.

Aranthur, focused on the *sihr*, led them into a blind alley behind the massive temple portico. Dahlia felt her way out, and moved to the left, then back to the south on a small street that grew narrower and narrower.

'Stop,' Aranthur said.

Dahlia, who was in the lead, came back.

'What is it?' she asked.

'We're not thinking. All the magelights are just giving us away. We need to think as if we're on a battlefield.'

'We're going to move through the fog in the dark?' Sasan asked. 'That's your plan?'

'Yes,' Dahlia said. 'He's right.'

The Masran priest spoke up. 'I think we should go back. I think we will all become food for this entity and to no purpose. We cannot stumble around in the darkness—'

'You can go back,' Dahlia said.

Aranthur took Sasan by the shoulder.

'Put the four shields in front – put Jalu'd and Haras behind. Dahlia, come to think of it, you're the most powerful – you get behind too. Then if something comes at us from behind, we have a sword and a shield at the back.'

'Behind us,' Ansu nodded, as if he hadn't considered all the possible directions.

There was screaming.

'Why is no one running away?' Jalu'd asked.

Without lights, their progress was much slower; every broken pot, every dead dog was an obstacle, and a load of fallen timber was like a wall. They inched their way along the street and then into a winding alley.

'This must be the Al-Suf,' Haras said. 'Yes. There are the perfumers.'

They could all smell the perfumers.

The ground began to slope. They were walking downhill on a narrow, cobbled street. The cobbles were fragments of ancient monuments worn smooth by thousands of feet passing over them, invisible now in the fog.

'Stop,' Aranthur said. 'It's ahead of us.'

A woman screamed.

There was a flash, like red lightning, and the fog just ahead of them was illuminated for less than a heartbeat. But it was not the sickly bile-yellow of their last entity, but instead, was lit with capillaries of scarlet, as if the fog had blood vessels . . .

'Shields,' Dahlia said.

Three shields flashed bright blue. In each case, the area covered by the shield was greater than the surface area of the material artifact.

'Lap them,' Aranthur said.

'Light,' Dahlia said.

'Oh, Goddess of Wisdom, save your children,' Sasan said.

All four adepts engaged their lights together.

Two red-veined tendrils shot out of the fog and slammed into their blue-lit shields. Aranthur expected a feeling of impact, but there was none. Nor did the red tentacles attempt to climb *over* the shields.

Ansu rolled a beautiful array of lights off his hands and began chanting a mantra. The pool of *sihr* shrank away like a kicked dog.

Dahlia and Jalu'd unleashed together. A beam of gold and an emerald green pulse struck the fog, and it writhed. There was *something* inside it, and it made a sound, like the metallic grating of an ungreased wheel.

Aranthur cast his *aspis*. He glanced back. Haras was working with a string of beads. Jalu'd was twirling, one hand in the air.

Behind them, illuminating them in a terrible parody of light, was a pit of *sihr*. It was black as pitch and deep as a thousand hells.

Aranthur sang his new *transference* and the *saar* flowed out of him and into the *sihr*. There was a glow like heated metal all across the malignant thing.

Dahlia whirled, already casting.

'Behind us!' Aranthur said, as calmly as he could manage.

In one of the bravest acts of his life, he turned to face the red-flashed thing in front, ignoring the threat from behind. With his *aspis* he batted away attempts to circumvent their defence, and he felt Jalu'd's back against his.

'Eyes front,' he said to Sasan.

Sasan was trying to look behind him, and he was breathing like a bellows.

Aranthur threw another *transference*. In fact, he realised how to roll such a casting in a continuous stream, the way Qna Liras did – it was like music, or like an argument in *mathematika*. He unleashed a chain of attacks and the red-streaked fog attacked, billowing in ever denser cords. His *aspis* couldn't be everywhere – a lash caught his left leg and the pain was intense – but the entity's attempt to dominate him with fear failed against his own concentration.

He drew his sword. It glowed a dull blue, as if the light came from deep within the metal.

Not unless there is no other choice, the sword said.

Haras, the priest, raised his right hand, his string of beads now a noose. He tightened them with two fingers until the whole string vanished into his hand.

The red-marbled fog flickered...

Ansu's light show intensified until it was like the heart of a lightning storm.

Aranthur turned, raised his sword over Jalu'd's head, and played his continuous beam of *saar* over the black maw behind them.

Dahlia was down. The Masran priest stood his ground, a crescendo of shields whirling around both of them. Jalu'd leapt, danced, and vanished into the cloud, whirling like a storm cloud of green light.

Aranthur's *saar* cut into the thing like a child cutting cake.

It fled. Its emanation rolled over Jalu'd and left him dancing alone, ten paces deep in the real fog.

Aranthur whirled, but Haras was rolling something between his hands. Sasan knelt by Dahlia.

'She's breathing,' he said.

'She overspent.' Aranthur put a hand on her forehead. 'Eagle. We'll have to carry her.'

'We got one,' Ansu said. 'And we defeated the other. We can do this.'

'Let's save Dahlia and then we can talk about whether we won or lost,' Aranthur said. He filed away 'got one' for another day.

'The shields work,' Sasan said, his voice a little shaky. 'Colour's coming back to her face...'

Indeed, by the light of their shields, Dahlia's face lost the white-grey of death.

Her eyes flickered open.

'Fuck,' she said, 'I'm not dead.'

Qna Liras held Haras' string of beads in a web of force. The others were gathered in a circle around the sacred fire in the sanctuary of Aploun. All of them were standing except Dahlia, who was sitting, and Sasan, who knelt by her.

'Incredible,' he said.

'Think of it as a proof of concept,' Ansu said.

Haras said. 'I only caught a very small piece. But the *working* you taught me—'

Qna Liras frowned. 'That's enough.'

'With the glyphs,' Aranthur said, 'you can rebuild the defences.'

'With the shields,' Sasan said, 'you can counter-attack when you must – and you can confine any break-in.'

'And with this –' Haras pointed at the beads – 'you can cut the entities off from their—'

'Gods,' Qna Liras said. 'The things that were released are ... like gods. While you were running off into the city risking the future for a little entertainment, I was deliberating with my order. What we think has happened...'

He was looking at the fragment of an *Apep-Duat*, trapped in the web of the string of beads.

'It is incredible. We haven't done this for centuries.'

Ansu smiled. 'Merely brilliant. Incredible is too much.'

Qna Liras shook his head.

'Tell us what happened,' Dahlia said. 'And tell us about harnessing these entities, since that is plainly what you do.'

Qna Liras hesitated. 'I'll do my best to explain. The Pure sent us offers last year, and in the spring they took Antioke, at the head of the Delta. Antioke is not necessarily yours – there was much debate here as to whether Masr was under threat. When your fleet appeared before Antioke, there was more debate.' He shook his head. 'I was here for none of this, you understand. Regardless, then, suddenly, an attack on the Black Pyramid. Only the gods know what they intended. The priest who survived says that the Disciple was looking for something.' Qna Liras smiled grimly. 'We assume he was looking for the Black Stone.

'When he didn't find it, he began destroying the ritual altars inside the Black Pyramid.' The Magos shrugged. 'Anger? Rage? Frustration? Some horrible intention of annihilation?' He looked around at them. 'Regardless. Something broke free. But it could not fully open the gate. Or rather, one prisoner broke free, and the others...' He shook his head. 'It appears that the others tried to restrain it. Of course, we can't understand them.'

'If they are gods,' Sasan asked, 'why are they wandering about killing villagers?'

'Metaphysikal insanity?' Dahlia asked.

'What a terrifying thought,' Aranthur said.

Qna Liras nodded. 'What best we guess, at least partly based on your little escapade, is that the entities are still caught in the framework of the... I can call it a gate, but it doesn't go anywhere. It's a gate to nowhere – a universe with a single door and no access to the *Aulos*. I'm sorry, this is not my area of study. The point is a practical one, however. The ... gods ... are still in there, except one or two, who escaped. And the ones still inside can emit these ... these killing things, powerful, although not full *Apep-Duat*. More like wraiths. They wander about, killing. Purely to gather *power*, so that the entities can grow and in the end, *eventuate*.'

Aranthur shrugged in his lack of comprehension.

Dahlia was as perplexed as he.

'How did they become so powerful in the first place?' she asked.

'The Disciple fed them,' Haras said. 'One of us saw him do it.'

Aranthur was shaking his head. 'What can the Pure hope to gain—'

'They sought the effect,' Dahlia said. 'Of course they did. The destabilisation of Masr, and the opening of a gate to the winds of magik.'

'But that's insane,' Qna Liras said. 'They caused the deaths of thousands – if that gate fails ... millions. Maybe everyone.'

Dahlia shook her head. 'The Master ... does not think the way we do. He takes risks. He assumes that your Masran priests will fix it. After it has accomplished what he wants.'

'Or he doesn't care,' Aranthur said. 'And in one raid, he knocked Masr out of the war.'

'Sophia,' Sasan breathed. 'How many of these ancient gods are in the Black Pyramid?'

'Ten thousand,' Qna Liras said. 'So far, according to what we have divined, we're facing between six and ten.' He took a breath. 'Listen – what I say is a secret known only to a handful of initiates. *This has happened before.* We have traps for *Apep-Duat* that escape – sometimes we even ... use them ...'

'Use them?' Dahlia was frowning at the beads.

'But now we know how to save this city, and we can limit the damage—' Ansu began.

'Until the food runs out,' Qna Liras said.

'Imperial fleet, major food lift, and a lot of magik support,' Aranthur said to Dahlia.

She nodded. 'This is not for us to fix. We need serious support.'

Qna Liras made a face. 'I would like to tell you that Masr will heal its own wounds,' he said. 'But I don't think we can last more than a few weeks, even with the glyphs and shields. Food – and more Magi.

I know, better than most of my brethren, how powerful the Academy is, and the *Studion*. Send me fifty Academicians. And we will close the rift. I agree that it can be done.'

Aranthur took a deep breath.

'I have to go to Antioke,' he said. 'And then I will go straight to Megara.'

Dahlia nodded. 'I will go with you.'

Sasan chewed his lip. 'I want to go back to Safi,' he said. 'Maybe that's just a dream, but—'

'It is a good dream,' Jalu'd said. 'I would go with you. But we are not yet strong enough. Bide, my brother. The tide has not yet turned.'

Ansu nodded. 'For my part,' he said, 'I am much closer to home here. And I think I can make a real contribution to holding this city.' He glanced at Haras. 'I will stay if you will have me.'

'Ansu!' Aranthur said.

Ansu shrugged. 'Pleasant as I have found this whole game of playing soldier,' he said with a fair amount of sarcasm, 'the awful truth is that we have come to a parting. I came west to bring a drake – and to look into the powers of the Pure. Now I have seen their works at first hand, and I can no longer dismiss them. Instead, I want to hurry home and prepare my own people to give them the reception they deserve. And who knows? Perhaps the way to defeat the Master is from the East.'

Aranthur threw his arms around the prince.

'I know,' Ansu said. 'I will miss you too.'

'And you owe us a year's rent on our rooms, you ingrate,' Dahlia growled. 'Now we have to find another room-mate.'

'Who knows? Perhaps I will return and study your ways of magik. In the meantime, I'm out of money... You've already spent it all on the shields.'

'I cannot abandon my city in the hour of her need,' Qna Liras said. 'So I will stay here. But I would appreciate it if you would take this young priest with you to be our ambassador to the Emperor. I would go myself, or send someone far more senior, but much of our hierarchy died eight days ago, and more have been taken since. We will need the survivors to hold the line. You say that the Master takes great risks. Now I must take one. Haras will carry our most precious relic with him. I cannot risk its fall, either to the Master or the entities.'

Aranthur met the Magos' eyes.

'You are now in ... command?' he asked.

Qna Liras spread his hands. 'Among senior priests, like the more advanced Magi, there is no "command". But most will follow my lead, now that I have returned.'

'Why did you ever leave?' Dahlia asked.

Qna Liras smiled without any warmth.

'I was exiled for my views. And now all that I feared has come to pass, they want me to save them.' He motioned for Haras. 'This young man will go with you, carrying something incredibly precious. Perhaps the anxiety will grind away a little of his arrogance. In truth, I cannot spare him – the most promising of the Magi of his generation – but spare him I must.' He looked around. 'And I will send one of the temple's most dangerous servants. To protect the Black Stone, and Haras, and even you.' He shrugged. 'She is a bit of a two-edged sword, but I have no stronger weapon. Also, a company of soldiers. I don't wish to lose a single soldier, but I have a small group who want to leave.'

Ansu smiled. 'Surely all soldiers, given the choice, might consider leaving.'

'I suspect that you underestimate our priest-soldiers. But these are mercenaries. They served us where ... political faction might have interfered ... Never mind. It does not matter. I will only say that they have done an incalculable service for us, and faced the Disciple, and lived. I wish them well.' He nodded to Aranthur. 'And they are your countrymen. They want to go home – you are going that way. The arrangement suits everyone but me – I need every sword I can raise.' He shrugged. 'So be it. I am gambling with someone else's money, as we say here in Al-Khaire.'

'There's an Arnaut here?' Aranthur asked.

It was as likely that he'd find dragon-head gable ends on an Al-Khaire balcony.

Qna Liras nodded. 'He'll meet you at your boat. I have an armed *trabaccolo* readying on the river. Or rather, because everyone is terrified of the riverside, I'm having the boat prepared in the Temple Canal. You'll launch from there, and you may have to fight your way out.' He smiled. 'I doubt it, though. Because we'll take back a piece of the Al-Jasr neighbourhood at dawn, with your shields and a lot of magik. Ansu, if you'd be so kind ...'

'At your service.'

'I expect that we'll distract the entity completely, but I have no idea how an insane monster with godlike powers, imprisoned for thousand of years and on the verge of escape, sees the world.' Qna Liras smiled.

Aranthur shook his head. 'I wanted a life of adventure,' he said.

Sasan smiled at him. 'I blame you, then.'

At dawn a day later, four companies of black-turbaned soldier-priests bearing glyph-shields moved off from the inner walls into the poorest neighbourhood in the city, the Al-Jasr. From the Temple of Lyra's prayer tower, Aranthur could see the new, red sun touching their spear points in the alleys to the east.

He leant out over the stone railing.

'Are we ready?' he asked.

'Not yet,' called an unfamiliar voice.

Down in the stone-paved temple courtyard, there was a man in a velvet coat and a white fustanella.

'Some of my little bastards are still in the arms of their temporary loves. Give me a few minutes!'

All this in the dialect of home. The man, clearly a Souliote, waved.

Aranthur shouted down, 'Quick as you can!' in his best officer voice. In Souliote.

Then he went back to watching the lower town.

From so high, it was relatively easy to follow the progress of the 'attack', although it was difficult to pin down exactly what the Masran warriors were attacking. They moved through the streets efficiently, though; as they came to intersections, they split into smaller bands, so that they occupied a united front.

Aranthur saw the moment at which they encountered the entity. There was a sparkle of blue, and the shrill sound of a shouted order, repeated.

And then a whirlwind of *Ars Magika* – too fast to follow. In a hundred heartbeats, the *sihr* was walled off by shields – enclosed – and overwhelmed.

The result was roughly the same as that of a young boy hitting a hornet's nest with a stick.

Suddenly, pools of *sihr* emerged from abandoned houses, or from the very streets themselves. It was more like a rising tide than an attack.

People screamed. There were still people living in the Al-Jasr, and they panicked, scattering away from the emanations.

Aranthur saw them as dust clouds.

And the entity across the river displayed itself as a firestorm of black-purple-white fire around the Black Pyramid. There was a cataclysmic crack, as if all the lightning in the world had flashed at once. A mighty bolt of black fire fell on the Al-Jasr.

And Qna Liras' seamless shield responded.

The outpouring of *sihr* and *saar* was so great that Aranthur's fingers tingled and his hair writhed.

With fearsome discipline, the soldier-priests opened ranks, let the screaming crowd past, and closed their shields across ten alleys and a dozen streets. Their line was ragged now, and assailed from every direction. In one case, the panicked people ran through their line and into a dark maw of voracious evil.

The Souliote came into the Temple court with a dozen men at his back. As many more were pushing through the gates.

'All present, Centark!' he roared.

The man had a deep voice and sounded so much like Aranthur's uncle that he had a moment of confusion.

'Go!' Aranthur yelled.

He took one more glance at the fighting – if the mute defence of six hundred soldiers against a wave of sorcery could be called a fight.

Then he ran down the long, twisting steps of the prayer tower.

He reached the bottom and ran along the towering wall, past the prayer arches, and past the long side of the pillared nave. The ground sloped down towards the river. There was a processional way where devotees of the god were taken after death, down to the canal-side docks where they could be transported to the necropolis across the river, in normal times. Now, there were hundreds of corpses close-wrapped in linen and stacked like a winter's firewood. Aranthur threw the tail of his turban over his face and ran down the ramp towards the muddy canal.

Somewhere to the east, there were three explosions that shook the ground. Aranthur watched the rapid plumes of smoke rise as buildings caught fire. He concentrated on running for the boat.

The riverboat was a *trabaccolo*, low and fifty paces long and black – a practical boat with little decoration, equally at home on the great river or at sea. Her pitch-coated black sides shone in the sun, and her two masts and long bowsprit stood out from the smoke. On board, Vilna stood amidships, shouting orders at men in the shallow hold. A dozen Arnauts in fustanellas were piling aboard, stowing their linen sacks against the netting with a skill that told of long experience on boats. The Nomadi and the Safians looked ill at ease with the sudden appearance of the Arnauts. In the bow and stern, a dozen Masran sailors in white linen kilts stood ready to cast off from lines already loosened on the pier's stone bollards.

'Get us underway!' Aranthur called

He leapt from the stone pier to the deck, which was crammed with gear, people, and horses.

The sailors in the bow looked aft. Aranthur turned towards the command deck; he'd been on ships before.

'Captain?' he called.

'Here,' shouted a woman in the bow.

She was tall and covered in tattoos where her brown skin showed. She wore black silk trousers, a black khaftan and a black turban with a veil, and had a large and very rosy *kuria* crystal on a black chain around her neck. Something about her gave the impression of immense strength.

Aranthur saluted.

'Aranthur Timos,' he said as he moved towards her, passing an angry Ariadne and stepping over a crate of unstowed chickens.

'Yasmina Inoques,' the woman said with a slight bow, in accented Byzas. 'Syr Timos, I am to obey you in all things save those required for the safety of my ship.'

'I'm very sorry we didn't . . .'

Aranthur waved in the direction of the Temple of Lyra, as if to excuse the whole war.

Another pair of explosions rocked the city.

'Get us underway, please,' Aranthur said.

'Doing my best, but I need all this detritus off my deck. Animals. Arnauts, too.' She pointed at the man in the velvet waistcoat. 'Get your marines . . . No. Tell your people to get these *horsemen* to clear my deck.' She glanced at Aranthur. 'I am not convinced that this entire attempt is not insane.' She enunciated every word in an unnatural way, as if she'd learnt Byzas from an automaton.

Ariadne disappeared into the maw of the hold, held by two leather straps under her belly.

Dahlia was standing on the command deck, just behind Myr Inoques.

'Something has gone very wrong. One of the entities was waiting.' She pointed to a viewer. 'I set this last night.'

Aranthur watched from a high vantage point. Dahlia's viewer was better cast than his own ever were, and she'd cast it on an object – a tall tower in the Temple of One Hundred Women.

The black-clad Masran priests were being systematically cut off and overwhelmed.

'Whatever it is, it can reach across running water,' Dahlia said.

'And our friends are in it.'

Aranthur was watching someone's Steppe pony going into the cradle. The ugly horse was the last big animal on deck. Two sailors were chasing a sheep. Other bundles were being thrown into the hold through the forward grating.

Sasan shook his head. 'We're never going to find anything again.'

'*Jaryah!*' shouted a tall man with a white kilt and intricate whorls of tattoos showing.

Myr Inoques nodded, shouted a long order. Aranthur watched the low hull drift away from the pier, helped along by four men and a woman with long pikes pushing against the shore.

'We are underway,' Myr Inoques said. 'It's going to be bad out on the river.'

Her Byzas was accented and he had to pay close attention to her to understand. She used terms he didn't know, like 'steerage way', that took him time and concentration to understand.

'Mera!' she shouted at the white-kilted man, and he answered.

Aranthur ignored them and went through the small leather bag in which he kept his store of *kuria* crystals, most of them looted from a certain shop in Megara.

'I have an idea,' he said.

Dahlia nodded. 'If that thing spots us, we're dead.'

'Where's the priest? Haras? I need a clear space of deck, maybe two paces by two paces, preferably amidships.'

The captain raised a tattooed eyebrow, but then shrugged.

'So be it.'

'And...' Aranthur grinned. 'And a...' He bludgeoned his memory for the word. Sailors had an implement... 'Loggerhead,' he said in Byzas.

She nodded. 'Yes, I know this thing.'

'Or, whatever you use to... heat. So you can smooth your pitch.'

Days on tramp freighters as a working passenger had given him a slight knowledge about seagoing tools and labour.

'We put the fires out when we go to sea. It takes fire to heat this tool.'

'We can make fire and heat,' Dahlia said. 'We are... Magi.' She glanced at Aranthur.

'I know,' Myr Inoques said, with a slight smile.

'What are we doing?' Dahlia asked with mock sweetness.

He was already clearing the centre of the amidships deck. The Arnauts watched him with open curiosity.

'I'm almost afraid to tell you.'

'Try me,' Dahlia said.

'We inscribe the glyph of warding on the ship.'

Dahlia laughed. 'Good. I thought so, too.'

'The glyph will only be as powerful as the *saar* we put in,' he said. She shrugged.

'My thought...' Aranthur was hesitant to give it voice. It was a stupid idea.

But tactically sound. They had to escape and the entities barred the river. As if they knew...

'My thought,' he said with false confidence, 'is to cut the entity or entities in the city off from the other shore. With the ship, and our... casting.'

Dahlia's eyes widened involuntarily. Then she gave him one of her twisted half-smiles.

'By the Goddess of Wisdom. That may be the best foolish notion I've ever heard.' She looked at the haze on the far shore, and the rippling, heat-distorted pyramids. 'But it will come after us.'

Aranthur shrugged. 'It's not good at surprises.'

'Hmm.' Dahlia waved at the lower city, where broken towers looked like the splintered teeth of a beaten man. 'We surprised them last night. Today, they are ready with ambushes.'

A sailor appeared with an iron bar that had a heavy copper teardrop riveted to the end. Ordinarily, this tool was heated in a brazier and used to melt a line of pitch to make the ship's seams tight and waterproof.

'I'll do it,' Dahlia said.

Without apparent effort, she made the copper glow a dull red in the bright sun. Aranthur could feel the heat.

He took his buckler off his pack and laid it at the foot of the mainmast. Then, working quickly, he copied the glyph on the buckler and burned the glyph into the deck.

The captain turned her head away, as if it was too painful to watch.

'Heat it again,' he said to Dahlia.

A sailor took a wet rag and ran it over the whole glyph. The other sailors watched with horror. All of them clearly feared the fire.

Aranthur took the newly heated thing and bored six small holes into the symbols of the glyph. He put all but one of his remaining crystals into the holes.

When he was done, the ship was moving slowly down the muddy canal. A handful of long oars protruded from each side.

'Tell me what happens next,' Aranthur asked the captain.

She was watching forward, over the bow. She shouted something in Masri and turned.

'In a very few minutes we come ... the mouth of the canal. We come ... *to* ... the mouth. Yes?' She shrugged.

'I understand.'

'Good. Then we turn into the current, and get the sails up. If we live to get them up, we go very fast indeed. Even faster if ...' She smiled mirthlessly. 'Never mind, foreigner. We will move fast.'

'I'd like you to stay near this shore,' Aranthur said.

She nodded. 'Yes. I have no wish to meet one of the entities.'

'What in a thousand iron hells are we doing, Captain?' asked a large, bearded Arnaut.

'I have no idea. Ask this man, he appears to be in charge.'

Captain Inoques turned away and called a string of orders down the now-cleared deck.

'Are we fighting?' the big man asked. 'I'm Kallotronis.'

'Timos,' Aranthur said, offering his hand the Souliote way.

The big man grinned. 'Flavi?'

'Over the mountain,' Aranthur answered. 'Schiavon?'

'*Po, bosi!*' Kallotronis said in Northern Souliote. 'Are we fighting?'

Aranthur pointed out over the pylons at the mouth of the canal, towards the looming bulk of the pyramids.

'You know about the *Apep-Duat*?' he asked.

'Little brother, I was fucking *there*.'

Kallotronis grinned, and his mouth was full of gold teeth.

'So, yes, we're fighting,' Aranthur said. 'But it's mostly Magi. We'll protect you.'

The big man grinned and his teeth glittered.

'Never yet met anything that could stand against a rifle ball. My lads dropped one of their *Exalted*.'

Aranthur didn't say, *I've put two down by myself.* He was tempted, because Arnauts played this game of bragging. But it was the wrong time and Kallotronis was not likely to be easily impressed.

'Stay ready, then,' he said.

'Here we go,' called the captain.

The river was choppier than the canal, and the steeply curved black bow bit into the waves of the river and the whole boat began to move like a living thing.

'Load!' called Kallotronis.

'I'm turning downriver,' the captain said to Aranthur, and he nodded.

Dahlia looked across the river, almost due south.

'I can almost *see* it,' she said.

Aranthur *invoked*. His *Aulos* sight flowed over his eyes, exposing the six long arms of black *sihr* that crossed the river like long, low bridges of malevolence. Now he could locate them precisely.

The captain came up beside him.

'You have my people terrified of fire,' she said. 'Please explain.'

'I'm finished,' Aranthur explained.

He pointed mutely at the glyph. Dahlia was kneeling by it, and even as they watched, she put *saar* into the pattern and it glittered like diamonds in the sun.

A tiny thrill, like the charge of a nearby lightning bolt, passed through the deck.

The captain's eyes met Aranthur's.

'What is this? I have no time for argument. Explain.'

'It is a sign of warding, a glyph that—'

'I have served the priests all my life,' she shot back. 'You have turned my ship into a *baraka* thing. Yes?' Her eyes spoke more than her words

– of authority ignored, of anger. 'This should have been discussed. Foreigner, do you even know what cargo this ship carries?'

She turned and shouted an order in Masri. A long yard was going up the foremast, and then, as if the ship was an insect shedding its cocoon, the great mainmast yard was cut loose from its place. The ship was turning into the strong river current; already it was moving faster in the deep green water.

Two sailors high above them belayed the long yard.

The captain was watching them.

'I bear a heavy burden. I cannot allow you to make my ship a target.'

'Your priests and soldiers are dying over there,' Aranthur said. 'We can help them – perhaps even secure a victory.'

'Where is the young priest?' Inoques asked, and then asked it again in Masri.

She shouted an order at the foremast, and a lateen sail dropped from the yard and filled. Instantly, the ship heeled with the wind, which blew almost straight downriver.

'We will be forced to fight the entity across the river either way,' Aranthur asserted.

They were perhaps five hundred paces from the first long arm of *sihr*.

With a growl like distant thunder, an almost invisible line of black shot across the river and detonated in the warehouse district along the shore. Debris, and a whole man, were thrown high in the air. The concussion hit the sails, and then came the sound.

The captain glanced at the new smoke, and then across the river at the cracked pyramid. Down at the glyph.

Haras, the priest, came up the fore hatch. He spoke carefully to the captain, as if he feared her. She waved a tattooed arm at the glyph and then called orders to the sailors in the mainmast. They cut the yarns that held the main lateen sail, and it came down. Sailors on the deck caught its trailing lines and belayed them.

Haras said something to the captain, with an emphasis that came through despite Aranthur's lack of the Masri language.

Haras glanced at Aranthur. He shrugged with genuine fatalism.

'Qna Liras told me to follow your lead in all things, unless it meant the destruction of my charge. You know what we carry.'

Aranthur was painfully aware that Haras meant the Black Stone, but he had no concrete idea of what it was or what it meant, save that it was a very holy relic and that the Pure had wanted it.

The Captain looked at him again, like his father sizing up a new pig at market.

'Very well.' She wasn't pleased, but she was obedient. 'We say, *Ma t'ayyatush 'ala fukharkum da luh 'umrzay a'markum.* Command me, foreigner.'

Aranthur smiled as best he could.

'I won't know what we're doing until we encounter the first . . . enemy. It's dead ahead, about two hundred paces.'

She didn't blink. 'I can see it,' she said icily.

Aranthur wasn't sure how the tattooed woman could see it if she lacked his spells, but he nodded sharply.

He looked at Dahlia. 'Ready?'

'For what?'

'When we cross the *sihr*,' he said quickly, 'we shoot what we can into the arm while it is severed.'

She nodded. 'Yes.'

Aranthur glanced at Haras.

'The ship itself should sever the arm,' he said to Haras. 'If you can work your beads . . .'

Haras grew pale. 'Gods,' he spat. 'Very well.'

Aranthur wrote in his mind the red *aspis* four times.

'Everyone down,' he said.

He had no idea what was going to happen when they hit the arm. It had no corporeal being; he couldn't imagine that the ship would 'crash' into it.

But he didn't know. He didn't really know anything.

'What did she say? *Ma tukktash* something?' he asked Haras.

The Masran priest gave a slight smile.

'It is a saying in Al-Khaire. Don't cry over the broken pot – you'll be ending the same way.'

'Ouch,' Aranthur said.

The combination of wind and current threw the ship forward, so that they were accelerating downriver. The ship pitched slightly, and the deck was at a slight angle. The wind at their backs was strong. Inoques stood on her command deck, and she was singing to her ship, or so it seemed to Aranthur. His magesight was up. Suddenly he saw that she was *puissant*, burning with the fire of the *Aulos*. Her signing was rich in *power* – she was controlling the wind. She burned like the sun with *saar*. And *sihr*.

He didn't have time to think.

'Ready!' he called.

The Arnaut marines and the Nomadi were crouched under the bulwarks. Those with matchlocks had their matches lit. The sailors were mostly on the foredeck, lying flat.

When the arm of *sihr* filled his forward vision, Aranthur put a hand on the largest *kuria* and ignited it. It powered the others to life, and a flash of blue-white *saar* raced outwards through the ship, up the masts, across the rigging, along the deck.

The bow of the ship struck the black fog. The white fire cut it the way a sword cuts, and the black fog roiled away.

The smallest crystal burned out, drained.

Then the second.

Aranthur realised that the rigging, not the ship, was doing most of the cutting of the arm, but the ship, as a giant ward, was functioning.

'It's too big,' Dahlia said.

The foresail burst into flame.

Aranthur put a hand on the ward and almost had his entire reservoir of *power* stripped from him. Years of dance and swordsmanship powered his flinch response, and he rolled away, breaking physical contact before all his *saar* was gone.

And then they were through. Dahlia cast something green, and Jalu'd poured jade fire on the flinching arm. But Haras made his loop of beads into a metaphysikal noose, a Möbius of *power*, and the arm of the wraith-god thrashed in his net.

And was taken.

'Sophia!' Aranthur said.

The whole severed arm of *sihr* began to dissipate like smoke in a high wind, caught in the net of the beads.

Dahlia flashed him a smile. Sasan slapped Haras' back, and the Masr priest smiled grimly.

'I'm still fighting it,' he hissed.

They had no more than three breaths before they struck the second arm. It was moving; Aranthur had the impression of a guiding intelligence flinching away, and then the bow and the standing rigging were ripping through the *sihr*-stuff. It was different, this time, more like a saw cutting than a sword.

Two crystals burned out together, going steel grey. The deck was hot. Dahlia knelt by the ward.

White fire played in the tops, and a sailor screamed.

Kallotronis was laughing, and his deep, booming laugh was like a battle cry.

The black fog was all around them, and the Arnauts began firing their *carabins* into the stuff. Vilna glanced at Aranthur; he nodded.

The Nomadi fired a volley into the *sihr*.

Aranthur grabbed Dahlia's shoulder and wrenched her away from the pattern on the deck. She fell back against the mainmast.

'The ship is too damned big,' she said between clenched teeth.

The last crystal, the largest, burst with a *pop*, spraying them with fragments. One cut across Aranthur's face like a hot knife.

The ship burst from the cloud of *sihr* as the stuff began to close in around them.

Inoques stretched her arms wide on the command deck and sang an invocation, and a web of purple-black hung over the ship – *sihr* and *saar* woven together.

Haras was down on the deck, wrestling with something invisible.

Jalu'd leapt onto the glyph and began to dance, singing in Safiri.

The second severed arm was writhing, losing substance in the *Aulos*, bleeding as if it truly was a severed arm, but it wasn't caught in a web, or trapped by Haras, and its thrashings were lethal.

'Shit,' Dahlia said, and her shields flared to gold. Aranthur got all four of his *aspides* out. The ship flared bright white, and a titanic purple flash blinded them.

'Now they know we're here,' Dahlia said.

The tattooed captain put a long-fingered, hennaed hand on the snake of *sihr* trapped among the beads of Haras' *working*. She grunted, but the *Apep-Duat* was forced into the net.

The mainsail was on fire. Aranthur didn't need anyone to tell him that the rigging and sails were the least efficient conductors of the glyph, and were delicate in too many ways.

Mir Jalu'd kept dancing.

Haras raised his head and glanced at Aranthur. There was a thin cheering from the bank; the glitter of steel told a story. Some of the priests had just been freed from the combat by the destruction of the black arms.

'I can...' Haras began, hesitantly. He was looking at Inoques. 'Do not trust her!' he spat.

'Ware!' Aranthur and Dahlia shouted together.

Four sets of shields burned and then singed away. Aranthur was knocked to the deck. There was blood on the surface of his skin. A dozen men and women were dead or dying; one sailor had apparently been turned inside out. The deck had blood on it, and...

'Use it!' screamed Inoques. 'I can't hold that thing alone!'

Aranthur tried to raise a shield and watched his forming thought shredded by a black hand in his head.

'Do it!' Aranthur shouted at the stunned priest. 'Whatever it is!'

Haras knelt by the glyph.

A third titanic blow struck the ship. Aranthur's shields were crushed as if they were paper. He watched the dark fog come down. Inoques alone stood, glowing with much the same purple fire as lashed them from above.

And then her web frayed...

Stretched...

And holes burned through.

Aranthur thought, *Damn. I was wrong. And now we all die.*

And then, between one heartbeat and another, the entire ship was encased in darkness. But it was not the oily evil of the *sihr*. It was as if they were framed in highly polished black marble, cut so thin that it was almost transparent.

Aranthur could just see Sasan, winding the lock of his puffer, Vilna, a powder horn in his hand, Dahlia, one hand on the glyph, ready to give whatever she had left. Jalu'd danced slowly, Inoques was on one knee, and Haras...

Haras stood as if holding an immense weight.

Aranthur experienced seeing all this, but he could not fully form a thought. Action was impossible. Time did not flow, or if it did, it flowed like honey.

Nothing seemed to happen at all. The universe was a black marble box, held by a priest, and it endured.

And then, in a blink, it was all back: the brilliant sun, the pitching deck, the sticky blood, the screams, the wind, the stench of burning canvas.

Sasan knelt by Dahlia, and she raised her head and kissed him.

'Fuck,' she croaked.

Aranthur was getting to his feet. Aft, past the stern, a thunderstorm seemed to be playing on the middle of the river. To Aranthur's senses, it appeared that the stumps of four arms were gathering, attempting to extrude a seventh. Now dozens of point attacks from the shore were pounding the cloud with lightning from the *outside*.

Dahlia pulled herself up a rack of belaying pins.

A crescendo of *saar* flashed against the black cloud and it flinched away, scuttling towards the pyramid shore.

'That was the Black Stone, I assume,' Aranthur said to Haras, who looked as if he'd run twenty miles. He tried to wipe the blood from his face.

Haras nodded. 'Yes. It was built as a prison, but it occurred to me that it could function both ways.'

'Brilliant,' Dahlia said.

Inoques smiled.

Haras shrugged.

Aranthur sighed. 'I guess my plan was a foolish plan,' he admitted.

Sasan was watching over his shoulder as the retreat of the black fog became a rout.

'Eh?' he said. 'The pot is not yet broken.'

The captain had new sails set in an hour. The wounded were safely stowed, the dead were wrapped in the remains of the mainsail and prepared for burial at sea. Two Arnauts, one Safian, one Nomadi, Batu, and two sailors were dead, with Omga lingering between life and death, badly burnt. Aranthur did what he could for the wounded, as he had more healing than the other casters, but it wasn't much. Kallotronis did as much with his rough and ready medicine, and a chest of drugs that included the Black Lotus for which Masr was famous in the Megara underworld. The powerful narcotic placed the burn victims beyond pain, at least temporarily.

'They will become habituated to the drug,' Haras said.

'Better than roaring their lungs out in pain, *boso*,' snapped Kallotronis.

'Separating a man from the Lotus can take months,' Haras said. 'Or they will become *Laji*, lost to the world, eyes black with the stuff...'

Kallotronis shrugged. 'But alive. The other choice is death.'

'The Lotus is a form of death.'

'Bullshit, priest. I've used it and I'm still me.'

Aranthur stepped in.

'I think that in our current state, Centark Kallotronis has done what was best for everyone,' he said.

'Centark. I like that.' Kallotronis grinned, his gold teeth flashing in the late afternoon light. 'Here, have a wet, syr.'

The Arnaut officer had a skin of respectable wine, and Aranthur took a long pull. Thus fortified, he went to face the captain, but her anger was gone with the heavy burden of combat, and now she was like oiled silk.

She bowed, and then pulled back the veil on her turban so that he could see her face for the first time. Her eyes were large and brilliant, with black pupils, and her eyebrows were tattooed with minute lines of script. Her small, elegant hand was not hennaed. It was covered in the same script, but in red.

'Antioke, syr. I understand. We must pass the Delta – I cannot go this speed amid the islands. With your permission, we touch at the first island, Dalmonna, or at Seta. This is best for wounded, and also for us. We need food and water, and perhaps even some small repairs.'

Aranthur blinked, unsure whether he was being asked or told, and suddenly so tired that nothing made sense.

'Captain,' he said, and then found that he'd lost the ability to speak.

She waited politely.

He shook his head. 'Whatever you think is best. I'm... very sorry about the first half-hour. I never had a chance to meet you – to discuss...' He shrugged. 'I'm sorry.'

She nodded, very serious. 'Good. That's good. I lost three men today – good men.'

She looked away, and he wondered what the lines of writing on her face meant. She had a strange beauty. She was as brown as the purest Byzas, but the lines of tattoos made her seem very exotic. She was as muscular as Dahlia, or even more so.

She turned back to him, her dark eyes on his.

'But...' she said, and then stopped. 'You are dead on your feet.

And nasty with blood. Swim, then go and sleep.' She reached out and touched his shoulder, and squeezed. 'Are you always this thin? Eat.'

He knew very little Masri, but one phrase he'd learned from priest-soldiers. He smiled.

'I obey,' he said in Masri.

Six hours later, the pitching of the ship awoke him. He got clumsily out of the hammock he had no memory of climbing into, got his feet on the deck and climbed a ladder to the main deck.

Myr Inoques was standing by the tiller with a helmswoman and another sailor.

'You are a sailor, I think,' she said.

'I'm a farmer. But I've been on a few ships, and fishing boats.'

She nodded, her eyes on the shadowy figure of a man in the distant bows with a lantern.

'We are entering the Delta. It is not really the river or the sea – it's between, like purgatory. And like purgatory, it is a *very* unpleasant place, unless you are a *kuramax*, of which there are far too many.'

Her Byzas was better already. He guessed that she had travelled widely; she was recalling a language she had once spoken freely.

The water of the Delta was choppier than the great river had been, and even by moonlight, Aranthur could see tiny islands, or perhaps sandbars with a tree or two on them, and floating logs.

The man in the bow called, long and low, like a Masran priest announcing evening prayers, and the woman at the tiller turned them.

As they turned, Aranthur could see lights – tiny oil lamps in houses – and a mud bank in moonlight, with fifty long, sinuous shapes...

'*Kuramax*.' The captain put a hand on his arm and then pointed.

'Lady,' Aranthur muttered.

'Don't worry, foreigner,' she said, her voice light. 'I'll protect you.'

The helmswoman laughed. Aranthur laughed too.

He stayed on the deck, smoked some stock, and Kallotronis joined him. They talked about the Souliote hills and drank wine. Before the stars had moved far, Vilna came on deck.

'I hate ships,' the officer said quietly. 'Like a prison, on water.'

He looked up, saw the Dark Forge and spat into the water.

'This will help,' Aranthur said, handing the nomad Kallotronis' wineskin.

Kallotronis lifted his fingers, deliberately mimicking the sign a priestess made blessing a congregation.

'I liked it when your men started shooting into the evil thing,' Vilna said.

Kallotronis nodded and took the wineskin.

'Probably not worth a shit, but it makes everyone feel better. And who knows? A lucky ball, and maybe you win.' He took a long pull.

'You have fought with . . . *eversham*? Before?' Vilna hesitated.

Aranthur realised that the nomad officer was shaken; that perhaps he was expecting too much from all of them.

Kallotronis leant back and stuck out his long legs.

'I'd take more of that good stock. Eh, *syr*. Do I really need to keep calling you *syr*?'

It was a peculiar moment. Aranthur knew that it was probably important to Vilna; the nomads, despite their freedom, valued hierarchy. But he also knew that among Arnauts, the whole idea of rank was . . . laughable, mostly.

Aranthur knew there was only one answer, with a fighter like Kallotronis.

'Call me whatever you wish. Just don't smoke all the stock.' He refilled the pipe, lit it, and handed it to Kallotronis. 'My friends call me Aranthur.'

Kallotronis smoked for a while.

'Good name,' he said. 'Vilna, I've fought fucking everything. Men, monsters, demons, *baraka, eversham*, ghosts . . .'

He opened his big, dirty linen shirt to show a chest full of amulets and scars. He reached into the fancy velvet doublet he always wore and took out a pistol ball.

Aranthur felt the *sihr*.

'Lady!' he spat.

Kallotronis, having got the reaction he wanted, grinned.

'Don't be a little girl. The Dark magik is the best for the killing.'

Aranthur made the sign of the Eagle without conscious thought.

Kallotronis took a pull at the pipe and handed it to Vilna.

'Eagle doesn't care what weapons we use. Kill your foes. Stay alive.' He shrugged. 'Eagle only cares that you kill the bad ones and let the good ones live, and even then . . .' He grinned. 'I don't make a lot of moral judgements when I'm fighting.'

Vilna drank some wine and nodded.

'How many of the *sihr* bullets do you carry?' Aranthur asked.

'Only two left. I keep them for . . . *eversham* foes. I shot a man with one, once. Didn't mean to, but he was the target that offered.' The Arnaut looked at the stars. 'Nasty. But very effective.' He raised an eyebrow, almost daring Aranthur to make a comment. 'I used one yesterday.'

'Who makes them?' Aranthur asked.

'Hedge wizards. The kind of self-trained idiot who isn't afraid to do a little blood sacrifice to make a little silver.'

'So you know what the cost is . . .'

'So I do, *syr*. Do you?'

Aranthur nodded. He had no trouble meeting the big man's eye. He was a big man himself.

'Yes.'

Kallotronis sat back and reached for the wine.

'Good. Then we don't have to discuss it.'

'I can make you ten balls with *saar*,' Aranthur said.

'Nah. The *saar* flows away. Unless you shoot it immediately. *Sihr* lasts. Because *it is death*.' Kallotronis nodded knowingly.

Aranthur had a moment of revelation. He had been about to refute what Kallotronis said, and then he understood . . .

Sigils and wards were devices for keeping *saar* active.

He reached into his pouch and found the three ancient sling bullets. He put them in Kallotronis' hand.

The Souliote mercenary looked at them carefully.

'Sling bullets,' Aranthur said.

'I know,' the older man said. He pulled his rich beard.

'The sigil would require to be powered. And I have no idea how long the *power* would last.'

Kallotronis frowned. 'If this works, why doesn't everyone do it?'

Aranthur shrugged. 'I don't know, but I'll guess, based on history. In the time of Tirase, the *power* was leaching away, and this sort of device was too . . . expensive, in time and money and *saar*.'

'So?' Kallotronis asked.

Aranthur exerted himself, and all three sling bullets suddenly glowed a fierce blue-white.

And they remained that colour.

Kallotronis whistled.

'Now...' he smiled, and his smile was wicked. 'Now, perhaps, we can fight these things.'

He put the three sling bullets in a horn cup, and they lit a portion of the deck.

'Let's see how long they last,' Kallotronis said.

Inoques came down from her command perch to look at the sling stones. In the darkness, she gave Aranthur a glance that in another woman might have been flirtatious. He didn't know how to read her.

'You are full of *power*,' she said. 'I see why the priest fears you. But you must be more wary – there are old things on this river, and they do not love us, or our powers.' She leant very close. 'You smell of *power*, man.'

'You are a practitioner,' Aranthur said with some embarrassment.

'My people call me *Alassahhr*.' She smiled. 'I might say "wind witch" in Byzas, but witch sounds so primitive, and what I do is very...' She shrugged. 'Careful.'

She smiled again. Aranthur decided that she was flirting. He smiled back. Even though he was sure she was hiding something.

'So please take care.'

'I will not cast again,' he said. 'I have much wisdom yet to learn.'

She nodded. 'Yes, it's good you know this about yourself.' She looked at him carefully, as if assessing the age of a horse. 'If you are the kind of man who can learn, I could teach you.'

He flushed, but it was dark. When she went back to her command deck, though, he found that Vilna was hiding a grin and Kallotronis was laughing quietly.

'She has your number, *boso*.'

'I think *maybee* she wants more than his number,' Vilna said.

Both men laughed. Aranthur had an urge, which he knew was foolish, to show resentment. Instead he smiled.

'I like her tattoos,' he said.

'Which shows that you have some wisdom, *Bahadur*,' Vilna said.

Kallotronis glanced at Vilna. '*Bahadur?*'

Vilna shrugged. 'You'll see, Arnaut-man.'

Kallotronis handed the lit pipe to Aranthur.

'Eagle! Heroes get people killed.' But he rattled the cup with the old sling bullets, which was still bright with new light. 'Still,' he said thoughtfully. 'Still.'

The Delta island of Seta had a great port on the ocean side and a smaller port on the river side. Both were crammed with fishing boats and local river ships, and three great Megaran merchant galleys whose long sides virtually filled the outer harbour, even partially beached on the mud flats.

Inoques made a face. 'Al-Khaire is under siege,' she said soberly. 'No one can run the river.'

'We did,' Aranthur said.

The tattooed face lit up as if the sun rose.

'So we did. But you had me,' she said, a flat statement of fact. But then she relented and smiled. 'Yesterday I was angry. Now I am proud.' She shrugged. 'I have much to learn, too. Emotion is complex.'

The small harbour was so full that she refused to risk her ship.

'We will anchor in the lee of this behemoth,' she said, pointing out the greatest of the Megaran trade galleys. 'And swim ashore.'

Aranthur immediately examined the mudflats and the sandy beach for monsters.

'I'll protect you,' Inoques said, and he couldn't decide whether he was being mocked or not.

'Vilna, go to the three galleys and tell the navarks of the battle and its result,' he said. 'Warn them of events in Al-Khaire. Look for their reactions. Ask what they've heard.'

Vilna saluted.

Dahlia made a face. 'I can do that. They're probably all people I know.' Then she paused.

Aranthur shrugged. 'Mayhap I'm being foolish, or stupidly secretive, like Drako. But something is clearly wrong. I think we need to be wary.'

He called all the troopers together, Safian and Pastun and all. He stepped up on a barrel of salt fish.

'We'll be here until the change of tide tomorrow mid-morning. Anyone not aboard is left behind.' He beckoned to Chimeg. 'Two lines, and we'll put a little coin in their hands.'

Chimeg gave a nod.

Sasan already had a table out, and Dahlia had the rest of Ansu's coins on the table. They managed to give each man and woman about three silver soldii – the price of a few cups of good wine.

Aranthur beckoned to Chimeg and Haran. With Sasan and Vilna, he had a sort of 'command council'. He glanced at Kallotronis, who shrugged and sauntered up as if he, and not Aranthur, were in command.

'I want to give them a night off,' he said. 'Am I being foolish?'

Sasan shook his head. 'No. No one wants to be marooned in this humid hell. But a cup of wine and a night of rest . . . Listen, let me find us a taverna. We can just take it over, keep them together.'

Haran and Vilna both nodded.

'That's the best way,' Vilna agreed.

Aranthur noted this for the future.

'Very well. Inoques says we swim ashore.'

Vilna nodded. 'We all know how to swim. We need to land all the horses and exercise them while the sailors do sailor things. Then we load all the horses back, and post a watch – show everyone where "our" taverna is.'

'You've done this before,' Kallotronis said.

It was obvious that the big Souliote and the wiry Pastun nomad had become, at least allies, and perhaps friends.

Aranthur went to the command deck, where Inoques was speaking with her first mate, the tattooed man in the white kilt. This morning, he saluted Aranthur by placing both fists to his forehead.

'Captain, it is our . . . thought,' he began, 'to choose a taverna and have all our people drink there, together. Could you help us choose one?'

'Immediately,' she said. 'I have a full day's work, but this is a fine notion. The tavernas will be crammed with sailors, but I know a place with a garden. Can you swim?'

'Well enough.'

'Good.' She unwound the black cloth from her chest and dropped her kilt. 'Put your clothes in a bladder,' she said. And then, with a wicked smile, 'You can use a bath, anyway.'

The first mate handed Aranthur an oiled bag.

He was still dressed like a Safian bandit, in voluminous trousers, a dirty shirt, a dusty khaftan that reeked of his old sweat, and a blood-soaked turban that had once been a handsome pale blue. He stripped them off, trying not to watch her muscled, lithe body, neatly covered in lines of script as if an entire book had been written on her – equally, trying to appear as unaffected by nudity as she was.

She prodded his khaftan with a tattooed foot.

'You can't wear this. It's disgusting. Mera?'

Her mate went below into the cabin under the command deck.

'He is my apprentice. A very good apprentice. In a year or less, he will have his own ship.'

She smiled at him again, as if he needed smiles to mollify him.

He tried to stand casually, naked.

She leant over and licked her thumb, and then ran it across his face. He had forgotten the cut there. It was exactly what his mother had done when he was young and had dirt on his face, and he grinned.

She licked her thumb as if tasting his blood, and her eyebrows went up.

'Ah,' she said.

She grinned back. It was not a natural look on her face – forced.

'Share my bed tonight, foreigner?' she asked. 'Since you like what you see?'

Aranthur blushed over most of his body.

The mate brought him a white kilt, which had a thousand pleats and which was not unlike a linen fustanella. Aranthur rolled it tightly with the man's help and put it in the oiled leather sack.

'Come,' Inoques said, and leapt over the side.

Aranthur followed, into the deep green water, and then he was swimming. He was a powerful swimmer, if not a particularly good one, and in moments he was on the beach.

He put the kilt on and let the wind dry his skin. Inoques wrapped herself in black, complete with a head-covering veil of light *katan*; she was almost completely covered. He followed her up the hot sand to a path that quickly became a street, lined in fish houses and net-dryers. Inoques led him up a side street full of cats, and she paused, squatted, and spoke to the cats, who milled around her. In seconds there were a dozen, then dozens, and then hundreds of cats, all attempting to rub against her.

She glanced back at him.

He stepped forward amid the flood of fur and patted an old tom with one eye and a huge head. The big cat rubbed his scarred face enthusiastically against Aranthur's ankles.

'They know me,' she said. 'Always.'

She laughed, and walked on. She snapped her fingers and the cats scattered, except the old tom, who stood licking Aranthur's ankle and then meowed loudly at Inoques.

Aranthur stroked his matted fur and his shredded ears and got bitten for his pains.

Then they went up a lane that smelt of azalea and jasmine and cat piss. They came to a gate, and Inoques knocked. A small man opened the gate, bowed, his ragged turban almost touching the ground, and the two had a rapid exchange in Masri. Aranthur caught a few words: wine; sleep; garden.

The man bowed, and Inoques led the way into a courtyard garden with a magnificent orange tree and towering bushes full of flowers – yellow, red, white, a riot of colour and scent. There was a sort of arbour with benches and tables. Half a dozen men and one woman sat about, obviously nursing the results of a night of heavy drinking.

Inoques moved through them like a queen, and the woman, at least, bowed her head as she passed. Two cats followed her, and Aranthur wondered why there were no cats on the ship.

He followed, aware, as one of the men looked at him with a certain wine-soaked malevolence, that he was completely unarmed. But no violence was offered, and he followed Inoques in to a cool room.

'Yes?' she asked.

The room was big enough for forty or fifty, with benches, and a pair of long, low, tables. Enormous red water jars, as big as grain jars at home, hung from the beams and cooled the room.

'Perfect,' Aranthur said.

She nodded. 'Don't tell the proprietor.'

They were led into another room, and then down an arcaded inner courtyard to a whitewashed room where a man sat on a carpet. He appeared very old, with a skimpy white beard and a magnificent silk turban.

He rose when Inoques entered, and then cushions were brought, and a pipe offered around. Inoques smoked a little, polite sips of smoke, and began to bargain. Aranthur could tell it was bargaining by the rhythm. There was a crescendo, frowns, the pipe was pushed away, offered again. Finally Inoques shrugged, truly annoyed, her mouth set.

'Sorry, this won't work,' she said in her accented Byzas.

Aranthur rose.

The turbaned man hid his emotions and reactions well, but Aranthur could tell he was surprised by Inoques.

He reached out an arm, and spoke forcefully.

She paused.

Aranthur was sure that the man was apologising. It was a tone of voice, a hand gesture.

She sat again, folding her legs under her.

'Everyone is so on edge since the sky broke open,' she said to Aranthur.

She spoke, and the turbaned man spoke at length.

'He agrees. He says that he is being very careful with his stores of wine and beer, because . . . everyone acts to excess. They think the world is ending.'

Her eyes met Aranthur's, and he saw the questions there. Inoques was one of the people who wondered if the world was ending. Or she knew things that he didn't.

The older man held out his hand.

Inoques took it, and clasped it, and the man rose and held both hands to his forehead.

Aranthur bowed.

She rose, cat-like, to her feet.

'We have an arrangement. We are welcome for food and drink any time after the afternoon prayer. Mats will be laid for sleeping.' She glanced at Aranthur. 'My priests will pay for all this.'

Aranthur nodded.

The old man looked at him, his eyes veiled – or perhaps drugged. But his voice, in Byzas, was sharp enough.

'You are an Imperial?'

Aranthur nodded. He hadn't prepared a deception.

The man sipped smoke. 'Someone in this town is killing Imperials. And there are men offering hard coin for news of many things. Temple things. God things. And Imperials. I offer this to you for nothing, because you are now my guest and a friend of my friend.' He closed his eyes, and then opened them. 'Inoques says you are trying to close the hole in the sky.'

Aranthur didn't see any reason to hide.

'Yes,' he said.

'May all the gods smile on you, then. Since the hole opened, it is as if it is in my own head, and there are many who suffer worse than I.'

Aranthur bowed, and followed Inoques out of the curtained room. But there she stopped and faced him. She smiled up at him; he was a head taller or more, and much heavier.

'Do you accept my offer?' she asked, without shyness. 'About tonight?'

Aranthur had never been quite so boldly propositioned, but he needed... It was not a moment to hesitate. It was like fighting. Her eyes had more challenge than love, but he liked her challenge, and he recognised that she was more powerful than he. He also found that since the moment with the cats, he... liked her. She was remarkable.

'Yes,' he said.

'Then Butun will marry us.'

Aranthur flinched, and Inoques laughed.

'Listen, hero. I have been in your country many times, but you are in mine. I am a respectable person, a temple servant. I request you for marriage for tonight. In the morning, we will be unbound.'

She smiled, and the smile held all sorts of promises.

Aranthur felt some of the excitement he felt when he fought.

'I accept.'

'Good! I'm sorry that we are not even well dressed. I am no *biddit*. But I have a ship to see to, so this is as it must be. Put your hand in mine.'

Aranthur did as she bid, and felt the warmth in her hard hands.

He also felt the *power* in her immediately: her *saar*, and also some *sihr*.

And something else. Something extraordinary, like a candle burning inside an already bright lamp.

She led him back into the curtained room. The old priest said the service in the name of the Old Kings – not a rite Aranthur had heard, and a very ancient one. He said it in Masri and in Byzas with great exactness. It was not long, but it was solemn.

'You may kiss,' the priest said. 'In fact, you must.'

Aranthur was swept into an unexpected maelstrom. Her lips were soft, and pliable, and not at all like...

Like...

Then Inoques broke away, her eyes dancing.

'Ah, there is good fire in the hero,' she said. 'Listen – now if I kindle, our child is legitimate. And the true gods smile on me and you.'

The way in which she said 'kindle' disturbed him, but Aranthur gave the priest a present – all the money he had on him, which was deemed enough. And the two of them walked back to the beach.

'But surely you won't kindle,' he said. 'You have a crystal . . .'

Inoques shrugged. 'That will be my choice, eh? Perhaps you will make me a daughter as full of *baraka* as you are – a woman to manage the river and the ships.' She smiled.

She was lying. He knew it.

Aranthur had a moment of fear, as if the water was closing over his head.

'Why the tattoos?' he asked.

She laughed. '*Power*. And a bargain I made.' She leant over and kissed him, and the touch of her lips was like a bolt of lightning, although they just brushed his. 'Perhaps I will even tell you, eventually.'

The horses were swayed over the side and swam ashore. Aranthur checked that Jalu'd was taking the wounded ashore in the ship's boat. He tried to find the Masran priest, Haras, to talk about the stone, but the man was nowhere to be found. Then he rode his Steppe pony across the island. They had to jump a *kuramax* that appeared out of the deep vegetation, but its snapping jaws were no match for the agility of a horse bred to the endless threats of the open plains. He fed the pony some sugar cane, and something that looked like a turnip but was not, and thought about names.

Then he took Ariadne out. This time, instead of being alone, he was with Dahlia, who was mounted on her white Nissean. They cantered along the beach, and then walked the horses to cool them in the heavy, hot, humid air.

'You *married* her?' Dahlia put a hand to her mouth. 'Damn!'

Aranthur shrugged. He felt oddly better for having told Dahlia.

'Well, I could tell she wanted you,' she smiled. 'I won't even say she has bad taste.'

They walked for a while.

'If Sasan—' Dahlia began.

'You'll go with him, if he goes to Safi.'

'I want to. But I know you're right about your hunch. Something is badly wrong in Megara – there should be warships here. Imperial warships, guarding the mouth of the river. Something is very wrong. And I know what strings to pull at home.' She tossed her short hair and looked at Aranthur. 'The thing is, I don't want to go home. Fuck it all – this is what I want. Sasan, and adventure. I don't give a shit about my marriage list – I'm never going back to that.'

Aranthur nodded. 'I feel some of that. I really haven't had time to think. But—'

'But the Academy?' Dahlia said. 'Can you imagine?'

Aranthur smiled. 'I can, though. I've learnt so much that now I might learn more.'

Dahlia looked at him. 'You are twice the caster you were even a month ago. I learn new principles every day. So do you. I feel as if the Academy was a machine to *hide* the real functions of magik, not to teach them. You and I are becoming something... But yes, I have questions for my masters.'

Something went through Aranthur like a bolt of cold lightning. It was almost painful.

'Oh, gods,' he said aloud.

It was as if a giant cascade of discovery played through him with Dahlia's words: the ancient well covered in glyphs; the sling bullets; the words of Tirase; the Black Pyramid.

Dahlia reined in. 'What?'

Aranthur was looking out over the Delta.

'I'm probably wrong,' he said, but his breathing was shallow.

'Speak,' Dahlia ordered.

'What if Tirase *wanted* magik muzzled? Because it was too dangerous. He didn't give magik to the people to empower them, but to strip *power* from the dangerous ones.'

Silence, punctuated only by the humming of insects and the distant yowling of a cat in heat.

'Endless wars fought with *power*. The gradual destruction of ... everything. Waves of refugees from heavy magikal combats, consuming everything in their path...' He was talking mostly to himself.

'Lady! So the Pure are right?' Dahlia spat.

Aranthur thought that he suddenly understood the knife edge that the Lightbringers walked.

'No. Or yes.' He stared into space. 'Do we trust Tirase? And anyway, think about those things at Al-Khaire. The *Apep-Duat*.'

Dahlia waved her fingers dismissively.

'I can already see how to control them. So can Qna Liras. Time, and *power*. That's all we need.'

Aranthur bowed with genuine respect.

'When you are the greatest power of our day, remember us little people.'

'This from you?' she said. 'You know why else I don't want to go with Sasan? Because together, you and I haven't been beaten. You know what I mean?'

'Yes.' Aranthur was embarrassed by her hidden praise – and deeply happy. 'And I miss Ansu already.'

'Me too. Keep this idea to yourself. I agree it fits the evidence – it won't help our cause.'

'Whatever our cause is.'

'Cold Iron,' she said. 'Keep that in mind. We save our own first – then the Empire, then the rest of the world. Masr is Masr. This is not our fight.'

'Says a woman who claims she's not going back.'

Dahlia nodded. 'Touché.'

Aranthur looked at her. 'I'm not sure you are right, Dahlia. Maybe because I'm Arnaut, I see this more clearly than you. It's not our own first, and then the Empire. It's everyone. We're playing for all the marbles, and there's no time to be selfish.'

Dahlia looked over at him. She was half-hidden in the shade of a beautiful flowering bush, and her hair in the sun was dazzling, but her expression was hidden.

'You have grown,' she said. 'I ... Interesting.'

Aranthur might have said more, but Ariadne was stung by a wasp, and that was all the time there was for talk.

The light on the Delta was ruddy when Aranthur finally made his way back to the garden gate. The bent old man opened it to him and bowed, fists to head. Aranthur returned his bow as best he could.

He had not yet taken a cup of wine when Vilna caught his arm and pulled him aside, through a beaded curtain to a small room tiled in simple mosaic.

'Listen,' Vilna said. 'I learnt many things, some important, some not so much. Here's the greatest – Myr Comnas, the lady who commands *Rei d'Asturas*, the long red galley, says there are bandits on the south bank trying to steal a ship. She thinks they are Safian – maybe even servants of the Pure. And she said, too, that the Pure have agents in this town. She has a guard at all times on her ship, and fears for her cargo. The navark of the *Leone* was killed in a tavern fight – she says it was a murder.'

He leant against the wall and crossed his arms.

In the courtyard, Chimeg's voice could be heard, a nasal *turomehn* song, and then the tambouras started.

'They all think that Myr Tribane lost the great battle,' Vilna went on. 'And there are no ships from the City.'

Aranthur groaned.

'They say the Emperor, may his name be praised, is sick,' Vilna added. 'And there is chaos in Megara. Martial law, maybe.'

'Grab a drink and come back here,' Aranthur said. 'I need a moment to think.'

He walked out through the door, past the garden where his friends and his people were singing, and through the gate.

He sat on the stump of a dead palm tree, smoking stock and listening to cats fight in the darkness. He thought it all through, and he came to conclusions. Then he knocked his pipe out against the old palm stump and got to his feet.

'Is a problem?' asked the old man at the gate, solicitously.

Aranthur thought a moment. And smiled.

'I think I can work it out,' he said.

The old man smiled. Aranthur went through the garden quickly, so that no one would pull him aside. He leant through the beaded door and saw Dahlia dancing sinuously to Chimeg's music. He waved to her.

She came with Sasan.

'Tell them what you told me,' Aranthur said.

When Vilna was done, Aranthur raised an eyebrow.

'Dahlia, I absolutely understand why you want to go with Sasan. But by the oath we swore – if it was up to me, you'd board the *Rei d'Asturas* and sail for Megara. You have the name to command the navark to take you home. I do not. Something is badly wrong at home and it is our business.'

'You mean, Cold Iron,' Sasan said.

'I do,' Aranthur said.

Sasan glanced at Dahlia. 'I agree.'

Dahlia gave Aranthur something like a look of pure hatred.

Aranthur stood his ground.

'Sasan, you need me!' she said calmly. 'You need my powers. Without me, you cannot operate against the Pure, even in the most cautious manner.'

Sasan nodded. 'This is true. So, I will come and be your sword in Megara. My bandits won't desert me. Maybe my dream is foolishness, anyway.'

'It is not foolishness,' Dahlia said. 'I'd rather be a bandit in Safi...'

'It's worse than that,' Aranthur said, steeling his voice. 'Dahlia, you need to go without Sasan. Too many people know him. Too many know you, but the two of you together—'

'You think I'm going to sneak into my own city?' she asked.

'As a Noble Officer on the *Rei d'Asturas*. Yes, that's exactly what I think.' Aranthur changed from commanding to a more pleasant voice. 'Dahlia, I can't even pretend to order you. But think about it as if you were Iralia or Tiy Drako.'

'Noble Officer?' Sasan asked.

'Most nobles who do not take a turn in the military or the civil service go to sea. I never did. I had the Academy.'

'Nobles have the greatest political stake in the city,' Aranthur said. 'So they have to serve. One of Tirase's reforms.'

Sasan nodded. Suddenly he smiled. His effusiveness seemed false to Aranthur, and yet he welcomed it instead of the storm of anger he'd feared.

'You must,' he said to Dahlia. 'Timos is right.'

She caught the falsity too.

'We need to tighten our guards on the ship,' Vilna said.

Aranthur looked around wearily.

'I'll go,' he said.

If Dahlia was really leaving on the morning tide with the *Rei d'Asturas*, he couldn't ask her to spend her last night with Sasan on board.

Dahlia and Sasan were staring at each other, and no one said 'no'.

Aranthur sighed.

'Did we get all our wounded ashore?' he asked.

'Jalu'd took them to the Imoter,' Sasan said.

'And then I brought them here,' Jalu'd said, brushing through the curtain of beads with all the drama of a dancer. He turned a pirouette and bowed, one hand on his heart. 'Omga is here, with a wine cup in his hand, thanks to a very thorough and very... hmmm... lovely Imoter in the port. Bored and able. I paid.' He smiled. 'In charm,' he added.

Even Dahlia smiled.

'I'm going back to the ship,' Aranthur said. 'To guard it.'

Jalu'd nodded. 'I will come with you. I have had my wine and I have... hmm... *danced* with a lovely partner.'

Chimeg rose as they went out. She held up two fingers, a *Mughail* sign.

Aranthur went to her.

'You go to the ship?' she said. 'I go. A little drunk, but good.'

'No, enjoy yourself,' he said.

She smiled. 'I have danced and had fuck. Come. Swim, maybe dance on ship.'

She scooped a deep-bellied amphora off one of the tables, and Nata, a small Qirin tribesman with a hatchet face, grabbed another and followed her. Nata was a good man – reliable, with near-perfect Byzas, so that he could relay any order and describe anything from scouting – and a wicked sense of humour. Now he raised the amphora and mimed drinking it, and then put a large cork in and melted wax across the top.

'Seawater,' he said in explanation.

Aranthur smiled at their ease with him. Without ordering anyone, people came to share the night watch. He looked back to see Vilna smoking a water pipe with Sasan, and Dahlia watching him. He shrugged, unwilling or perhaps unable to make any more decisions.

He grabbed the mate, Mera.

'Where's the captain?' he asked slowly.

The man bowed. 'I left her in the market, *Shaib*. She was bargaining for greens, and told me to go drink for her.'

'That's a good captain,' Aranthur shouted over the growing noise. 'Tell her that I'm sorry, but someone had to watch the boat and I chose me.'

Mera smiled. 'This is a weight off me, *Shaib*.' He put his hands to his forehead. 'Now I can drink in peace.'

Aranthur led the way, and they walked down to the beach, two streets away. Aranthur and Chimeg stopped to talk to cats. They emerged to the starlit sky and the murmur of the crowded harbour – lanterns on the ships, and oil lamps along the waterfront. They stripped and swam to the ship. Chimeg showed her immense agility by climbing the anchor chain into the bow and then diving back into the sea with a hiss of disgust.

'Anchor chains are filthy,' Aranthur explained.

He took the opportunity to swim slowly around the ship, aware that there could be *kuramax* or other enemies in the water. He spread his awareness wide, but he found nothing. Nata gave him a hand over the side, and he was handed someone's old cotton turban cloth as a towel.

The two Nomadi were dexterous enough to have swum out with full pitchers of wine, which went around. Aranthur had a cup, and then passed. He was walking up and down the deck, trying to decide what the best way of watching was.

In the end, he elected to put a very small amount of *power* into the glyph carved into the deck. And he put a monitor on it inside the *Aulos*. He asked Nata to swim around the ship and the wiry Qirin splashed about until Aranthur had the limits of his detections.

An hour later, as he passed a pipe with Chimeg, now decorously wearing a uniform shirt, a tone sounded inaudibly in his head.

'Visitors,' he said.

They had loaded *carabins* in the rack just by them; each of them took one and knelt.

'Anyone aboard?' called a voice.

There was the sound of a boat coming alongside – a squeal of an oar in a rowlock, and then the thump.

'Someone should be on fucking watch,' the voice grumbled.

The man tossed a coin to his boatman and then turned away.

'Fuck,' he muttered.

They heard him take out a noisy tinderbox and go through the laborious task of lighting his pipe. When the coal was glowing like a cherry, he turned back to find Chimeg's pistol aimed ... not quite at him.

'Welcome aboard,' she said.

It was Kallotronis. He grinned.

'I knew the best party would be here. Look. I found *arak*.'

'Aren't we on watch?' Aranthur asked.

'I've killed more men drunk than you'll kill sober,' Kallotronis said.

'I think it's rude to kill people when they are drunk,' Jalu'd said, and they all laughed.

They sat, and things passed – stories and the pipe, wine and memory. Overhead the stars turned.

'There was a smuggler once,' Jalu'd said.

He was the best storyteller – better even than Kallotronis, who was also both sharp and funny. They all fell silent.

'Every day, he crossed the mountains from Armea to Safi. Every day, the Shahinshah's guards stopped him, and asked him his business.

' "Smuggling," he said, each day.

'Most days they let him go, but some days he went to the captain of the guard, and the captain would try to get this old man to confess.

' "What are you smuggling?" he would ask, and the old man would smile and put a finger alongside his nose.

'And the guards would search the old man and his donkey, basket by basket, but all they found was straw. And each night the man returned home by the higher pass. Finally one day, the man came to the border post on foot.

' "I am retired now, and only wish to go see my children," he said, like many other nomads.

'The guards sent him to the captain. The captain fed him, gave him *quaveh* and a pipe, and bade him good cheer, and then, when the man had eaten, drunk, and smoked, he said, "Oh wise one, you are now retired. Please, satisfy my poor intelligence and tell me what you took every day across my border to sell in my master's land."

'The old man smiled. "Swear on Aploun that you will never harm a hair on my head, nor my family."

'The guard captain, who was quite a decent man for the job, swore.

'The old man laughed. He rose, picked up his stick, and gave the captain a deep bow. "Donkeys," he said.'

When Jalu'd was done, they all roared with laughter. Aranthur leant back, and his alarm sounded, and he was on his feet. One look at him and they all moved. Kallotronis and Jalu'd continued talking as if nothing had happened.

This time it was Inoques. She pulled herself up to the stern rail.

'Don't kill me,' she said. 'It's my ship.'

Chimeg let her weapon off half-cock, and Inoques climbed over the rail and jumped down, naked and glistening in the darkness.

'We have wine,' Chimeg called.

Inoques took the pitcher. Aranthur sat down against the mast and she came and fitted herself beside him. She smiled at him.

'I do not give up easily.'

He found that he was grinning. 'I hoped.'

She shrugged. 'You can do little wrong with a captain, by guarding her ship.'

She leant over and kissed him, her lips cool in the warm air.

Chimeg gave a muffled laugh.

'Get a room,' Kallotronis said.

'We had a room,' Aranthur said quietly, suddenly bold. 'But someone had to guard the ship—'

The alarm went again.

'Damn it,' Aranthur spat. 'Someone coming.'

He still had the *carabin* in his hands and he rolled over, eyes searching the darkness.

'Careful. Probably more of ours.'

'Everyone will end up out here ...' Chimeg mocked.

The sound of muffled oars came plain across the water, and Chimeg's playful comment died away.

'We could play cards,' Kallotronis said loudly.

'I wish I had my tamboura,' Aranthur said, playing along with Kallotronis and his deception. Then he moved.

'You can't play it for shit anyway.' Kallotronis sounded much drunker than he was. 'I can, though. Give it here.'

Somewhere amidships, Inoques said, 'Shut up, you lout. I want to hear *him* play.'

There were three boats crammed full of people. More important, there was a glamour – a fairly subtle *working* on all three boats. Aranthur was confused, because the *working* was an Academy *working*.

The boats were close.

'More wine!' roared Kallotronis.

'It's mine!' shrilled Inoques, sounding like a harridan.

Something familiar in the caster. A feeling that Aranthur knew very well.

A whisper under the bow, in Safiri.

On the count of three…

Aranthur stepped back, and Chimeg stepped aside.

He shook his head violently, and made the Nomadi hand sign for 'capture'.

Chimeg nodded, a puffer in her left hand, a belaying pin in her right. She stooped behind the bowsprit fitting.

A man crawled over the bow with more strength than grace. He made plenty of noise, dropped to the deck, looked back, and Chimeg struck. Her belaying pin tapped him behind the head and he fell to the deck.

The second man appeared in seconds, jumped down with a rattle as his scabbard caught on the railing, and froze.

'Khan?' he said in a stage whisper.

Aranthur moved. The man turned, raising a puffer, and Chimeg hit him. Aranthur took the puffer as if the three of them had practised this dance many times. But the blow caught the man's turban, and he was not out; he croaked a warning.

The third man had just his arms over the rail, but he was smaller and faster. He vaulted the rail even as Chimeg struck the wounded man again. Aranthur reversed the puffer…

It took too long.

The small man raised his own puffer.

'He' triggered a *working* with a word, *Lucit.*

An Academy word.

Everything happened at once. The puffer's steel barrel centred on Aranthur's forehead as his own puffer came up to the target. The flare of light outlined the downed man's white turban, his Safian features, the second man's scarred face.

The third 'man' was a woman.

It…

was…

Kati.

Aranthur raised the barrel even as his finger tightened on the trigger, and he stepped back.

Kati flinched with the effort she made *not* to pull the trigger.

'Aranthur?' she asked. Her puffer was still steady on his forehead.

Another man jumped down behind her.

'Stop,' Kati ordered in Safiri.

And another man.

Chimeg stood up, a *carabin* on Kati and a puffer covering the second man.

'Drop your weapons,' she said.

Another figure dropped to the deck.

'I have five shots,' a voice said from the darkness above them. *Kallotronis.*

'And I have three,' Inoques said. 'Drop your weapons.'

'Kati?' Aranthur said. 'I knew it was you when I felt you cast.'

'Aranthur?' Kati's barrel was steady. 'What in ten thousand hells are you doing in Masr?'

Aranthur thought as quickly as he'd ever thought in his life, as all the pieces fell into place.

Safian bandits, the Pure, the attack on the Black Pyramid, Kallotronis saying they were 'Safian warriors...'

Between one breath and another, he guessed much, and he made a leap of faith.

'I'm putting my weapon on the deck. Kati, I beg you to talk to me. And I promise you that if you fight, most of you will die.'

'All of them!' called Kallotronis.

Aranthur ignored him and knelt, placing his loaded puffer on the deck. Since Kati held her shot, he put a hand on the downed man's head and felt his pulse at the neck.

'He's alive,' Aranthur said. 'No one's been killed. Kati, did you attack the pyramid?'

Very slowly, as if her arm was melting in the heat, Kati's puffer descended. Aranthur could feel the line that the barrel traced along his body almost physically, and then the weapon was pointed only at the deck.

'I am not surrendering. But I will talk.' Kati shifted. 'Are you really Aranthur Timos?'

'Penknife,' Aranthur said. Then he spoke up in Safiri. 'No one will be harmed unless you act with violence, or move too quickly.' And in Byzas, 'Hold your fire! Please let me talk. I know this woman well.'

He rose to his feet and no one pulled a trigger.

'Half-cock. Everyone. Come on. Let me hear the clicks.'

He looked at a scarred man beside Kati and pointed to his own weapon on the deck.

In Safiri, he said, 'Make it safe.'

'Fuck your mother,' the man said.

Aranthur met his eyes. They weren't crazy – merely feral.

'Mikal!' Kati said.

Mikal shrugged. 'I'm tired of running and I won't be a slave. I say, fight.'

Aranthur knew the man was about to shoot him. He could feel the dark energy building – not *sihr*, but human will.

'I will not fight.'

Aranthur deliberately turned his back on the man. His whole body shook with his fear of the action he was taking, but he couldn't see another path.

Now he shoots me.

'Kati, no one will be a slave,' he said.

He was looking up into the mainmast rigging. Kati's light *working* was so powerful that he could see Kallotronis on the platform of the mainmast, his body covered by the step of the mast.

'These people are my family and my family's friends,' Kati said. 'I have loyalties you cannot imagine, Aranthur.'

Dear gods, send me Sasan. Please, Lady, if ever you heard a prayer. Sasan. Come to me!

'Do you serve the Pure?' Aranthur asked.

'We did.' Her words carried a heavy freight of emotion. 'Aranthur, you really can't imagine—'

'Enough talk,' Mikal snapped.

'There is always time to talk,' Jalu'd said, in his beautiful, courtly Safiri. 'You must not be in such a rush to die, my brother.'

He danced out from the main deck. He twirled – a neat pirouette – and from his hand trailed a hail of rosebuds. The scent of roses pervaded the deck.

Mikal's mouth opened.

Jalu'd took his puffer from his hand with a graceful movement, and then bowed and returned it to the surprised man, butt first.

'But you are one of us!' Mikal said.

'We are all *us*, my brother.'

'You have a *Seeker* among you?' Kati asked.

'We were just in Safi,' Aranthur said. 'I'm going to guess that we crossed the desert just behind you – maybe four days behind.'

'Gods,' Kati said. 'Aranthur Timos. The last person I expected to see on the deck of a ship in Masr, much less with a war band and a Safian Seeker.' She knelt by the downed man. 'He is our leader, and our cousin.'

'He will recover,' Chimeg said, and Kati was startled by the Steppe woman's proximity. 'I know how to hit people.'

'Draivash?' Kati asked.

A tall, rail-thin man pushed out of the crowd in the bows.

He shrugged. 'There are only seven people on this boat. But they are very well armed. I say, *talk*. The Khan would say the same. Especially,' the bandit chuckled, 'as he will be the first to die.'

'No,' Aranthur said, turning slowly. 'I'll be the first to die.'

The one called Draivash had the same feral look as Mikal, but his smile was broader.

'True for you,' he said.

Aranthur managed a slight smile.

'What do you want?' he asked.

'We want to go home,' Kati said. But she didn't sound sure at all.

'We need to get across the river,' Draivash said. 'There are more of us. So far, we've only managed to steal three little boats, and one of them is sinking right now.' He shrugged. 'So I'm willing to talk.'

Aranthur nodded. 'What if I said we'd take you across the Delta?'

There was a muffled squawk from the foremast above him. He assumed it was Inoques.

'What if we told you that you were on the wrong side?' Jalu'd said. 'What if I sang to you of the harm the Pure are doing to our people?'

At Aranthur's feet, the prone figure stirred.

Kati knelt by him and started to croon. It wasn't a *working* Aranthur knew, but it followed precepts he knew. A healing *volteia*. Something simple.

The man sat up, groaned, and held his head.

'He's been hit on the head before,' Draivash said.

'Speak to us, Khan,' Mikal said.

'Gods,' Val al-Dun said. 'Hells.' He spat. His voice was thick, but his words were clear. 'You don't have to fucking tell me the Pure are poison.'

Mikal stepped back, so that he was against the bulwark of the bow. Draivash relaxed. Other men and women finally released the catches on their puffers and *jezzails*, or pointed them over the side.

It was as if the world exhaled.

'Boats coming off the shore,' a Safian voice called.

'That will be the rest of our soldiers,' Aranthur said.

Tension returned to every figure; tense muscles, tense jaws. At least one click as a half-cocked weapon was pulled back to the firing position.

'May I go to the rail and talk to them?' Aranthur asked.

The man holding his head raised it.

'Who are you?'

'He's Aranthur Timos,' Kati said. 'I went to school with him in the Empire. Please, I trust him, Val al-Dun.'

'He didn't kill you,' Draivash said. 'Seriously, Khan. He didn't.'

The injured man looked up, his face almost white in the burning light of Kati's casting. He managed an ironic smile.

'Well, thanks. Sure, talk.'

Aranthur stepped to the rail, deliberately passing next to Mikal.

'Sasan!' he roared out.

All around him, men looked at him.

Kati folded her arms.

'Sasan!' Aranthur roared.

'Here!' Sasan called.

'I need you, and only you. The others, stand off! We have a . . . a . . .' He looked around. 'A negotiation.'

'Understand!' Sasan called.

'Who is this Sasan?' Kati asked. 'He is one of us!'

'We are all called Sasan,' Mikal said.

Aranthur knew that, as soon as the man spoke to him, something was better.

He could feel Sasan climbing the side; even a fifty pace long hull moves when a big man climbs aboard. Sasan jumped down into the midships and then walked forward.

'Aranthur?'

'Here. Sasan, I believe we've found the Safian bandits.' He indicated Kati. 'And this young woman is—'

'Sasan!' Kati said.

'My mother's cousin,' Sasan said, his hand on his heart. He bowed.
Kati bowed.

The injured man stumbled to his feet.

'You are *the* Sasan?'

Sasan shrugged. 'That died with my father.'

Kati was in such shock that her magelight sputtered and died.

Aranthur stood in the darkness, watching the Safian men and women
bow to Sasan, and wondering if the gods did, indeed, play a role in
human affairs.

Later, when most of the Safians had been returned to their shore,
and an arrangement patched up to embark them the next day; later,
when calm had returned; when Sasan had admitted that yes, his name
implied a noble rank, and Aranthur had been confounded because he
had known that at some point; later still, when Aranthur had drunk
quaveh with Kati and Val al-Dun, asked them questions and answered
theirs as honestly as he could; even later, after he'd hugged Kati and
handed her down the side to Sasan and Dahlia to row ashore, Aranthur
stood, exhausted, and watched the very first fingers of dawn touch the
darkness.

He dropped his borrowed kilt and slipped into the water, hoping it
would clear his head. He swam down the length of the ship. He was
just turning under the stern when Inoques leant out over the captain's
rail.

'Syr Timos,' she said. 'Come up my ladder.'

He found himself in her tiny stern cabin under the command deck.

'I make it a rule never to make love here,' she said. 'But this night
has been so very full of events that I think I must make an exception.'

Aranthur was so tired, so at the end of various tethers, that the words
formed to decline her, even as her lips touched his.

But then he had no sense of himself. His passage from careworn
leader to lover was virtually instant, and then there was no world for
him but her lips, her hair, her hard brown body and the lines of tattooed script that ran...

Into all sorts of interesting places.

But even as they rose into union, he could feel the heat of her – not just lust, or love, but some fire in the *Aulos* that filled him with awe and a little fear.

They ended with her lying atop him, her legs astride, and she lay breathing calmly.

'So,' she said. She was smiling.

He smiled back at her.

'You are a person who carries more *power* than you reveal.'

'This is your Byzas idea of love-talk?' she asked, and licked his lips.

Aranthur was tempted to summon his magesight, but he let it lie.

She ran a hand down his chest, and then paused.

'My body is entirely human. Other parts of me are not so human. Can we leave it there?'

Aranthur grinned as her hand continued its searching.

'And we're married,' he said.

'Oath-bound,' she said in an odd voice.

4

Antioke

They made odd sea fellows, the low black hull of the Masran *trabaccolo* and the Megaran great galley. Even odder was the empty sea around them. In the busiest sea lanes in the known world, the horizon was clear from the long, low coast of Masr falling away to the east, all the way around. No sails nicked the horizon, white or black or Megaran red. Only, low over the marshes of the northern Delta, above the wheeling birds, stood the Dark Forge, like a dark vein in otherwise white marble.

Captain Inoques was relaxed in a folding chair placed under the stern awning that carried Myr Hangelika Comnas' magnificent arms and the lion, eagle and triangle of Megara. The great galley was the largest ship Aranthur had ever been aboard. The deck seemed as large as the hippodrome, and the whole galley was decked over. Although there were row ports piercing the sides, the ship mostly moved under sail; the oars were only for moving in and out of port. Just beyond Inoques' tattooed legs stood a pair of helmspeople at a large wheel connected to the enormous curving rudder by a complex series of pulleys. The great galley represented the very highest level of Megaran technology, complete with the slim young man who stood by the helm, a weather Magos, a graduate of the *Studion* named Ectore Comnos. By him stood Dahlia, now in the red doublet of a Noble Marine. Behind them stood Haras, the Masran priest, who looked deeply uneasy.

'It's larger,' Myr Comnas said. She was pointing at the Dark Forge. Dahlia looked at the helm.

'I don't know...' she said, tentatively.

She wasn't sure yet of her role; aboard the red great galley, they were back in Megara, and Dahlia was caught in the web of power and class that dominated the lives of the aristocracy.

But Myr Comnas wasn't power mad. She nodded at Dahlia, as if approving her question.

'I do, Dahlia. I have instruments – I'm both an astronomer and an astrologer. It is wider – worse, the crack in the sky has lengthened. In fact, with precise instruments, you can see that it is wider every day.'

Ettore, the weather Magos, nodded. 'I can confirm that.'

Katia ai Faryd also had a folding canvas chair. Val al-Dun stood behind it. Kati was looking away, out at the western horizon.

'It's all our fault,' she said softly.

Aranthur shook his head. 'No. First causes. It's the Master's fault, and his Disciples.' He paused, because he felt too young to even be a part of this council; he was younger than Kati, younger than Dahlia. But the words came to him, and he spoke them. 'And regardless, blame is useless now.'

Sasan nodded. He was at the rail; he was watching the coastline intently, as if it held some answers.

'Agreed,' he said. 'Forget how it happened. Now we have to fix it. The people on this deck know more about what's going on than perhaps any other group in the world.'

'Wine,' Myr Comnas said to one of her sailors. She sat forward and looked at Sasan. 'Gods, Sasan, that's the most terrifying thing I've ever heard. Do you have any idea how great a responsibility it is to take this monster through the water? I have the economic fate of twenty houses in my holds – marriages and alliances can break and fail if I fail. It pins me to my deck – the worry, the constant calculations of wind and sun, of *power* and the sea. And you want me to take on the hole in the sky and the threat to Masr—'

'If I may,' the Masran priest said. His arrogance was mostly gone, replaced by seasickness and an oppression of responsibility. 'The... artifact I guard is literally the only shield we have. And I must insist that its preservation be always the first priority, because its loss or capture would immediately spell the end...'

Inoques raised her eyes. 'Would it, though?' she asked quietly.

Haras would not look at her. 'And I protest her presence. *Its* presence.

It is a tool of my Order – a weapon. But it is not to be trusted – I protested its inclusion on this mission.' He spoke without anger; he sounded tired. 'It is using sex to gain your confidence,' he said to Aranthur.

'I am not "it", priest,' Inoques said. 'I am currently "her". Keep a civil tongue in your head.'

The weather Magos winced. 'What are you, Myr?'

'*It* is a construct. Something that should not be!' Haras spat.

Inoques rolled her eyes like an outraged adolescent.

'I am what I am. I saved you all in the fight on the river, and I have –' she smiled salaciously at Aranthur – 'other commitments to you now.'

Aranthur spread his hands and looked at Myr Comnas. Her eyes encouraged him.

'Can we move on?' He wondered where the soft steel in his voice came from. The voice of command, Vilna called it. But he looked around. 'I think we have no choice but to trust Myr Inoques, and for my part—'

'You married her,' Dahlia said. She laughed.

Haras looked stricken. 'You *what*?'

Aranthur blushed. But Inoques laughed her rich laugh. She accepted a beautiful Muranese glass of white wine from the steward, lay back, and glanced at Haras.

'Relax, priest. I am bound by oath. Marriage is as sacred to my kind as yours. And even if I were not . . .' She shrugged. 'I am already bound like a slave by your priests. And again, even if I were not, here, in this case, against this enemy, I would aid you.'

'It is manipulating us—' Haras said.

'You all manipulate each other constantly,' Inoques said. 'I play by your own rules.'

'Enough,' Comnas said. 'You are some sort of bound demon?'

Inoques shrugged. 'Untrue, but sufficient as an explanation.'

Aranthur, who observed things, blinked.

'You are bound to the Black Stone?'

She smiled bitterly. 'How astute of you.'

'You are one of the Old Ones?' Ectore asked.

Haras looked away.

Aranthur looked at Dahlia.

'I can guess. So . . . This is not the first time the Old Ones have tried

257

to escape from the gate, am I correct?' He looked at Haras, who looked away. 'And at some point, your order found a way to capture pieces of them and bind them to bodies. To create superbly powerful Magi who were nonetheless utterly under the control of the priests.'

'Not utterly,' Inoques smiled.

'Mistakes were made in old administrations,' Haras said.

'Draxos' dick, as my father used to say.' Comnas shook her head.

'I just want to note in passing that our "side" appears to indulge in some fairly dark practices.' Aranthur looked at Haras.

Haras shook his head vehemently. 'You have no idea what pressures are on us, you soft northerners. You do not have to keep the dead in their graves. You do not have these ancient things crawling through your dreams like maggots ...'

Aranthur watched Haras, keeping himself in check as he would if a gate guard was searching him. But inwardly he felt loathing; inwardly he was experiencing the same doubts that he had felt when he confronted Tiy Drako. But still ...

'Can we move on?' he asked. 'Haras, I have heard you. But Inoques ...'

Dahlia laughed, and put a hand on Inoques' shoulder. The bound woman smiled a very human smile.

Aranthur shrugged. 'Perhaps I have a special interest.'

Comnas laughed too. 'I agree. I've only known the captain for a few hours and I say, move on.'

Haras shook his head. 'You will rue this. It is not a person.'

'Noted.' Aranthur didn't like Haras, and yet he understood the man all too well – and the weight of his responsibilities. And the narrowness of his experience. 'Can we decide anything before we raise Antioke?'

Sasan turned from the rail. 'If al-Dun and ai Faryd will support me, I will go to Safi from Antioke.'

Val al-Dun stood with his arms crossed, rolling with the ship. The swell was growing, as if there was a major storm somewhere in the west.

'I am not a hero.' He shrugged. 'If you go home and raise your banner, everyone who follows you will die.'

Kati looked at Aranthur. He smiled at her.

'It's a long way from a garret room in the Academy,' he said.

'As soon as I saw you,' Kati said, 'I thought, "Now I can go back to the Academy, and all this will be a bad dream."'

Aranthur looked at them all, still wondering why he, and not, say,

Captain Comnas, seemed to be in charge of the discussion. And in his mind he was struggling with even the simplest decisions. It appeared to him that events in Megara demanded Dahlia – and that the work on the Safiri grimoire, the *Ulmaghest*, required Kati. But that was not his secret.

He hadn't shaved in days, and that gave him a short beard to run his fingers through.

'Sasan, I think we need to at least see Megara before you launch an expedition into Safi.'

His friend gave him the 'this from you' glare.

'That is not the tune you sang two nights ago,' he said. 'I will ride east from Antioke, regardless of who joins me.'

Dahlia bit her lip.

I'm not good at this, Aranthur thought.

The sea remained utterly empty. They had a two-day blow from the east – a wind so strong it carried the scent of the birch forests of the south continents. A flock of seabirds took shelter in the great galley's rigging.

Inoques spent the whole day and night on deck. She seemed able to work forever, without fatigue, without diminution. Aranthur wasn't quite sure how to approach the reality that his 'wife' was one of the *Apep-Duat*, like the arms attacking the city of Al-Khaire. For the most part, he tried to ignore it. As the wind abated and he no longer needed a lifeline to survive on the *trabaccolo* foredeck, he went topside with a wooden mug of warmed wine for her.

She drank it off. At a glance, Aranthur could see the enormous *power* that was bound within her – and could also see the web of weather-*workings* and protections she had woven over her ship. Off to the west, the great galley hung, invisible in the darkness, but visible to his magesight as a web of *puissance* that strengthened sails and calmed the howling winds, or deflected them.

"He's very good,' she said. 'The weather Magos, Ectore.' She drank the wine off. 'We have been co-operating these last hours – you people are very good.'

'Humans?' Aranthur asked.

She grinned, kissed him, and then stepped back.

'No. Those of you who learn in the *Studion.*' She nodded. A patch of cloud whirled away, revealing stars. 'It is almost over.'

'That wasn't so bad.'

She looked at the helm, and then forward. 'You think so? Listen, the sea can always kill you. Or me, for that matter.'

She was looking up, and he followed her eyes; the Dark Forge was gradually revealed by the retreating cloud.

Larger.

Aranthur groaned.

'Can I tell you something?' Inoques asked. 'If you have *power*, it is always like this. The sea is the perfect model. There is no time that the sea cannot kill you. A gust of wind on a beautiful day – a squall – and your ship is laid on her beam ends, and everyone aboard drowns. Or a storm, or insufficient fresh water, a leak, dry rot...' She shrugged. 'And so, with *power*. Someone is always trying to conquer. The multiverse itself is fraught with perils equivalent to storms, and there's no malevolence involved. And then every sentient race is well stocked with arsehats craving dominance and fools to follow them.'

'So...' Aranthur looked at her, trying to read her expression through tattoos and darkness.

'So, if you still fancy me, I'd like to make love, and enjoy this body, and you.' She pointed at the Dark Forge. 'That will be there in an hour, whether we mate or not.'

'Can we defeat it?'

She shrugged. 'You know that I am basically a slave. And slaves learn fatalism.'

'You are no slave.'

'You may be surprised. You may be surprised at what I am. But know, too, that I like you, and come what may, I will not harm you or your friends.'

'I suppose you mean that as love talk?'

She laughed. 'Damn it, Aranthur. You are deeper than I thought. You grow on me.'

Aranthur found that he was very easy with her, despite what he knew. So he made the same quip his father often made when his mother complained about something.

'You married me.'

*

260

Antioke rose with the dawn. The sun rising in the east silhouetted her truncated towers and the soaring majesty of her ancient Temple of Light. Well off the port, a low string of islands with little white towns, stained pink by the rising sun.

Aranthur raised his magesight as soon as the orb of the sun was clear of the horizon.

'No fleet,' he said. He had hoped, very hard, to find the Imperial Fleet in the secure harbour of Antioke. 'But a lot of small stuff in those island ports. Black sails.'

'Pirates,' Inoques said. 'Killikans.' She looked at the veritable forest of black masts.

'The *Rei d'Asturas* is beating to quarters,' Mera, the mate, called.

Captain Inoques had dressed in Byzas clothes after they made love: breeches, a fine shirt, a sash and a magnificent waistcoat cut for a woman. She looked more like a pirate than an Imperial officer.

'The Imperial Lady seems to know her business. Let's follow suit.'

'You have guns?' Aranthur asked.

'We have one big gun each side amidships. But they take an hour to get into place, and—' She was looking up. 'Where away?' she screamed to the masthead.

Above her, a slim woman was waving to the west.

There followed a long exchange in Masri.

'I'll be getting the guns into their cradles,' she said. 'Aranthur, can you get Kallotronis and Vilna to ... man my guns?'

'Can't you just sink things with your dread sorcery?'

Aranthur had decided that a little humour was required in dealing with his wife, the demon.

'I can, but it takes energy and concentration and all the usual things. And I love the smell of the powder.' She smiled.

Aranthur spent the next hour with Mera and Omga and a dozen other men, moving the heavy bronze tubes carefully to the right place where they could be swayed up out of the hold and into the gun carriages that the carpenter assembled at the low-slung gun ports. But as a piece of the deck was folded away on smoothly oiled hinges to reveal the gun positions, he understood that the guns were too big to remain on deck all the time – useless or worse in a storm or a heavy blow.

It took an hour, and a lot of sweat, but the guns were up, and with them, powder, shot, shot wads, and all the tools, rammers and scoops

261

and sponges to swab; buckets of seawater; quills full of powder for priming.

The guns fired marble balls, each one hand-chipped to round. Aranthur was unsurprised to find that every ball had a deeply carved mark, and was latent with *sihr*.

He came up on deck, stripped to the waist, with Kallotronis behind him.

'Ready, captain,' he called.

Antioke was fully visible, perhaps four sea-miles off the starboard bow. The rise of the hills behind the town was now visible, as were the scars of the recent siege.

And the smoke.

'Darkness,' spat Kallotronis.

Inoques turned around. 'I've seen a few wars. I'd say that was an army.'

Aranthur tried to make sense of what he was seeing. His first assumption was that his information had been wrong, and that the city was still under siege by Imperial forces. He was vaguely aware that Myr Elena Kallinikas had gone to serve in the siege of Antioke, for example. And General Tribane had referred to the expedition several times.

But the Lion and Eagle was clearly visible in the far-seer, over the citadel, which also bore the scars of a siege.

Aranthur watched for a while and shook his head.

'We hold the city,' he said.

'Unless the flags are false,' Inoques said.

The eastern horizon was now nicked with sails – a dozen or more. Coming out of the little fishing ports on the islands.

'Small ships. Like mine.' Inoques was watching the shore to the north. 'And it looks like two more are coming out.'

Aranthur continued watching.

'We have to decide soon – into the port, or back out to sea and try and leave those bastards behind. I don't like them,' Inoques said. 'It looks to me as if we are running a blockade.'

Aranthur moved his *volteia* back and forth, watching the beaches.

'Lay me alongside the *Rei d'Asturas*,' Inoques said to her helmswoman.

One of the *trabaccolo*'s guns fired. Kallotronis waved.

'Practice!' he called.

'Gods, I love the smoke. Best thing humans ever invented,' Inoques said. 'Myr Comnas!' she bellowed.

One of the effects of her strange dual nature was that her voice was enormous.

The stern gallery of the great galley towered over them like a palace above a hovel. Myr Comnas' greying black hair appeared over the side, framing a very worried face.

'Run for the sea or the port?' Inoques bellowed.

'Guns on the headland!' Comnas shouted down.

Two sailors with boarding pikes poled the *trabaccolo* off from a near collision.

'Mind your helm,' snapped Inoques.

'There's a current, ma'am,' said the helmswoman.

Aranthur began a *working*. It was *so* complicated; in effect, it was a far-seer *occulta* with gongs and whistles. But he was trying something new, and he'd had days at sea to build himself a glyph. He unrolled it out of his private *Aulos* and wrote it on the crystal wind, and he was looking at Dahlia. She was upside down.

'Fuck,' he said.

She laughed. 'Timos? Where are you?'

He closed the *occulta* and tried again.

The image was still upside down. He projected a tablet of light and wrote a message on it.

Dahlia understood immediately.

'Inoques?' Aranthur said a moment later. The exchange in the *Aulos* had been very rapid, and Dahlia had corrected his misrepresentation of some matter of optics. He re-inscribed his glyph. 'Captain?'

She glanced over and saw a life-sized representation of the Imperial captain floating on the deck.

She smiled at Aranthur. 'You people are so inventive.'

She had to speak to one side, so that the two captains appeared to be speaking at angles, but the *occulta* worked – a two-way communication device between two Magi, line of sight only. Castable almost instantaneously.

'Stand off,' Inoques snapped, as they scraped a finger's width of paint and wood off the *Rei d'Asturas*.

'I cannot risk my cargo,' Comnas was saying. 'Except that truly, it's a risk either way.'

'Why don't we *know* anything?' Inoques asked.

Aranthur spoke quietly to her. 'There's no *sihr* in the city or the citadel. None I can find readily. Lots of death.' He looked at her. 'My people hold the city. I'd wager on that.'

'We are wagering,' she said. 'Myr Comnas, my bet is the port.'

'Those ships coming in from seaward look like blockaders,' Comnas said. 'How do we ever escape?'

'Sixteen sails!' called the masthead. 'Make that seventeen!'

'We can't take them all,' Comnas said. 'Port it is. I'll lead the way – if it's a fight, I've got the weight of metal.'

The closer to the port they came, the more obvious it was that there was an army moving into siege positions around the city. They had seized the low hills and the long sand spit that led to the stone fort that guarded the harbour entrance, squat and deadly, but the Imperial flag flew from it and the hasty trenches of the sand spit were being reinforced by cut logs. In fact, it appeared that the sea fort's attackers had just arrived.

'The Pure,' Aranthur said, after he'd seen two of their milk-white flags and a scarlet-cloaked *Exalted*. He passed his thoughts to Dahlia.

'We're going to pound the sand spit as we pass,' she told him.

He passed that to the captain,

'Excellent,' she said. 'Colours – Masr, and an Imperial Lion under our flag.'

Mera saluted and the Golden Sphinx of Masr on a black background flew up the halyards and broke over the ship. The great galley seemed to blossom – six banners, including a huge swallowtail that had its own spar.

The fort dipped its colours and ran up a black wooden ball.

The great galley raised two blue pennons and a black wooden triangle.

The colours on the fort dipped again, and three wooden triangles ran up.

'That's the current signal,' Dahlia said. 'Myr Comnas says her codes are twenty-four days old. But that was all correct.'

Aranthur passed this to Inoques.

'Codes,' she said. 'You people. In we go, then.'

The mouth of the outer harbour was almost a mile wide, with big forts on either headland. The sea went from dark and blue to light as they passed over the ancient river bar. Then they could see the bottom;

kelp, rocks, and shoals of fish flowed by under the pale blue sea in the brilliant sunlight.

'Tell Kallotronis to fire whenever he wishes,' Inoques said.

Aranthur ran down the deck and passed the order. Everyone else seemed to be doing something.

All of the Nomadi, and all of Kallotronis' men not used as gun crews, were in the rigging or along the bulwarks.

He had the big port-side gun loaded, and traversed as far forward as the gun would bear.

Ahead of them about three hundred paces, the great galley was firing. She had heavy metal in her bows and lighter guns in among the row benches, and she was under full sail, a daring move so close to shore.

On the sand spit, hundreds of men and women were struggling to adjust to this new development, re-pointing big guns to hit the ships.

Kallotronis fired.

Through the far-seer *volteia*, the shot cut a terrible swathe through the human wheat. A big bronze gun was dismounted on the sand, and crushed the little people in its ruin.

The *Rei d'Asturas* pivoted, her oars out now, and her bow artillery fired down the line of the enemy entrenchments.

Kallotronis roared, and then the port-side gun fired again.

Aranthur looked at the Arnaut through the smoke.

'Grape,' he said with glee.

Aranthur found the one-sided slaughter sickening, but he continued to perform his duties, which were mostly maintaining several unlinked *workings*.

There was a scattering of *occultae* from the beach, easily parried by the various Magi aboard the ships.

When the workers and gunners on the sand spit broke and ran, the galley hunted them down the spit. There was no cover, and the two ships moved along with leisurely precision, their marksmen and gunners wagering as the fleeing besiegers were massacred.

'Must we?' Aranthur finally asked.

Inoques was grinning from ear to ear as they sank a series of fishing boats that the enemy were clearly using to shuttle supplies. The boats were laden to the gunwales with fleeing people.

'I suppose we could stop, and let them come at us tomorrow?'

She glanced around to be sure no one was watching her. Aranthur sensed rather than saw her transference of *power*.

The sole surviving boat sank. Its timbers rotted before Aranthur's eyes, and so did the people in it.

Inoques smiled smugly. 'You make me feel young,' she said.

He repressed a shudder. 'But this is just murder.'

'It's all murder, love. And they're just as dead whether I boil their blood or Kallotronis hits them with grapeshot.'

'Most of those people are drafted slaves. They have no choice.' Aranthur couldn't look away.

'Yes. So?' She pulled his head close, like a lover about to deliver an erotic kiss. But instead, she whispered, 'Do you imagine that slaves do not revolt? You lay your plans, and you are slow and careful, and in the end, you have your revenge. If these people want to save themselves, they should do as I do.'

She kissed him, and let him go. She was inhumanly strong.

Aranthur felt the ice go down his spine.

Kallotronis fired again. They were deep in Antioke's lagoon, almost against the shore, with their shallow draught. They were so close that when Kallotronis' hail of grape struck the mob trying to cross the open beach that connected the sand spit to the mainland, Aranthur could see the spray of blood and hear the screams.

Far off, in the low hills to the east, drums were sounding. A massive *working* launched from far off to the east, but it was slow and ponderous, a fire *working* at extreme range. Ectore swatted it down among the hills before it was ever a real threat.

Now nothing could save the enemy troops fleeing the isthmus. Their fate was sealed by a troop of cavalry appearing from the city and rounding up the survivors, who surrendered immediately.

The cavalrymen looked tired, and their horses were skin and bones. But they waved at the ships, and they were receiving cheers from the walls of a high black basalt redoubt that covered the sea gate on the landward approach. The cheers were thin, and sometimes resembled the screaming of gulls, and Aranthur's feeling of unease deepened.

The Vicar was older than Aranthur expected – old and tired, with deep lines around his mouth and a wispy grey-white beard that was stained from smoking too much stock. Vicar was an old rank, from the first empire, like Legatus. It implied a quasi-religious status, but Vicar Dukaz was, effectively, a senior Imperial Vanax and Aranthur's dispatches were addressed to him.

Now he sat at an enormous oak table covered in charts, maps, and loose papyrus and parchment, all endangered by the wax from twenty candles. They were deep in the maze of frescoed stone corridors behind the magnificent Temple of Light. There were still dead men, and women, in those corridors. There were flies everywhere, and sand, and the Imperial Army had a haunted look – not enough sleep, and not enough food.

The Vicar was reading through Aranthur's bag of documents.

'Sophia!' he said, about forty heartbeats after finishing his empty compliments on Aranthur's speed and dedication as a messenger.

He looked up, and his old eyes had a fire in them that Aranthur hadn't expected.

'Get me the Chief Engineer, and Ippeas,' he said to his orderly.

The man bowed. 'Ippeas is in the trenches. Kallinikas is asleep.'

'Fetch her,' the Vicar growled, and went back to reading.

A slim young woman in a black breastplate over a very dirty buff coat came in, walking the walk of the exhausted, using her hips to control her weight.

'Where's the fleet?' she asked as soon as she came in. Then she stopped. 'I know you. You were at my brother's funeral.'

She shook her head, as if to clear it. She had black marks under her eyes as if she'd taken a few punches.

Aranthur bowed. 'Myr Kallinikas.'

'Sophia's tits, was that just two weeks ago?' Kallinikas threw herself into a chair. 'You bring word from Megara?'

'No, milady. From General Tribane.' Aranthur pointed at the dispatches.

Kallinikas nodded. 'What's she have left?' Her voice was flat.

'She apparently *won*.'

The Vicar tossed a scroll tube to Kallinikas and opened a second.

'What the fuck?' the young woman spat, and seized the scroll. 'When? Were you there?'

Aranthur nodded. He wasn't sure if he should salute, and he felt foolish.

'I was there. It was . . . a brilliant victory.'

'Based on your years of military experience, young man?' The Vicar rang a bell, and another officer came in, carrying a glass of wine. 'You should hear this, Vardar.' But he smiled, and he looked younger, as if some of the care had come off him. 'Gods above. You are a Centark? In the Nomadi?'

Kallinikas glanced up. 'Damme, Timos. You weren't a centark two weeks ago.'

The Vicar looked up again. 'We've been sold a fake pig, Kallinikas. Vardar, read this. Ten thousand hells. What does it mean?' He turned. 'Vardar, this young fellow is Timos, Centark in the Nomadi. He came here from the General, through Safi. Vardar is my chief aide.'

Aranthur chose to salute. Vardar neither returned the salute nor bowed. He raised one eyebrow.

Kallinikas was reading a third document. She looked at Aranthur.

'Swear to me on my brother's death that you saw a victory, Timos.'

Aranthur went down on one knee and put a hand on his sword.

'I swear on the death of my friend Mikal that what I say is true. The General, and the Capitan Pasha of Atti won a victory. We took or destroyed most of their host and took all their *gonnes* and all their baggage.'

Vardar's eyes narrowed. He was tall and thin and well dressed, in a uniform that had more gold lace than either of the other officers'.

'This is not possible,' he said carefully.

The Vicar shrugged. 'I already believe him. There's a codeword in these that was missing in the supposed Imperial dispatch, and I know Alis' writing. Fucking hell! What's going on at home?'

Kallinikas looked up. 'Tribane sent General Roaris home in disgrace?'

'Yes, Myr.' Aranthur nodded.

She shook her head. 'Only . . . Roaris seems to be in the War Ministry. We had Imperial dispatches from Megara. By pigeon, yesterday.'

'Saying that the General was defeated in Safi and was withdrawing, having lost most of her army,' the Vicar said.

'There must be some mistake,' Vardar said. 'General Roaris is the Empire's most loyal officer and her finest general.'

Aranthur couldn't stop himself. He sneered.

'*General* Roaris declined to obey his orders and attempted to abandon the battle line.'

'I doubt you understand what you saw,' Vardar said, 'so I will forgive your treasonous talk.'

Aranthur shook his head. 'Syr, no difference in rank can stop me from saying this. Roaris attempted to sabotage the Imperial army. I was there, as a messenger on the staff. I heard his comments with my own ears. He was arrested, and sent home.'

'You lie!' Vardar spat.

The Vicar rose, a look of displeasure warping his face.

'Silence, both of you. This serves no one. Roaris' disgrace, however unlikely, appears to be a matter of fact, Syr Vardar. I would appreciate it if you apologised to Syr Timos.'

Vardar drew himself up. But when he turned his head, he wore an unctuous smile.

'I'm so sorry that such an outrageous... phrase escaped me, Timos.' He bowed. 'I am afraid that my enthusiasm for General Roaris carried me away.'

Aranthur bowed.

'Where's Tribane now, Timos?' Kallinikas asked.

'Myr, she is withdrawing. She's out of food, and needed to link up with the fleet.' He glanced around. 'And when the sky opened—'

The Vicar met his eye. 'I know. It was bad here. We'd only just stormed the city six hours before. We had to fight step by step for the Temple – they were doing something and we interrupted it. Grisly work – lost ten Magdalenes and a hundred regulars and some knights in the fighting.'

'How much food do your ships have?' Kallinikas asked.

Aranthur shook his head. 'Food? No idea.'

The Vicar rubbed his dirty beard. 'Any idea where the fleet is? Truth is, we rather hoped you were the fleet.'

Aranthur shook his head. 'There are two more great galleys in the Delta. But we haven't seen the fleet. Only the black ships off the port.'

Vardar spoke quietly. 'So in fact, it does sound as if General Tribane lost.'

Kallinikas sat back. She rubbed her eyes.

'I still don't get it. I came late to this party. The Chief Engineer was killed and the Arsenale sent me out to replace him.'

'And she took the city,' the Vicar said to Aranthur.

'Ippeas took the city,' Kallinikas said. 'I just made it possible.'* She leant back again. 'We were in the city six hours when the gods' damned Dark Forge appeared in the sky, and about thirty hours when the first tendrils of a new army came over the hills. And we left them a complete set of siege lines.'

The Vicar shook his head. 'It never occurred to me to order our trenches slighted.'

'This place is out of food and we were running out too.' Kallinikas shook her head. 'Before I even arrived, the fleet left to take the General's army to gods know where. There's too much secrecy, too many compartments, and not enough planning and no logistics central command. We're short of everything but enemy. Food, ammunition... We have a good sized artillery train and lots of tools. We have a few hundred cavalry horses as back-up food, and so far, our erstwhile opponents are astoundingly incompetent at opening a siege. You helped today – we're making them afraid of occupying our old lines. I have all my diggers working to wreck our trenches opposite the black redoubt. I have a mine under the main sap.' She shrugged. 'A mine with most of our powder in it. Really? We won't last ten days. Maybe fifteen. I'm just playing the game to the end.'

The Vicar nodded. 'We only beat their army into this city by hours. And now they'll take it back.'

Aranthur made himself smile. 'My lord, the General herself told me she was marching to relieve you. She'll get here, probably with the fleet. And I'm going to guess that the fleet is loading her troops, and that's why we haven't seen them.'

'Your words to Sophia's ear,' the Vicar said. 'This scroll here tells me that you were promoted Centark for heroism on the battlefield. Do you have further orders from the General?'

Aranthur didn't have an easy answer, and he didn't know where to place his duties to Cold Iron against his military duties.

'Vicar—' he began.

'First, what troops did you bring?' Kallinikas asked. 'Anyone?'

'A dozen cavalrymen with our mounts,' he said. 'And another company of Arnauts from Masr.'

* See 'The Storm' in the anthology *Art of War* edited by Petros Triantafyllou.

'Mercenaries?' the Vicar asked. 'I'll take them.' He leant back. 'I don't have many centarks, I have to admit.'

'We lost a lot of officers in our assaults,' Kallinikas said. 'Assaults have to be led from in front.'

'I'd like you to command a force. It'll be rag-tag and bobtail – probably your Arnauts—'

'The Twenty-second City lost all their officers in the Storm. Only a couple of dekarks.' Kallinikas shook her head. 'There's about eighty of them, yesterday's muster.'

'Good. You'll take the command?' the Vicar asked.

'I have no command experience . . .' Aranthur said.

'Come, come,' Vardar said, smiling. 'No false modesty. This says you were promoted for heroism, and that's exactly what we need.'

The Vicar smiled faintly, as if he disagreed but didn't need to say so.

'Actually, I assume you can write and figure?'

'Yes, my lord,' Aranthur said.

'Good. I need you to count everything on those ships before you look at your scratch command. It's more important.'

'Everything?'

'Yes, centark. Everything,' Kallinikas said. 'This city has been drained of everything from food to ink by a month of siege, and now we're under siege again. *Everything.*'

Aranthur hesitated. In his head, he could see it on Tribane's huge charts of the western Area – the army he'd seen marching on the plains of Safi. The Imperial advance, pinning it in place; and then Tribane's retreat, allowing that army to move west, to strike at . . .

'Immediately, centark,' the Vicar said. 'My people are hungry.'

Aranthur moved through both ships for half a day in stifling heat and blind darkness. The *Rei d'Asturas* was well run and had excellent documents, but even aboard the great trade galley it took constant attention to list every useful thing. When he found an entire tier of powder barrels hidden in the hold he began to doubt the ornate bills of lading.

Myr Comnas took him aside into her great cabin and served him wine.

'There are things aboard that would be inconvenient for me and my investors to have discovered,' she said bluntly. 'I'm pulling various nuts out of various fires, young man. I don't need to have all my little secrets blared to the world.'

Aranthur nodded, trying to imagine what he was supposed to do.

'And I believe that we have a common interest.' She smiled thinly. 'I'd like to make sure that nothing in hold four or the second tier of my lower hold is reported. Is that blunt enough? In exchange, I'll make sure that no one ever sees your horses.'

She put ivory spectacles on to look at her bill of lading.

'I believe you and your Nomadi place an especial value on horses? The Vicar is butchering cavalry mounts for food.'

Aranthur was reminded of Qna Liras' comments on being a Light-bringer. A knife edge. This was corruption. And yet.

Aranthur loved Ariadne. It was foolish and possibly ignoble, but the loss of Rasce had hit him hard. Ariadne deserved better than to end as stew. And he liked Comnas for her honest dishonesty.

'Done,' he said.

Inoques, still his wife, was much harder to deal with than Myr Comnas. She made it clear that she resented his lists, and she followed him through the ship, muttering under her breath and at times obstructing him.

'You can't just take my *gonnes* and my powder,' she said.

Aranthur shook his head. 'I'm not taking anything. But the Imperial Vicar needs to know what you have.' He turned to her. 'Listen. Tell me what you want to hide and I'll hide it.'

She shook her head. 'Will you, though? I think I'll just hide what I want to hide, and save you the soul-searching.'

'He only wants to know—' Aranthur felt defensive, and he spat the words.

'So he can seize it. Haras and I have a task – to get the Black Stone to Megara. This is a city under siege, and by your own account, it could fall. Let us take on water and run. And if we run, let's have enough powder to load our *gonnes*, and enough *gonnes* to fight off the hoard of blockaders off the harbour mouth.'

Aranthur bowed, but he kept counting.

'Aranthur!' She grabbed the point of his bearded chin and swung his head around. She was very strong. 'I am duty-bound to the Black Stone. I have to take oaths and vows very seriously. I promise you. I was designed and ensorcelled to be so.'

Aranthur frowned. 'I wish to save this city from falling to the Pure again. And also get you to Megara.'

She leant against the damp partition in the forward hold.

'And if you cannot do both?'

'I will . . .' Aranthur looked into her eyes, which had a faint inhuman glow to them. 'I will put the Black Stone first.' He shrugged. 'I know how important it is.'

'Listen to me, man. You do not know how important it is. If the Black Stone is broken, I will be free of this shell, which is, for me, good. But all my . . . kin . . . will also be free, and many among them are mere ravening maws of chaos. Or worse.' She leant close. 'That stone is the cornerstone of your world, and without it, the Pure will seem benign.'

Aranthur kissed her. 'I have an idea.'

She laughed. 'So human.'

But then she returned his kiss with a ruthless hunger.

'We are still married,' she purred.

A day later, kisses were not even a memory. Aranthur was in the trenches behind the rubble breach in the Black Redoubt. The breach had been blown ten days earlier by Imperial *gonnes* – huge siege monsters firing almost point-blank, from just two hundred paces away, overcoming ancient stonework and ancient spells with modern powder. Black rock chips and rubble were everywhere. The final Imperial assault which carried the town by storm had entered through this breach and this bastion.

Now, the engineers and the hundreds of pioneers had dug deep trenches and thrown up earthworks across the former parade ground of the bastion, creating, in effect, a diagonal wall from corner to corner of the ruined square. Further to the right, they had begun work on a long trench behind the old curtain wall, a trap for an attacker who might believe that he'd scaled the main defences. The enemy guns and their potent Magi had trouble reaching the new earth and timber wall, because the height of the surviving black basalt walls still deflected most of their rounds, because no Magos could strike what he could not see, and because they had neither the number nor the weight of guns that the Empire had had.

Aranthur was in a long trench under a firing step, pretending to know how to be in command of a company of Arnauts and another of City militia. His six Nomadi had become his runners. He had been given two dekarks: Kouznos, a grocer from near the Aqueduct, and Stathi, an out-city farmer. Both had deep lines on their faces and neither had bathed in a week.

Both were prepared to listen to Vilna, and perhaps even Aranthur Timos. Aranthur had very little time to get to know them. He knew that there were some Keltai and some Easterners and a handful of Byzas in the company, and he didn't know any names yet.

'Just give the orders,' Vilna said, as if Aranthur knew what he was doing.

But Aranthur worked out that he could discuss with Vilna, get advice from Kallotronis, who made clear that he didn't take orders very seriously, and perhaps, coached by the two of them, he would not make any major mistakes.

All they'd done for seven hours was to dig in the dark, with the trench line itself lit with small magelights and torches. They dug steadily, improving their line, adding saps to the rear, and mounting two small falconets from the great galley to cover the corners of the entrenchment, masked *gonnes* that could not be seen or reached by enemy batteries. Aranthur finally realised that they were digging an enormous trap for an attacker.

'I hate fighting on foot,' Omga said.

'I hate anything that isn't a horse,' Vilna said. 'This is a stupid way to fight.'

Chimeg nodded. 'Unsafe,' she said, which made Aranthur laugh.

He translated their Pastun for Kouznos, who laughed and passed the joke on to the militia.

Aranthur walked all the way along the trench, wondering what a real officer would do, and stopping to talk to the Keltai and the Arnauts. The Keltai were all fisherfolk, caught by the war, and willing to fight; they wore long maille shirts and carried long rifles and heavy swords. They were led by a woman who called herself 'Cleg'. She shook his hand in the darkness. She was as tall as he, with fish-belly white skin and red hair and as many tattoos as Inoques.

Aranthur ordered more fresh water brought forward. He listened to a lot of complaints, and then he found Myr Kallinikas beside him in the darkness. She had on a white shirt and breeches, and she had a rifled *carabin* slung over her shoulder and two pistols in her belt.

'They'll attack you at dawn,' she said.

'Why?' he asked, feeling stupid.

'They have every morning. They just push slaves or "volunteers" up the scarp to see what we do.' She shrugged. 'If you have no morals and unlimited fodder, it's a justifiable tactic.'

Vilna skidded down the earthwork from the firing step.

'*Effenda*, we should send patrols out into the darkness to . . .' He struggled for words. 'To hit them as they form up, my lady.'

'Who do you recommend?' Kallinikas asked. 'Me? You?' She shrugged. 'There's no point to the trap I'm building here if their scouts find it. I need you to keep them off.'

'The Arnauts,' Vilna said, waving at Kallotronis. 'They're brave enough, and bored. And our Keltai. They know the life.'

'*Exalted?*' Aranthur asked. 'The scarlet-cloaked killers? Are they out there?'

'Not since we shot one down the first day,' Kallinikas said. 'But there's at least two more.'

Aranthur wondered why they were all looking at him until he realised that in this moment he was actually in command. It made him laugh and feel like an impostor, all at the same time.

He thought of the long-ago night when he'd watched a middle-aged woman dance as the voluptuous goddess of love, Aphres, in the opera. She had been neither young nor beautiful, until she danced, and for as long as she moved, he had believed in her completely. He drew himself up.

'Right,' he said. 'We'll catch them as they rise out of their trenches . . .'

He looked at Kallotronis, who nodded. Vilna also nodded.

'Firelocks only – match will give us away. Vilna, find twenty volunteers among the militia – ask Myr Cleg first.'

'Lang Cleg, syr.' Vilna, who was a head shorter than Aranthur, grinned. 'She is tall.'

Aranthur managed a smile. 'If you insist. Lang Cleg, then. Kallotronis—'

'I'll choose my own devils,' the Arnaut said.

They crept down the front of their own earthworks an hour later. Aranthur, who insisted on leading the left wing, swore that he'd put steps into the damned rampart if he ever held this wall again. He already hated siege warfare; the level of tension was insane. While he tried to hold the Black Bastion, he had no idea what was going on in twenty other positions – on the weak sea wall, for example, or the Royal Tower.

He slipped, and then slid down the front face of the earthwork. The slide was noisy and drew a fusillade from the darkness, but none of the rounds hit close enough to do any damage. Aranthur landed badly, rolled forward, and then spent time finding a lost puffer in the darkness. Then he crawled to the position that Kallinikas had indicated, or so he hoped. The moonless darkness was lit only by stars. The Dark Forge made the sky even darker, especially as the bastion faced the eastern sky.

He skidded across gravel on his breastplate and wriggled in close to the shattered edge of the black basalt wall. Vilna followed him, and then an assortment of militiamen and women, all with their faces blackened: 'his' militia from a City regiment raised in the Docklands north of the Academy, small crafts, the Keltai, and a handful of longshoremen.

A big woman in a black maille shirt whispered 'last', and they all went to ground.

Not a rustle or a whisper betrayed the movement of the Arnauts.

Aranthur lay watching the Anvil for long enough to almost fall asleep, and then something began to bite him under his breastplate. Each bite was like a piercing blade; whatever it was bit him repeatedly.

'Shit,' Vilna muttered. 'Razor ants.'

As quietly as they could, they moved away from the nest. Aranthur continued to be bitten for a long time. It was as miserable as any time he'd ever spent, including being tortured by Pure agents.

Just before dawn their adversaries sent a patrol. But the men and women sent to test the new defences were *augmented* and the burst of *power* alerted Aranthur. The moment the patrol moved into the open ground, they were caught in a crossfire between the militia and Kollotronis' Arnauts.

There was a sudden barrage of *power* in the *Aulos*. The red *sihr* fire fell on Aranthur's company, but jade shields like the scales of an artichoke flashed to cover them. The terrified militia crouched amid the rubble and razor ants until the light show moved on.

As the sun tinged the horizon a deep pink somewhere to the east, a whole battery of mortars began to fire from behind the bastion

– perhaps as many as ten. The rounds whistled past the broken walls of the once-proud bastion, and the shells exploded among the not-very-distant trenches of the former Imperial lines.

The smoke and dust was thick.

'Let's get out of here,' Aranthur said to Vilna.

The twenty of them scrambled back up the face of the redoubt. The enemy fired at them, but the response was thin and not accurate.

Aranthur was scratching furiously, but he paused with the oncoming centark.

'I need to get my Arnauts back inside,' he said.

The older man raised an eyebrow.

'Captain Kallotronis came in an hour ago,' he said.

Aranthur wondered at the man's tone. He understood it better when he climbed down the improvised steps to the covered way between the bastion and the city wall, where the mortar battery was.

Kallinikas was there. She raised an eyebrow.

'Centark?'

There was sarcasm, and more than a little criticism, in her use of the rank.

'Myr?' he asked.

She waved at the little mortar battery. A hundred sweating men and women lay around, drinking water.

'An hour's work for a hundred pairs of hands. Sweaty, dangerous work.' She shook her head. 'Any idea what I'm talking about?'

Aranthur shook his head.

'Sophia, you are green. Centark, what was your plan for extricating your sally from the front of the redoubt when the sun rose?'

Aranthur met her eye. 'I didn't think about it,' he admitted.

He'd imagined the ambush, the fighting...

Shit.

'Well, I didn't either. So we're fucking idiots together. I threw this together when Kallotronis told me you were stuck out there.' She shook her head. 'Any time you go out, you have to plan how to get back in.'

Aranthur felt the weight of his ignorance.

'I'm not bad on a cavalry patrol.'

'I'm good at designing bridges,' Kallinikas said.

*

The next day the enemy launched an assault on the Black Bastion when Aranthur was asleep. It proved to be a ruse, to occupy the defenders. Then they blew a mine under the Royal Tower.

Several hours later, Aranthur lay at the edge of the new line of earthworks inside the collapsed wall of the tower and along the old curtain wall that led to the Black Bastion. The tower had been ancient and huge; the stones were the size – each one of them – of a wagon. To his left, Kallotronis had a wall gun, like a small, rifled artillery piece, or a musket that someone had made for a giant. It had a heavy iron axe that locked it to the wall. Kallotronis was watching the enemy artillery pits for targets. Behind him, three of his 'devils' loaded three more wall guns.

'They're at least as incompetent as we are,' Kallinikas snarled. 'They blew their mine, and all they did was to drop the tower on their assault force.' She wrinkled her nose. 'If they'd dug another twelve feet in, we'd all be dead now.'

Aranthur rolled over, laid his *carabin* on the parapet, and tracked the earth being thrown up by a single poor bastard shovelling at the head of the enemy sap. Their men were digging deeper trenches and improvising a wall behind them. For the moment, a handful of tired officers and snipers were all that was holding the rubble, in shallow scrapes or behind the huge stones.

Aranthur tracked his target by signs: thrown sand; a little flash of metal from his shovel. He was no doubt clearing sand off the collapse of the tower so that his own side could dig trenches. The enemy – the Pure, or whatever they called themselves – had carts full of earth and big pavises rolled into position. Aranthur tracked the man's shovel as it sparkled above a cart; a shovelful of sand flew over the next pavise and then another.

Aranthur was already focused on the gap – the very narrow gap – between the two wheeled pavises. They were heavy, built of thick timber painted with a black oil. He didn't think his *carabin* would penetrate one.

There was a very slight flutter between the next two pavises.

Aranthur didn't fire.

Kallotronis did. The big wall gun spoke with a flat crack, and the fluttering movement stopped. There wasn't even a scream.

But Aranthur saw the movement in a gun position, two hundred paces away. Without conscious thought, he cast his *aspis occulta*. He kept several ready almost all the time; his casting was so smooth that it was like pouring liquid from a pitcher.

The falconet ball struck the *occulta* and richocheted away as if it had hit solid stone. Before an enemy sniper could fire, Aranthur's second *aspis* came up and covered Kallotronis.

The Arnaut was lying very flat, his arms crossed over his head, but none of the rounds directed his way struck home. They were all stopped on Aranthur's shields.

'You are *puissant*,' Kallinikas said.

'I'm getting a great deal of practice.' Aranthur bit his lip.

A heavy, *sihr*-based *occulta* shot from deep in the enemy lines. Aranthur was the target. He flexed his shield and raised another. Two more emanations struck at him.

'Shit,' he said out loud.

They were tracking him by his casting, and targeting him the way the snipers targeted men digging.

He threw his new *displacement* back down the line of the first attack. Then he was enveloped in a layer of someone else's shields – Dahlia's. He knew her at once.

A stream of green fire washed over a distant position. Off to his left, Jalu'd was dancing his *power* straight into the enemy lines. Aranthur, the pressure off, rippled off the continuous *saar* assaults he'd spent the summer learning. They had effect on things – earth flew. But no real effect on people, because force based on life was not particularly *puissant* in causing death – like trying to use water to start a fire.

And, of course, the *sihr* to cause death directly was *right there*.

Now the enemy's return fire had artillery, and also the coherent red fire that Aranthur associated with the *Exalted*.

But Dahlia's shields held it all, and more. There were other casters on his side, a choir of them. Off to the east, a set of shields went black and collapsed, and suddenly there was silence in the *Aulos*.

'Still with us? Can you hit that *gonne*?' Kallinikas asked, pointing at the falconet that had fired at Kallotronis.

Aranthur sighed. 'Perhaps.'

He was tired; he had just expended more *saar* in thirty heartbeats than he used to gather in a week.

'But you do not want to.'

Aranthur shrugged, scratched his bites, and thought confused thoughts.

'I ... don't like ... It feels like murder.'

Kallinikas nodded. 'Well, tonight I'm blowing my mine under their forward sap. That'll kill maybe a thousand of them.' She shrugged. 'Look, they want to kill us or make us slaves. I'm untroubled.'

Aranthur thought, *You can't see their souls as life force in the Aulos.*

As if to punctuate their discussion, Kallotronis' wall gun spoke again, with authority. Far out across the sand and grit of the siege, a woman with a rammer in her hand had her lungs blown through her chest, and fell across the mouth of her *gonne*.

Another falconet fired. This time, Aranthur hadn't spotted its position. The cannonball struck a huge stone from the collapsed tower, sending a spray of deadly stone chips across the open rifle pits and marginal cover.

Kallotronis was bleeding from a cut across his face, but he rolled and gave Aranthur a thumb's up. But the next man was Chimeg's partner, Nata. He lay curled around his right arm, his face grey. He was silent, but the pain was obvious.

Flies gathered around him.

Aranthur's khaftan was cut across by stone chips in two places, but thick, filthy fabric had actually prevented lacerations.

'They are trying to kill us,' Kallinikas said.

'I know,' he said. 'Listen, Myr. I have killed quite a few people.'

In fact, he could see them all, when he thought about it. It was as if he was carrying a satchel of dead. Sometimes.

He was watching the distant *gonne* positions when it occurred to him that she might not know that her parents were dead. The very day he'd left – two days after she'd sailed for Antioke, he thought. He lay there, his barrel tracking no target, squinting, sweating in the brutal sun, trying to decide if he should mention that she was Kallinikas Primas. Wondering how he'd just survived a brutal and faceless magikal duel. Except it wasn't a duel.

Of course she didn't know about her parents. She'd be using the title.

'Myr,' he said.

She half-rolled to face him.

'Syr?' she answered with her usual sardonic lip twist.

'I'm sorry, I don't know how to do this. Do you know that ...'

She leant closer. 'What?'

She was so close he could feel the warmth of her breath.

He breathed out. 'Damn. I'm sorry, Myr. Do you know that your family palazzo was attacked by—'

Her head snapped back.

There was a volley of artillery from the other side.

Aranthur's sword hilt, pinned under his left side, pulsed with energy and he raised his head.

'Fuck,' Kallinikas spat.

Several hundred Safian Tufenchis rose from their trenches in broad daylight, their dull, dusty red coats interspersed with black robes and brilliant orange robes that Aranthur hadn't seen before.

His front sight stopped on an obvious officer with a gold-mounted sword. His morality vanished in powder smoke as he shot the man down.

To his right, Vilna began to sound an alarm by beating his bronze canteen with a knife hilt. Every man and woman working behind them on the hasty earthworks dived for their weapons.

Aranthur bit the bullet off the top of a prepared paper cartridge, put the weapon on half-cock, primed his pan, flipped the cunning little pan cover closed, and rolled on his back to load.

Kallotronis fired again.

Aranthur got the bullet down the barrel and put the rammer back in its pipes. He rolled back on his stomach.

'Time to leave,' Kallinikas said.

Aranthur had seen the flutter of scarlet robes in the centre of the line. It was like a kick in the gut; he hadn't fully realised until that moment how badly he feared another encounter.

But the *carabin* kicked against his shoulder and he was moving, reasonably certain he'd hit it. He and Kallinikas slid down the outer face of the new ditch, and then they had to scramble up the face of the new wall.

Behind them, the Tufenchis were cresting the rubble of the old tower, and there were shots.

Kallinikas screamed.

Aranthur grabbed her wrist and pulled. He was a big man, and she was a small woman, and he pulled her along like a sledge.

More shots. She was hit.

A volley from just over his head, crisp, ordered, and Vilna's voice chanting the ritual of reloading.

Aranthur bent and got his arms under her. Kallotronis appeared from below, put a hand under her, and pushed. The three of them tumbled over the scarp and into the new works.

Aranthur got a hand on her chest, pushed in with *saar*, and stabilised the blood flow around the wound. The rest needed an Imoter.

He raised his head.

Vilna snapped 'Fire!'

The whole wall erupted in fire.

Tufenchis fell like wheat under a scythe, but there were hundreds more, and the *Exalted* burst from the middle of them. They were in the ditch now. In the very heart of the trap.

Masked *gonnes* at either end of the ditch fired grape into the packed men, and the carnage was total. In the *Aulos,* black *sihr* welled up like water from a spring.

The *Exalted* was gone as if it had never been, and the destruction was so total that there were very few wounded. Silence fell over the ditch; a handful of dying men kicked.

The amount of blood was horrible – enough to make the bottom of a sand ditch wet and black.

Most of the militia turned their heads away, or fiddled with their matchlocks.

Aranthur was still watching the ditch. Smoke was drifting, and far out over the sandy hell of no man's land, some ruthless bastard decided the assault had failed and ordered the enemy siege *gonnes* to reopen fire.

'It's still down there,' he said.

Vilna was lighting his pipe. He shrugged. 'For heroes.'

Aranthur looked along the wall, east and west. They hadn't lost a man or woman.

Kallotronis was carrying Kallinikas down the back wall, shouting 'Imoter!'

'Off the wall,' Aranthur ordered.

The militia were all too happy to comply, tumbling back into the safety of the trench behind the new work.

Chimeg was left with Aranthur, looking down.

'Still down there, *boso.*'

He nodded. 'I'm going to ... cast something. *Malas. Baqsa* stuff. And then I will move very fast.'

She took his *carabin* and checked the prime.

'I'll cover you, *boso*,' she said, simply.

Aranthur cast his *enhancement* so easily that it was difficult to remember how much effort it had once taken. He drew the old sword, and slid down the front face of the inner wall in between artillery rounds.

He landed in the blood and sand at the bottom. The bodies were a thick carpet, the dead men curiously flat, and horrible to walk on. The smoke was dissipating, but the dust hung in the air. Already, the world looked different, as he moved and lived faster.

It occurred to him that the gonners on the masked *gonnes* at the ends of the pit trap might think he was a Tufenchi. His red Nomadi khaftan was of almost the same colour that most of the Tufenchis wore. It also occurred to him that he was a blur to them, like the *Exalted*.

He missed its move. He was trying to wave at the gonners, and the pitiless thing exploded up out of the wet corpses, scarlet robes dark with the stains of dead men.

The *Exalted*'s bright swords cut.

He crossed the first cut late and something burned his forearm like fire. He stepped back on the awful carpet, his back foot skidding on a head to rest in entrails. The second cut he also covered, snapped a counter-cut down the same line and the *Exalted* stopped. It just stood, both bright swords over its head, something like smoke dripping from its shoulder where he'd cut it.

'*Who are you?*' it asked.

Aranthur saw the face, the puzzlement, and he understood something in that moment. Something very important.

Aranthur also saw the indecision – the war on its face, the conflict in its lips, the pain – and then it ran. It went straight up the face of the ditch as if it ran up a grassy bank, and then it was gone into the smoke and the *gonne* fire.

He didn't follow it.

Aranthur went up the inner face with more care. When he looked back, there was only smoke and dust and brilliant sunlight. He cancelled his *enhancement*.

He stayed on the wall until their relief came – an hour in intense pain. His right arm felt heavy, and he couldn't stop eating: first the biscuit he kept in his ration bag, and then some hard military cheese begged from the Imoters. It wasn't until he was back in the shade of the cathedral, with Dahlia cutting away his sleeve, that he realised what was familiar. His arm was turning brown, exactly as it had with the *kotsyphas*, the Black Bird. It seemed a lifetime ago, in his garret in Megara.

5

Antioke

But one thing that the Vicar's force had aplenty was *Studion*-trained Magi; Imoters and *polemagi* too. Dahlia held his arm while two young men cleaned the brown tinge off his skin with repeated applications of ritual, and a liquid that smelled like good *arak*.

The younger man, who had long black hair, smiled, poured a little into a cup, and handed it over.

'Good inside, too,' he said.

'Do you have any food to go with that?' Aranthur asked.

'Food's rationed now,' the Imoter said.

'I can find you something,' Dahlia said. 'You look like shit, if I can be blunt.'

'Aren't you always?' Aranthur said. Whatever the Imoter was doing hurt.

'Always, but you look like a *thuryx* addict – you're skinny as a corpse and all the bones in your face stand out.'

Aranthur shrugged. 'I'm fine.'

'Sure. Listen, then. Sasan wants to be fighting.'

'I wondered where you'd all gone,' he admitted. 'I missed you, and I worried about Sasan.'

Dahlia waited until the two Imoters were finished. Farther down the nave of the great cathedral, under a gilded and painted statue of Sophia, Aranthur could see Haras working on a table full of implements – alchemy, he guessed.

The dark-haired Imoter gave Aranthur a light slap on the shoulder.

'Enjoy my magik elixir,' he said. 'You're good to go, syr. Should be getting some sleep.'

'This is particularly good on an empty stomach,' Aranthur said. 'Gods, I'm drunk.'

He was lying on the cool floor and saw no reason to move.

Dahlia came and sat with him and took the cup.

'I have some food, as long as you don't ask where it came from. Better yet, come to the ship and sleep safe, and eat your fill.'

Aranthur considered the morality of it.

'No,' he said. 'I should be with my people.'

Dahlia nodded. She wasn't angry. But she was . . . empty. Or possibly . . .

Aranthur looked up at her.

'What's wrong?' he asked. 'And what are you doing, while I fight for the Empire?'

She laughed. 'You never used to be sarcastic before.'

'I hadn't seen a war yet.'

She nodded and sipped his *arak*.

'Listen. I've been looking at this place. They actually stopped the ritual here. The Magdalenes burst in and saved most of the ritual sacrifices – they were fighting around the altar. Their Great Sword says that several of the knights actually saw into the . . . the *Hyperaulos*. I don't have a better name. But the "gates" were open.'

Aranthur had already assumed as much.

'So they meant this to happen—'

'At the same moment that they took the Black Stone and opened the gate at the pyramids.' Dahlia sighed.

Aranthur managed a smile. 'I know what Kallinikas would say – my new mentor in everything to do with war.'

Dahlia polished off the *arak*. 'What?'

'You drank all my medicine.'

'Toby left the bottle.' Dahlia refilled the cup. 'I did healing arts with Toby first year.' She shook her head. 'Blessed Sophia, first year seems a lifetime ago.' She looked at him. 'Anyway. What would the estimable Myr Kallinikas say?'

'She'd say it was a stupid plan. Anyone who thinks they can win two major battles simultaneously and time things like rituals amid violence isn't god-like. They're just arrogant. The Pure planned to knock over three or five sacred places?' Aranthur was warming to his subject. 'But instead, they lost a field battle and their Disciple in Masr fucked the whole thing away, released a bunch of dead gods, and failed to break open the sky. And here... Instead of doing the obvious and doing their dark ritual while they held the city, some arrogant twit ordered them to hold to the very end so that they could keep the timing...' He shook his head. 'Idiots.'

Dahlia nodded.

'What's Sasan doing?' he asked.

'More than five hundred "Pure" surrendered or were taken wounded when the army stormed this place. He's questioning them.'

'He's recruiting,' Aranthur said.

Dahlia nodded. 'Of course.'

'And Kati?'

He caught the hesitation in Dahlia's face.

'They are doing it together,' she said, without much tone.

Aranthur understood too much, which was how he had begun to feel all the time.

'Let me tell you something, in case I take a ball out there. The *Exalted*. They're constructs, exactly like my *wife*.'

Dahlia exhaled. 'Of course they are. Thousand hells.'

'I'm going to guess wildly,' he said. 'But haven't you wondered about their... lack of gender?'

Dahlia shrugged. 'No. Gender – who cares?'

'They're amalgams. Someone is building super-sorcerers by binding three or four people in one body.' He shrugged. 'That's what I think I see.'

Dahlia shuddered. 'Oh, gods.'

Aranthur shrugged. 'Masr does it, so we've probably done it, too.'

Dahlia was shaking her head. 'Round up your political opponents who have *power*, and bind them to a healthy body and a mind that's politically reliable—'

'You can see how the "Master" could start very small and grow very quickly. I should message Qna Liras. Except that the more I learn about Inoques, the less I trust any priest of Masr.'

Dahlia raised an eyebrow. 'It's not just the sarcasm. You've changed.'

Aranthur took the cup and drank some. 'I'm tired of a number of things. I feel like a swordsman committed to defence, who parries and parries instead of taking the initiative and attacking. Every day we keep this up, people die, and the poor fucking Tufenchis are victims as much as our militia.'

Dahlia sighed. 'Will you take Sasan?'

'Of course. Why didn't he come in the first place . . . ? Oh. His own people.'

'Almost all of them. There's some Armeans out there, but mostly it's Safians.' She took the cup. 'And your *wife*.' She smiled when she said it. 'She scares me, Aranthur. What's under those tattoos?'

He considered various half-truths and outright lies.

'*Power*. And a person as complicated as the rest of us.'

Dahlia watched him for a moment, took a slug of *arak*, and shook her head.

'You like her?'

Aranthur looked down the nave, where two Imoters were removing a severed arm from a bin. Two young girls were washing the area around the operating table, as if kneeling barefoot in old blood was their everyday lives. And perhaps it was.

'Yes,' Aranthur said.

She reminds me of you came to his lips, and he realised how true it was – the self-assurance and the ruthlessness and even the humour.

And a terrifying thought.

If a superhuman entity wanted to seduce me, would it immediately read my relationships and then duplicate . . . ?

He paused, and then shook his head.

'I don't really know her,' he admitted.

'No shit. None of us do. I thought Haras hated her, but yesterday they were thick as thieves.' Dahlia put the *arak* bottle carefully aside. 'Be careful. I speak as a Magas and not as a woman – be careful. This is a temporary marriage? Unbind it. You are bound to something much more powerful than we are.'

'Powerful and yet a slave.' He shrugged. 'As to Haras . . .' He watched the man siphoning a bright yellow liquid, intent on his work. 'He and Inoques share a common goal. And I'm not going to speak of it here. Listen, Dahlia. I'm worried that . . . this is not where we ought to be. The Pure. The Black Pyramid. This place, the ritual. The bone plague. Think about that. I understand what role this place plays, but it's not . . .' He looked around. 'It's like what we talked about in the

Delta.' Which seemed like a hundred years before. 'It's not a Cold Iron problem. It's an army problem.'

'They need us,' Dahlia said, but even as she said the words, her lack of assurance showed what she thought.

'They need to know the fleet is coming, and they needed our food. But let's face it – they have better magik than the General had, and the Vicar, Kallinikas and Ippeas seem—'

'Very competent,' Dahlia agreed. 'The Vicar's in over his head, but the other two hold him up, and he's canny. And the troops like him, exactly because he's old and tough.' She glanced around. 'But when the food runs out, it will get ugly.'

'He's cautious,' Aranthur said. 'In storybooks, soldiers love a rash leader. But in the trenches, they like an old man who knows their names and doesn't get them killed.'

Dahlia leant over and kissed him on the forehead.

'I'm scared, Aranthur. It's all too big and it moves too fast.'

He got up with uncharacteristic care; he really was drunk.

'It makes me angry,' he said with sudden truth. 'I'm sick of being a tool.'

Dahlia shook her head. 'You are fucking dangerous. I said so to Tiy Drako the first time I met you. You are some sort of vortex, and you draw everything to you.'

Aranthur's vortex at that moment was a faint tendency to wobble on his feet. He waved dismissively.

'I need to go and pretend to be an officer.'

He went and saw his own wounded: a dozen militiamen and women, including a wheelwright's apprentice he knew from the Square of the Mulberry Trees. He sat with the young man.

'What are you doing in the Twenty-second City?' he asked. 'You're from Northside!'

The boy smiled. When he spoke, it was in the shoreman dialect.

'Nah, syr. I'm a longshoreman. Well, my da's a longshoreman, an' I have the tats. But Nella gave me work when I needed it, and I liked the wood. Still a shoreman born.'

Aranthur nodded. 'Seems a long way from the City.'

'You think we'll hold, syr?'

Aranthur knew full well that the 'boy' was perhaps a year younger than he was himself – perhaps two years. But the young man's trust was absolute.

'Fleet will come in a few days,' Aranthur said. 'Trust General Tribane.'

'We heard she was some sort o' traitor.'

Aranthur shook his head. 'I know her.'

'Well, then. People talk a lot o' shite when they're afraid, aye.'

Aranthur nodded and moved on. Two pallets down was Chimeg's partner, Nata. When Aranthur approached, he turned his face away.

Aranthur knelt down next to his pallet.

'Nata?' he said cautiously.

'Go away,' the tribesman said.

'Nata, can I do something?'

'Give me my fucking hand back,' Nata spat.

He held up the stump of his right hand. It had been severed cleanly.

'Blessed Sophia!' Aranthur was surprised, in a way he didn't think he could be surprised. 'That's—'

'Your fucking Imoters saved me.' The little tribesman's voice was dead, devoid of real emotion, or exhausted. '*Saved* me. You know what life is like on the Steppes for a man missing his right hand? Now I can eat with the same hand I use on my arse. Just kill me.'

Aranthur had no words – no banter – for this.

'Just fucking kill me,' Nata spat. 'Or if that's too much, pay someone.'

'I'll get Chimeg...'

Nata looked at him with pure hatred.

'Yes. Yes, *Bahadur* who thinks everything can be fucking *fixed*. Get Chimeg. She has the balls you lack.'

Aranthur found himself backing away from the small man's rage.

'You can live without a hand,' he said.

'Yes, *Bahadur*. No doubt I can. Criminals do, after all.'

Aranthur backed away from the man's anger. He stopped in one of the Temple's labyrinthine cross-corridors under a very dark depiction of the eviction of Draxos from Heaven. Draxos was not innocent, in this depiction. Aranthur shook his head at the relish the artist showed for the smith-god's degradation, and then smoked some stock to clear his head before he went back to his wounded.

He visited every wounded person he had. Then he found Kallinikas, her feet up, on a once-grand settee, manipulating a *saar*-filled tablet.

She glanced at him. 'You saved my life, I hear.'

He shrugged.

She shrugged again. 'Half-rations as of tonight. Two hours after midnight I will blow our countermine. Expect to go with the assault wave.'

He stood, stunned. 'Assault?'

'I'm going to try for their gun line. What the hells? We're doomed, Aranthur. We have maybe three days. Why not attack?'

'The Vicar is backing this?'

'Vicar and Great Sword. Vardar is against it. Sorry, Aranthur. It's bad. We're holding on by *luck*. Like the direction in which the tower fell.' She shook her head.

'I still haven't met Ippeas.'

She smiled. 'He's leading the assault. You should be about five feet apart.'

Aranthur succumbed to temptation and swam in the sea. The harbour was still clean; almost untouched by the siege, it was like a different world from what was going on around the walls.

Then he went aboard the *trabaccolo*. It was dark, perhaps three hours to midnight. He'd need an hour to make his arrangements for the assault.

Inoques met him at the rail. Her tattoos glowed very slightly in the dark. Aranthur didn't think that had been true before.

She laughed. 'The Black Stone binds me. And it's right there, under my deck.' She laughed again.

'Why are you laughing, then?' Aranthur asked.

She took his hand and led him aft to her cabin, where Mera laid out a feast of old salt cod and ship's biscuit beaten with sugar and rum.

'I'm already drunk,' he said. 'Listen, Inoques. I owe you – you are, after all, my wife.'

Just saying it made him smile, and she returned his smile.

'I agree, it is droll. I have no regrets, though. You are an interesting man, and your youth is pleasant. Since I met you, I have thought some thoughts I have not had in an aeon. Truth, loyalty, glory, honour. These things are not part of the quest for power.' She shrugged. 'Nor part of being a slave.'

He nodded. 'We're attacking tonight. In about four hours. It's a desperate gamble and no one expects it to succeed. We're at half-rations and we have perhaps five days left to hold, or so says Kallinikas.'

'But you could fall tonight. If they catch me in the harbour, even with Haras and your Dahlia, even if we make them build bridges of the dead, they will take the Black Stone.' She shrugged. 'Which we were foolish enough to bring here.'

She poured something dark into his glass, and he drank it without thinking.

'Damn it, now I am *drunk*,' he said.

She began to pull her linen shirt over her head.

'I'll sober you up,' she said. 'This carnality is one of the things I had forgotten. So long since I had a body as nice as this.'

He thought of her rotting the boat full of desperate people fleeing the ship's *gonnes*; but that was nothing beside the reality of her – her scent, and her skin, and her hair, and her obvious delight.

He awoke to moonlight. She was stroking his cheek.

'And there you are,' she said.

'What time is it?' he asked, sitting up.

'Plenty of time for you to run and die. Listen, love. I . . .' She showed actual embarrassment.

He laughed.

She smiled. 'I think it is the reality that you *like me* that continues to haunt me. I have taken a great liberty. I entered your mind.'

He drew back.

She shrugged. 'I built you something. I promise you would have come to it in time. I only accelerated the process a little.'

He tried not to flinch at the notion of her inside his head.

'I'd like you to live,' she said. 'Oath-bound.'

He kissed her, and rose to put on clothes. He found they were all clean, a small, household miracle.

'Mera did it of his own free will,' she said from the bed. 'You spend a great deal of time with Myr Kallinikas,' she said suddenly.

'She's my mentor in this bloody business.'

'If you sleep with her, I will kill her.' Inoques' voice was calm, and in a normal human, would have been rational. 'We are oath-bound.'

'Blessed Sophia! Sleep with Kallinikas? Are you mad?'

'She was in your mind.' Inoques was naked, the lines of her immense binding ritual glowing well enough for him to button his doublet by their light. 'I am sorry. It was foolish of me to go in, but you were asleep, and I want you to be strong, and live.'

'What have you done?' he asked, his voice sharp.

'What needed to be done.'

Aranthur pursed his lips, and decided that he had too many battles to fight, for this to be one of them. So instead, he took a steadying breath.

'I need some silver,' he said. 'Maybe a pound.'

She changed directions as quickly as he.

'A pound is possible. Here – some spoons. For what?'

'A casting.'

She nodded, as if she had not just invaded his head, and found him silver. And then she rowed him ashore.

'I'm sorry,' she said.

He kissed her. 'Another time, we'll argue.'

'Don't die,' she said. 'I like you.'

Aranthur went to the nave of the ancient temple, where he found Haras, still working.

'I need an alembic and a ladle to cast silver,' he said.

Haras nodded. 'That I can provide. You work alchemy?'

'Only the simplest kind,' Aranthur admitted.

He melted the silver with a small brazier and, when he was impatient, a blast of his own *power*, which was too easy.

'*It* is altering you,' Haras said.

Aranthur turned to Haras.

'Look,' he said, raising his hands and stepping back, as if afraid of Aranthur. 'I mean no offence. I need it to perform my mission, but I fear it.'

'*Her*,' Aranthur said.

Haras shrugged. 'If you insist. *She* is a shard of an ancient, alien consciousness bound to the body of a young woman who is effectively dead. And that combination – that construct. It's at least three hundred years old.'

Aranthur shrugged. He took out the mould he'd made in a *huril* shell he'd picked up on the beach, the way farmers did it in Souli. *Huril* shells were soft on the inside, and yet incredibly resilient; you could press a shape into them, and then cast into it dozens of times. People made charms and fish-hooks that way. He'd duplicated the Varestan glyph of *penetration* in the shell's soft interior. Now, working quickly, he cast the sparkling silver into the shell and watched it cool and become solid. In each case, the solidification was sudden, as if some inner impulse suddenly frosted the metal and then it was done. He used the tip of his eating knife to pry the new bullet out and drop it in water, where it would hiss for a moment. Each time, he checked the bullet to make sure the glyph was clear. With each, he gave it a dose of *saar* to ignite the glyph.

'You are very *puissant*,' Haras said. 'Will you listen to me?'

Aranthur had been crouched over his mould, but he only had enough silver for nine bullets. He rose, his thighs burning.

'I am listening. Haras, I think you imagine that I am a witless foreigner without a sensible thought in my head, a tool of this dangerous ancient thing...'

Haras' face betrayed that he thought something like that.

'You have to imagine that perhaps I have some idea of what's happening – out there in the darkness, up in the sky, and with Inoques.'

'You can't imagine—' Haras insisted in his patronising tone.

'You have no idea what I can imagine. And perhaps your Byzas is good enough to understand one of our sayings.'

'Try me.'

'War and politics make for strange bedfellows.' Aranthur smiled. 'I mean no offence, but at the moment, I trust my wife more than I trust you. I will do my best to protect the Black Stone. Otherwise, be cautious.'

Haras nodded. 'You are honest. An honest fool.'

Dressed and armed, he found 'his' troops in the new ditch by the collapsed tower: Vilna and Lang Cleg and thirty militia, Kallotronis and twenty of his Arnauts. He went to Kallotronis and handed him the silver bullets.

Kallotronis nodded slowly. 'Damn, I owe you, Timos.' He gave Aranthur a bear hug. 'I feel naked without something to shoot the... witches.'

Aranthur returned the squeeze, slapped the big man's back, and went along the lines of his people at the base of the trench. He looked them over in the moonlit darkness; checked on their powder, made sure that every weapon was loaded.

Almost all of the assault party had borrowed some armour, from Lang Cleg, a tall Keltai woman with maille and a breastplate and a heavy morion, to the smallest of the Arnauts, who had a maille collar that hung almost to his belt. Beyond his people were the Magdalenes, as steel-smooth and enigmatic as they were in the streets of the City. There were thirty of them, all in steel, so well polished that the lantern lights reflected from all of them.

'Timos?' a voice asked.

The voice was connected to a suit of armour, smooth and seamless.

'Syr Ippeas.' Aranthur didn't know whether to bow or salute. 'Great Sword.'

He bowed. Ippeas was that imposing.

'Not a noise or a shot,' Ippeas said. 'When the mine blows, it's possible it will hurt us. The essential thing is that we have to go into their trenches the moment it blows. We cannot give them time to recover. And then straight for their *gonnes*. And their magikers, if we can get them.'

Aranthur nodded. 'Yes, syr. I can ... shield us. Against some of the effects of the mine.'

Ippeas nodded. 'I know. At least, I think that's why young Kallinikas chose you.'

The ditch was becoming packed with people, and more were coming out of the sallyport.

'Aranthur!' Sasan shouted somewhere close by.

He turned. In the darkness and enforced quiet, the voice was loud, and desperate.

He grabbed at Sasan. 'Silence,' he hissed.

'You must come!'

'I'm in the assault—'

'Now!' Sasan said. 'I beg you.'

Aranthur caught Vilna's wrist.

'I have to go. Sasan—'

'We have half an hour,' Vilna said.

Aranthur followed Sasan back down the dark and dirty zig-zag sap to the old sallyport.

'They're going to kill all the prisoners,' Sasan said, his voice choked.

295

'What?'

'To save food.' Sasan paused. 'And there's a bone plague outbreak.'

'Bone plague doesn't just—'

'I know. Damn it! Come. Someone is trying to kill them, and to manipulate the rest of us.'

'Thousand hells!'

Aranthur followed Sasan into the walls, up the narrow stairs, and into the city. The Safian led the way through a web of alleys.

'I've been doing this for three days,' he said. 'I'm getting good at slums.'

Aranthur was breathing hard, as he was wearing armour and carrying forty rounds of ammunition, food, and carrying a helmet and his *carabin* and a long sword.

They went under an arch and they were in the ancient stadium, past a pair of guards – men of the Seventh Geta Regiment. Getans were hard-working farm-folk, and tended to be very serious about the Empire. But they saluted Sasan as an officer, and saluted again when they saw Aranthur's crimson sash.

The stadium was very like the hippodrome in the City. Aranthur could see several hundred people lying, standing, or sitting at one side. At the other side, a company of one of the Getan regiment, drawn up in ranks.

The prisoners were clearly terrified. And among them, he could see Kati and Haran and Val al-Dun.

Aranthur cursed.

Syr Vardar was standing with two officers at the head of the Getans. He glanced at Aranthur and frowned.

'Timos? Aren't you with the assault? This is none of yours – ugly business.'

He turned to one of the officers, an Arnaut in wide Souliote trousers and a velvet waistcoat, with two silver-mounted pistols in his sash.

Aranthur stepped in. 'I disagree.'

'*Eks kajak synnina pasha? Sri inna?*' he said to the Arnaut.

What has he told you to do? The officer?

Vardar turned, real anger in his eyes.

'Timos, really. I will overlook this, but go back to your troops or I'll have to arrest you. This is nasty, but it must be done.'

'Nasty?' Sasan spat. 'You are going to kill half a thousand men and women in cold blood.'

Vardar shrugged. 'Your fellow feeling does you credit, no doubt. We have a food crisis and the Vicar has decided not to feed these enemies any longer. And be sure they are enemies. We took them in arms.'

'Sophia!' Aranthur grabbed Vardar's arm. 'You can rationalise anything, Syr Vardar. But they are prisoners!' He stood in the other man's face. 'And some of them are *my people* and not prisoners at all. From here I can see a woman who is an Academy Student.'

Vardar shrugged. 'I have orders.'

'I will stop you.'

It just came out, like so many of his other decisions.

Vardar turned on him. 'You what?' He looked puzzled.

Aranthur put himself between the Getans and the Safian prisoners.

'Gods witness,' spat Vardar. 'You Arnauts disgust me. We do all the fighting and all the governing, and you people steal and lie and serve as mercenaries, as if the Empire isn't worth your spit. And now here you are, having some sort of crisis of conscience because your precious Safian friend wants to save these people. They're the enemy, and now that I think about it, you Arnaut thief, I wonder if you aren't the enemy too. You lied about General Roaris, and—'

'*Do not obey this man,*' Aranthur said in Souliote.

The Arnaut officer spat.

'*I heard the Byzas fuck,*' he said in the same tongue.

'What was that?' Vardar snapped.

Aranthur nodded to the Arnaut officer.

Vardar grabbed at Aranthur's collar, where it hung over his breastplate.

Aranthur let him grab the collar, and then, in one pivot of his hips, he captured the man's elbow. He rolled him, and threw him face down, with his right arm twisted behind his back.

'Syr Vardar, I arrest you for violations of the honour code and for conduct unbecoming an officer,' Aranthur said smoothly. 'Personally, I think you are the kind of man who thinks that Arnauts will kill whomever they are told to kill. Surprise – that's not true. I'm going back to the assault force. Feel lucky I don't just throw you to the Safian prisoners you planned to butcher.'

'You fucking idiot – the Vicar ordered it, you traitor—'

'I choose not to believe you. And I note you are not accompanying the assault.'

'You dare—'

Aranthur laughed, and tripped a simple *lethe* spell. Awareness faded from the man's eyes.

'When he wakes,' Aranthur said in Souliote, 'insist that it was all my doing.'

The Arnaut shook his head. 'Fuck that. I'm going back to barracks to get some sleep.' He beckoned to Sasan. 'This isn't my duty. And fuckhead won't be awake for an hour. He sent the real guards away.' The man grinned. 'These Getans are good lads and lasses. They'll march away. I'd recommend that you and these poor bastards just... wander off.'

'Thanks!' Aranthur said.

The Arnaut smiled, and then frowned, troubled.

'I couldn't decide what to do.'

Aranthur nodded. 'My one talent.'

He had no time. But he went to Kati.

'Kati,' he said.

She shrank away from him.

'Kati,' he insisted. 'it's not all like this. I'm sorry – I'll see to it that the orders aren't carried out—'

'Is this how it's going to be? I wanted to go back to the *Studion*. But a Byzas officer just ordered my execution – I'm not even a prisoner, or so you once assured me.' She shook her head. 'And look at you – you reek of violence. Is this your life?'

'I often try to prevent violence—'

'With your sword and your *carabin* and your puffers?' She shook her head.

Aranthur thought of ten thousand things to say; explaining would take a hundred hours, or none.

'Sometimes, violence works. Like, when you are being attacked.'

Kati nodded. 'I have killed. Masran priests.' She shrugged. 'But it was wrong. It is all wrong.'

Sasan came up. The guards were gone, as if they'd never been.

'No idea what we're going to eat, but I know a place we can hide—'

'Don't tell me,' Aranthur said.

'Right.'

'Get food from Inoques,' Aranthur said. 'Tell her I asked.'

Sasan embraced him. 'You are a good man, Aranthur.'

Aranthur picked up his lobster-tail helmet.

'I try,' he admitted. 'Now I will go and kill.' He glanced at Kati. 'Sometimes...'

He shook hands with Sasan and headed out into the darkness beyond the gate. For a few ugly minutes he thought he'd spend the night lost, and then – a miracle from Sophia – he found himself at the sallyport steps. In a matter of a minute he was at Vilna's side.

'Where the hell were you?' Kallinikas put a hand on his shoulder. 'I need to light my fuse. Where were you?'

'Vardar was about to kill all the Safian prisoners,' he spat.

Kallinikas nodded. 'We don't have the food to feed them. Laws of War.'

Aranthur took a deep breath. 'I put Vardar under arrest. I won't accept it.'

Kallinikas laughed. 'Damn. Damn, you are quite the idealist. I have to light the fuse. You're right in one way – if we fail in this sortie, no reason to kill the poor wretches.'

'Thousand hells, Kallinikas, you mean you approve?'

'We have no food!' she hissed. 'We have four thousand soldiers! We can't feed five hundred Safians!'

He shrugged. 'I can do *arithmetika*. Five hundred mouths scarcely changes the day count.' He leant close to her. 'And frankly, if we kill prisoners, how are we better than the Pure?'

'They're forcing us—'

'Bullshit!' Aranthur spat. 'Bull *shit*! When you kill helpless people, that's on you.' He took a grenado from Vilna without turning his head, checked the priming in his *carabin*. 'I'll do whatever you people ask, but I will not stand for this.'

She looked at him for a long time.

'I need to light my fuse. If you happen to have any friends among the gods, pray.' She put a hand on his breastplate. 'I'm so fucking tired. Maybe you are right.'

'Go and look at them,' he said. 'Go and look them in the eye. Talk to five of them, and then tell me you approve. Sophia! It's all murder.'

'Exactly. And I'm about to kill a thousand of them, I hope.'

'Different,' he said.

'Really? Bah. Later.'

She shook his hand and ran off into the darkness.

'Five minutes,' said Ippeas.

He walked over to Aranthur.

'What was that about?'

Aranthur considered his options, and chose honesty.

'The Vicar has ordered the Safian prisoners executed. I have stopped it, at least temporarily.'

'Despicable,' Ippeas spat. 'Is this what my brothers and sisters are fighting for?'

Aranthur breathed. Despite the danger of the assault, he felt relief, and he wondered at his own feeling. But he had no time for self-analysis. A dozen men and boys were handing out wax earplugs. The entire assault force were putting in their earplugs and lying down against the earthwork rampart and crossing their arms over their heads.

This must be the posture in which the whole enemy assault force died when the tower fell on them, Aranthur thought.

He reached into his own mind to prepare his shields, the way a student will touch the facts in her memory when she sits to take a test. But like a lucky student who finds more information than she ever memorised, he found more than he thought he knew – a whole . . .

A whole *occulta*, with options and extensions.

Power wasn't an issue; there was so much *power* lying in the *Aulos* that he had no fears for the casting. So he brought the new *occulta* to the surface of his mind. Built like a glyph. Actually, as if it was a glyph of glyphs. He understood it immediately, even the parts he couldn't read.

'Two minutes,' Vilna said.

'The moment that the mine blows, we go up the ladders,' Aranthur said. 'We will go from right to left, by files.' He'd heard Vilna say it twice. 'I have five gold sequins for the first man into the enemy *gonne* line.'

A whispered chuckle of approval.

'Two minutes,' Vilna called softly.

'This is going to be bad,' Aranthur continued quietly. 'Stay alive, and help your mates, and we'll make it.'

It was his father's harvest day speech, the year that they had crops standing in every field at the same time due to the odd weather.

'One . . .' hissed Vilna, and the mine exploded. Very early.

It was never an *explosion* in Aranthur's memory – more a curious blackness, an absence of anything but light and sound. He unrolled his shield sequence almost instantly. He was pounded as he had been the day before when a dozen enemy sorcerers attacked his shields, except this time, the blows just rolled off.

His hearing was gone. He felt as if he'd been stuffed with fur, somehow – padded, and yet shocked. And the explosion seemed to take forever. The dirty smoke stank of rotten eggs and death, and it was thicker than fog.

But the most stunning thing of all was the sequence of his shields, which spiralled out of his reaching left hand like a dragon's scales. He almost lost the casting, he was so stunned by his own *occulta*, but even as it expanded, it stopped the flying splinters, the stones, the red-hot sand and the sniper bullets and crossbow bolts too.

Aranthur shook himself. He felt . . .

Powerful.

He reached up and got a hand on the ladder. He was shouting, and the sound of his shouts was peculiar in his ears and in his head.

He started up the ladder. It only had ten rungs to the firing step above. They flew by, as his shields continued to ring with the flying gravel and flung detritus of the mine – a human jaw, a whole musket.

Aranthur reached the head of the ladder. To his right, in all the smoke, he could see the flash of steel armour; to his left, the giant form of Kallotronis.

He could hear nothing, and the smoke filled the dark like a curse.

He was sliding down the front face of the wall. He knew what to expect – day-old corpses – and there they were, their sweet and horrible smell suffusing the sulphur fog.

There were people following him, and he lit one of his magelights to show the way, and put it on the back of his lobster-tail helmet. He stepped on something bad, hard and then squishy, and then pushed through, and he was climbing, this time climbing the ditch's outer face.

It wasn't so much a silence as a roaring in his ears. Without audio cues, he wasn't even sure where danger might lie; was the enemy firing on the old breach above?

He pushed his shields out ahead of him, and they rippled smoothly away. Whatever Inoques had done, it had something to do with this.

301

The new defence was vastly more sophisticated than his simple red *aspides*, however strong they were as point defence.

He topped the ditch and crossed the top of the breach, where he'd lain in a rifle pit the day before. Now he could see.

The whole enemy siege line was firing. The lines were a blaze of light, long tongues of dragon's fire spitting from the tubes of sixty *gonnes*.

Except in the centre of the arc. There, the whole line was dark. He couldn't see anything there – not a gaping pit, nor a rising column of smoke, dust, and up-thrust dirt. He had no idea. It was like a black maw – a grounded Dark Forge in the firmament of fire.

And his shield was holding.

There was no room for thought, or choice.

Aranthur went forward into the fire.

Somewhere to the left, a powerful Magos began to unlimber a set of attacks on Aranthur's shield complex. But his attacks slid away as if they were balls of butter thrown at a wall of glass, and Aranthur continued to stumble forward. The enemy sorcerer raised the *tempo* of his attack, and then was suddenly gone, taken by a massive *occulta* from the choir in the fortress above and behind him.

Aranthur was clambering down the rubble of the collapsed tower. Two thousand year old stonework lay tumbled like the fallen blocks of a child's tower.

A volley of purple and turquoise fire hit his shields and lit them up, an enemy choir's concerted effort.

The shield shed them, and Aranthur felt Dahlia and Jalu'd, the Seeker, and Ettore, the weather Magos, reaching through the *Aulos* to pinpoint the attack. *Sihr* and *saar* criss-crossed like the flames of the firing *gonnes*. The light and the black light of the charge of *puissance* lit the deaths of a thousand men and women.

But nothing was touching the assault force. Now they were through the rubble field and crossing the burnt open ground that led to the old Imperial trenches. Aranthur could see the outline of the burst mine, a gaping maw in the earth, with sulphur smoke still eddying from burning beams and backlit in his magesight by the absolute darkness of *sihr*.

He went to the left, where the mine had done less damage. Men were passing him, now. The assault force was eager to cross the killing ground and get to grips. A burly longshoreman leapt down into an enemy trench and began to use a pick to clear it. Aranthur noted that it was Jase Nero, first man into the enemy *gonne* line.

In his moment of inattention, Aranthur was *located* by a Magos. The first flash disoriented him, but his new crystalline shields held, even at point-blank range. Aranthur's snapped discharge of *saar* blew into his opponent's shields and cut his opponent in half.

The sword was in his hand, and he felt, not fear, not rage, nor even disgust, but a sort of joy, a pleasure like singing, like making love. The battle, the enemy gun line, the flashes of *power*, were beautiful, the way a sword blade could be beautiful, even held by an adversary.

'*To your left*,' the sword said.

He picked up the motion – saw it as *sihr* – and guessed, correctly, that this was an *Exalted* at night. He cast his *enhancement* and then unleashed a torrent of *power* at the *Exalted*.

It returned two thin red beams of pure *sihr*.

The two of them walked at each other, and the *tempo* of attacks increased as they closed, until, almost at the point of going sword to sword, the two shields all but merged. They spun off shards of failed realities from the event horizon of the powers of change.

Aranthur had never been so *puissant*. It was as if something inside him had been unlocked, or unleashed.

But even as his sword moved to engage, the *Exalted* half turned, and fell, cut almost in half. Ippeas, the Great Sword, had passed unnoticed through *its* shields and now continued forward as if the dispatch of an *Exalted* was an everyday event.

Aranthur followed Ippeas into the enemy's second line of trenches. Off to his right, Magdalenes, polished steel armour a malevolent reflection of the fire-crossed dark, were destroying a *gonne* battery, spiking *gonnes* or blowing the iron tubes. To his left, Kallotronis leant over a trench and shot down into it.

Aranthur rolled his shield around to face new threats, but the attacks were slowing – the ripples of red fire dying away.

Off to the left, there was chaos.

Ware said the sword, a soft woman's voice.

Aranthur turned to the left, and there was another of them. It was in among his Arnauts – a man eviscerated, a woman beheaded.

He ran to meet it, and it saw him.

'*You*,' it said.

Aranthur stepped forward. 'I know who you are.'

By the light of their shields, he could see again the rage and confusion in the shoulders and the neck. The face was untroubled – that ivory-pale face. Up close, its constructedness was obvious – the face itself was an attached mask.

'I could release you,' Aranthur said.

The thing raised a puffer through his shields and fired.

The ball smashed into Aranthur's breastplate. The ball didn't penetrate, but the blow knocked him down, and the pain was intense. Ribs broke. The sword spun out of his hand with an audible wail of despair.

The *Exalted* drifted forward, invulnerable, victorious, glowing with potency. It put a bloody, bare foot on Aranthur's breastplate and pressed him into the sand, grinding his broken ribs. And his vision tunnelled. He was unable to breathe. The pain was immense.

Who are you? it asked again.

Aranthur lay looking up at it, and in his mind he was running a hand over Inoques' tattoos. He'd come to know them quite well. And he'd had a day to think this through, although he'd hoped to have a little more calm to try . . .

He knew the binding. He'd copied it amid the blood and despair of another battlefield, and it was written in his mind.

He reached up and put a bare hand on the *Exalted*'s leg. He unwrote the binding in letters of fire on the crystal surface of the *Aulos*, all of which was pure mental allegory, but he imagined the whole of the *binding*. Then he imagined the Safiri characters unwriting from left to right, backing the text across the page of existence.

The *Exalted* stood stock-still for a moment, and then it unknitted.

The release of *saar* from the unwritten glyphs was tremendous, but the *saar* didn't burn him, but rather, almost refreshed him.

Its scream wasn't harrowing; it was more pathetic, as if it welcomed death, or mourned something lost. The scarlet robe fluttered for a moment in the firelight like the flag of a beaten army, and then fell to the ground.

Aranthur rolled onto his side. He was empty of *power*. It took him two attempts to get to his feet, and even then he stood and swayed. Then he stooped, despite the broken ribs, and put a hand on the sword.

You live! it said.

For the first time, he answered it.

I need you, he admitted. The voice came to him as naturally as speaking, but it was in his mind.

Chimeg came out of the darkness and got a hand under his arm, and Vilna steadied him.

'Orders?'

The fighting didn't end because the *Exalted* were destroyed, and in many ways the withdrawal was going to be more demanding than the assault. The assault had needed only bravery; the withdrawal would require discipline and attention to detail, and Aranthur could feel days of fighting and short rations compounding.

Trumpets sounded on the walls behind him, and a red rocket rose over the battlefield. It still took him a hundred heartbeats to realise that these were the recall signals. He managed to get a knee under himself, and his helmeted head seemed to weigh more than his body. He struggled, wobbled, and knelt. Everything hurt – dehydration, partial rations, weeks of stress. And the *Exalted*. In the unbinding, he had somehow cancelled his *enhancement*. The hunger was already on him, and he had to function.

He could see his own militia ahead of him; by the light of a hundred fires, they were spiking a row of heavy *gonnes*. Lang Cleg had a bag of iron spikes, and beside her Daud, his half-shaved blond hair lit by the magery all around, swung a mallet driving the soft iron into the touch holes of the *gonnes*. As Aranthur watched, the two of them looked like actors in an opera about Draxos the Smith, the fires of all the hells burning around them as they forged the weapons of the gods.

Weaving like a drunkard, he made his way over the upcast of sand where the enemy had tried to protect their gonnes. Two Byzas women were setting fire to a stack of prepared wicker gabions, as yet unfilled. An older man in a black breastplate was pressing a huddle of prisoners towards the city.

'Let them go,' Aranthur spat. 'Do you want to feed them?'

The man frowned, but obeyed, and the terrified men and women scattered.

'Drummer!'

Aranthur was afraid for a moment that he was spent, but he had *power* and he hadn't even tapped the crystal on his chest.

He *enhanced* his voice and called, 'Drummer, on me!'

Every head turned. The boy who carried the company banner, an elegantly painted Sophia with her sister Magdala on plain white silk, ran to his side, the banner almost red-gold in the firelight of the battle.

'Rally!' Aranthur called. 'On me!'

His drummer, a big Byzas man with dark skin and blond hair, ran out of the darkness, trying to sheathe his heavy cutlass.

'Syr!' he called.

'Rally!' Aranthur called.

Off to the right, he could see the flash of armour – the Magdalenes were also rallying. He grabbed a dekark.

'Kouznos!' he called. 'Rally and hold.'

'Aye!' the man called.

Aranthur made his legs work. He turned to the left and ran along the smooth boards that floored the battery, tripped over a corpse, and climbed up a short ladder.

A ball took the cheek-plate off his helmet.

There were enemy out there in the darkness; he saw movement, and lit matches.

A volley crashed out to his left, and the tongues of fire of forty matchlocks, and he could hear the orders in Souliote.

He put his head down and ran. He tripped over something soft and went down, twisting his neck, and the pain in his chest from the ribs. Then he was up again, and in among the Arnauts.

'Kallotronis!'

'Here,' yelled the big man.

'You saw the signal?'

'No!'

'Time to withdraw. Can you hold here for . . . two minutes?'

Kallotronis shrugged. 'A year, if you want. No one out there wants a piece of us. They're shit-scared.'

'Listen, and tell me if I'm insane. I pull back to here – along the chord of the circle—'

'No idea what you mean.'

'Never mind. Along the enemy lines. The Magdalenes retreat to the militia, then both to you, and then together we back across the sand.'

Kallotronis hesitated. 'We should attack their next line. They're fucking panicked, Timos. We could break the siege.'

'With a hundred soldiers?' Aranthur said. 'No.'

Kallotronis looked as if he was going to disobey.

'If you had any balls—'

Aranthur grabbed the other man.

'Listen to me! On a battlefield of twenty thousand, one hundred cannot triumph. Now obey.' He paused. 'Please. I ask it.'

Kallotronis looked over his shoulder.

'Well, perhaps there are more devils out there in the dark than I think. Tell me again.'

'Look,' Aranthur insisted, and he drew it in blue fire on the air, with little arrows. 'We collapse from right to left, so that we're all together here, at the end of the battery if we have to make a stand.'

'Yes. I never thought I'd follow a fucking warlock into the dark, but lead on.'

'Two minutes!' Aranthur said.

Running across the gap between positions was one of the bravest things he had ever done. His shields were gone and his reserves were spent, and it was totally different from fighting the *Exalted*, or a duel. Death was grim and impersonal and very close, and no amount of his own cleverness was going to save him. His red shields were still up, but he now knew from experience that a close-range musket ball was not deterred by magik. There were field pieces of some sort firing out in the darkness – or perhaps the enemy had a third line. Even as he forced himself to run across the open ground, he heard the unmistakable ripping-paper sound of a cannonball and felt the heat of its passage. It had come through his weakening shields without difficulty.

His chest hurt, and he found breathing difficult; he wondered how many ribs he'd broken. He ran anyway. This time he didn't fall. His shield *occulta* flickered, and he had to lie in open ground and summon more *power* in the *Aulos*, which was rich with *power* tonight.

The enemy seemed hesitant. There were many soldiers out there, but they were not coming forward. Instead, they were firing into the dark, at very little.

Except Aranthur.

The effort of will to get to his feet and run, facing the fire of his enemies and the near exhaustion of his muscles, was like the effort of will of launching a major *occulta*. But then, he had lots of practice. He stumbled to his feet and moved, reached the head of the ladder down into the battery held by his own people, slapped Vilna on the shoulder, and ran past the banner. He headed for the next battery in the enemy's second line arc, held by the Magdalenes. He saw Ippeas instantly – the man's armour shone in the *Aulos*.

'Great Sword!' he called.

Syr Ippeas turned. His knights had just repulsed an attack. There was a wrack-line of corpses in front of them.

He didn't even attempt speech. Instead, he raised his diagram of blue fire, a broad red arrow showing his suggested path of retreat.

Ippeas glanced at the diagram.

'The militia are in the next battery,' Aranthur panted. 'The Arnauts just beyond.'

Ippeas nodded, his steel-visored face utterly inscrutable.

'Yes,' he snapped. 'On me!' he roared.

The whole armoured line turned like one being and ran. Aranthur, carrying a breastplate and a helmet, couldn't imagine the effort required to sprint through the firelit darkness in full harness, but the Magdalenes ran like pacers, heads up, leaving a line of corpses behind them. Four of them carried another. Aranthur scrambled along beside the wounded knight, found the wound, a deep puncture inside the left elbow. He stopped the blood flow as best he could at a run in the darkness – two *occultae* cast simultaneously, a thing that he would have thought impossible ten days before.

The Magdalenes came into the battery held by the militia from the east, and formed like the molten metal hardening in the bullet mould; suddenly they were there, a wall of steel.

'Load!' called a feminine voice among them, and they began to load their long puffers. A few had long *fusils* or *carabins*.

Kouznos saluted. 'Centark?'

'Load and hold. The Magdalenes will pass behind us. Give them a count of one hundred to cross to the next position, and then fire and run like hell.'

Aranthur held up his diagram.

Syr Ippeas shook his head. 'Never let it be said that my brothers and sisters had to be saved by militia, Centark. We will be the last out – your people can fire and retire.'

Aranthur shrugged at his dekark; Ippeas outranked him, and was probably right. He began to load his own *carabin*, which had remained slung on his back since the attack began. He opened the pan to find it primed and loaded.

He'd never fired it.

'Do you have a target?' he asked Kouznos.

'Not really,' muttered the dekark.

'Vilna?' Aranthur called.

'Here, *Bahadur.*'

'See anything out there? Off to the left?'

'Aye, *Bahadur.* Just there.'

Chimeg aimed a *carabin* and fired.

'Just there.'

Aranthur saw the dim shapes of men in the darkness, and he could see the glow of the enemy's lit match. Tufenchis. He aimed and fired, with no thought of morality.

Kouznos bobbed his head. 'Got it.'

'Do it!'

'Make ready!' Kouznos roared. 'Look left! See the burning match? Take aim!'

Fifty musket barrels moved to the left, glinting in the light of the burning gabions.

'Fire!'

The volley crashed out.

'Go! Go! Go!' Aranthur rolled, *augmenting* his voice. No point to secrecy now.

The militia picked up their wounded and went up the ladders to the open, sandy ground. It was Aranthur's third time across the darkness, but whatever the effect of the last volley, the enemy fire was slackened. Aranthur found himself with Kallotronis. It occurred to him in a moment of battlefield clarity that it was easier to cross open ground with comrades.

He had a moment to catch his breath, which slammed against his broken ribs. The Arnauts were firing, a rolling fire, men choosing targets or firing into the darkness in their own time.

'Five rounds a man left,' Kallotronis said.

Overhead, a cataclysm of *occultae* criss-crossed the air, and made the stars and moon pale by comparison. A flash of purple-black left lightning lines on Aranthur's retinas, and then an answering curtain of jade green, and a detonation off to their right, as if an entire siege battery had fired together.

'Eagle. Draxos. Fucking hells!' Kallotronis spat. 'All the big boys. I need better amulets for this shit.' He shook his head.

There were a dozen almost consecutive flashes, like the height of a deadly lightning storm, except in colours: black-lit purple, white and red and green and gold. Most if it was high overhead – Magi on the city walls exchanging vast gouts of *power* with enemy Magi in the foothills. But one fist of red-black *power* struck full on Aranthur's remaining shields, and burned through in a dozen places. A woman died, incinerated. A man boiled, and the burning-soap scent filled the air and the smell of scorched flesh and superheated sand was added.

Aranthur found that his shields healed themselves, weakened but still intact. He finally understood what Inoques had done. In a flash of insight, he understood the principle, and how his red *aspides* were only a chrysalis stage of a wider principle of defence.

Ware, said the sword in his hand, so clearly that Kallotronis turned his head.

Aranthur threw his will into his shield, and then emptied his *kuria* into his will.

'Sophia!' his dekark spat.

'Centark's a warlock, lads!' cried a voice. 'We're safe as fucking houses.'

Vilna growled, 'Make ready!'

The ranks locked up, the three companies like one. Ippeas was locked in the magikal combat, one hand on a talisman. The knights obeyed the little Nomadi dekark because his voice held the absolute assurance of a veteran.

Another storm struck, but this one took longer and the pulses were easier to deal with singly.

I should be spent, Aranthur thought. *How am I even functioning?*

Trust me, the sword said,

The enemy infantry that had lurked out in the dark for so long came forward. Aranthur had now made enough war to feel their hesitancy. He walled off the part of his mind that maintained the shield, and demanded that it hold. Then, with *power* he should not have had, he tossed a string of simple, brilliant magelights.

They hung in the air, illuminating the mass of the enemy.

'Present!' Vilna sang.

A hundred barrels came down – muskets and puffers and rifled *carabins* together, like a single arm commanded by a single will – pointing into the illuminated mass that hesitated . . .

'Fire!' Vilna roared.

The volley pierced the darkness and the smoke billowed out into the brilliant magelight.

'Charge!' Aranthur said.

It was the only order he'd given, but he knew it was right. The mixed line exploded through their own smoke, but the enemy broke, unprepared for the switch from predator to prey. The moment they ran, there was no point to the charge; Aranthur was trying . . .

'Halt!' called Ippeas, clear and high. It was like a *subjugation*. The whole line halted as if on parade.

The barrage of magik had moved. Something had changed, and Aranthur felt like a swordsman whose opponent had made an error in timing.

'Now!' he said to Ippeas. 'We need to get out of here.'

'Agreed,' Ippeas said. 'Militia first. Load, and run.'

Aranthur waited to the very end, holding his shield up much the way his banner bearer was clutching the colours, as using the banner staff to hold himself erect. But whatever prompted the firestorm of *power*, it was gone, off to find a softer target, or perhaps itself defeated, bleeding or incinerated. Aranthur had no way of knowing.

He walked back with Syr Ippeas, and there was no resistance after they left the siege lines – no pursuit, and almost no fire. The shooting was dying away along most of the lines out in the darkness. Fires flickered, but the ongoing flashes of *puissance* were few and far between, exactly as if a cell of thunder and lightning had passed over them and was now being blown into the distance.

Aranthur was the second to last soldier to tumble down the wall of the ditch. It was part of the logic of fighting in a siege that the moment he put a wall of sand and earth between himself and the enemy he felt a lethargy creep over him, and his mind relaxed.

Ippeas took his hand.

'Well done, young syr,' he said. 'Even if you did attempt to give me orders.'

His helmet was open, his tired face visible in the light of the torches at the base of the trench. He was smiling.

There was a reserve waiting on the firing step; men and women who had been in the nave, wounded, stood ready with lit matches. Ippeas gave Aranthur a hand up the inside wall, and spoke out the password several times.

'Wouldn't do to get shot by someone a little too eager,' he said. 'Coryn's Sword, Coryn's Sword,' he called.

The people on the firing step were cheering.

Aranthur got a leg over the parapet, and for the first time, gave Ippeas a hand.

'I confess it,' Ippeas said. 'I'm tired.'

The men and women of the Twenty-second were coming up the wall, and Aranthur called out the password.

'My folks coming back,' he called, first in Byzas, then in Souliote, because the people on the wall were cheering, but they were twitchy, too alert, with too much pain and not enough sleep among them.

'Incredible.' Kallinikas grabbed Aranthur's hand and wrung it like a drowning man clutching at floating wood. 'You did it. Their *gonnes* are silent.'

Ippeas allowed himself to be embraced, and his stoic face split in a broad grin.

'We did, too,' he said. 'The mine was perfect.'

'Thousand hells, yes!' Kallinikas laughed. 'It was perfect. And the Magi – they had a plan of their own, and they used your whole sortie as bait.' She was wild, her hair plastered to her forehead. 'Come on. The Vicar will want to see you.'

'I want to see my people off the wall,' Aranthur said.

'Same,' said Ippeas.

As it proved, by the time the seven companies that had made the sortie were assembled in the covered way, the Vicar came out. Aranthur was counting with Kouznos; it didn't seem possible that they'd only lost three dead and a dozen wounded, all retrieved. While he counted, he ate a large wedge of military cheese. He was ravenous.

'Centark Timos,' the Vicar called.

Aranthur turned. 'My lord?'

'Arrest him,' spat Vardar.

A pair of the Vicar's Black Lobsters stepped forward.

'Sword, syr,' said one. The voice was impersonal.

A frisson seemed to run through all the troops in the covered way.

There was enough light to see; the two Black Lobsters were in full armour.

Syr Ippeas was less than four strides away. He turned very suddenly, and almost as if he was *enhanced*, he suddenly stood between the two Black Lobsters.

'What's this?' he asked.

'None of your affair,' Vardar snapped. 'Do your duty.'

Syr Ippeas turned, and flipped down his visor.

'I am doing my duty,' said the impersonal voice of the helmet.

The Black Lobsters stepped back, drawing their weapons.

The Vicar raised an arm. 'What is this? Syr Ippeas? I have ordered this man arrested. Please do not interfere.'

Again, a movement among the assault troops.

'For what?' Ippeas asked.

'He used magik on me, and released the enemy prisoners!' spat Vardar. 'Even now they are no doubt preparing to seize the town.'

There was a long silence. Ippeas' helmet nodded once.

'Of course, you ordered the execution of the prisoners.'

The Vicar's eyes narrowed. 'I realise that you are used to being an absolute authority, Great Sword, but I do not debate my orders – not in public, not in the face of the enemy. Stand down, or I will have you arrested too.'

Silence.

'You are a fool, Vicar, if you imagine that arresting this man at the end of the assault was wisdom,' said the helmet. 'Or that you can arrest me. Ever.'

The ranks of the assault force were growling. Even at the point of both exhaustion and victory, men and women leant in, listening. Most of the assault's left wing knew they owed their lives to Aranthur's shields; some took a step forward, or two, or three.

At the word 'fool', something in the Vicar snapped.

'Damn you!' he spat.

One of the Black Lobsters raised his puffer.

Kallotronis leant over Aranthur's shoulder, his long *jezzail* pointing unerringly at the Vicar.

'What in a thousand hells is going on here?' Kallinikas ran into the circle of officers. 'Sophia's tits.' She saw the *jezzail*. 'Stop this!'

Aranthur made his decision. He raised his hands.

'I will be arrested.' Loudly and clearly, he said, 'We do not need dissension.'

'I'll back any play you make,' Kallotronis said. 'I can command this army better than this old fool.'

'Walk away,' Aranthur said to Kallotronis. 'Arrest me,' he said to the Black Lobsters.

He unbuckled his sword belt and handed the old sword, not to the Black Lobsters, but to Ippeas. The man had to take it, and he stepped back.

Loudly, he said, 'Three more days and the General will be here. Everyone stand down.'

Vardar was struggling to speak.

Aranthur dropped his helmet on the ground. He saluted the Vicar.

'Whatever you say, my lord.'

Ippeas flipped his visor open.

The two Black Lobsters relaxed slightly. Both lowered the muzzles of their puffers.

'In irons,' Vardar spat.

The Vicar flicked a glance at the other man and frowned.

'No. No. In the nave, one hour. All of you.'

He took Aranthur by the arm, as if they were old friends, and started walking him along the gravel path to the sallyport.

The assault force stood in loose ranks, still not dismissed.

Aranthur waved, as if he was merry.

The Vicar led him through the sallyport.

'Why in all the hells did you release those Safian dogs?' He sounded more tired than angry.

Aranthur shook his head. He was too tired to mince his words. He found that instead of being afraid, he was mostly angry.

'My lord, you were about to commit a great wrong, and I put it beyond your power to do so.'

'Traitor!' Vardar spat.

'Traitor to what?' Aranthur shot back. 'An Empire whose nobles endlessly place self-interest before even simple patriotism?'

'No matter how we dress you people up, you remain savages,' Vardar said. 'You cannot even remain loyal to the hand that feeds you.'

Aranthur shook his head. 'Foolish debate. You ordered five hundred people killed in cold blood. This is unacceptable. I'd rather die than allow it.'

'Grow up,' spat the Vicar. He looked old and as tired as Aranthur felt, but there was no sympathy in his old face. 'Grow up. Welcome to the real world. We aren't idealists. We kill people. I can't feed them. No one should have taken them – they should have died in the storm.'

Aranthur thought of Kurvenos.

'If you kill defenceless people, then all you are is a murderer,' he said.

'Oh, shut up,' the Vicar said. 'Your adolescent morality is misplaced and stupid. Put him somewhere.'

'First, tell us where they are,' Vardar said.

Aranthur shrugged. 'No idea.'

Vardar slapped him.

Aranthur felt the rage, but it was distant. It was almost as if he was bored. His fatigue was total. Nothing mattered. Even the pain in his face, and the humiliation. The weight of the people he'd killed lay on him like wet black felt, and cloaked any real anger he might have felt. His broken ribs were much closer to the surface of his reality than a face slap.

'He's colluding with them,' Vardar said.

The Vicar glanced at him.

Aranthur took a deep breath.

'My lord, if you don't mind' – he allowed himself more than a little sarcasm – 'I've had quite a day. If I am under arrest, I'd nonetheless like a bowl of soup and a clean shirt. I think you owe me as much, frankly.'

'He's allied with—'

Aranthur turned his back on the other officer.

'My lord, I have a hundred witnesses that I led the fucking assault, and unlike this woodlouse, I just fought. And with the help of many other people, we conquered. We bought you some days. If you think I'm some sort of enemy spy, then I, too, think you're a fool.'

The Vicar was angry. Through his own fatigue, Aranthur could see that the man's age, and exhaustion, were making it harder and harder for him to see through the haze of decisions. He could see it, but it was as if he didn't care.

The Vicar was trapping himself into a set of decisions.

I should not have called him a fool, Aranthur thought.

'Cell,' the Vicar spat. 'Irons.'

6

Antioke

The cell was dark, and damp, and smelt of old despair. Aranthur had no water to wash, and a single candle; and air, and room to stand. And despite the Vicar's orders, no one put him in irons, but then, no one offered to get him a clean shirt, either.

The candle burned down. About six hours.

No one brought another. The hunger was the worst; he'd cast a great deal, and he'd used the *enhancement*, and now he had no food. After the first hour, he lay on his face on the wet, filthy floor with spikes of pain that shot into his gut and stayed there, like a sword thrust. Every few moments it would fade, and he'd start to sit up, and then the pain would strike again. When he wriggled in pain, the broken ribs would torment him.

The pain and the dark brought on the . . . the other.

Aranthur was never able to decide if what happened was real, or his imagination – a tentacle of the *Aulos* intruding into the real world, or just his guilt and his fatigue.

It occurred to him many times that there might actually be no wall of 'reality' which separated his guilt and imagination from the *Aulos*.

But he was alone, writhing in pain. And then he looked up, and there was a man sitting in the darkness. He was thin, and pale, and light seemed to shine from him, because there was no other light.

'Remember me, do you?' the man spat.

Aranthur didn't remember him.

And then there was another man, broader in the shoulder.

'Remember me, cocksucker?' he said.

Aranthur backed into the corner, away from the hole in the floor, and hunkered down.

'Doesn't remember us,' the broader man said.

He turned to speak to the thin man, and when he turned, his profile, which glowed slightly, showed that the back of his head was missing.

Aranthur gagged.

'Now 'e knows us,' Broad Man said.

''E knows you,' Thin Man said.

'I killed you,' Aranthur said.

'There oughta be a prize for yer honour,' Thin Man said. 'You fuckin' kilt me too.'

'An' me,' said Crossbow.

Then they were quiet. But there were others beyond them in the darkness, glowing a sickly pale green and pressing forward, murmuring.

Crossbow came closer. 'What do y'say to me, eh? You what killed me.'

'An' me!' Thin Man said. 'I was alive. No better than I ought, maybe. But fuckin' alive.'

'You were going to kill me,' Aranthur said.

Thin Man shrugged. 'I doubt it. Really, I didn't even know you was there.'

'Boy, you fuckin' came back and kilt me. I was lettin' you run off. You came for me.' Crossbow was angry.

'You were paid to kill me.' Aranthur wasn't sure that was even true.

'So what? You could ha' just *ridden away.*' Crossbow shook his head. 'You wanna be a Lightbringer? You *like to kill.*'

The other figures behind Crossbow pressed forward.

There were a great many of them. Including some Safian women, their hair lank, their eyes bright with despair. They spoke in Safiri, and he could understand them perfectly.

'I never wanted to hurt anyone. They took my children. They tortured me. They made me a thing, a flesh weapon, and you killed me.'

A Safian cavalryman.

'You were like a whirlwind of death.'

A Pindari, who smiled, and spat.

'Death is the thing that unites us,' he said, and laughed.

317

A Tufenchis officer with a bullet in his heart, his khaftan soaked in blood.

'You shot me yesterday,' he said.

And behind them, more, and more.

'You killed me,' they said. 'I was alive. You killed me. I had a life, and you took it.'

You killed me. Youkilledmeyoukilledmeyoukilledmeyoukilledme youkilledmeyoukilledmeyoukilledmeyoukilledmeyoukilledme.

They came to him, each telling a story, yelling, or just complaining, as if he'd cheated them in the market.

The real horror came when they passed through him. Each one *entered into* him, and as they passed into his cowering, shaking body, he felt the death, the moment of separation, the loss...

When it was over, Aranthur awoke, shaking, damp, lying curled in the corner of his cell. It was absolutely dark, and there were no phantoms, no voices complaining of death, and he was alone. His gut hurt, and his fingers and toes felt as if they were on fire. Every injury and wound he'd sustained in the last year hurt, and he felt an echo of the deaths that had passed through him.

For a moment, he lay in the darkness and thought he might, in fact, be dead. He heard an odd sound, and he tried to place it. It took him a long time to realise it was his own weeping.

He tried to pray. He tried to visualise Sophia, or the Eagle – to see them as they appeared in statues – but when he thought of Sophia all he could see was Nenia, and when he thought of the Eagle, he could think of nothing. So he thought of Nenia, and despite the pain, or because of it, eventually Aranthur went to sleep. He was already afraid of a bewildering array of things, from the angry ghosts of his dead, to being executed by his own side, to being captured by the Pure. If the fortress fell now, he'd be taken. He had time to imagine being *bound* to an *Exalted*. He understood the process now.

I would make a particularly effective Exalted.

But his body was too tired to stay afraid forever. He fell asleep in his sweat-sodden clothes, and woke, freezing cold. There was nothing in his cell to warm him, and he lay, teeth chattering, wondering if he'd contracted a fever. The darkness was total. Fear rose to choke him, and he tried to see anything – Nenia, or Tribane, or Tiy Drako. No faces came to him. He lay and shivered . . .

He managed to piss into the hole in the corner of his cell – a particularly foul hole with an ancient, musty smell. Finally he put his sweat-soaked doublet back on, and something crawled on his skin. He had a moment of terrible panic, fell back, and hit his head, and lay moaning, but the pain helped him fight the panic, and he seized on it. Then he recovered from that brink, and realised that he had slept enough to have *power*. A little.

He warmed himself, dried his shirt and his doublet. Made a light.

How long had passed?

He had no way to know.

He had no water, and that was going to be a problem. He called a few times, but something of the quality of the silence told him he was absolutely alone. It occurred to him that in the heat of a siege, a prisoner could be completely forgotten. He didn't even really know where he was: somewhere deep underneath the old Temple complex, he thought. Maybe the citadel. It was all connected underground; they'd walked a long way, the two Black Lobsters silent.

Yes, a man could be forgotten.

Aranthur went to the door of his cell. It was ancient oak, thick as his arm and heavily reinforced with iron. He could think of a dozen ways to open it. He couldn't imagine who would be stupid enough to leave a trained Magos in a normal cell.

Unless they want me to try and escape.

That sort of thinking was all very well, but the more he explored the idea, the less likely it seemed. He could sense no one within his range – maybe a hundred paces. Certainly no latent magik.

He shook his head. It would have to be an elaborate trap arranged in the middle of a siege by tired, angry men and women.

Didn't seem likely.

He lay a while longer, and then he rose from his crouch and lifted the bar with his *power* and stepped out into the corridor. He was afraid, and he couldn't put a name on his fear. He pushed his fears about the dead who had come to him down, and moved off to his right. He kicked a wooden bucket, almost fell, and then stood listening to the rattle and clack of the bucket echoing off the walls.

Is there a way of doing all this without killing?

319

He reviewed each of the deaths he could remember as he inched down the corridor. Eventually there was emptiness under his left hand, and he paused for an age, listening.

Nothing.

Very cautiously, he went across the corridor and felt carefully.

Nothing. So the hallway that held his cell was crossed by another, wider corridor. He couldn't remember which way he'd come.

He inched back the way he'd come until he found the wooden bucket, which he then carried back.

'This is stupid,' he said aloud.

He lit a magelight. Now anyone could see him, and anyone who could detect *power* could find him, but at least he could see.

He left the bucket to mark the corridor and turned left, because that was his best guess and the air seemed marginally fresher.

He counted a hundred steps, and then another hundred. The floor under his feet was smooth, but curiously uneven. On examination, it proved to have been hewn from the rock. Black basalt, by the look of it – the same stone as was used in the oldest parts of the Black Bastion.

He remembered that they'd walked for a long time. But when he'd counted to two hundred, he lost confidence, and stopped. He breathed for a while and went on. Thirty-seven paces further he came to a cross-corridor at an acute angle.

He didn't remember it at all, and he stopped. The corridor to the left turned away at an acute angle and seemed to slope down; the corridor to the right curved.

He stepped back from the junction and took a deep breath.

He heard something.

Instantly he raised his shields and put out his magelight. He ignited his magesight and the *power* of the thing coming at him down the curving corridor was so great it appeared to light the tunnel.

Aranthur stepped back. His new shields would not uncoil, and he realised how little *power* he had.

The bright thing came on, moving confidently.

Aranthur tried to back down the corridor but he was too clumsy and his heel caught and down he went. It was all he could do to maintain his red *aspides* as he fell.

The brilliant glob of *power* turned into his corridor and ignited its purple-black shields, a dense and terrifying display of *power*, meshed discs of dark crystal like a scale armour covering the corridor and reflecting Aranthur's puny red shields like the thousand eyes of a malignant insect.

Aranthur stumbled to his feet. He had no sword, and no dagger.

He raised his head.

'You are a remarkable human,' said Inoques' voice. 'They arrest you, and you escape.'

He smiled, but he almost slumped to the floor in relief. In those last seconds he'd convinced himself that an *Exalted* had been sent to kill him.

'You came for me,' he said.

She settled gracefully onto the stone floor, folding her labyrinthine shields away like wings beneath her.

'Let me tell you something. I have my ship loaded – enough water to sail across the whole South Sea, enough powder to fight every pirate in the great green.' She smiled mirthlessly, and the tiny lines of calligraphy that replaced her eyebrows raised. 'Haras has wanted to leave for days. I agree – this place is doomed. Even after your fight the other night – you know that Haras and Jalu'd and your Dahlia smashed the enemy's choir?' She shrugged. 'Haras loosed the *Apep-Duat* he captured on the Azurnil, and it destroyed their casters. And still this place is doomed. I was ready to leave.'

'And?'

She laughed. 'I am a poor slave. I do not like to have my will balked. And at the same time, you have wakened something in me. I came back for *you*.'

Aranthur smiled despite his various misgivings.

'I suppose I should escape,' he said. 'But then I really am a criminal.'

She shrugged. 'The shades of your obedience or disobedience to the laws of people who don't value you are of little importance to me.'

'Tell me something, Yasmina?' he asked.

She nodded. 'Perhaps.'

'If I leave, will the city fall?'

She shrugged. 'You are not so important, and I have never been able to predict the future. I can only tell you that if the Pure take the Black Stone, your . . . side . . . is finished.'

Aranthur sat back. 'I believe that General Tribane will get here.'

She shrugged again. 'Perhaps. Not my problem.'

'Tell me what's happening out there?'

She looked at him. 'Very well. Almost nothing. The Vicar is hunting these Safian prisoners, and they are nowhere to be found, mostly because Dahlia and Kati are hiding them very effectively in plain sight, and none of the Vicar's magikal staff would do anything to harm Sasan or Dahlia. The Vicar is very unpopular... The Pure are attempting to rebuild their siege, but they are having difficulties with their slaves, who won't do any work. The loss of all of his *Exalted* has left their Disciple with almost no way of commanding his slaves, much less attacking, and Haras and Dahlia have virtually exterminated their casters. Likewise, after your arrest, the combat troops in the city are nearly mutinous. Neither Ippeas nor Kallinikas are doing anything to change that – both treat the Vicar with contempt, and he responds with anger. Your friends are starving – so, to be fair, are the Pure. It is like some black comedy of human frailty and wickedness being played out for my delectation.' She smiled. 'I admit I rather enjoy it. But the first force to receive either food or reinforcements will win utterly, and the other side will be destroyed.'

'I understand the hunger. Food is almost the only thing I can think of.'

Inoques leant over and kissed him.

'I might have brought you some food,' she said, 'but I knew you'd want to suffer with your friends.'

'Are you really so wicked? Or is this just a role you play? To keep your distance from me?'

Suddenly, the two of them were facing each other in the darkness.

'I am oath-bound to a mortal,' she said softly. 'A mortal in a world of mortals, where I am a freak and a weapon.'

'Yasmina, I have avoided asking you this until now. But, what are you?'

'You know,' she said bitterly.

'I don't. I'm really a third year Academy student pretending to be a Magos, an apprentice pretending to be a military officer, a Souliote pretending to be a Byzas. I know you are *bound.* Is there still a human woman in there?'

'No,' his wife said bitterly. 'They killed her to give me her body.'

'And you have been enslaved for three hundred years?'

'Three hundred years of hunting and trapping and killing *my own kind* at the bidding of my masters.' More softly, she said, 'We fight among ourselves all the time, of course. Like you.' She laughed without mirth. 'I cannot even avenge myself on the men who did this to me. Their bones are dust.'

Aranthur said, carefully, 'And yet, you can see through your hatred to know that we need to preserve the Black Stone, even though its breaking would free you.'

She shrugged. 'It would also free a torrent of my kin and my foes and creatures and *Apep-Duat* as alien to me as I am to you.' She shook her head. 'Every malign thing that has ever come through the gates. I would not destroy the world to be free.'

'You do not seem so alien.'

'Yes,' she admitted. 'Three hundred years in these bodies, and I have warped. Or merely bent. I know it. At some point, I began to laugh. And at some point I realised that there were aspects of my life that I enjoyed. Like any slave. I adapt. Listen, *husband.* I love sailing on the deep water – when the wind rips the surface, and throws the spray in my face – when my ship runs through the waves like a gazelle over the desert.' She smiled. 'And when your hands close on me in a certain way, and I know you find me desirable. When you tilt your head and *listen*, as if I was a person.'

She stood up. 'So. Enough confession. Shall we go?'

But instead of moving away, she leant close to him, and he kissed her.

For a long time.

Aranthur stood. 'I confess that I don't want to make love on this floor.'

She laughed. 'Nor I. You stink. And I'm not precisely choosy.'

'You really didn't bring me any food?'

'Did you enjoy having the shield structure of a god?'

'Yes,' he said. 'It was a great gift.'

'I could perhaps make it permanent. Come, I imagine there's food somewhere.'

Together, they walked out into the corridor, and then, slowly, up out of the darkness. They emerged into a corridor with magelights, and then, after listening at a door, they passed into the nave, where a dozen Imoters were working on wounded men and women. Everyone moved listlessly.

'You don't intend to confront the Vicar,' she said.

'I'd like to find Ippeas,' Aranthur said.

If any of the Imoters recognised him, none of them called out; the listlessness of deep fatigue and hunger had its effect. Aranthur walked the length of the ancient nave. Even in his own hunger, he looked up at the ancient frescoes and the magnificent mosaics that glittered on the domed ceilings with awe.

Then he turned to the right, crossed the great square in front of the Temple, and went to the door of the square chapel of the Legate Giorgios.

A Magdalene stood guard at the entrance, visor closed, in full armour.

'Aranthur Timos,' the guard said.

'To see Ippeas,' he said.

The visored face nodded.

'The Demon must stay here,' the voice said. 'No rudeness is intended, but we do not know you, *Apep-Duat*.'

Inoques raised her chin. 'I doubt that you could stop me, knight.'

The visor nodded again. 'True. But then, if you attack me, you validate my position that it is unsafe to admit you.'

Inoques laughed aloud.

'Oh, well said. Go, *husband*. Meet this Great Sword. I will wait right here, and exchange barbed witticisms with the gate guard.'

The outside air made Aranthur fully aware of how dirty he was, but he went into the chapel with as great a show of confidence as he could manage. A squire, one of the young people training to be a knight, took him to a side chapel where Ippeas sat alone.

Syr Ippeas looked up.

'A cup of water for my guest,' he said, as if he was a great lord in a hall.

Aranthur sat when bidden.

'I assume you escaped,' the Great Sword said.

'Yes, syr.'

'And now you are walking around in broad daylight.'

'No one was guarding me.'

Ippeas sighed. 'Discipline has all but collapsed. There is no food – that, at least, was fairly allocated. If the enemy could mount an assault, they might break in – or perhaps we'd muster the will to fight.'

The squire brought a cup of water, and Aranthur drank it thirstily and was refilled from a pitcher.

'I was thinking of reporting to the Vicar as if nothing had happened,' Aranthur said.

'Why are you here?'

Aranthur shrugged. 'You have my sword. And you are my ally in this, I think. I guess that you share my outrage.'

Ippeas smiled. 'War is terrible. There is no morality to it but what decent people bring with them, and even that is eroded like a sandbank in a flood. Outrage is too strong. Indeed, but for your protest, I might have been silent.' He shrugged. 'I have committed so many sins in this war that I fear I will not have enough life left to do penance. And at this point, I will confess to you that I would do almost anything to keep the rest of my people alive.'

'Murder prisoners?'

'No. That's just stupid. At any rate, I owe you my thanks. Here's your sword, which, let me add, is an artifact as old as my own sword, or older.'

He looked up and met Aranthur's eyes as the squire handed Aranthur the ancient sword.

'I might have let the massacre happen, occupied with my own cares.' He sighed. 'It's difficult to thank a Lightbringer for anything.'

Aranthur sat back. 'I'm no Lightbringer,' he said.

Ippeas smiled. 'Of course not. Shall we go and see the Vicar?'

'Is Kallinikas with us?' Aranthur asked.

'She's young, and her desire to win outweighs her ethics. Which may just be sensible. I don't know any more – I haven't eaten for two days.'

The man was still in full armour. He rose to his feet slowly, and the two of them walked out into the brilliant sunlight.

Inoques inclined her head.

'Great Sword,' she said.

Ippeas returned her greeting. He managed a smile.

'This is the effect of hunger,' he said. 'I'm dreaming that I'm having a pleasant conversation with an *Apep-Duat* in front of the Cathedral of Light.'

'Exactly,' Inoques said.

Kallinikas was crossing the square, walking quickly towards them, her coat open and a plumed hat on her head.

She raised both hands. 'Aranthur,' she said. 'Where are you going?'

Aranthur didn't bow. 'The Vicar.'

'No violence,' she said. 'Listen, Timos. There's no food. There's . . . nothing. We have nothing left. There's no point in squabbling—'

'The General will be here soon,' Aranthur said. 'Let's finish as we began, as an army.'

Kallinikas was so skinny that she looked as if a breeze on her feathered hat might blow her away, but she planted her hands on her hips.

'Fine. I agree. So go to your troops. I'll see to it that the Vicar rescinds your arrest. No confrontation.'

Ippeas nodded. 'Sensible.'

'One shot in anger, and the army will dissolve in chaos,' Kallinikas said.

Aranthur thought of twenty horses in the hold of the great galley, and an unexplored tier of casks and barrels.

Oh, Ariadne! he thought. But he was ready to allow his beloved horse to become stew.

Including the Safians, there were about four thousand mouths to feed. A few horses and some fine foodstuffs wouldn't even touch their hunger.

But his own . . . Another spike of pain in his gut, and he was almost brought to his knees. It was all he could do to stay on his feet.

'There is no way out,' Kallinikas said. 'Unless your General comes, we start dying tomorrow.'

Inoques smiled. 'I think we should just sail away.'

Kallinikas glared. 'Who's she?'

Aranthur shook his head. 'My wife. Very well, Myr. I will go to my troops. You know I was left unguarded.'

'I have never, ever been described as someone's appendage before. Your *wife.*'

Aranthur smiled. 'Partner, then.'

'I know you were left unguarded.' Kallinikas rolled her eyes. 'Who do you think sent your guards back to their duties? The gods.'

As they walked away, Inoques glanced at him. Most of her tattoos were hidden; she wore a veil, and away from the power of the Black Stone, they didn't always show through her skin.

'You aren't coming, are you?' she asked.

'Now that we come to it, I find that I can't abandon Vilna. Or Kallotronis.' He shrugged. 'Or Chimeg or Omga or Kouznos.'

She made a motion of disgust. 'Do you people ever think rationally?'

Ippeas bowed. 'Well, Syr Timos. You are an idealist. I can only promise you that if they arrest you again, I'll have the next cell.'

Behind them, the sun hung in the west, a round ball of fire; the greater moon was already rising in the sky.

'Weather's changing,' Ippeas said. 'That storm to the west is moving. The breeze is nice.'

He walked off towards the Chapel.

'I'm leaving,' Inoques said.

'I'm not,' Aranthur said.

'I suppose I could just make you.'

'It's ironic,' he said. 'Because if I had time, I could probably unbind you. Which makes me more powerful than you.'

She paused. 'You what?'

He shrugged. 'Never mind. You're leaving.'

'You bastard,' she said. 'Anyway, I have my own path to salvation.'

'Do you really?' Aranthur saw her from a great distance. He was so hungry he couldn't really imagine having anything else to worry about. But he said, 'The black ships will still be there. One more day.'

'Come aboard and eat a meal.'

He shook his head. 'When Kallotronis can eat, and Vilna.'

'When did you become this holy?' she asked. 'It's fascinating, but possibly lost on this audience.'

Aranthur smiled. 'I need to sit down. Maybe I could be clean and hungry?'

He blinked. He thought he was seeing Kurvenos, the Lightbringer, standing in front of him.

'I'm seeing visions.'

She looked at him, and then, like a priest, she put a hand on his forehead.

'There,' she said. 'My bride price.'

She brushed his lips with hers and walked away.

He sat on the steps of the cathedral, watching her. The square was quite large, and he watched her go, saw the little swirl as people unconsciously got out of her way. Then, with a massive act of will, he got to his feet and started to walk to the billets where the Twenty-second and the Arnauts were living. He knew the way; his feet were having difficulty getting there.

She had walked away.

She had come back for him and then walked away.

It was the strangest relationship of his life, and he was clear-headed enough to realise that he didn't really have enough experience to know... anything.

He stopped, leant against a whitewashed wall, and swore.

When his head cleared, he walked round the corner and found Kallotronis and Kouznos rolling dice. They weren't really playing. Each man would name a large amount of money, and roll the dice, and then the other would take the dice and the cup and do the same.

'Aranthur!' Kallotronis shot to his feet.

'Back on duty,' Aranthur said. But again he could see Kurvenos, and the man was waving – yelling...

Kallotronis laughed. 'Good! Let's attack the fucking Pure and take their food. That's my plan and I think it's brilliant.'

'I concur,' Kouznos said, sounding exactly like Kallinikas.

Aranthur smiled. 'I am not the General or the Vicar.'

The manifestation of Kurvenos scared him. Or he was losing his mind.

Kallotronis looked around, then reached into the bosom of his fustanella and his hand came out with a length of garlic sausage.

He cut a piece and handed it to Aranthur.

Aranthur found that he'd eaten it before he even wondered where it had come from.

Kallotronis, who was a good host, cut a small piece for Kouznos and then a smaller piece for himself.

Aranthur sat with them. 'Where's Vilna?'

'There was an alarm on the desert wall,' Kouznos said. 'He volunteered.'

'The Eastern wall?'

Kallotronis shrugged his huge shoulders. 'I agree. No one should be coming at us over the eastern desert.'

Aranthur drank some water. The piece of sausage hit him like a drug; he felt immeasurably better, at least for a moment. He heard a roaring in his ears.

It wasn't in his ears. He heard roaring.

'Gods!' he said.

'Ten thousand hells,' Kallotronis spat. 'General alarm.'

'It was a feint,' Kouznos guessed. 'The Eastern wall.'

Men and women ran in every direction, collecting weapons. Daud, the biggest of the Keltai men, had been in a bath. He emerged naked, his tattoos covering most of him in a brilliant woad blue, carrying a snaphaunce rifle and wearing a bandolier of horn cartridges and a bullet bag as his only raiment.

But Aranthur was proud of how fast his companies turned out. He left his breastplate and his helmet by the whitewashed wall; he was too tired to bear them. Kallotronis handed him his puffers.

'Kept 'em for you. Both loaded. One of your fancy rounds in the pretty *gonne.*'

Aranthur checked the prime automatically, and put both puffers in his belt, locks out.

Kallotronis was on his feet and grabbed his long *jezzail.*

'That's not cheering,' Kouznos said.

Aranthur didn't want to believe it – or rather, was afraid to believe what he thought. So instead, he ran with the rest of them, up the long street and steps to the ruins of the seaward bastion at the head of the street, and then, heedless of enemy sniping, up on the wall.

Off to the left, a thick column of enemy was assaulting the Black Bastion.

'They have reinforcements,' Aranthur said, stunned.

But he didn't hesitate more than a moment, although Inoques' comment haunted him.

'*The first to get reinforcements...*'

'We must hold!' he shouted. 'Follow me!'

He ran along the top of the wall, and a dozen rounds struck around him, but the wall top was ten times as fast as the back alleys. He ran as fast as he could manage, cursing any number of things, and then pushing it all away to raise his new shield structure. It rose not as a single *aspis*, but like a factory making the round, red shields. Faster than he could actually imagine them, they rolled out of him and each joined the last, like a vast interlocking wall of round scales, or knit maille.

The Keltai cheered. Lang Cleg screeched a war cry and yelled 'Warlock!' Other men and women took it up.

Sniper shots sparkled against his shields and ricocheted away.

329

Aranthur paused at the sallyport. Two terrified Getan militiamen stood guard; the quarter guard had already charged into the rubble of the Black Bastion.

'Gods, syr!' the dekark said. 'Do we close the gate?'

Aranthur looked at Vilna, but for once, the little Nomadi dekark had nothing to offer, and Aranthur thought of it – the doom of the city.

'Lock it after us,' he said.

Every man and woman in his two companies heard him say it, dooming them all to death.

He got up on the trellis that supported the gate's chain.

'Listen up,' he snapped. 'I'm going to try and hold the Black Bastion.' He shrugged. 'I'd rather die out there than wait in here. Make your own call. I don't think we're coming back.'

Before he was done speaking, Kallotronis jumped up on the wall.

'Die or fucking win!' he shouted. 'Let's stop talking and go!'

Lang Cleg licked her lips, as if this was a party. Kouznos showed his fear, but fear only made his resolve plainer.

'Ready, then?' Aranthur turned to the Getan dekark. 'Lock it behind us, mind. Password?'

'Niobe's Children,' said the terrified dekark.

There were other soldiers coming down the alleys, but no officers.

Aranthur's smile was dark. 'Of course.'

The mother who committed hubris; the mother and her children murdered by the gods in revenge for a very small sin.

It was a sign. Not a pretty one, but an apt one.

'Let's go,' Aranthur said.

He ran out of the gate, and across the covered way. There in the ditch to the right were ten mortars, all dug in; no one was manning them.

He grabbed the militia drummer.

'You. Run to the citadel. Tell anyone you meet that the Black Bastion is under attack. And get me . . .' He shook his head. 'Dahlia Tarkas and some Magi.'

'Yes, syr,' the man squeaked.

Aranthur took a breath and dashed across the covered way. He had to run about seventy paces in the broiling sun between the massive Black Bastion's walls and the towering red brick of the city walls, unmarked because no *gonne* could touch them until they'd battered the bastion to flinders.

He turned towards the low gate to the bastion. The bastion's front was, of course, battered away to non-existence, but for ten days the Imperials had dug a new wall and trenches behind it *inside* the old bastion, and the trenches started at the old back gate.

Aranthur made himself run up the ramp, although fatigue, insufficient water and too little food had caused every injury of the last month to burst into pain. His face hurt where the bursting *kuria* crystal had flayed him, and his broken ribs hurt, and his leg. Everything hurt, and every muscle seemed to scream as he ran, but nothing hurt as much as his inner despair.

He kept going. Then through the gate, and he had all the militia at his heels, led by the Keltai, and they flew along the zig-zag trench. Just from the sound, Aranthur could *feel* the fight. And when he turned into the third line trench behind the new wall, he could see tall soldiers in blue khaftans coming over the parapet; they seemed endless.

The men and women in front of him were the same Getan Militia as held the gate behind him, or perhaps the hastily summoned quarter guard. They fought with exhausted desperation, with the butts of their matchlocks, with rapiers and side swords. The enemy were taller, stronger – implacable . . .

'Clear this line.'

Aranthur pointed to the left to Kallotronis. The Arnaut went left, leading his own company. Aranthur looked back at Lang Cleg.

'We have to win this trench. Now!'

He led himself. There was no thought. He merely pushed his shields out over the edge of the third line trench to wall off the enemy and then turned right, where half a dozen Getans were fighting with a determination and desperation that kept them alive.

Aranthur burst past them, the *enhancement* already burning. The tall warriors were murder victims – no faster than any other mortal – and this time, without hesitation, in despair and anger, he used all his *power*. His stream of *saar* broke bones and crushed flesh. He misused it, cruelly – *saar* as a flail, *saar* as a club – and his sword finished the wounded. At the angle of the trench, well down the line, he paused. The Keltai were right behind him; anyone he left alive, they finished.

He turned, facing the distant wall and the flood of new foes. The third line was cleared and retaken.

All around him the black *sihr* pooled, ready for uptake. With *sihr*, he could kill faster, more efficiently...

He wouldn't do it. He told himself that, but it beckoned – more efficient.

War is just killing. Who cares what means you use?

He could use it. Morality melted away like sand before an incoming tide of foes. He was unwilling to lose these people who had followed him, and he was damned...

Damned.

Damned if he was going to lose the bastion if he could keep it.

'*No!*' screamed the sword in his hand.

He ignored the sword, and he opened himself to the *Aulos*, dark *sihr* and bright *saar* together.

'*Come and get me, Disciple!*'

He screamed it into the *Aulos*. Then he cast through his shields, because of course, when shields are layers of little overlapping round crystalline shapes, you can also order them to open and close, like the port-lids on a line-of-battle ship.

Do not do this.

Aranthur stood balanced on the knife's edge, his soul full of *saar* and *sihr*. For a hesitant eternity, he wrestled with himself, the desire to kill and the desire not to kill perfectly balanced: the tools to retake the bastion; the knowledge that retaking the bastion might itself be a meaningless gesture.

But Lang Cleg and Vilna and Kallotronis were real. Omga and Chimeg and Daud were real.

He struck, and the *sihr* rolled from him like black fire, efficiently harnessed and efficiently released, and the blue khaftans died. Aranthur, who a moment before had been exhausted, still had the *power* and the time to identify the Magi among them: to isolate them; to crumple a shield here; to push a Magos off a rock there; to detach a mind from the *Aulos*; to strip another's shields. He was a fountain of raging *power*, and he burned them like an inferno.

But by the time he was closing on their Magi, he was also advancing; his militia threw grenados. They sailed through the air with laughable slowness and exploded, and the two companies were in the second line. Aranthur ignored the blue khaftans to concentrate on their Magi.

Some fled, and others wailed their despair in the *Aulos*, and ever

Aranthur felt the draw, the seductive pull to draw more *power*, to be a Dark god of the battlefield.

The shock of his attack began to bleed away. The blue khaftans were terrible in their stubborn strength. They didn't give back or break, as Aranthur had hoped, and they had an incredible proportion of Magi; he felt like a boar surrounded by dogs. The attack cleared the second line with an effort that cost his people twenty lives. Then they were done, and more blue khaftans were coming down the inner face of the wall of rubble.

Even in the grip of an eldritch rage, even throwing all caution and all morality to the winds, Aranthur wasn't going to retake the redoubt. And people were dead – his own people.

Damned.

'Back,' Aranthur ordered.

They ran back down the sap, and more grenados sailed into their attackers as the second trench was won and lost. But they made the blue khaftans pay, and pay again. Cleg fell at the corner of the sap, her axe broken in her hands. Omga died loosing one last arrow off his horn bow as the second line was abandoned.

Aranthur saw both of them die.

Damned.

It was clear that no help was coming. The Getans, the handful of survivors, were exhausted. Somehow, in fifteen minutes of fighting, Aranthur's people had shot away all their ammunition, and still the enemy came on.

'Back,' he said.

'Gates locked behind us,' Kallotronis said, as if this was an everyday problem.

'Go to the Sea Gate,' Aranthur said.

His fire was gone. He had little interest in watching Chimeg and Kallotronis and Vilna follow Omga and Cleg into death.

Kallotronis looked at him. 'And you?'

'I'll hold the little sallyport here. Long enough for you to go.'

Kallotronis narrowed his eyes for a moment. Then he nodded.

Vilna had taken a thrust through his gut. Chimeg had him over her shoulder.

'Don't do it, *Bahadur*!' Vilna shouted. 'Come with us!'

Aranthur ignored the small Nomadi dekark, despite the constant quality of his advice.

Kallotronis looked back at him. There were already blue coats prowling along the walls.

'This is really what you want?' he asked.

Aranthur took a puffer from his belt. 'Yes.'

Kallotronis smiled. It was an enigmatic smile.

'Stupid,' he said very clearly. And called 'Follow me!' in Souliote.

The third line began to empty.

The blue khaftans hesitated, fearing a ruse. A handful of grenados were thrown by the Arnauts, and Aranthur sprayed black fire at the corner where Cleg's blue eyes stared sightlessly at the white sky. Then he buried her, by the simple expedient of pointing at the earth wall of the sap and blowing a piece of earth as big as a carthorse off the wall, collapsing the trench.

Then he backed slowly into the ruined bastion's back gate, surmounted by an ancient lion that predated anything made by Megara or Ulama.

A pair of enemy clambered over the collapsed trench wall. One was a Magos; he raised his hand and a blue fire rolled in a wave to break on Aranthur's shield. Aranthur raised his golden puffer and shot the Magos through both their shields. He fell, his lips working. The glyph-warded ball had gone straight through his shields; his puzzlement was written in his death throes.

The other came forward, wielding a slim sword that was five feet long.

Aranthur allowed him to get close enough to confirm his fears.

It was no man. The soldier was Dhadhian. His face was blank, as blank as a corpse's face.

Aranthur took his second puffer from his sash. Then he spent a long heartbeat trying to find and breach the *subjugation* that he knew must be on the Dhadh. He located the *occulta*; it was as smooth as polished steel, and it burned from within the ancient creature.

The Dhadh was fuelling his own *subjugation* with his own will. Exactly the way Aranthur's *enhancement* functioned.

It was terrifying, and he lacked the resources to breach that adamantine wall. Wearily, he raised the barrel of his puffer and shot the creature from five paces away. The ancient thing fell, his eyes unfocusing. The *subjugation* rode the dying creature all the way until death, still powered by the thing's own corrupted will.

'Aphres!' Aranthur spat.

The Goddess of Love was the only one he could imagine, just then.

He began to load his puffers. He could see the 'enemy' moving along the top of the bastion, but then there was a burst of supporting fire from the walls of the city. That raised his heart; somewhere, someone had got the message.

I will die here.

This is a good time to die.

Nonetheless, he leant out and shot one, and then another, with both precision and revulsion. Shooting Dhadhi was, literally, doing the will of the enemy.

He was still *enhanced*. He could load quickly, and when four of them rushed him down the sap, he killed them all: cut, cut, parry, cut, thrust.

Finish the wounded.

Swordplay had never seemed so banal, so routine. So like murder.

He reloaded his puffers.

Murder. Murder of people hundreds or thousands of years old, bound somehow to their own destruction.

His anger rose and rose.

He saw the Dhadh on the wall as the man's barrel covered him. He stepped back under the ancient lintel, and the shot rang out, too late to catch him.

Aranthur stepped back, raising a puffer, but he was gone. Aranthur threw a curtain of fire into the angle.

It was hard to explain, even to himself, but he was perfectly prepared to die. He'd lost something – some belief, some sense of purpose. It was as if the enemy, willing to use women and children and ancient creatures as assault troops under *compulsion*, had robbed him of his sense of proportion.

At the same time, his anger rose to choke him. And he considered things for the first time – in hatred of the Master and his works, and in despair.

He thought of how easily he could work *sihr*. There was enough in the Black Bastion for him to make a firestorm of black terror; to clear the bastion completely.

That thought, the thought of mastering the *power* that lay all around him in death, twinned with his self-loathing. The killing – the deaths he had himself inflicted.

I used to try and heal them, he thought. *Now I just kill them in dozens.*

He thought of the Dhadhi who played music for feast days. He thought of running in the woods with his sister, pretending they had met elves and faeries.

It's all so fucking wrong.

The sword in his hand was so warm he could just hold on to it, and it vibrated as if it had been struck.

The Disciple is attacking your mind.

Aranthur stood still, one puffer still trickling smoke, the other cocked in his hand, and his eyes widened. Still the temptation lingered...

He thought, in that moment, of Iralia. Of Tribane. Of Tiy Drako and Dahlia and Sasan and Ansu, of Kurvenos and Qna Liras.

All flawed. All capable of evil.

All fighting as best they could.

Yes. There is only the struggle. Did he think that, or did she whisper it to him?

He was just too stubborn to succumb. The *sihr* lay there like poisoned food in front of a starving man, and he let it lie.

Better to let himself die. And while the *enhancement* lasted, he still had a great many advantages over his opponents, who, however many advantages of physique and magik they may have enjoyed ordinarily over mere humans, were hesitant now.

Aranthur called out, in his best Varestan, 'I see your precious Disciple won't come and face me.'

No one answered.

'I don't want to kill you,' he said, with brutal honesty.

But when the sniper on the wall moved, Aranthur seared him with white fire so quickly that he never managed a scream.

He was, in fact, almost out of *power*. He ran a mental hand over his shields, which were intact, and incredible – almost literally, the shields of a god.

He shot left-handed at a Dhadh moving at the corner of the bastion, and missed.

Two shots, and a grenado. He batted the grenado aside with *power*, and it exploded on the other side of the angle of the sap. One return shot destroyed the Capitan Pasha's beautiful puffer in his hand, and the other struck the lintel behind him. He flinched away, and a knot of them rushed him. It was hand to hand, and he took wounds, and he was slowing. Even the eight of them that reached him over his carpet of white fire were not a match for him. Their blank faces couldn't register the despair they felt, but he matched it. And they were fast – quicker than mere men. Their long slim swords flickered like a steel fire.

The old sword refused to let him die. It flashed with its own fire, and it sheared through the Dhadhian weapons – through armour and through ancient bodies.

He wanted to weep. He wanted it to be done. He'd learnt something, but he also knew that he wasn't capable of just letting go and lying down. He'd just go on.

Instead he cut up, fastidiously, behanding the last Dhadh facing him and then splitting his head on the downstroke.

He stood in the gate, as the *enhancement* faded from him, as the last of his *power* ran out through his fingers. He was panting like a dog that has run all day, and his hands were covered in other creatures' blood, and his anger was as black as the storm clouds that scudded across the western sky.

He heard them coming from behind him. He turned, back to the wall, prepared for the end, and was stunned to see Sasan at the head of a crowd of Safians, all armed – and Kallotronis, and Kouznos. They filled the ditch, and there was Kallinikas, leading a dozen gonners to the mortars.

And Dahlia. Jalu'd. Kati.

And Inoques. In front of all of them. In the *Aulos*, she burned like a torch.

'I was ready,' he said.

She shrugged. 'Too bad. Your friends love you.'

Book Three
Risposta

A counter-attack launched in the time immediately following the attack of your opponent. Two elements are essential in a risposta: first, that the opponent's blow is fully and completely parried, so that his blade can be left; second, that the response is immediate, and confident.

Maestro Sparthos,
unpublished notes to the book *Opera Nuova*

1

Antioke

'I don't even understand what happened,' the Vicar said. He had his head in his hands. 'I don't understand—'

'Their Disciple won't fight,' Dahlia said. 'He threw his very best shot at us, and Aranthur stopped it.'

Syr Vardar frowned. He muttered something about 'under arrest'.

Aranthur was still on some high place – the place he had gone to prepare to die. So he said nothing. The rage was still there, and now it had no outlet. So was the hunger.

But Kallinikas raised an aristocratic eyebrow.

'Well, we were saved by the Safians we'd planned to execute to save food.' She looked around.

'The Laws of War—' Vardar began.

Kallinikas looked like a scarecrow in a good shirt. Her brown skin was burnt almost black, which failed to hide the bruises under her eyes and contempt she could still generate.

'Tell yourself any story you like,' she said. 'Listen. It changes nothing. We held a few hours more, is all. We're out of food – most of our troops are down to three or four rounds.' She shrugged. 'Been good to know you, boys and girls. Really – there aren't even rats to eat, much less dogs or cats.'

'The Pure are *subjugating* Dhadhi,' Aranthur said suddenly. 'The assault was Dhadhi. Imagine what that means. The Master uses them against us, and we kill them for him.'

'Imagine the sheer volume of *power* it takes to subjugate so many Dhadhi,' Dahlia said.

'The Disciple has to handle it all, because we've killed all his *Exalted*,' Aranthur said, his tired voice implacable. 'And we beat him. Let's make our little victory count for something. I say, we go for the Disciple.'

Dahlia looked at him. 'We don't have a Lightbringer.'

'You have half a dozen military Magi in a choir, and Haras and you and me, and Jalu'd,' Aranthur said. 'And Kati. And Inoques, if she'll come. I am guessing that she could probably beat the Disciple alone.'

Inoques' face moved behind her white silk veil, but she gave nothing away.

'Where is Ippeas?' the Vicar asked.

Dahlia nodded. 'In the Black Bastion.' She looked at Inoques for a moment and then back at Aranthur. 'You have a point.'

'It's an insane risk,' the Vicar said. 'All we need to do is hold out a few more days—'

'He's living in a fantasy where we have a few days,' Dahlia said.

Aranthur had seen his own militia curled in the shade, racked with the tremors of total exhaustion, where the body begins to consume muscle to stay alive. He felt above the pain, but he was aware that as he had *enhanced* himself, he was actually worse off than most, unless the last little piece of sausage had magikal powers.

'Tomorrow?' Kallinikas asked. 'Tonight? Moon will be bright...'

Aranthur shook his head. 'Now. How many of us will still be able to walk tomorrow?'

Dahlia looked at him. 'Maybe a little over-focused, there, *Baradur*?' She used the Safiri word for 'hero' with contempt. 'I don't think you can walk all the way to the enemy camp, even if they threw down rose petals in your path instead of grenados.' She walked to him. 'You were going to die. You're still on that path. I'm not. What if we start ferrying the garrison to Masr?'

'What?' the Vicar demanded.

Kallinikas raised an eyebrow.

Dahlia raised a sparkling screen of light.

'The great galley will take five hundred,' she said, 'and come back with a week's food. And then another five hundred away, and another week's food.'

Aranthur saw the flaw in it, but also her resolve. He didn't care.

Inoques came and took his arm.

'Come,' she said.

He allowed himself to be led away, much as the Vicar hid his eyes, unable to look at his people starving in the shade.

'Twice you've come back for me,' he said.

'You are a very strange man. Also very dangerous. I already wonder if I have made you too dangerous.' She handed him something.

He took it. It was a large piece of salt beef, wrapped in rich white bread.

'What?' he mumbled, but the salty, dry meat was in his mouth, and he was chewing and swallowing. Almost immediately the pain came – cramps in his gut – and he fell to his knees. She lifted him.

'Eat,' she said.

He felt that he was betraying something. But he had cast *sihr*.

What betrayal is left?

But his body demanded the food, and he ate it, the meat that was a product of death. And the delicious bread.

Unmoved by anything he was thinking or mumbling, she handed him a canteen. He drank, and almost choked; it was wine, not water.

She smiled.

'Don't die,' she said. 'I would be angry.'

That made him almost smile. 'Do you have enough—'

'No. No, I'm not here to salve your tender conscience. I'm here to keep you alive. Nor will I fight this Pure thing – the Disciple. It is like me – a broken thing bound to a dead thing.' She smiled crookedly. 'Perhaps not so dead,' she said with a certain humour.

'Your body, or the Disciple's body?'

'You are so instantly alive, and interested, when I discuss your *enemies*.'

Aranthur ate the last scrap of bread. His gut felt as if it might explode.

'I think I need to lie down,' he said.

'I'll walk you to your billet.'

She seemed to be laughing, and he could not imagine what she found funny.

343

They crossed the empty square. No one was moving; there were no rats, or dogs. Even the big flies seemed to have gone.

'I cast *sihr*,' he said suddenly.

She smiled. 'I know. I can taste it on you.'

'What does that make me?' he asked her.

She laughed, her laughter rich and genuine, echoing off the ancient stone of the cathedral.

'Human. But I promise you, I am not the one from whom you'd wish absolution. I am *constructed with sihr*.' She smiled wickedly. 'You might say you've been mating with death.'

They went past the Chapel, and into the warren of side streets behind the Cathedral, until they turned on to the Corso Nuovo that led to the sea wall.

'Sophia,' Aranthur spat.

Once again, the ringing in his ears. But it wasn't in his ears, and it wasn't the sea.

Screams. And a roar.

He stopped. Looked at Inoques.

'Not again.' His eyes wouldn't even lift off the street. 'I'm done.'

She shrugged and walked rapidly towards where his companies were lying in the street and along the benches of an ancient *quaveh* house. Kallotronis was up, with his *jezzail*. Kouznos was having trouble standing, and Aranthur could see the advantage of training and some salt beef. He was walking, and Kouznos looked as if he might fall, and two longshoremen, but most of the Keltai lay like tired dogs.

'Sea Gate,' Chimeg said.

She snapped something in Pastun, and the other Nomadi got up. Stoga, the tallest, staggered visibly.

'They're cheering,' Vilna said.

'Draxos' prick,' Kallotronis spat. 'What are they cheering?'

Aranthur had his *carabin*. He stumbled down the street, towards the crumbling sea wall. He made his thighs push him up the line of old crenellations where the wooden hoardings had fallen in during the last siege. Kallotronis was with him, and Inoques, who was inscrutable in her veil.

Aranthur was the first to the sea wall. The cheers were thin. Down on the docks, a woman was screaming – repeated, long bursts of sound.

There, to the west, was a long line of sails – more than Aranthur could count. The brilliant red sails of the Empire's fleet.

He watched for a long time, first unbelieving, and then again, to be sure. And while he watched, the whole line tacked together, and came closer.

2

Antioke

When it was all over, Aranthur walked out to the Black Bastion. He wore no badge of rank, nor weapon; he wore only a stained fustanella and a blue turban.

He had imagined that, after the General's victory, the broken bastion would be empty, but of course it was not. Hundreds of men and women, like self-actualising ants, scurried over the walls and the surface. A burial party moved the corpses, some of which were twenty days old. Other parties filled the ditch that the Imperial army had dug, and the trenches behind. A dozen people were mixing mortar. Aranthur could smell the lime that was being burned somewhere on the other side of the great black walls.

At the base of the breach stood a dozen heavy wagons, each of which had hauled one block of the dark stone that gave the big fort its name. Aranthur picked his way down the breach, even as soldiers and workmen cleared the shattered stone away.

'There's a quarry, just across the fields,' a man said. 'Thousands of years old.'

Aranthur didn't at first recognise the man. He was middle-aged, had a small beard and moustache, and looked Byzas.

'Thousands of years.' Aranthur shook his head. 'And we'll rebuild it, of course.'

The other man smiled. 'You don't know me. I'm not offended – it happens to me all the time.'

With a smile, he held his hands around his face, hiding most of it...

346

Like a helmet.

'Great Sword,' Aranthur said.

Syr Ippeas smiled. 'Did you come here to commune with your dead?'

Aranthur blinked. 'Yes.'

Syr Ippeas nodded. 'Your own losses, or all the people you killed? Both, I assume.'

Aranthur writhed. 'Yes,' he choked.

Ippeas nodded. His mild blue eyes held no accusation.

'Do you pray?'

'I used to,' Aranthur admitted.

'If the gods forget us as easily as we forget them, much of the world as we know it is explained,' Ippeas said. 'You thought you'd be alone here?'

'Yes.' Aranthur was watching Kallinikas lay out the new angle of the new front walls. She was still as thin as a Souliote scarecrow. 'We just build it again. And in a hundred years or a thousand, another army comes – another would-be conqueror will drive his slaves before him, and new weapons will grind people to paste.'

Syr Ippeas had found a place to sit, at the very edge of the sabre grass where it grew to the base of the old breach.

'Careful, there are razor ants,' Aranthur said.

Ippeas nodded. 'I led the assault here.' He pointed into the tall grass. 'I crawled right up the tongue of grass. The ants were everywhere.'

Aranthur sat next to him.

The silence went on for a long time.

'I feel as if I went on a trip and I didn't come back,' Aranthur said.

Ippeas nodded. 'I know that feeling.'

Aranthur frowned. 'Is it all pointless?'

Ippeas was looking out over the sabre grass.

'You have friends – people who love you – comrades. Cling to them. They are your lifeline. Fight the urge to walk out on them. People can always help.'

'People,' Aranthur said. 'I have killed so many people. It was never my intent.'

He looked out over the dirty ground, where just a day before, the Imperial Army had crushed the remnants of the besiegers, driving the survivors into the hills. The pursuit still went on. Aranthur knew what 'pursuit' meant.

'But?' Ippeas's mild eyes locked with his. 'You have more to say. Say it.'

'I enjoyed it.' It wasn't quite a sob. 'By the Eagle, I killed them, and I felt...'

Ippeas smiled enigmatically.

'Like some sort of Dark god,' Aranthur confessed.

Ippeas put a hand on his shoulder.

'When I do something wrong, I struggle with why and how I did it. And there is always the temptation to believe that actually, I did no wrong. There's a taste to that sort of self-deception – a sickly-sweet taste, like a children's candy. You did not enjoy it. You are merely becoming accustomed to it, and you prefer victory to defeat, like all of us.'

Aranthur could see where his raging *saar* fire had fused some of the old black stone and charred the rest. Where his *sihr* had stripped the life out of the Dhadhi as if he'd been killing insects. He shuddered.

'I am tired of killing. I swear, I must find another way. Or I will become...'

Ippeas smiled. 'That would be a noble thing. And in that, I hear the Lightbringer that you want to be.'

'I want to be – how can I be a Lightbringer? I cast the blackest fire.' He sagged. 'And I revelled in it.'

Ippeas nodded. 'Now you know the temptation.'

'You are a good priest, Syr Ippeas.'

Ippeas smiled. 'In this case I am merely a comrade who has killed more innocents than you.'

Aranthur shook his head. 'I feel... tired. I want it all to stop.'

Ippeas leant back. 'Listen. The first time I was in battle, we were fighting very ordinary pirates, and one of them snapped a puffer at me – maybe ten paces away. And the bullet creased my armour and broke my wrist, and I remember thinking "He shot at me! But I'm... different! And people love me!'

Aranthur laughed, as he had had similar thoughts.

'But immediately afterwards, I was exhausted. Fear? Near death? My wound?' Ippeas shrugged. 'Everything we know is under threat. Even if we triumph, a triumph none of us can foresee now, our world will never be the same. I'm tired too. But I will not stop, nor will my sword sleep in my sheath, until I am dead, or the Pure are destroyed.

I see no remedy besides killing.' He shrugged. 'The best I can do is to not love the killing, or the power to kill.'

Aranthur brushed a razor ant off his hand.

'You inspire me,' he said.

'Good.'

'You are a Lightbringer,' Aranthur said. 'Aren't you?'

Ippeas shook his head. 'I prefer simpler choices,' he said after a moment. 'I chose to commit myself to a saint, to a path, because I know so well what I would be if I didn't find some ... limits.' His mild eyes crossed Aranthur's. 'Unlike you, I actually like to kill. Every death I cause – it's like a contest I have won. Yet I can still discern right and wrong ...'

Aranthur met his eyes. Ippeas was waiting to say something; in fact, he put a hand on Aranthur's shoulder to speak. And then his head turned, and he smiled, as if relieved.

'Now, you see that woman coming into the bastion?'

'Dahlia,' Aranthur said.

'Very lovely,' Ippeas said in a very un-celibate voice. 'But what I mean is, I can tell she is looking for someone. And she is, herself, someone. Hence, I assume she is looking for either you or me.' Syr Ippeas stood and brushed razor ants off his hose. 'General Tribane was summoning a military council.'

Aranthur nodded. 'Thank you, Great Sword,' he said formally.

Ippeas glanced at him.

'You came out to commune with your own dead, didn't you?'

Ippeas nodded. 'I lost ... a good friend.' He glanced at the sky. 'Right about here.' He shrugged. 'And I killed a great many helpless victims.'

'Oh, gods. Refugees?'

'No,' Syr Ippeas said. 'No, they were soldiers. But when you have twenty years of training, perfect armour, and comrades, all the militia in the world are just so many lambs waiting for the knife. War is not a fair contest. War is terrible, deliberate murder. But you know that, don't you?'

'Yes,' Aranthur said.

Ippeas smiled. It was terrible, feral and bleak at the same time.

Two women with a wheelbarrow approached, and they glared at the two loafers in the shade.

'Let th' Engineer tell 'ems to move,' said one in a thick Armean accent.

'We're moving,' Aranthur said in Armean.

A moment later, Dahlia saw him.

'Both of you!' she said. 'Alis told me to find you.' She smiled at Ippeas.

'Dahlia Tarkas, this is Syr Ippeas, Great Sword of the Magdalenes,' Aranthur said.

Dahlia bowed like a swordsperson, right leg back, knee almost touching the ground.

'Your servant,' she said.

Syr Ippeas bowed as deeply.

'Your humble servant.'

Aranthur had once thought that the courtesies of the aristocratic class were empty and foolish; then he'd aped them as protective colouring at school. But on a bastion, between peers, they were somehow fitting, as if, with their bows and courteous words, they rose above the smell of death and quicklime. He thought about Tirase, trying to make everyone an aristocrat.

Tirase, who'd apparently made quite a few decisions that were affecting Aranthur's life.

'Let us go and attend the General,' he said, in the same courteous language. 'It would never do to keep her waiting.'

Alis Tribane wore high boots and a black silk under-doublet over a snowy white shirt. Her feet were up, and she was writing on a lap desk. Around her were members of her staff; Syr Klinos waved at Aranthur as if they were old friends, and so did another staff officer Aranthur only dimly remembered. Coryn Ringkoat pushed effortlessly through the crowd of officers, Magi, and sailors to shake his hand.

Aranthur didn't know half of the men and women present. He was introduced to Vanax Kunyard by Centark Uschar. Equus, also a Vanax, shook his hand and congratulated him on his promotion, as if it was a normal day at the great gate of the City.

'Well done, eh?' Equus said, twirling his mustachios. 'Have you seen your commission, young Timos?'

'No, syr,' Aranthur admitted.

Equus grinned. His uniform was perfect: a scarlet doublet with tiny

350

gold buttons; a small scarlet jacket that seemed to function as a half-cloak, lined in fur, on his shoulder; thigh-high boots as black as the General's, and a tawny-gold fur busby with a green plume.

'And you brought Vilna back alive,' he said.

'He brought me back,' Aranthur said. 'He was wounded in the Black Bastion.'

'Just so,' Equus said. 'He'll recover. He's made of leather and steel.'

There were some thirty chairs at the long table, and then another hundred seats, benches and stools around the outside wall of the room. Aranthur sat with Dahlia behind Equus. Ippeas sat close to Kallinikas; neither sat near the Vicar.

The General finished reading the dispatch she'd been handed, and then she took her feet off the table, stood up, and drank off a cup of white wine.

'*Hetaeroi*,' she said, using the ancient Ellene word for companions.

The soldiers stiffened to something like attention. The sailors nodded; the Magi stopped talking. She smiled up and down the table.

'We have won a second victory. It's not a decisive victory, but as long as we hold Antioke, we make it virtually impossible for the enemy to strike in Masr. And while our opponent thinks that people are expendable, I'm going to wager that he's running low on even the most expendable bodies.' She looked around. 'That said, our scouts indicate that there is another army marching here. Long-range scouts –' and here she smiled at Aranthur – 'detected them two weeks ago, and now we are contesting their approach.'

Her smile could only have been described as sinister.

'We will meet them here. But only after we've bled them for a hundred leagues. In the meantime, I need a massive lift of supplies from Masr. Capitana del Mar?'

The Megaran admiral stood.

'Majesty, I understand that there are foodstuffs in the Delta, but that Al-Khaire itself has... requested food. From the Empire.'

Tribane looked down the table.

'We have a nested set of problems—'

'Surely we can get food from Megara or Lonika?' Syr Vardar asked.

Tribane glanced at him. 'The City is currently in a state of turmoil. An attempt was made on the Emperor and he is recovering; and I do not trust—'

'We are being cautious,' the Capitana del Mar said to Vardar. The admiral was sitting next to Myr Comnas, who nodded.

Vardar rose to his feet.

'General, isn't it true that you have been ordered, directly, in the Emperor's name, to take the fleet and army home?'

There was a sudden buzz of talk.

All eyes turned to the General. She smiled.

'If my cousin the Emperor so ordered me, I would ignore him. He's not here and could not understand the situation.' She shrugged. 'As it is, the order was signed only by a discredited Imperial officer whose recent behaviour suggests that he is not competent to command a quarter guard.'

Vardar remained standing. His brown skin mottled with fury.

'We are ordered home!' he shouted.

The General ignored him.

'We're not going home while the Pure have an army in the field. And Atti is still in disarray – we're all recovering from the *event*.' She raised an eyebrow at the admiral. 'Can you fetch me food? We'll need about fifty tons a day.'

'Lenos and Octos will have reserves,' the admiral said. 'I need to work it out, and send out scout ships, and if possible I'd like the co-operation of the merchant marine.'

Lenos and Octos were islands – large ones, part of the Empire. Lenos was the location of the Imperial Heart of Stone, the source of the best *kuria* crystal, a rich island and a reasonable source of grain. Once again the admiral nodded to Capitana Comnas, who nodded slowly.

'We could help. We can lift huge amounts of grain or flour, but my goods would have to be warehoused and I need absolute promises of indemnities for my owners. I'm sorry, Majesty. I would like to make a ringing statement of loyalty, but the sums of money involved...'

Tribane nodded curtly. 'I'll find you indemnities, and a banker to cover them.'

The council moved on with painful slowness. Most of it was about food and water and finding horses, as the cavalry were using up horses almost as fast as the fleet used water. Aranthur went to sleep and Dahlia woke him with a tap. A little later, he found Dahlia's head a weight on his shoulder, and listened to her snoring softly.

Twice Aranthur was asked to rise and speak, both times about matters in Masr. Both times, the Vicar smiled at him, as if he was one of the Vicar's cronies. Equus and Kunyard were tasked in detail; the entire meeting began to devolve into minute logistical planning.

Myr Jeninas, Buccaleria Primas and chief of the General's staff, rose to her feet. Her lungs were of brass and iron, or so it seemed.

'This general war council is at an end. All of the following will remain.'

She read off a list, which seemed to principally consist of Aranthur's friends.

The senior officers rose, saluted, and left, followed by their junior officers, most of whom cast glances – curious, admiring, envious or anxious – at Aranthur and Dahlia, Sasan and Val al-Dun, and Jalu'd , who seemed unaffected by the siege, looking about himself curiously, like a small child in a tavern full of adults.

'I've never thanked you,' Aranthur said to the old robber, 'for retaking the Black Bastion.'

Val al-Dun, known among the Safian refugees as 'Il Khan', was fifty. His skin was burnt the brown of an old tree's bark, and his eyes were as bright as diamonds. Kati said that he was a famous bandit; Sasan said that he was utterly trustworthy.

Val al-Dun nodded. 'Sasan said we had to fight the Pure.' He shrugged. 'I owe them nothing. They tried to burn my mind.' He shuddered.

'He spent a few minutes under a *subjugation*,' Kati said. 'When the Disciple broke the – I don't even know what to call them – the "worship receptacles" in the Black Pyramid, he was released.'

Aranthur was interested. 'Why, I wonder? Because the Disciple died?'

'Died?' Kati asked. 'It's still alive, in the pyramid. I could feel it, until we got far enough away. It kept trying to *subjugate* me.'

Dahlia was taking notes.

'Why don't you all sit?'

Tribane waved to Myr Jeninas and the last unwanted staffers were swept out of the room.

'This is a meeting of Cold Iron,' General Tribane said. 'Which at this point might be called "the conspiracy to save the world".' She looked at Aranthur. 'Syr Timos, would you care to outline what we know?'

Aranthur sat up. 'Majesty, I'm not sure I'm the best informed—'

'I'm quite sure you are,' Tribane said. 'Outline the threats.'

Aranthur stood. He knew everyone present: Equus was still there; so were Syr Ippeas and one of the *polemagi*; the other people were all his companions and friends.

'Very well. First, in Masr, the breaking of the Black Pyramid threatens to release a flood of *Apep-Duat* that a reliable source refers to as a "ravening maw of chaos". One or more of these wraiths had opened the rift in reality that we are calling the "Forge of Darkness", which is growing. I think I can speak for the other Magi here present when I say that the crystal winds blow with increasing force every day.'

Dahlia nodded, as did the Weather Magos from the *Rei d'Asturas*, Ettore, and the Polemagos, who seemed unsettled.

Aranthur locked eyes with Myr Tribane.

'It seems to me that the first order of business must be closing the rift in the sky.'

'Give us the rest,' she said, from a serene face with lowered eyelids.

'General, I can't speculate as to what has happened in the City, except that it must be bad.'

Tribane nodded. She sipped wine.

'In Ulama, a dozen assassins tried for the Sultan Bey. He was badly wounded, and the resulting search for traitors is doing more damage than the assassination did. In Megara, we do not know exactly what has happened to the Emperor – only that he is sick, and accusations have been made that he is not actually functioning. I'm worried that Roaris has concealed my orders about him and is actually trying to gain and hold power. I need to send a high-level messenger over his head.'

'Roaris,' Aranthur said. ' I remember that Drako asked Roaris to fix things . . .'

Tribane nodded. 'Yes, it needs to be said out loud. It now looks possible that Roaris is an active enemy – maybe an independent player, or maybe, worst case, a servant of the Pure.' She frowned. 'I find that very difficult to believe. That he's a Lion, yes, obviously. But a man can be a damned fool for power and not be a traitor.'

'Blessed Sophia! He's my great uncle!' Dahlia said.

The Great Sword, Syr Ippeas, nodded.

'This would be terrible news if true. And I am a veteran not only of war, but of the bitterness of court politics. Majesty, could it not be simply that General Roaris refused to accept your orders from personal antipathy?'

'Totally possible. And yet, he knew almost every member of Cold Iron,' Tribane went on, speaking slowly. 'So maybe everything is blown. Or at least, it may be blown. I have to worry about the worst case.'

'What do we do?' Sasan asked.

'I'm here to ask you. As a general, I'm the absolute commander of this expedition – I can even make treaties. But in Cold Iron I'm just another agent of change, hoping that someone will make the right decision.'

'Majesty, my role is almost purely military.' Sasan was on his feet. 'I want to take all the Safians who will volunteer, and ride for Safi. With some eldritch support, I think that we can be a thorn in the Master's side – and perhaps pull my country back from subjugation.'

'How many of the prisoners would go with you?' Tribane asked.

'All of them.' Val al-Dun stood up and joined Sasan. 'We are done running. You only have to experience the *Exalted* once, up close, before you know what they are – a collection of live corpses.'

Kati also rose. 'All of the Safians will ride against the Pure.'

'And for ... occult matters?' Tribane asked.

'I'll go,' Dahlia said.

'As will I,' said Kati, with a hard look at the blonde Byzas aristocrat.

Tribane put her chin in her hand.

'The Dhadhi in the assault tell me a great deal. They tell me that the Master is running out of bodies to do his fighting. They also tell me that while we covered Masr, however ineptly, the Master is now in full possession of the *Altos* and the Attian highlands. That and the recent attacks will force Atti into a defensive posture ...' She sat up. 'I think in terms of armies. The Master must have a main army – I believe it's in the highlands, mopping up the poor Dhadhi.' She shook her head. 'Anything you could do to shake the Master's hold on Safi would be a godsend.' She raised an eyebrow. 'I needn't tell you it's insanely dangerous?'

Mir Jalu'd, the Seeker, who reeked of patchouli and had just oiled his hair, laughed a merry laugh at odds with the gravity of the situation.

'For much time that I ought to have spent in contemplation of the infinite, I thought instead of how to resist this Master. I think I have some resources.'

'I find that ...' Tribane shrugged. 'Reassuring. Despite knowing nothing about you.'

'I am a person of infinite resource. I know many things and many rare words. I know poetry from before there were humans. Also, I am an expert lover of both men and women.'

Tribane smiled. 'I'll keep that in mind.' She looked at Aranthur. 'What do you intend?'

He looked around. But he'd already made up his mind.

'I think that I should go back to the Empire as your messenger. I share the General's fears for our friends there. The General cannot go, and I see why Dahlia and Sasan are needed here. But someone needs to find out what is going on, and stop it.'

He looked around. Neither Inoques nor the priest, Haras, were present. He wondered how many of his friends knew what lay on board the black *trabaccolo*.

'How safe is this city?' he asked the General.

She shrugged. 'I don't know how big this third force is. How many armies can this Master raise? This city could fall. You know that – you almost saw it happen.'

Aranthur narrowed his eyes in thought. *He knew too much.* He looked at Dahlia. The complications rolled away from him like his shields unrolling from his hands; only he knew the details of the Master of Arts' intentions for the *Ulmaghest*. And since Masr, he was increasingly convinced that it held secrets that needed to be learnt. That had been his mission before any of these missions appeared – before war overruled everything. And the Black Stone – really, only he knew exactly what they carried.

He was tempted to share the knowledge with the General and let her be the leader; she had the skills. But it didn't work. He couldn't think of any reason to distrust any of them. But he wasn't going to speak of the stone, or of the *Ulmaghest*, in front of people who could be captured by the Pure in Safi. It made his guts churn to think of it, but he made himself consider it all. Time stood still. He looked at the problem from several angles.

'I was hoping to give you a command,' the General said to his silence. 'Equus said you could command the Nomadi, if he was nearby—'

Aranthur laughed. 'I'm a terrible officer. I just do what Kallinikas and Vilna tell me to do.'

Syr Ippeas laughed. 'You're the only one who thinks so.'

Aranthur glanced at the General. Made his decision.

'I think I must accept that I am your messenger to the Emperor. I think that we must be sure... that our city and our government are secure,' he said in the language of war.

She nodded. 'You are correct that I was going to send an officer with dispatches. It is usually a high honour – people would die to be sent with dispatches of a victory.'

Aranthur made a face.

'Vardar is a protégé of Roaris,' the General said thoughtfully.

'At least,' Ippeas commented. 'I'd hold him close, Majesty.'

'Imagine the worst, Majesty,' Aranthur said. 'Imagine Roaris seeks to control the government. What good will sending one officer with dispatches do? He'll never let me go – worse, he'll know I'm Cold Iron.'

She grimaced. 'It can't be that bad – at worst, you think on your feet.'

'Too often,' Dahlia said.

'All right,' Tribane said impatiently. 'What do you intend?'

Aranthur looked around. 'I think I'll keep my plans to myself. I think we have to be very careful now, Majesty. I think our foe underestimated us, but no longer. And I think...' He paused. 'I think I need to go to the City.'

She met his eye, and then nodded. 'Very well. Aranthur, remain. Sasan, I will write you a commission and arrange supplies. I'd like you to move as soon as we can supply you.'

Dahlia glanced at him. She was trying to tell him something with her eyes.

He mouthed 'later'.

Sasan shot him a smile. It was not a very genuine smile; not false. More... sad.

Aranthur nodded, and then moved to the seat nearest the General. Neither of them spoke until the room was empty.

'Clear as day, you're telling me that you know things I don't know,' she said.

Aranthur sat back. 'Yes, ma'am.'

'I hate "ma'am".' She smiled suddenly. 'You have earned the right to call me Alis. In almost all situations.'

He nodded. 'Very well. Alis...' He shook his head. 'I know too much,' he admitted.

She nodded. She was as hesitant as he was. So they sat in hesitant silence for a long time.

Finally she spoke.

'It is possible...' she began, and then she looked up. 'Fuck it. It's possible that I'm the Imperial government right now. So please. I need to know whatever you know.'

Aranthur stood the scrutiny of her mild, wide-set eyes. He couldn't think of any reason *not* to tell her. Except the caution he'd learned in the last months.

But he shook his head, because in fact, he knew that too much caution was the death of decision making.

'Damn,' he said. 'Very well. Two things. First: in Megara, I am in charge of a research project—'

'The *Ulmaghest*. My cousin the Emperor told me in detail.' She breathed out. 'Thank the gods, I thought it was something deadly.'

'Second,' he said, emboldened, 'on board the black *trabaccolo* is the capstone of the Black Pyramid, sent by the priests of Masr to be protected.'

She blinked.

'It is some sort of... existential...' Aranthur shook his head. 'I have experienced it. It's not like *anything*, Alis. It's... possibly our only defence against the *Apep-Duat* released by the Pure. Or... recapturing them,' he ended weakly. 'I don't even know—'

'A magikal artifact,' she said in a matter-of-fact voice.

Aranthur was going to let it go, and then he paused. And leant forward.

'No, Alis. As far as I can tell, it is *the* magikal artifact. All the others pale in comparison. It is the key to a one-way gate that controls...' He shrugged. 'The most dangerous components of the past. I can't think of a better way to express this.'

'Sweet Aphres' cunt.' Tribane shook her head. 'And Draxos' prick. Are you kidding me? This thing is in my harbour, right now?'

Aranthur paused. 'Yes.'

She shook her head. Now she was pale.

'How bad is it in Masr?' she asked, pouring him wine.

'Very bad, Alis. So bad that they sent this precious thing with us, assuming our city was safe.' He met her eyes. 'Their... chief priest begged me to return with food, and with fifty *Studion*-trained Magi. And the stone.'

'Why didn't he keep the stone, then?'

Aranthur looked away. 'Because if it falls to the Pure, Qna Liras – Harlequin—'

'I know who you mean.' Tribane was like a wife dealing with her husband's death. Strictly business. 'Go on.'

'Harlequin says that if the Pure get it, or if the entities took it, we'd be done. All done – the whole world.' He shrugged. 'For what it's worth, I've had this confirmed by another source.'

'What other source?'

He looked her in the eye. 'Not my secret.'

She smiled crookedly. 'Why'd the Vicar arrest you?' she asked suddenly.

'I wouldn't let him execute the Safian prisoners.'

She nodded, and drank off her wine.

'Aranthur, why in ten thousand hells are you the centre of this?' She shook her head. 'Over and over again, since we first started watching you, you have been at the very centre of the struggle with the Pure. Why you?'

Aranthur met her eyes. 'I think it's the sword. Qna Liras says my sword is one of the Seven. The one with the woman.' He sat back.

'Blessed Sophia. You have Myr Orsin in your scabbard?' The General looked at him. 'I admit –that would explain . . .' She steepled her fingers. 'Well. Regardless. Sophia, I'm tired of making these decisions. But to the best of my knowledge, the City is a safer haven for this thing than this cursed place. If it was safe in the Treasury at the Academy, I think we'd know we were secure.'

'Even from treason?' Aranthur asked.

Tribane blinked. 'I no longer know what I believe,' she said, and for the first time, he heard the despair and the exhaustion. 'I'm like a punch-drunk fighter in a prizefight. It's all I can do to come up to scratch at the beginning of each round, and keep swinging. We need to fight back – we need to counter-attack and stop reacting. If this were a sword fight, I'd say we need to steal the initiative.'

'Give me a month with the *Ulmaghest*. I might find you a tool.'

'Really?' she asked. 'Is this what the sword says?'

'I've never asked.'

Go to Megara, the woman said. *Save the Emperor.*

He sat up as if he'd been hit by a shock.

Tribane shook her head. 'I heard it too,' she said, and leant forward to touch the worn hilt. 'Sweet Sophia. You give me hope, old lady.'

Aranthur swallowed.

'Really. Listen – it's not just the sword. Dahlia will back me. I have a way to . . . *unravel* the *Exalted*. They're constructs. We didn't know that before. I think the Disciples are similar.' He shrugged. 'I don't want to get your hopes up. But I think . . . I think I know where to look for the keys. I think I know why we were brought the *Ulmaghest*, and I think I know what the Master has done.'

'You, the twenty-two year old third year Student.' Tribane smiled.

'Exactly.'

Aranthur grinned. He couldn't help himself. At some point since the Black Bastion, he'd lost hope, and found it again. Between Inoques' ruthless pragmatism and Ippeas' bent morality, perhaps.

She sat up. 'Damn, Timos. I want to believe you. Very well. You take the dispatches home. Get me a massive resupply for the fleet and what the hells, get us fifty *Studion*-trained Magi to send to Masr.'

'Yes, ma'am.'

She grimaced. 'You need Myr Tarkas.'

He hesitated.

'Timos, the world is at stake, and Myr Tarkas' love life cannot influence you. Or me.' She raised an eyebrow. 'No one would ever take her for a Safian, either.' She sighed. 'Very well. I'll write a lot of orders.'

3

Megara

'I ought to fucking hate you,' Dahlia said. The beaches of Lenos were visible in the morning light to starboard, and the *trabaccolo* was running free, quarter reaching with her big lateens full of wind. 'Your little friend—'

'Kati is a grown woman—' Aranthur said.

'Oh, I know,' she said. 'Very grown. Very clever. Never mind. What's done is done. I know my duty. I don't need you to tell it to me.'

Aranthur remembered exactly how arrogant she had sounded when they'd been together.

'I'm sorry,' he said.

'Are you, though? It's like a nursery game, except that when you all fall into bed with someone, I'm left alone.' She turned and looked at him. 'You look like death, by the way. Maybe that's why the construct fancies you, eh?'

She turned on her heel and walked off.

Inoques came up behind him.

'Do you still love her?' she asked.

Aranthur thought about that for a moment. He turned and looked into his wife's eyes.

'Yes,' he said. 'But not in any way you should read as a threat.'

'I'm fairly astute at reading you people,' she said mildly. 'There is a point when you move beyond mating to actual...' She shrugged. 'To something better than mating. Why is she so angry?'

'Her chosen mate is going on ...' Aranthur was caught in an endless web of trust nets. 'On a mission. A different mission.'

'With another woman.'

'Exactly.'

Inoques looked out at the island sliding by.

'You know what I wish?' she asked.

'What?'

'I wish we had more time. I wish I was more ...' She turned away. 'Human.'

Aranthur thought of replying. Instead he put a hand around her waist, and they watched the island's magnificent beaches slide by, the water as blue as the sky above, the sun, which at Antioke had been a sort of enemy, now just a kindly and brilliant light in the sky. There were whitewashed houses with red-tiled roofs, and little harbours dotted with fishing boats.

'I'd like to run this boat ashore, and wander off,' he said. 'We could lie on the beaches, steal fish from the traps, and lie under the stars—'

'And watch the Forge grow. But yes. Every fishing boat we pass – every woman washing clothes, every village – I wonder what it's like to be them.'

At the end of the deck, Kollotronis was dancing a sailor's dance. Aranthur was pretty sure he was trying to attract Dahlia, and wished him luck. Later, when Inoques went to con her ship among the shoals at the north end of the island, Aranthur went and learnt the dance. Then he and Kollotronis fought with sticks. The sticks had leather hilts to cover the hand; it was the way the Masran sailors practised repelling pirates. The other soldiers gathered around, including Chimeg and Vilna, who had remained with Aranthur, and Nata, who never seemed to leave Chimeg's side.

He had become a bitter man, his humour extinguished. When his eyes rested on Aranthur's, he had to wonder if the man blamed him for his wound, which was terrible enough. But when Aranthur approached him on deck one night, the man was all smiles and false humility, and Aranthur didn't want to press him.

He tried to ignore the wounded man, and Vilna's raised eyebrow, and the rest of them, and so he knew the moment Dahlia appeared on deck. His back was to her, but his opponent leapt forward and threw a whole flurry of blows with a showy leap. Aranthur allowed

362

himself to be backed to the edge of a hatch cover in four successive parries, and then on the fifth parry, he didn't retreat. In fact, he stepped forward into his cover, caught his opponent's wrist, and disarmed him. Kollotronis was minded to struggle. Aranthur passed an arm across his throat and caught his opposite shoulder for the throw, but Kollotronis was an experienced wrestler and evaded the grip, retreating. Aranthur still had both swords.

Kollotronis grinned.

Aranthur also grinned.

Dahlia came down the deck and stripped off her doublet.

'This is just what I need,' she said.

When Aranthur made to step away, she smiled wickedly.

'Oh, no,' she said. 'I mean you.'

She hefted the oak stick, and then saluted, as if they were at Master Tercel's School of Defence.

It was a long time since Aranthur had faced Dahlia, and he was cautious. But she made simple attacks, and by the third cover, he thought he had her *tempo*. He stepped into the parry as he had with Kollotronis, took her weapon, and she punched him in the jaw.

At least, that was her intention, but he dropped both swords and spun her by her punching arm.

He let go before he formed the shoulder-breaking lock.

'Damn you,' she spat. 'That hurt.' She looked at him. 'You are very fast now.'

This time she attacked with a very simple, well-executed deception, a high cut and a deceptive thrust following. Aranthur parried the first, and then the second, and struck a *risposta* from her thrust, tapping her in the head.

She saluted smartly and came straight back at him. He covered and countered. He threw a deceptive attack of his own, but the third bout went on and on, or so it seemed. She thrust to his leg, he voided and counter-cut to her head, which she parried and carried around to back-cut at his wrist. He parried moving forward, but this time she stood her ground. Their hands went to each other's elbows, and then they were locked together, both of them gripping their sticks at the hilt and again halfway down the blade, at the so-called 'half-sword'. Point, and then pommel, and then point – strikes as fast as heartbeats, and parries to match, and then they moved apart. As they retreated, she flicked a rising cut off her last parry.

It caught him on the wrist because he thought he was out of distance. He smiled, and so did she.

'I remember when you weren't very good,' she said.

'I had good teachers.'

She smiled. Her smile included Kollotronis, and even Inoques.

'So you did.'

That night, in the little cabin under the command deck, Haras and Inoques sat at one end of the captain's table and Dahlia, Kollotronis and Aranthur sat at the other end. They drank *arak*, and Aranthur explained his plan.

Dahlia heard him out.

'You are taking all the risks,' she said.

He shrugged. 'In many ways I'm the most expendable. In a worst case, I'm captured and you are still free. Best case, I put up the signal and you run in and I'm on the customs boat. If the whole thing is wrecked, I put a red light up and meet you at Lonika.'

Haras nodded. 'I am ageing every day we're at sea. One storm, and the best hope . . .' He shook his head.

Inoques laughed. 'I've never lost a ship, priest.' She looked at Aranthur.

'When we're under the batteries of the City, we are very much at their mercy. We need to *know*.' He glanced at Dahlia. 'You know that we're going to be in time for the Autumn Session at the *Studion*.'

Dahlia leant back and laughed.

'I don't really care a rat's arse about the *Studion*.' But a slow smile spread over her face. 'We've only been gone two months . . .' She laughed. 'I'd like to take advanced battlefield concealment and perhaps a research class. And then, more serious, 'I don't think you should pass a gate. If they have our names . . .'

Aranthur paused. 'I have a new idea,' he said.

The last night, as they entered the vast straits dominated by the twin cities of Ulama and Megara, Aranthur put a belt of gold around his waist and chose clothes he could wear wet.

'You've smuggled things into Megara?' he asked Inoques.

She shrugged. 'Not precisely. But I know the currents. You're not that good a swimmer – you can't be daring. If I sail past the city in the darkness, I can put you in the water two hundred paces from the beach below Petros Island.' She looked at him. 'Do you know someone you trust absolutely?'

Aranthur thought of Tiy Drako and smiled.

'Not absolutely,' he said. 'But for this.'

She reached out and caught his hand.

'I want to tell you something.'

He sat next to her on her swinging hammock. It was more a box bed that swung on heavy ropes; it was very comfortable, and he'd enjoyed the four days sailing from Antioke very much. He'd also learnt that he looked like a scarecrow.

'I'm pregnant,' she said.

He thought for a moment, and met her black eyes.

'You always intended to be pregnant,' he said.

She continued to gaze at him. 'You are perceptive.'

'So . . .' He leant towards her. 'Why would you want to be pregnant, oh Ancient One?'

She smiled. 'That needs to remain with me for a while. I promise again, no harm will come to you or your friends.'

Aranthur nodded. 'That's not as reassuring as it sounds.'

She nodded.

Two hours later, he was out on deck in wool hose, simple linen braes, and a good wool doublet – the clothes of a gentleman. He found Dahlia and handed her the old sword, wrapped in his sword-belt.

'I wish you were taking a sword,' she said.

'I've come to believe this sword is almost as important as the Black Stone,' Aranthur said. 'And I can't swim with it. Keep it for me, and if I don't return, consider . . . carrying it.'

'Complete with its guardian angel. Is she the woman in armour who saved us when the sky broke open?'

'I think so.'

Her hands closed around the scabbard, and he let go.

Dahlia looked at him, her eyes round with amazement.

'It spoke!' she said.

Aranthur nodded. He felt an enormous sense of loss, and even jealousy.

Dahlia glanced at him. 'You know you are thin as an old board, eh?'

'I know.'

'I think that *enhancement* is burning you away. I think I know how to treat you, but I think you have to stop using it.'

'It's all that is keeping me alive—' he began.

Dahlia shrugged. 'I'm trying to help.'

'Mark twelve. By the mark six. By the mark five.'

The man in the bow had a dark lantern and the lead, which he threw very rapidly, testing the shoaling water. The Northside neighbourhoods of the City were so close that Aranthur could smell the *polpo*, the octopus grilling in the bars and tavernas along the waterfront.

'Two green lanterns anywhere along the Angel,' Aranthur said. 'Every night after dark until midnight, if you can come in. Red lanterns if you should sail for Lonika.'

Dahlia nodded. Inoques stepped in close, as if to kiss him, and then changed her mind. Kollotronis took his shoulder.

'I still think I should come,' he said.

Aranthur shook his hand. 'See you in a day or two.'

'By the mark four,' Mera called from the bow, very softly.

'Ready about,' Inoques said. 'Ready, there,' she said gruffly to Aranthur.

He stopped, grabbed her waist, and kissed her.

She smiled. 'Don't die.'

Then he stepped up to the rail facing the city. It was slack water; the tide was neither rising nor falling, the notorious currents around the city walls at their lowest speed. He could see the Aqueduct, lit from below by the fires of the refugees, and he could see the clock face on the Temple of Light. The palace of crystal was dark, but the Temple of Light was well lit, and the whole north side of the city sparkled with life.

He leapt into the sea, and began swimming for shore. When he was close enough to hear the conversations of the privileged who ate in the taverns of the beachfront neighbourhoods, he turned and swam up the Little Canal, passing under the bridges, and then south. He rested against an ancient stone bollard, surprised at his own temerity.

He couldn't have imagined swimming voluntarily in the canals before the war.

Then he swam on. He swam past the ruins of one of the Northside palazzi, destroyed by a poisoned *kuria* crystal, and he followed the bend until he came to white marble stairs, green where the tide washed them. The *fondemento* was empty, as far as he could tell. He climbed out carefully and dripped for a few minutes, savouring the relative safety of dry land.

He had to lie down on the steps when six strong porters carried a chair past him on the bridge above. When they were gone, he felt ready for the next leg. He didn't want to use magik until he had an idea of what was going on, so he didn't dry his clothes or warm himself.

He walked up the Gully, the little valley that separated the Pinnacle from the Academy, avoiding honest neighbourhoods, using alleys when he could, because until his clothes dried he looked wrong. He passed under High Bridge with a regretful glance back; somewhere above him, the Master of Arts . . .

He set his damp shoulders and walked on along the dark path that edged the stream that ran down out of an ancient leak in the Aqueduct. He'd walked this way many times as a first year student, but now there were refugees living in the Gully. Tiny fires winked on either hand, and he was cautious, which was just as well, because there were corpses on the path: bloated victims of the bone plague, but other corpses too; perhaps victims of brutal robbery, but possibly unburied victims of *the darkness*. The Gully stank, and Aranthur, who had survived the Black Bastion, found himself afraid.

Eventually he climbed the short flight of wooden steps set into the mud bank and came to the neighbourhoods he knew, below the Academy on Southside. He walked to the little square with the wellhead and pretty bridge, where once, he and Mikal Kallinikos had fought three thugs in a fixed duel. He took one of Dahlia's red ribbons from his pocket and tied it to one of the four bronze lions, each of whom bore a bronze ring, left over from an ancient time when people tethered horses to wells in the city, perhaps the time of Tirase.

It was his signal. A member of Cold Iron would see it, and tell Tiy Drako.

The ribbon shone against the dark brown of the bronze and the white of the wellhead. Aranthur smiled and walked away quickly, before the rising sound of aristocratic voices coming from the seaside neighbourhoods.

This time he walked with purpose, across the bridge, along the walkways, across another bridge until he reached a familiar blue door. It was late, but not impossible.

He knocked.

A pretty child of ten answered his knock.

'I know you,' she said. 'You look very thin. Have you been in prison? You called me Demoiselle once. And you are very damp.' She blinked. 'Patur is eating his dinner.'

'May I come in?' Aranthur managed.

'You are very damp,' the girl said. 'Daddy! Daddy! It's one of your students and he's very wet.'

Maestro Sparthos appeared from the back of the house.

'What the devil...?' he said, and then stopped. He was perhaps three strides from Aranthur.

Aranthur learned a great deal in that one moment, when their eyes crossed.

'Do I know you, syr?' the maestro asked.

Aranthur bowed. 'I have been your student.'

Sparthos smiled at his daughter.

'This is a friend. Go eat your nice biscuit and honey.'

'But I like him—'

'Run along,' Sparthos said firmly.

She looked back and Aranthur bowed.

'Is this politics?' Sparthos asked. 'You are Timos, aren't you? I didn't know you at first.'

'Yes, Maestro.'

'What do you want, coming like this when the school is closed, wet to the bone?' Sparthos said sharply.

'I need to get dry. Then I will leave you,' Aranthur said.

Sparthos considered for a moment. 'Of course. Come.'

He led Aranthur out of the back of his house, into a very small courtyard, only just big enough for a tangle of clothes lines. The little yard was clearly shared with three other houses.

'Sapu's visiting his father. Here's his room. Let yourself out.' Sparthos paused. 'Can I get you something to eat?'

'Yes, Maestro.'

Sparthos returned with good rich cuttlefish pasta and a heap of bread and garlic, as well as a tall glass of beer. Aranthur ate it all.

'Were you with the General?' Sparthos asked.

Aranthur nodded.

Sparthos looked away. 'Was it terrible?'

It was the most human thing that the sword master had ever asked him.

'Yes,' Aranthur agreed. He thought of killing the women in front of the Yaniceri trench; or the fighting in the Black Bastion. After a long time, he said, 'You know we won?'

Sparthos' head snapped round.

'What?' he asked.

Aranthur's fears were confirmed. He had the satisfaction of having guessed correctly.

'We fought a major action on the plains of Armea, and defeated the Pure with Atti as an ally. Two weeks ago, General Tribane defeated them again at Antioke.'

Sparthos sat back. 'Impossible,' he said.

'I was present at both battles.'

'So Roaris is a liar,' Sparthos said. 'No news there.' He sighed. 'How is your bladework?'

Aranthur thought for a moment. His smile was genuine.

'I'm here.'

Sparthos laughed. 'In other words, adequate. Well said, Timos. Should I ask any more?'

'Probably not,' Aranthur admitted. 'May I ask you some things?'

Sparthos nodded.

'Tell me what's happened here in the last month.'

Sparthos got up, put out all the candles but one, and paced nervously.

'The fleet sailed, and everything was quiet. Then the bone plague grew worse – a great many Easterners died. And then ...' He shrugged. 'The Dark Forge came to the sky and *the darkness* came to people's minds. It was ... terrible. And there were attacks in the streets – people going mad, or acts of terror. I can never tell.'

He coughed, and settled into a chair. He coughed again, and took out a handkerchief, which was spotted with blood.

'I thought the world was ending,' he said, 'and I do not succumb to fancies. My daughter held me, as if she was the adult and I the child. People died – up in the Academy precinct, it was as if there'd been a riot.' He was looking into the candle. 'They say that the Emperor is still lying in his bed, staring at the ceiling.' Sparthos shook his head silently for a while. 'That's when things began to go mad. There were looters, and some of the Easterners attacked an aristocrat's farm outside the city, or that's what we heard. I heard there were roving gangs of Easterners. And then Roaris returned, the same day or a day later...' He stopped. 'And they say that the Emperor appointed Roaris to command the Watch. I've heard that the Emperor can't speak. Regardless, Roaris is widely believed to have saved the city. He crushed the Easterners and ended the looting.' Sparthos sat back. 'Except that then he began arresting people.'

Aranthur nodded. 'What people?'

Sparthos shrugged. 'I try not to take sides in politics. But mostly, he arrests prominent Whites. He claims they are in league with the Easterners to overthrow the city.' He shrugged again. 'Almost no one believes that except Lions.' He glanced at Aranthur. 'But suddenly there are quite a few Lions. Even lower-class lions, if such a thing could exist.'

Aranthur nodded. He could almost see it.

'And the Academy?'

'Roaris has demanded the Master of Arts' resignation,' the maestro said. 'She appealed to the Emperor yesterday.'

Aranthur nodded. 'And the Emperor?'

'Is in the Crystal Palace with his guards,' Sparthos shrugged. 'That's what the broadsheets say. There's a lot of open talk against the Emperor now. Because the guards didn't do anything to stop the riots.'

Aranthur said nothing.

'You look like you need sleep,' the maestro said.

'I do,' Aranthur admitted.

Sparthos thought for a moment. 'You can have Sapu's room until he returns next week at the start of the Autumn term.'

'I'll be gone in two hours. If I return... we'll talk.'

'You are very sure of yourself.' Sparthos rose. 'More food?'

'No, thanks. My duty to your daughter.'

Sparthos frowned. 'I wish it had been I who answered the door. I would not like to see her interrogated by the Watch.'

'It's like that, is it?'

'Everywhere,' Sparthos answered. 'The Watch themselves aren't so bad, but there are a good many young men, mostly Lions, in black and yellow cloaks who are "deputised". Yellowjackets, people call them.'

When the maestro went to put his daughter to bed, Aranthur went through Sapu's small room. He had an armoire, a big one, and in it, Aranthur found his student robe, which he'd left months before.

He stripped off his doublet and put on the gown. It was not cleaner than the last time he'd worn it, and he had a moment of temporal confusion buttoning up the familiar buttons, his thumbs seemingly working of their own accord.

The hour rang. He ate a piece of garlic bread. He was supposed to visit the meeting place every six hours, under certain conditions. It was all very foolish, unless things were very bad. But now he thought that things really were *that bad.*

He went back through the *corte* with the wellhead and the four bronze rings an hour later. The ribbon was still tied there. Recrossing the Aphres Bridge, where the goddess's voluptuous statue flirted with pedestrian traffic, Aranthur saw four men in black and yellow parti-coloured cloaks loitering at the end of the bridge. It was too late to turn around, so he walked up to pass them, but they fanned out.

'*Hola*, Student!' called one. 'Where are you going at this hour?'

Aranthur didn't sense that they were after him, exactly; more, seeking entertainment.

He bowed with all the subservience that Arnauts saved for Byzas officials.

'I stayed too late with friends.'

'Carrying a weapon?' the short one asked. His face was the meanest – pinched and angry like a ferret's.

'No, my lords,' Aranthur said, bowing again.

'Let's just search him,' said Ferret.

Aranthur had a range of choices, but he chose to be searched.

Ferret's fingers closed on his *kuria* crystal.

'This is too nice for an Arnaut boy,' he said.

'Stop that, Ypsila,' said the tall man. 'Stop, I say.'

'He probably stole it,' Ypsila said, in an ingratiating voice.

'I've told you before,' the tall man said, his voice a hoarse whisper. 'The way we treat the lower orders defines us. If we are noble, we must be noble in our behaviour.' He stood back and waved. 'You there. Get off with you. Be careful in the streets.'

Aranthur walked away, feeling their eyes on his back.

The same bridge was guarded by four more Yellowjackets six hours later, when he came back. He spotted them from above, and he walked across one of the Academy terraces to look down on the little group. He leant over the elaborate marble railing to look down...

Into the eyes of Djinar, looking up.

Djinar recognised him instantly and shouted. But Aranthur wasn't just twenty paces higher – he had instant access to the labyrinth of alleys and paths inside the Precinct. He crossed the Great Square by the chapel of Sophia, went through the Gate, and entered the Long Hall, which had been technically forbidden to him as a Second Year.

He could remember when such rules had mattered to him. Now, he walked boldly down the Long Hall and crossed the 'Small', a lush green courtyard with a garden behind the Long Hall. The Master of Arts' magnificent windows gave on to the Small, and he was again tempted to try and obtain an interview, but he knew she would be watched.

But he did think of Edvin, her notary. He knew where Edvin lived. He filed that thought away and turned back towards the Ravine, this time by the back gate of the Small, which led to a dirt path.

He crossed the Ravine, a longer trip, all the way down on muddy, seldom-used steps. At the bottom of the Ravine he could hear the Yellowjackets accosting tradesmen on the bridge above. Just at the edge of the stream that ran down the Ravine to become the Great Canal further along, he found not one but three bloated bone plague victims like evil puddings. One long tendril of skin showed how a dying man had tried to scoop water from the stream even as his bones melted.

Aranthur shuddered. But he climbed the far side of the Ravine, passed through a small host of beggars almost without comment, so threadbare was his robe, and emerged into the web of streets behind the *corte*, approaching the wellhead from a new direction. He passed maids going to work, manservants opening palazzo gates, and vegetable carts making deliveries. Everyone looked tense – even terrified. People looked at him as if he was out of place, and Aranthur began to reconsider his Student guise.

He emerged from a filthy alley between the walled gardens of two great palazzi into the *corte*. The ribbon was still there as he walked by.

He was crossing the next bridge when a canal boat full of furniture was poling along in the early morning light, and the boatman was singing 'The Battle of Cowry'. Aranthur hummed the tune himself and wished for his tamboura. And a sword. His arming sword was hanging in his rooms, which were paid for.

Was it a risk?

Was there a point to all this cloak and dagger?

Aranthur continued across the bridge. He never stopped moving. He watched the canal boat go under him, and saw another boat loaded with stone coming down the cross canal, and then he was on the Thousand Steps, going up to the level of the Academy, out of all the fine houses and the best neighbourhoods. He turned from time to time, until he found a 'landing' about halfway up the steps from which he could see down into the *corte*. The ribbon was a spark of red below him.

He climbed up to the Precinct, watching the Yellowjacket post on the bridge and cursing himself for his own daring. There, he bowed to Tirase, and then walked along High Street to where Kallinikos had been murdered. Almost every lower storey window was boarded up; some he saw with many panes shattered, and there was a door that had clearly been beaten in with stones. It was ugly, and unexpected. He'd always thought of the Academy as inviolate, despite the Black Bird attack on him.

His own door was still a chipped and ugly yellow.

It was seven in the morning.

On a whim he looked into Kallinikos' rooms. They were obviously unoccupied, the shutters closed and a board nailed over the door. Kallinikos' own window remained unboarded. The next house was also boarded. The bone plague had killed more than a dozen people here, and the riots had clearly done more harm.

Aranthur looked up and down the street, and then stepped up onto the corner of the stone under Kallinikos' window. It held his weight, as it had before.

Even encumbered by the robe, he wriggled through the window, past the badly nailed boards. The bed on which his friend had been murdered was gone, and Aranthur dropped carefully to the floor. It smelled musty, but the walls had been freshly painted in elaborate patterns; there was a good fresco of Sophia on the ceiling.

Aranthur explored the house, and found the back gate with a string to its simple lock – clearly the way people were intended to come and go; workmen, for example.

After a while, Aranthur went to the sixth floor, and lay under the eaves in the hot attic, watching his own former rooms across the street and the door far below.

They were occupied. He watched two, and then three young men get up and move about, passing in front of the glass window. He muttered imprecations about the dishonesty of landlords, and then cursed the loss of his sword and his tamboura. And his spare clothes, his bed hangings...

'Bastards,' he said.

But another hour of watching and he'd discovered that at least one of the young men had a black and yellow cloak, which put it all in a very different light. And then two Yellowjackets met in front of the yellow door below him.

One was Djinar.

'He was right here!' Djinar spat.

The other Yellowjacket's reply was inaudible.

'How can you have missed him? If Timos is abroad in this city, the threat is... incalculable. He is a traitor, a servant of the enemy!'

Aranthur blinked. And then lay, awash with fear and anger. The anger roiled along like some act of Dark magik. He grunted aloud at the thought that Djinar, who knew perfectly well what had happened in the battle on the Armean Plain, also knew who was the traitor...

Djinar.

'Darkness rising,' Aranthur spat.

He sat up and banged his head on the slates of the underside of the ancient roof.

It was all worse than he thought.

He descended the stairs and slipped out of Kallinikos' former lodging. He hesitated in the street. He walked up a square towards the two great courtyards and the ancient buildings around them. He thought about the last year and again decided against visiting the Master of Arts. The idea of some authority who would help him was seductive, but he was increasingly aware that he was on his own. The logic was the same – she would be carefully watched – and he turned. He walked along a tunnel he knew that ran to the back side of the Precinct, and then he walked back through the Small Garden, breaking one of Drako's rules about reusing a route. This time he was lucky and the Small was unwatched, and he went out of the Gate and past the statue of Tirase. It all made him nostalgic for a simpler time. He looked out to sea from the height of the Pinnacle and tried to identify the *trabaccolo* through the haze, and then he went back down the steps. The red ribbon still showed on the wellhead. He went back to Sparthos' courtyard, lay down on Sapu's bed, and slept.

He borrowed a brown cote of Sapu's to go out in the afternoon, but the ribbon was still there.

Aranthur had expected a more immediate result, and now he fretted. He had expected Tiy Drako to appear, almost instantly.

Now he'd been out in broad daylight, twice, and Djinar had seen him. He was watching as well as he could, looking for people to recur, watching for unlikely sightings, but he was running out of time.

'Timos? I could use you this evening,' Sparthos called from his back step. 'Despite your sudden notoriety.'

'Notoriety?'

'The Watch has been ordered to take you for questioning. I heard this when I went to get a licence for two students to fight.'

Aranthur felt himself flush. 'I can't—'

Sparthos shrugged. 'No one here will know you. But I will ask you to be gone in a day or so.'

Aranthur found Sapu's fencing clothes and put them on: canvas breeches; a plain leather doublet with a removable, washable lining. He had longer arms than Sapu, but the fit wasn't bad.

He had second or third thoughts on the landing, climbing to the fencing *salle*, but Sparthos shook his head.

'No one you would know. All incoming first years.' Sparthos shrugged. 'And not many of them. The bone plague is keeping people at home. All the ugly rumours. And your own mother wouldn't recognise you. You look like a scarecrow.'

Indeed, Aranthur didn't know any of the students, and he moved among them, the junior teacher, correcting basic postures, asking one student for more fluidity. He was mostly quiet.

He was surprised at how quickly he fell into the role. When the class put their weapons into the racks and began to file down the steps, the maestro smiled.

375

'If the world ever returns to normal, you are welcome here. You have become a blade. There – it's said.'

Aranthur frowned. 'I doubt I'm any better than when you saw me last, Maestro.'

Sparthos smiled. 'Have you ever known me to be generous with my compliments?'

He coughed again. He coughed and coughed, and eventually took a handkerchief from his sleeve and used it.

Aranthur couldn't miss the blood on the white linen.

Sparthos gave him that look – the poisonous look he'd worn when he'd almost died in the Inn of Fosse, a lifetime before. As if the blood on the handkerchief was somehow a failing.

'Don't tell my daughter,' he spat.

Aranthur shook his head.

The sword master stepped closer. 'I'm serious, Timos. You have settled into excellence. Your sword work is like the best craftsmanship – stripped of adornment. I hope you will come back here. I hope all this nonsense ends...'

Aranthur frowned. 'It is not nonsense, Maestro.'

Sparthos shrugged. 'Is it not?' He nodded. 'Please do not get caught. Note that I ask nothing.'

He bowed and went down the stairs to his own chamber.

Aranthur wondered how many of the inhabitants of the City, or indeed of the whole world, thought that the crack in the sky and the incursions of the Pure were annoying interruptions of wheel-making, ceramics, sword fighting, or a hundred other pastimes.

Somehow the thought gave him room to breathe.

He changed back into his student's robe, and went back out into the night. This time he paid to be floated past the little *corte* and the wellhead in a gondola. The ribbon was still there, lit by the torches on the corners of the richer buildings.

Aranthur felt too exposed, even in the darkness. But even as the gondolier rowed them along with his single oar, a young girl crossed the bridge. Aranthur saw her stop, and then run to the wellhead, where she untied the ribbon, and put it in her hair.

'Blessed Sophia,' Aranthur said.

Of course silk ribbon was valuable. Was she a Cold Iron member? Or just a poor girl who wanted a scarlet ribbon?

But what gave him a little hope was that she'd been in the colours of the Palace.

He went back to Sapu's and got a few hours of sleep. At midnight he rose, convinced by then that he was wasting his time, and went across the first bridge to the broad piazza behind the noble's palaces. The piazza ran down to the water, and was commonly called the Angel because of the statue there, reputed to be solid gold.

The Angel had appeared to Tirase, or so it was said. He looked at the statue, and then out to sea. Aranthur's military ship had sailed from just there... He walked along the square, under the powerful magelights that shone on the Angel. It was his rendezvous, if the signals system had been working. He wondered about Inoques and Dahlia, who were probably close offshore, waiting for two green lights. He thought of Tiy Drako, and his network of agents. And of what it meant that Djinar was looking for him.

Something was very wrong. *Everything* was wrong. He'd feared as much, but the reality was worse.

The Angel was almost deserted. Aranthur was not ready to leave the square, because he knew in his heart that when he walked away, it would be to fetch a red lantern – an admission that the City was not safe.

He looked at the Angel. The sculpture was superb; the body of the angel sculpted with incredible attention to detail.

Including the lines of engraving around the angel's wrists and neck.

Aranthur paused. He looked around. The great square was almost empty. Granted, the Academy was two weeks from opening, but on a pleasant summer night, the Angel should have had a thousand people, courting, gaming, or just strolling to be seen among the dozen tavernas.

Instead, there were fewer than two hundred people. There was one big, raucous party at the eastern end. The revellers were very well dressed.

He stepped up onto the rail that surrounded the statue. An alarm sounded – a thin, piping sound – and he jumped down, feeling like a fool, but with enough self-possession to pretend to be a drunk. He'd seen the *writing on the Angel's wrists*. Like tattoos.

He was still in a state of mental shock as he walked unsteadily along the waterfront, and the alarm stopped. He looked out to sea, and was afraid.

He turned for the refuge of the fencing *salle*. In ten minutes he'd gone from hope to real fear. He could feel the fear throughout his body. He didn't even understand. He was just afraid.

Tirase's angel was a construct? The sculptor wanted people to know that?

He wished for a weapon. For friends around him. He began to walk more quickly.

A figure detached itself from the loud group – the *only* loud group, a dozen young people who were all drunk by an elaborate tent. Nobles.

Aranthur headed for the first bridge.

The slim figure from the drunken group moved faster, pacing him, and Aranthur felt the ice in his spine. He didn't dare to run, and he had neither sword nor dagger.

He came to the middle of the arched bridge, and looked back. The slim man in high boots was crossing the lower bridge parallel to him. Aranthur turned away, and the sound of the slim man's boots followed him.

Aranthur turned again, afraid of getting lost in an unfamiliar part of the City. He decided to go uphill. He passed out of the prosperous neighbourhood, and began to climb muddy steps.

He passed his first bone plague victim, a pile of rags and flesh, and his bile rose in his throat. The smell was cloying, sweet and grotesque.

He looked back, and the man in the boots appeared from an alley below him.

They were perhaps twenty-five paces apart, and Aranthur had no place to run.

'Who in the thousand hells are you?' asked the figure. Aranthur knew the voice immediately.

'Iralia!' he said. 'Oh, gods!'

It was indeed Iralia. She looked tired, and she wore men's clothes and no make-up. She looked nothing like the glorious beauty who accompanied the Emperor in public. Whom he'd saved in the snow, fifteen months before.

She had a dagger in her hand. 'Who are you, syr?' she asked.

'Aranthur Timos,' he said.

She flinched. 'Aranthur? Blessed Aphres, Aranthur. Almost all of us

378

are taken. I got your message... I thought Tiy had escaped or some miracle had happened. Where have you been?'

He looked back over her shoulder.

'You're being followed,' he said.

'That's not news.' She flattened herself against the building. 'What are you doing here?'

He looked behind her. 'Tribane sent me. To the Emperor.'

She squeezed his hand. 'General Tribane is still... alive?'

Aranthur nodded. 'Alive? Still fighting. She is victorious. Roaris was sent home in disgrace.'

He was watching the two dark figures who were trying to appear casual, leaning against the balustrade of the old steps he'd just climbed. Plain cloaks.

She looked down.

'I can hide us,' he said. 'I have other problems...'

She shook her head. 'I'm still safe in the palace. So are you. Come with me.'

Aranthur shook his head. 'Damn. Where's Tiy?'

'They arrested him yesterday. I only came out to see if there was anyone left to help me... rescue him.' She glanced at him, her face set. 'The Emperor is very sick. Even...' Her voice bubbled but did not break. 'Even dying,' she managed. 'Aphres, Aranthur. I am not a poor weak woman by anyone's standards, but you are a sending from the gods.'

'The Emperor? And Tiy Drako arrested?' Aranthur whistled. 'Let's move. These two gentlemen do not have our best interests at heart.' He glanced at her as they started to walk, and tentatively he reached out to her. 'The Emperor... Is it... *the darkness?*'

Iralia looked at him again.

'I'm no Imoter. You know that,' she said. Then, in a rush, 'I think I'm supposed to think he has "*the darkness*". But I think it's poison. I try all his food. The Palace is a sieve. Aphres, Aranthur – this place—'

'Where's Drako?'

She was moving up the steps rapidly, and he followed her.

'Held at the Lonika Gate,' Iralia said.

'And Kurvenos?'

'No one knows. Drako went to find him. I thought you might—'

'You don't even have a knife to spare me?' he asked.

Iralia smiled. 'We have better weapons than knives,' she said with something of her former brilliance.

Aranthur considered, somewhat bemused, that he had just been missing his lack of a weapon; what Iralia said was true. Yet he felt a strange repugnance to use his powers directly to harm, even after the Black Bastion, or perhaps because of it.

'I'd still be happier if I had a sword.'

Iralia flashed another one of her brilliant smiles and turned right, crossing High Bridge. It was one of the few places in the City where the ridge that dominated the centre was cleft by a deep watercourse that became the Great Canal far below. It was a sort of public park, with waterfalls and secluded bowers much beloved of courting couples, but it tended to split the north side into two, crossed by two ancient and very ornate bridges, both dating to the First Empire. The Low Bridge was still a respectable fifty paces above the Great Canal. The High Bridge, at the very top of the park steps, linked the back of the Academy to the rest of Northside.

Aranthur followed her across. In the middle of the bridge they stopped. He put his arm around Iralia's waist, and she put her arms around his neck.

'Now there are three of them,' she said. 'You are all skin and bones!' she added.

Aranthur was looking the other way, where there were also three shapes moving in the magelights that marked the edge of the Precinct on the north side.

'Who are they?'

'Lions. I don't think they're from the Watch. They're not very good. But I suspect they plan to take me. I am a notorious harlot and rake, and taking me this far from the Emperor will allow them to say . . . anything.' She leant against him. 'We should just be able to walk through them.'

Aranthur walked with her, his arm still on her waist, leaning slightly as if a little drunk.

'Stop!' shouted one of the men ahead of them, on the Academy side. He'd *augmented* his voice, and it sounded deep and almost ridiculously pompous. 'Stop and be searched!'

Aranthur kept walking.

The three men were perhaps fifty paces away, and now those behind were hurrying to catch up.

'Put a barrier behind us,' Aranthur said.

Iralia hummed, and then turned. She stood for a moment and then followed him.

'Is this the Precinct?' he called out to the Yellowjackets ahead. 'Are you from the Academy?'

'Halt!' called the deep voice.

Another voice, shrill with apprehension, said, 'She just used *power*! I saw it!'

Aranthur identified two of the three men at the Academy end as Magi. They were second or third year students, and he did not want to hurt them. So he reached out with Ansu's trick, learnt what seemed like an aeon before, and when Deep Voice tried to cast, Aranthur cut his casting off as he summoned *power*, the Zhouian way. Deep Voice was too inexperienced to have seen this simple tactic, and he stood, stunned, when he couldn't access the *Aulos*.

Aranthur was then less than twenty paces away with Iralia just behind him.

'Draw! Draw!' called Deep Voice.

His voice was no longer *augmented* because in his initial panic at losing the *Aulos* he'd also lost his concentration.

All three men drew their swords.

Iralia gestured, and a plane of pale lavender fire sprang out of the bridge. At a nod from her, a second plane intercepted it at an acute angle, like the prow of a ship, and the two of them followed it. The three men with swords were simply excluded by the two fields, which they could not penetrate, and Aranthur and Iralia walked past them. As soon as they were past, Iralia closed the two planes of light as if they were gates, walling the three men on the bridge.

'How long will that last?' Aranthur asked. 'Beautiful, by the way.'

'Not long. But long enough. Line of sight.'

The two of them took a long, circling path that went up to the level of the Academy but kept the High Bridge apron in sight the whole way. At the top, Iralia cast something else – something very colourful, directly onto the surface of the bridge – and then cancelled her shields. The two of them entered the Precinct, stepping across the inscribed gold line.

'Let's run,' she said, and Aranthur followed her down towards the Spice Market.

'Aren't we going the wrong way?' he asked.

'Trust me,' Iralia said, and Aranthur found that he did.

They sprinted along familiar streets, utterly deserted, past Kallinikos' former apartment, and his own yellow door. Then up into the Academy proper, where they slowed down to breathe before descending the steep marble steps into the valley that separated the Academy from the Precinct. In the light of both moons, they could see High Bridge behind them, white and graceful. The play of light on the bridge meant that Iralia's last *working* was still functioning.

'Illusion,' she chuckled.

But when they reached the base of the Academy steps they were in the slums below the Pinnacle, and they were too well dressed. Aranthur had not been in the Pinnacle since he had returned. He was shocked at how much worse the tent city on the steep slopes was – how it stank, how crowded it was, and how many dead he could see as huddled piles of boneless flesh.

'Yes,' Iralia said. 'Someone is pushing the plague. Someone truly evil, with a great deal of *sihr*. A new Servant? Or perhaps a Disciple?'

'Sophia,' Aranthur spat, trying to breathe through his mouth.

As soon as they passed in among the tents and hovels, they were followed. Close in were a handful of silent, persistent beggars; farther back, someone better trained or perhaps more sinister.

Just as they passed under the Black Aqueduct, Iralia scattered some silver soldi in the moonlight. They emerged from the darkness under the stone water trough without any beggars and started downhill.

'It's not black,' Aranthur said.

Iralia glanced back. 'No, silly. In the First Empire, the racing teams repaired and maintained the aqueducts. Red, White, Black, Gold and Lions.'

Aranthur would have laughed, but a pair of very large men stepped out of the darkness.

Iralia stopped. 'Don't get in my way,' she said.

One of the men smiled nastily.

'Honey, I don't even have to ask if you have anything I want.'

Iralia also had a particularly nasty smile.

'I'd prefer not to kill you,' she said.

The man clutched at his chest, and blood came out of his mouth, black and slick in the light of two moons.

Iralia smiled at the other man.

'Truth? I dislike people who threaten me, and I have the power to make my dislike strike home.'

The first man was flopping on the ground like a fish pulled from the water. His face screamed silently; his agony was obvious.

The second man turned and ran.

Iralia raised an eyebrow. 'Now we run again, I fear,' she said.

'Footpads?'

'*Al Ghugha*,' Iralia said, and started down the hill.

Aranthur had to exert himself to catch her. They raced side by side through the lower slopes and past the tenements of Northside, where most of Aranthur's Twenty-second City Regiment had been raised, and then, breathing hard, in the great piazza above the Spice Market. Even at this hour, there were shops open in the market. Lamps burned, and men and women struck deals, and in the canal behind the market, a long line of gondolas waited for late-night patrons.

Iralia dropped into the first in line, and Aranthur stepped down behind.

'Take us to see the Stars,' Iralia said breathlessly.

The gondolier, a heavy woman with a red scarf on her head, leered.

'Oh, the Stars,' she said.

She used her long oar as a pole to push the slim black craft away from the Spice Market pier, and then they were coasting on the smooth canal water.

'You can raise the screen there if you want more... privacy,' she said.

Iralia sat back on the cushions.

'I love the Stars,' she said.

The Stars were a series of three very new fortifications built to protect the entrance to the private harbour of the Imperial Palace: three star forts, with modern cannon and magikal defences that the Emperor's father had built to complete the sea walls he'd designed himself. Because they were lit up at night and had lighthouses, they had a spectacular, other-worldly look. Visitors loved to be rowed out to look at them.

Aranthur sat next to Iralia, aware, as he always was, of her proximity, her femininity, and her allure, even in men's clothes and covered in sweat.

She smiled at him. 'Thank Sophia you came home. Tell me about the General. Tell me everything.'

Aranthur raised an eyebrow and glanced at the gondolier.

Iralia smiled. 'We are murmuring sweet nothings to each other. I do these things quite well. Speak! She can't hear you.'

Aranthur narrated the campaign in Armea as best he could, from his arrival with Ansu, Sasan and Dahlia until they left for Masr. Twice, in the midst of his recitation, Iralia smiled at him, and he leant closer...

Both times she laughed and pushed him away, leaving him confused.

'Too much verisimilitude,' Iralia said the second time. 'As in, no.'

Aranthur flushed, but then nodded. 'I'm sorry.'

She nodded back. 'I'm sure I was sending mixed signals.'

Aranthur's embarrassment deepened. 'I'm a fool,' he said. 'Please pardon me.'

Iralia shrugged. 'Apology accepted.'

Aranthur turned away to cover his annoyance at himself, and there were the Stars – all three of them. The two end Stars were attached to long fortified breakwaters that defined the outer harbour of the palace. The third, the middle fort, was on a small islet, and was higher, larger, and even better armed.

'Take us in to the Palace Harbour,' Iralia said.

'Can't do that, ma'am,' the gondolier said. 'Forbidden.'

Iralia held up a badge that lit in her hand.

'Palace business,' she said.

The gondolier sighed. 'And now no tip, I suppose,' she muttered.

'On the contrary,' Iralia said. To Aranthur, she said, 'the Lions tend to be country people, and they don't think of the City as surrounded by water. Drako and I use boats as much as we can.'

She lay back. Again she gave him her brilliant smile, but Aranthur believed that no meant no, and he was not led to try again.

Instead, he sat up. 'Does the Palace Harbour have its own customs boat?'

'It could if one was ordered.'

They had come to the narrow harbour entrance. Only Imperial pleasure boats and very small military ships ever entered the Palace Harbour.

'I have to stop, milady,' the gondolier said.

Iralia stood up and held her crystal aloft, and it glowed a bright lavender.

'Pass,' called a voice above them, and the watergate was opened.

Aranthur leant over, but not to kiss her, despite her glory.

'I have an idea,' he said. 'Do you want to rescue Drako?'

'Before they torture him?' Iralia said, her eyes suddenly as brilliant as diamonds. 'Most assuredly.'

'How soon can you get us a customs boat?'

'Half an hour at most.'

Iralia stood up. They were coming alongside the Palace pier, a white marble confection slightly marred by some very green seaweed clinging to the base of the arches.

Aranthur turned to the gondolier.

'If you will wait a few minutes, I'd like to go to the Angel,' he said.

'Don't worry, we'll pay,' Iralia said.

The woman in the red scarf grinned. 'Anywhere you like, my honeys.'

An hour later, two green lanterns appeared on the waterfront by the statue of the Angel. An Imperial Axe placed them there, and no one questioned him.

Two hours later, the Customs Service cutter ran alongside the *trabaccolo* half a league south of the Stars. Mera saluted with both hands to his forehead, and the Customs officer stepped aboard, followed by Aranthur.

He kissed Inoques, and then turned to Dahlia.

'It's bad. Drako's taken, and Iralia's thinks he's being tortured. We're going to get him.'

'When?' Dahlia asked.

'Right now,' Aranthur said. 'Are you in?'

'Of course.' She smiled.

Kollotronis grunted. 'Am I invited to this party?'

'May I ask how this ship has passed...?' The Customs officer had Inoques' bill of lading in his hand. 'Good gods! From Masr? And Antioke?' He looked at Aranthur. 'We have orders not to allow any foreign ship to land, or any Imperial ship from overseas, unless we have permission from the Watch.'

Aranthur nodded. 'And you have the Emperor's orders to allow this ship to land at the palace,' he said.

The Customs officer swallowed. 'Gods. All right. Gods.'

'You plan to do this without killing anyone,' Dahlia said, as the low *trabaccolo*, its topmasts struck down, crept through the watergate to the palace.

Aranthur nodded. 'If it can possibly be avoided. Subterfuge and non-lethal force.'

She smiled. 'I'm willing to try. But if it fails—'

'Just try and remember that almost everyone, even the most virulent Lions, are merely people. Imperial citizens. Misled—'

Dahlia laughed. 'Aranthur, you are sometimes the most patronising man I know. They're my friends from childhood, most of them!' She shrugged. 'I don't want to kill them. Perhaps one or two. And Roaris...' She shook her head. 'I don't believe everything you've said. He's a hero, Aranthur. Old-fashioned, loud-mouthed, a bit of a bastard...' She shook her head. 'Not a traitor.'

An hour after first light, General Roaris rode into the hexagonal fortress that dominated the Lonika Gate, accompanied by a dozen staff officers and a troop of the Noble Guard in their scarlet doublets and plumed hats. The officer in charge of the General's guard saluted smartly, and answered the password contemptuously, as if it wasn't worth her trouble to talk to her inferiors.

The military guard indicated the immediacy of the Emperor's favour. None of the officers in the Gate fortress could remember any general who was granted a Noble Guard. Likewise, the general was in a fine, expansive mood, and he took a few minutes to turn out the gate's guard, militia from the Twenty-first Northern Border Regiment. He looked them over, complimented their astonished officer, and then went into the fortress proper.

His staff stayed with him, but the escorting Nobles demanded wine and went to the kitchens on the City-ward side of the fortress.

'Wine at eight bells?' asked the Watch officer.

The Watch had its headquarters in the South Tower, across from the military headquarters. Mocking the military was a professional duty, despite the fact that most of the men and women on the Watch were military veterans.

'Look out, lads and lasses, his nibs is coming this way,' said the Night Sergeant.

As eight o'clock was just ringing in the Temple of Aphres on the other side of the 'Long Canal' behind the gate fortress, the Night Sergeant was technically still on duty, although she was already putting her weapons into the rack.

'Why not just get his precious Yellowjackets to do the Night Watch?' muttered a duty officer.

A dozen beautifully uniformed staff officers, each more poisonously disagreeable, early in the morning, than the last, took up a great deal of room. The Watch's outer office was suddenly flooded with fine cloaks, fur-lined dolmans, braided jackets, and elaborate moustaches and coiffed hair.

'General the Prince Verit Roaris,' announced a gigantic military courtier, and several of the Watch bowed.

Roaris himself was affable. He was a big man and he projected his size as confidence. He swept through his staff, at once apologising for their arrogance and enjoying it.

'I need to have you bring out a prisoner,' he said. 'Immediately. Order from the Emperor.'

The Night Sergeant looked at the seal, which was very solid. She passed it through an aperture on her desk, and a bright green light shone.

'Genuine,' she said. 'My lord . . .' She read down the document. 'Syr Drako. My lord, I have a request here that his mother be allowed to visit him.'

'Denied,' Roaris said. 'I'm sorry. But I'll be taking him to the palace.'

The Night Sergeant nodded. 'Yes, my lord. If it is not impertinent, my lord . . . Is the Emperor . . . ?' She paused.

Roaris smiled. 'Your loyalty does you credit, sergeant. The Emperor is very sick. *The darkness* – we all know what it is.'

'Sixteen officers not reporting for work,' the oncoming Day Sergeant said, mostly to get noticed by the general. 'I'll fetch Drako.'

The Night Sergeant tried not to show what she thought of the Day Sergeant. Most of the Watch stood in various forms of attention, and the staff took up too much space and looked around. No one spoke.

'How bad has crime been since *the darkness*?' Roaris asked the Night Sergeant.

She frowned. 'We've sent you our reports.'

'I wanted to hear it from your own mouth.'

'I am only a sergeant. Syr.'

Her dislike was unmistakable – a woman who did not hide her disdain for superiors she regarded as less than perfectly competent.

Roaris' eyes narrowed. 'I asked you a question,' he snapped.

Her shoulders sank slightly, as if she had sighed.

'There has been very little trouble since the initial burst of rioting, and the violence in the Academy,' she said. And then, greatly daring, 'We have a rash of complaints against your Yellowjackets.'

'Deputies,' snapped one of Roaris' staff, a slim woman with the most elaborate hair the Night Sergeant had ever seen on a soldier. Even a staff officer.

'Here he is.'

The Day Sergeant emerged from the direction of the cells, and gave his prisoner a gentle shove.

The prisoner was in irons. He had been beaten, and his hands looked like melons.

'What the hells?' the slim staff officer said.

'We were ordered to keep him this way,' the Night Sergeant said. 'The Captain protested.'

Drako didn't raise his head. He'd been badly beaten in the head, and his flesh was puffy, the way soft tissue is before the bruises have time to rise to the surface.

'Take him,' Roaris said. 'Give the sergeant the quitclaim.' He turned and gave the sergeant a little bow. 'I'm sorry that . . .'

The Day Sergeant was shaking his head.

'I thought Roaris hated Arnauts,' he said to one of his officers.

The man, who had been standing at attention, looked at the big staff officer who was holding Drako.

'I'll be damned,' he said.

'Shit,' the slim staff officer said, and stepped back.

Roaris was already out of the door and the big man who had Drako's chains was next. The slim staff officer smiled at the Watch officers standing around. They were all staring at the retreating staff.

She bowed and gave them all a brilliant smile.

'I'm truly sorry for any misunderstandings,' she said, and the stone portal was suddenly full of a lavender fire.

Then she turned and followed the general's staff, who were not going to their horses in the courtyard, as might have been expected. They moved to the east, across the marble-paved octagonal parade ground between the two main towers. There was a barracks block, as well as the ranges, the practice courts, the kitchens, and, of course, the access to the canal.

A knot of staff officers were just emerging from the elegant marble gate to the Military Tower across the courtyard.

Roaris walked across the courtyard toward them as if he was the Emperor himself. Most of the staff officers bowed formally, but one checked himself in mid-bow, and instead cast. His casting was quick and fluid, and General Roaris' face seemed to run like an actress's make-up in the rain.

'Damn,' Aranthur said.

Alarms were sounding. One of the real staff officers shouted. Another drew his sword, and the tall man who'd thrown the disruption came forward.

Aranthur, no longer concerned with keeping up his complex *guise*, turned to cover the two men carrying Drako.

The man running at him was Djinar. The young noble burst into a blossom of shields.

Aranthur emanated his own shields, which flowed out in a brilliant scarlet display to those who could see such things.

Djinar actually paused when he saw the *puissance* of Aranthur's shields. He looked back to see if he was supported. Aranthur glanced back at his people, all of whom were still in their *guise*, which was still confusing their adversaries.

By the gates to the barracks block, stood two of his Noble Guard, who fell in behind his chief of staff.

Aranthur, secure behind his shields, replaced his *guise*. Djinar was demanding that a pair of military guards go forward.

The last of the Arnauts passed behind Aranthur and entered the barracks. Aranthur bowed to Djinar just in time to see General Roaris emerge from the Military Tower behind Djinar. Aranthur backed into the barracks gate, cast a simple *transference* that moved an immense quantity of real smoke into the courtyard, and ducked back into the barracks. He went down the steps to the kitchens, collecting the rest of his 'Noble Guard' on the way. Out in the marble court, there was an alarm sounding, and pounding feet, and a shot was fired. Everything smelt of woodsmoke, and people were coughing.

A dozen cooks looked out from various stoves and hearths, and were surprised to see Verit Roaris himself striding along the kitchen's corridor, followed by most of his staff and twenty Noble Guards, one of whom closed and locked the hall's main door. She threw the key out of the window into the shining surface of the canal. Then all thirty of them walked out onto the kitchen's private pier, where the massive supplies of produce were daily landed from canal boats. Above them was the main bridge into the city. They could hear the portcullis coming down, and shouts.

General Roaris stepped onto the lighter that waited, tied only by two light lines to bollards. It had a limp sail up, and no oarsmen; only a single veiled woman stood in the stern, under an awning.

The staff and the Noble Guards came aboard, even as the shouting above them rose to a fever pitch. Someone was hammering at the hall door to the kitchen corridor, and the hollow sound echoed off the stone walls of the canal.

Roaris raised a hand, and the veiled woman nodded.

The sail filled with wind even as a pair of Masran sailors tossed the lines into the lighter and stepped aboard.

With her sail suddenly and perfectly filled, the lighter coasted away from the dock – at first slowly, but gathering way as she moved.

Up on the Lonika Gate Bridge, a soldier shouted.

The lighter sailed along the canal. Smaller craft scattered to get out of her way, and a gondolier cursed, colourfully and long, as his beautiful boat's black enamel was endangered by the bow wave that the lighter was throwing as she brushed past.

The soldier aimed his matchlock musket, but his dekark stopped the match.

'Don't be a fool,' he said.

The soldier looked chagrined. 'They're getting away!'

The dekark shrugged. 'Who is? General Roaris? Laddie, we have no idea what's going on. Let's not shoot anyone until we do.'

Aranthur dropped his *guise* as soon as the wind filled the lighter's sail. He was grinning from ear to ear.

'And no one hurt,' he said.

Dahlia, dressed as a Noble Guard, had seldom looked so completely like what she was – a member of the oldest of families in the Byzas nobility. She was sombre, her lips pursed.

'We're not done yet,' she said. 'And Tiy is most definitely hurt.'

Aranthur looked back at Inoques, who was slowing the lighter for the turn into the open sea from the Long Canal. There was a fortification at the opening in the wall, and it was possible . . .

The lighter was in the midst of a dozen other vessels: gondolas, other lighters, a big canal-boat full of stone for building, and passenger boats.

'Everyone down,' Iralia called.

All of the Magi had shields ready to deploy, but to cast them was to give themselves away to watchers with the talent to see such things.

The fort gave no sign.

The lighter passed under the fort's guns, but no alarm had been raised and none of them were run out. Aranthur looked up to see a soldier smoking stock in one of the embrasures. He waved.

He felt almost light at heart.

He knelt next to Drako in the bow. The man's eyes were unfocused.

'Tiy,' he said.

Drako didn't look at him.

Iralia knelt next to him.

'Shit. It's not just that he's been tortured,' she spat. 'He has *the darkness*.'

Drako spat. A froth of tiny bubbles came to his lips.

He spat again, as if clearing his mouth, and his eyes flickered open.

'Not actually,' he muttered. 'Gods, Iralia, have I mentioned how beautiful you are?'

Aranthur breathed again.

'Timos, the harbinger,' Drako said. 'Gods . . .' He looked at Aranthur.

'You don't have *the darkness*!' Aranthur said.

Drako swallowed and shook his head.

'Everything is falling into the hells. Roaris has the City, and the Pure took Kurvenos.' He blinked. 'You came for me!' he said softly, and began to cry.

Aranthur was trying not to look at the man's ruined hand, his bloated, beaten face.

'Of course we came for you,' he said.

Iralia took one of his hands – the right, which was swollen to a terrible size – carefully, tenderly.

'We'll put you to rights . . .' she said.

'It's too fucking late,' Drako said. 'Kurvenos is dead. We're doomed.'

Aranthur shook his head. He looked at Dahlia.

Dahlia smiled. 'We're not beaten yet.'

The End
Of 'Dark Forge' Book Two of Masters and Mages
To be completed in Book Three, Bright Steel.